Father Aloysius

The heroic Priest

By

Charles Shaylor

Copyright © 2024 by - Charles Shaylor - All Rights Reserved.

It is not legal to reproduce, duplicate, or transmit any part of this document in either electronic means or printed format. Recording of this publication is strictly prohibited.

The Novel is dedicated to the Author's wife & family. Any royalties will go to the refurbishment of St. Mary's Church, Lasham, and the Anglican Dioceses of Karamoja and North Karamoja to be used to support the Diocesan Training Centre.

Acknowledgement

Lorna Forrester, Anthea Del Mar, Antonia Goor, Maurice Goor, and my daughter Rebecca Shaylor for their initial proofreading, and the staff of A. M.Z Publishing Company for their invaluable help.

About the Author

Charles Shaylor was born in Uganda in 1943 and educated in Kenya before coming to England to train as a teacher. His teaching career took him to India as a VSO and Kenya before returning to England in 1973. He retired in 2000 from his position as headteacher of a small primary school in Hampshire, trained as a Lay Minister, and was involved in fundraising for the Dioceses of Karamoja. He is married with two children.

Contents

Foreword 1
Chapter One 2
Chapter Two 10
Chapter Three 15
Chapter Four 22
Chapter Five 38
Chapter Six 54
Chapter Seven 68
Chapter Eight 75
Chapter Nine 88
Chapter Ten 95
Chapter Eleven 103
Chapter Twelve 108
Chapter Thirteen 117
Chapter Fourteen 122
Chapter Fifteen 131
Chapter Sixteen 143
Chapter Seventeen 148
Chapter Eighteen 158
Chapter Nineteen 169
Chapter Twenty 177
Chapter Twenty-One 189
Chapter Twenty-Two 196
Chapter Twenty-Three 207
Chapter Twenty-Four 214

Chapter Twenty-Five	223
Chapter Twenty-Six	228
Chapter Twenty-Seven	235
Chapter Twenty-Eight	243
Chapter Twenty-Nine	263
Chapter Thirty	269
Chapter Thirty-One	293
Chapter Thirty-Two	313
Chapter Thirty-Three	325
Chapter Thirty-Four	338
Chapter Thirty-Five	353
Chapter Thirty-Six	402
Chapter Thirty-Seven	420
Chapter Thirty-Eight	451
Chapter Thirty-Nine	476
Chapter Forty	501
Chapter Forty-One	526
Chapter Forty-Two	544

Foreword

Karamoja and Alton Deanery

The character Father Aloysius had his genesis in a Junior School in 1981 when the author was appointed as a deputy headteacher. He was a classroom teacher, but one of his many other duties was to take morning assemblies and to organise the rota for class assemblies one morning a week. The rest of the week was up to him. He found subject matter hard to come by, so he eventually started telling his own stories. Father Aloysius was a leading character from one of his more popular series of stories. Later, Father appeared again at another school, where he was appointed headteacher in 1987. In the year 2000, he retired and decided to devote some time to writing a novel that featured Father Aloysius. However, he also had to earn his living as a supply teacher. The novel took second place and eventually was put on hold. When the first COVID-19 Lockdown was imposed, he dusted off the file and started again.

Chapter One

A Knife is Sharpened on a Stone

Father Aloysius was brown and sweating. The beads of perspiration shone in his hair and trickled down the furrows in his broad brow, finally dripped from the end of his gleaming nose to puddle on the tabletop below. His breath, hot in his throat, whistled through his white, white teeth, and the whites of his eyes bulged.

His ears rang with the deafening screeches of a hoard of screaming faces that crowded in on every side, but for all the noise and the strain written in his contorted face, his eyes never lost their fixed focus. Unflinching, his gaze fastened in fierce concentration on the face opposite, less than a breath's distance away.

Sid's face, too, was contorted and puce with his own efforts. His breath came in grunts, deep from the breadth of his heavy chest and huge belly. A dark red lock of hair creeping from under the grimy rim of an old woollen hat that had been pushed back from his freckled forehead clung damp across its furrowed surface, and a pulse bulged at his temple.

"Sid, Sid, Sid, Sid," the incessant chanting pounded on and on. Sid's cracked lips drew back from a set of broken, discoloured teeth in a distorted grin of triumph, and his blue, bloodshot eyes gleamed with the scent of victory. His huge hairy hand, his broad fingers entwined with those of the African, was gradually forcing his opponent's hand downwards. The tendons in his wrist stood out as taut as a bowstring, and his huge biceps bulged. His ears were full of the sound of his own name as the children of the youth club pressed ever closer in their wild encouragement.

It was Father Aloysius's second day in Pondreath. He had been talking about the village to Miss Farrow. She had been designated by the bishop to be his housekeeper, and she had mentioned at the end of a list of worthy institutions that included the Women's Institute, the British Legion Club, and Bingo in the village hall on a Tuesday night that there was a youth club that met in the school hall. The priest, at a loose end, had decided to pay it a pastoral visit, his third of the day. Earlier, Miss Farrow had driven him in her battered old Morris to Falmouth Hospital to see Edna Towzer, who was having her varicose veins seen too. He also saw Duncan Evans, the headteacher of the school, who had been sent in for a series of observations. His second had been to see the Rector of St. Jude's, the Anglican Church.

Like the villagers at the hospital and the Rev Burns of St. Jude's, Mr and Mrs Tarrant, who ran the youth club, had been both surprised and pleased to see him. They had never had a Catholic priest visit the club before, let alone an African. The club catered to the children of Pondreath and the surrounding rural area. It was popular not just because there was, in reality, little else on offer for the youngsters to do of an evening between the age of seven o'clock bedtimes for the playgroup set and going to the pub at any age you could convince the landlord you were eighteen, but more because both Mr and Mrs Tarrant were cheerful souls who worked hard to provide a relaxed, casual, drop-in sort of a club which also, from time to time, had the attraction of special events, like trips to Falmouth cinema or to Plymouth to see Argyle play.

Father Aloysius was an easy mixer. He quickly got chatting to groups of children and had been enjoying playing table tennis and pool with them when the idea of an arm wrestling competition had been mooted. At first, the priest was an umpire, but then he became somewhat reluctantly involved as a participant. Larry, being the largest and the oldest of the lads, was the club champion and somewhat of a hero. He was, in reality, too old for the club but came along ostensibly to help. The truth was, he was there because he had been banned from the pub. He quickly disposed of the few half-hearted challenges to his supremacy. Rachel, whose admiration for Larry was only exceeded by her loathing of Anna, innocently suggested that the priest wrestle with Larry. Larry clearly had more than a passing interest in Anna. It was not a good match. Father |Aloysius, in his early thirties, was an athlete of some prowess. A cassock is not designed to show off a man's physique to any great advantage, and Larry was somewhat naive with regard to clerics. Father Aloysius made a generous pretence of having to struggle to beat the lad, but the result was never really in doubt.

When the priest finally forced Larry's hand to the tabletop, there was an uproar of rejoicing and indignant protest. Those who resented Larry's somewhat swaggering dominance were happy to congratulate the cleric; those who valued Larry's tolerance were eager to show him that they thought it was a fix.

In the middle of the pandemonium, Sid Trevinian arrived. Sid was Larry's uncle. He was a huge man with the ponderous gait of a lorry driver, used to manipulating leviathan-sized trucks up and down the narrow Cornish lanes. Sid was also acknowledged to be Pondreath's strong man. Any family resemblance between the boy and his uncle was confined to the eyes. Both the Trevinians had cornflower blue eyes, but while Sid was big and ginger, Larry was slight and dark in hair and complexion. He had the refined features of his mother. His father and mother, having finally split up after an unhappy marriage, both fled the county in search of greener pastures. Larry and his sister Philippa had been left with Sid and his wife. The arrangement was more a financial one than one based on any feeling of family affinity. Sid, often away for days on end, hauling goods up and down the country, left the children with his spouse. She received a monthly cheque from the children's father, who, so rumour had it, was making a fortune in the City.

The money did not linger long in the bank. Charlotte, a pale, wan creature when she was not hanging about the pub scrounging cigarettes from the fishermen and regaling them with stories and jokes of a somewhat dubious nature, was reputedly cleaning at the Smugglers Arms, a run-down pub-cum-motel on the main road to Pendon Bay.

The children received rather less in terms of financial benefit from their father's cheques than did the landlord of the pub. Why Sid had turned up at the youth club that night was never established. Philippa, or Flip as the gang called her, was filled with a strong sense of foreboding.

Sid rarely showed any interest in the children, and when he did, it was invariably trouble. Larry, however, immediately saw a way of deflecting the interest from his humiliating defeat and getting his revenge on the priest. He decided to engage his uncle to arm wrestle with Father Aloysius. Sid was not at first happy to rescue his nephew's honour, but when Larry darkly hinted that the priest might be more than a match for him, his pride got the better of him. The priest, too, was again a reluctant participant, but his newly won admirers eagerly pushed him forward.

The lorry driver and the cleric were squared up, belly down across the long, heavy oak table - a legacy of long gone days in education when things were expected to last. The two protagonists lay legs astride, arms raised. Larry had fussily made sure their elbows were in line, and ushering the eager spectators back into a circle with haughty instructions to give them air, he called for the contest to begin. Father Aloysius felt Sid's thick fingers squeeze his in the grip of iron. The big man grunted. Slowly and inexorably, he began to force the priest's hand back and down.

Father Aloysius fought every inch of the way. His contorted face showed the huge determination he had to make Sid battle right to the end, but the gleam of victory clearly shone in his opponent's eyes. He gritted his teeth. From his straining toes to his fingertips, he called on all his strength to pull back from defeat.

"Sid, Sid, Sid," the gang chanted, but there were, too, a few somewhat plaintive exaltations for Father to do his best.

"Faaaather, Faaather!" Anna, much to Larry's chagrin, had chosen it seemed to be the priest's champion and leaned over his shoulder, begging him to try harder. The locked hands quivered just above the tabletop, then were still.

"Sid, Sid, Sid," came the chants. There was a tremor in Sid's heavy forearm. Then, bit by bit, Father heaved his hand up, up, up to the vertical.

"Sid, Sid, Sid!" the cries were more urgent now. The hands stopped again. Sid summoned all his reserves to halt the downward pressure on his arm. A pause was won. The two arms were again motionless, again locked, shivering for a long agonising moment. It was down to will, which wanted the victory the most, would it be Cornish pride or the steely resolve of the enigmatic African. Father Aloysius stared hard into the face opposite him and then, with the sweat dripping from his chin, forced his opponent's hand downwards. The collapse was sudden. Sid's reserves were spent, and his strength was all consumed. The priest's indomitable spirit and his stamina had won. Sid's huge hand hit the table with a thump. There was a long moment of studied silence. The gang could not believe what had happened. Then a small voice blurted out,

"Chocolate drop has won, would you believe it!" Titch, or Small Si as the Gang affectionately called him, stared incredulously at the priest. Sid sighed and, slowly flexing his fingers and massaging his forearm, got up.

"Huh," he grunted, "Another of God's miracles. Might have been different if I hadn't wrenched my wrist jacking up the motor last week, but I guess you did well for all that." Father had his face buried in the crook of his other arm. His body trembled under his black cassock. He looked up and grinned, "Well done to you too." He managed to stammer. He'd won. Slowly, he got up. Big Sid towered above him. Gingerly, the huge man again flexed his fingers.

"Reckon, you must have had God and his angels pulling for you," he muttered, "No one has done that to me before, or least, not since I was a nipper Larry's age." He shook his head in disbelief. Suddenly, just as suddenly as the end had come and the club had gone quiet, it erupted into noise again. Small Si leapt onto the priest's back and waved his skinny arms in the air.

"The new champion of Pondreath! Roll up everyone and feel his biceps, a penny a pinch." Father Aloysius sagged. It was Anna, with her blue eyes wide and shining, who steadied him. She pulled Si off the priest's back.

"Get off, Si, leave the man alone, can't you? You can see he's done in. Anyway, that's no way to treat a visitor."

"Visitor," chirped Simon irreverently. "He's no visitor. He's the vicar."

"All the more reason to act respectfully," Anna insisted.

"Respect!" snorted Si. "Respect? What do you know about respect?" He stood defiantly, staring up into Anna's face, his body taut with indignation.

"You're a fine one to talk. What respect have you shown to anyone lately? Skiving off with the surfies instead of being at college as your dad told you to be, and now you come here, having been away for how long, beyond imagining, and you start to order us around as if you were big Miss Bossy Boots again!"

Father Aloysius held up his hand. It trembled with fatigue. "Peace, peace, please." He said. He walked away to get a drink of water. Big Sid did not stay long. He had a brief word with Larry and Philippa, and then he ambled off, stumbling through the door, his huge frame filling the small school porch as he let himself out without so much as a farewell.

Larry left soon after, taking Anna with him. On her way, she wished the Tarrants a polite "Goodnight," and then, coming up to the priest, she gently touched his arm, "We'll see you about," and then more archly added, "Champion." Father Aloysius smiled,

"Certainly," he replied and watched the couple slip away. Gradually, the others left, saying their farewells to the Tarrants on the way. For each, there was a cheerful reply and a bit of friendly bantering advice.

"Now, just you take care of your mum, Ollie. Watch out for Old Arthur's dog, Em. Mind you say your prayers, Jacob, or the new Champ will be after you." The priest grinned and shook his head in disbelief. He helped the Tarrants clear up.

"What did you say your name was?" asked Mr Tarrant as they came to lock up.

"Father Aloysius," the priest replied.

"Father Aloysius, eh? Well, Father, you've made a bigger impact on the youth of this village in one evening than all the priests that's been here in the last twenty-seven years." Father Aloysius smiled gently and shook the hand extended to him.

"Perhaps God has made an impact," he replied and then added. "If he's done it through me, then I'm glad, but some seeds may take a long time to germinate. Good night." The priest quietly walked home to the presbytery. As he walked, his thoughts were full of the events of the evening. He could have done without the arm wrestle. It had been a real test of his resolve. What was that old saying, what doesn't kill you makes you strong," then there was another in the same vein, "A knife is sharpened on a stone." They were an interesting group of children, and the Tarrants were clearly doing them a valuable service. He wondered about Larry and Anna; she was a pretty girl. It was a weary priest who knelt beside his bed for his final prayers of the day before retiring to sleep.

Chapter Two

O, beware my lord, of jealousy; it is a green eyed monster which doth mock the meat it feeds on

-William Shakespeare

Outside the school door, Larry had paused. He gazed about at the familiar surroundings and then at Anna. How often the two of them had come tumbling out of that door together at the end of a school day, swinging their satchels and calling out to their friends. Avoiding their respective mothers, who were invariably talking, they had gone charging about the playground, playing at being jet pilots or kicking some quickly screwed-up ball of paper about, rejoicing in the freedom of having escaped from the restraints of the school room. They made the most of the brief opportunity to assert themselves before they were recaptured by another regime. Now, suddenly, Larry felt a similar need. The need to reassert himself in Anna's eyes. He had been humiliated by the priest at the arm wrestle, and the way Anna had taken the cleric's side in the match with his uncle had really rankled him. He swore and, driving his heel hard into the worn tarmac, turned on Anna.

"Fancy him, do you?" he accused. All his pent-up anger and emotion came grating out in the harshness of his voice. There was, too, an accumulated frustration that he had lived with over the years. He was younger than Anna, but for as long as he could remember, he had looked up to her and loved her. As a little tot when he first went to school, he had worshipped her from afar; she used to organise the milk and help in the infant class at lunch times. Later, for a brief time, they had even been in the same class at the top of the school. She had been head girl in her last year at the primary school when he had graduated to the top class. She had been especially kind to him when his mother had left. Then, he had been aching with resentment at everyone and everything. Lessons were a long purgatory of wondering and worrying, his mind far away from the tasks Mr Evans set. His breaks and lunch hours were full of fights and battering as he worked out his wild rages on the other children, or times of punishment when he had to catch up with work unfinished, redo work done badly, or just stand facing the white wall and reflecting on his latest rough house escapade. Anna, then it seemed, was the only one who had tried to understand him, and they had become friends of a sort, as friendly as any boy of that age could be with a girl. Secretly, he had cried the day she had left to go on to the secondary school in Falmouth. That had been the year when once more he had had to admire her from afar as she came and went on the bus each day. On occasion, she would come back to the Primary School. Old Evans, her father, was a wise head. Apart from encouraging Larry in every practical activity he could, he also used to arrange for Anna to help him with his homework. Poetry almost became enjoyable. At last, Larry, too, had graduated from the little school and had joined Anna on the bus. It was at first hard for him. Anna, understandably, had other friends. He had had to cope with the hot surges of jealousy that almost threatened to overcome him as she mixed so easily with her contemporaries. She was an able student and was gifted at sports; she had charm and style and was always the centre of things, popular with her teachers and her peers. But she had, too, a caring sensitivity for others, and unlike some of her other friends, she did not look down on those younger children starting at the big school but often had a cheery word for them. This was especially so after the setting up of the new youth club by the Tarrants. In that informal atmosphere, all the youngsters were encouraged to mix and get on together. The former club had been run by a previous Rector of St. Jude's and his wife and had met in the church hall but had folded when they left. The new club met in the village school. It had been a proud moment for Larry when he had at last beaten Anna at table tennis, but he was even more proud when the two of them paired up and won the mixed badminton competition.

The secondary years had seen the two of them grow in very different ways, and yet Anna still had found time to talk to him and even, on occasion, sat next to him on the bus. It was at Sixth Form College that Anna started to change radically. She had found a whole new set of friends, and suddenly, from being the blue-eyed 'Miss Conformity,' she had become little 'Miss Rebel.' At first, it was music and clothes and bands and boys and then the surf. Larry did not know how to relate to the new Anna. Anna the rebel, but they did now have something more in common. For years, he had felt like an outsider. For years, he had struggled with himself and the moulds that people wanted to make him fit himself into. Now, she, too, had decided to cross the tracks and be different.

Strangely, however, it was not with Anna that he felt his sympathies lie; inexplicably, he found himself feeling for her parents. Anna had fallen in with a very different set of young people. Brown-limbed, muscled youths who worshipped the waves were now her friends. Larry felt the old feelings of jealousy rekindled. And then she had returned tonight to the club. The club she had left, the club where he, independent of her, had achieved some status. For a brief moment, he had thought there might be common ground again and opportunities for them to be together, but then she had gone and spoilt it. The feelings of the years all found expression in those few hard words. The unsuspecting Anna had felt very differently as she had emerged onto the playground. She had enjoyed being back at the club. It was good to see Larry again. He looked so grown up, too, in his black leather jacket, but her mind was already racing ahead, planning how she would spend the rest of the evening. Larry's explosive accusation had startled her. His possessive bearing and aggression sparked off her own resentment. Her retort was equally sharp.

"For heaven's sake, Larry, I haven't seen him before tonight, and anyway, anyone would be preferable to your uncle."

"Uncle, just you leave my uncle out of it, at least he's Cornish and not black."

It was Anna's turn to swear, "Now you just listen to me," her voice was strained with anger, "I'll fancy just who I like. It's time you started to grow up, Larry, and to get rid of your small-minded village ways. This place just makes me want to scream. The sooner I can get out of here, the better."

Humiliated further but not entirely cowed, Larry sneered his reply, "I see, so Miss High and Mighty, we are not good enough for you now. The kids you sat next to at school, the ones who shared their break with you and picked you up when you fell over blubbering, are now not up to your oh-so-high standards, you with your 'surfie' friends and black sympathies. Well, I hope you know what you're doing with that lot from Pendon Bay because if what I hear about them is true, you're heading for a fall, and this time, I won't be there to pick you up." With an angry toss of his head, Larry strode through the school gate. Anna stared after him. His tirade had left her speechless. Too late, she gathered her whirling thoughts and wished she had called after him.

With a deep sigh, she, too, left the playground and made her way through the night down the hill.

Larry's anger was still smouldering inside him when he reached the bottom of the hill and the bridge. Who did she think she was, coming back to the club with all her airs and graces. Even little Si had found her to be far too bossy. He mooched along the front. The lights of the pub opposite shone in rectangular blocks of yellow on the dark waters of the estuary, and the noise of its famous, restored jukebox blared out over the water. He dropped down off the walk onto the narrow beach. A car's headlights flashed on the white walls of a cottage half way up the hill. Larry traced its descent to the front, watching for the glimpses of light as it sped round the bends to emerge at the bottom of the hill, full beam in the little car park. His mind was still full of Anna as he idly watched the car. It paused for a moment and then proceeded slowly along the quay. As it passed under the solitary street light at the end of the car park, Larry identified a beach buggy. It disappeared behind a lorry. The car stopped, and its lights went out, but Larry could still hear the engine running. There was movement along the side of the lorry, and Larry could just hear whispering and then the scrape of metal. Suddenly, all thoughts of Anna were driven from his mind; his senses were on full alert, and crouching down, he strained his ears to hear what was going on across the water. The lorry door swung open. There were further fumbling noises, and then the door closed. The car lights suddenly went on, and it shot off out of the car park and up the hill. For a moment, Larry crouched, frozen to the spot. He could hear his pulse throbbing in his ears and the soft lapping of the water on the pebbles at his feet; the jukebox was blaring still, but what had he just witnessed? He was in no doubt. Someone had been tampering with the lorry. What should he do about it? Slowly, he straightened up. What should he do about it? The thought filled his mind as he made his way home.

The sound of the jukebox followed him up the hill.

Chapter Three

Without faith a man can do nothing, with it all things are possible

-Sir William Osler

The cruet clinked as Father Aloysius fumbled with the glass stopper to the bottle. It was his first Mass in St. Prodricks. It had gone well. It had gone moderately well. He revised his reflection as he folded the brouse and tidied the altar linen. Miss Farrow had intimated that there would be no more than five people at the service... there were eight. The hymns Miss Farrow had chosen were well known, and the congregation led by Miss Farrow, who played the ancient organ and sang at the top of her reedy voice, had been sung quite cheerfully, if not completely tunefully. The congregation had even kept awake in his sermon. Mind you, he had, on Miss Farrow's advice, kept it short, very short by African standards. Ten minutes at the outside, she had said, and he had said all he had to say in nine, but the points had been made, and he was happy that there was some teaching there, for that surely was the purpose of preaching. Preaching was teaching, teaching the Gospel story. Father Aloysius strode down the aisle, his cassock swishing against his long legs. He stood at the door to shake hands with the congregation as they left. He was smiling cheerfully.

"Thank you for coming, Mrs?"

"Hughes, Father, Muriel, and this is my husband, Anthony," said Mrs Hughes helpfully. Mrs Hughes was a grey little woman with bright brown eyes and had a beautiful Cashmere shawl draped over her narrow shoulders. Her husband was tall with a military bearing. He walked with a limp.

"Wouldn't have missed it for the world, my man, not for the world," he said as he limped off with his little wife down the gravel path.

"Pleased to meet you, Mrs and Mr Hughes. Goodbye," Father called after them, wondering what it was, Mr Hughes wouldn't have missed for the world, and hoping whatever it was, that he would be back for more next week, for Mr and Mrs Hughes were two of the congregation who had turned up, who had not been on Miss Farrow's list of regular attenders.

The congregation filed past, one by one, and Father Aloysius thanked them all, shaking their hands warmly. The last to leave before Miss Farrow was Mrs Hazelmere.

Mrs Hazelmere was a formidable-looking lady of large proportions. She made herself look all the taller by having her thick brown hair piled high up on her head in a most intricate style. The whole creation was held in place by shiny tortoiseshell combs stuck in at strategic points. Mrs Hazelmere was a widow and a stalwart of the church. Her husband had been a banker. He had been much older than she and had died of a heart attack some years before, leaving his younger wife fairly well provided for. There had been no children, and now that Mrs Hazelmere had returned from the City to her native Cornwall, she had adopted St. Prodricks to be the focus of her love and attention. She squeezed Father's hand warmly. It was all Father could do to prevent himself from flinching; his fingers were still stiff and bruised from the vice-like grip of huge Sid Trevinan and the arm wrestle.

"Well, thank you, Father, an excellent sermon, thank you," then leaning closer, she whispered conspiratorially, "I bet Enid put you up to that, she can't stand long sermons, anyway," Mrs Hazelmere reverted to her normal booming voice.

"Anyway, I look forward to seeing you for lunch. Twelve thirty, please, if you don't mind." Father didn't; he was looking forward to the lunch already. Mrs Hazelmere was an excellent cook, or so Miss Farrow had maintained when they had received the invitation. Miss Farrow had helped the priest clear up in the church. She was a neat little lady with deft hands, and the business of clearing away in the vestry, counting the collection, what little there was of it, and putting things right for the next service was soon accomplished. Father Aloysius was grateful for her help. His first service had gone well. The pair then returned to the presbytery, Miss Farrow scuttling along beside the long-striding priest.

"I thought we could just put these things away, have a cup of coffee, and then perhaps go for a walk. It's such a fine day for March. We've got a bit of time before Mrs Hazelmere's lunch. We can work up an appetite, and I can show you a bit of the village. Father smiled his appreciation.

"Thank you. I'd enjoy that," he replied. He was not so sure about the coffee. Miss Farrow, so far, had tended to make his coffee rather strong and never put enough sugar in it for his sweet tooth, but the walk certainly sounded a good idea. Fortunately for the priest on this occasion, Miss Farrow acquiesced to his suggestion that he make the coffee while she put the collection in the little safe, entered the amount in the account book, and dealt with the dirty altar linen. Father Aloysius hummed happily to himself as he made the drinks. It did not take him long to find what he needed in Miss Farrow's sparkling little kitchen. Everything in Miss Farrow's life was neat and ordered, the priest observed as he opened the cupboards to look for the mugs. The bishop, who he assumed had chosen Miss Farrow for the job of looking after the priest in charge of St. Prodrick's, had chosen well. Miss Farrow was a treasure.

"Coffee to your taste?" Father asked when Miss Farrow joined him at the kitchen table. The house keeper took a sip and wrinkled up her nose, "You've been a bit mean with the granules," she observed, "But I'm sure, as it's Sunday, it'll be fine."

"What's that English saying?" asked Father. "What's right for the …"

"Good for the goose, may not be good for the gander," interrupted Miss Farrow.

"Something like that," agreed Father.

"Precisely that," corrected the housekeeper, Miss Farrow, Father Aloysius decided, as he ran his eye along the neat shelf of saucepans, each one exactly equidistant apart, was a very precise lady. He also reflected that he had fallen, presumably, into the same error that she had when she made his coffee. He had made hers too weak because he preferred his that way.

"Different but the same," he said quietly to himself.

"What was that?" asked the house keeper.

"Different but the same, we are all different, yet the same," explained the priest.

Miss Farrow merely smiled. Clearing away the cups, she replied. "Walk."

Father Aloysius decided the tone of her voice made it sound more of an order than a suggestion.

Perhaps I'd better fetch my lead, Father thought, restraining himself from giggling out loud. Heel Father! Now, what sort of dog should he be? He followed his housekeeper out on their walk.

The sun was shining, and Father was glad to be out in the fresh air. Miss Farrow took him up the hill away from the village. The houses were fewer up here on the high slopes of the hill and more modern, Father noticed, except for the large brick building at the top that looked out over the cliffs and across the bay.

"Commander Nesbitt," Miss Farrow explained when Father had asked who lived there. "Retired Naval man. House been in the family for years, Victorian pile."

"Victorian pile?" queried Father.

Miss Farrow laughed. "Of course, you wouldn't understand a large house built in the reign of Queen Victoria to a particular style." She explained. "Most of the houses here at the top are more recent. In the old days, before cars, people didn't want to struggle up here. Nearly all the families in the old days were fisher folk; they didn't want to be far from the water." Miss Farrow paused to catch her breath, and they looked back down the hill at the village. The houses, closely packed, clung to the steep hillsides of the valley. To the priest's eye, they seemed to be huddling together to keep out of the wind. The roads between the dwellings, he noted, were narrow and the alleys even narrower. His eyes rejoiced in the variety of colours of the older homes. Higher up, he observed, the modern houses all seemed to be bungalows, white and cream; the older homes of the fishing families, as well as white and shades of creamy yellow, displayed a whole variety of colours, blue, green, ochre, and dark red.

"There," said Miss Farrow, pointing across the green waters of the estuary to the river and then with her finger leading Father Aloysius's eyes upstream into the harbour to the quay.

"You see that thatched cottage there, the one with the brown oak door. That's Mrs Hazelmere's." Father Aloysius picked out the long, low, thatched cottage and, then, one by one, found the other buildings that his housekeeper identified. The Ship Inn, just down the quay from Mrs Hazelmere's cottage, the old customs house, now the home of the doctor, the bridge, and, leading down to the quay and the bridge, the main street that would become the road to Pendon Bay.

"And there, of course, is the Anglican Church," Miss Farrow said, pointing to the square red sandstone tower of St. Jude's just visible over a cluster of tiled roofs.

"Where is the school?" Father asked.

"Ah," said the housekeeper, picking up her basket and setting off up the hill again.

"Just there across the green, they wanted the children to have a bit of a field to play in, I guess."

At the top, overlooking the cliffs by the war memorial, they stopped to gaze out across the blue expanse of the sea. Gulls, calling plaintively, soared and dived along the cliff face. Way below, a solitary fishing boat lay still on the calm waters. Further out across the bay, a yellow-hulled yacht made full sail, stretching out every stitch of white canvas to catch all the breeze it could. The priest's eyes explored the coastline, tracing it from the far green smudges of distant headlands along to the waters that fringed the narrow sandy beach at the base of the cliff. He marvelled at shades of colour, the faded blues of the hazy horizon, the dark expanses of water where the weed grew, to the lovely lighter transparent colours of the shallows where the sea bed was sand. He traced the sun's silvery passage across the waters and noted how passing clouds high above changed the whole complexion of the scene. His eyes eagerly explored the cracks and crannies of the rocky outcrops where the closer headland crumbled into the sea, scanning the dark fissures where the pounding of countless waves had cut deep caves into the rock face and had carved out pillars and even archways. Like some giant sculptor creating a magnificent coastal cathedral.

"Beautiful," Father exclaimed in an awed voice.

"Beautiful and always changing," the housekeeper agreed. "Never the same from one day to the next, always changing, but always, always beautiful."

"Thank you." Father felt compelled to express his gratitude, "Thank you for bringing me here."

"Don't thank me, Father, thank God. I do every time I come here, which is most days." Miss Farrow laughed. "Now come on, or we will be late for our lunch. Mrs Hazlemere doesn't like to be kept waiting." By the time they had walked on up the hill past the school, its playground deserted, save for the rustle of an empty crisp packet that travelled in fits and starts across the tarmac in the light breeze, and down through the village, pausing every now and again when Miss Farrow was accosted by a passer-by and regaled with the time of day, to cross the iron bridge at the head of the harbour, it was almost half twelve.

Chapter Four

Those who love dogs know something about God.

-Fakeer Ishavardas

Father Aloysius was ready for his lunch. Miss Farrow led the way down the quay to Mrs Hazelmere's cottage. Mrs Hazelmere, accompanied by two yapping Pekingese, met them at the door. She beamed a welcome, and then hastily undoing her apron and shooing the dogs before her, she led the way in through a narrow hall to her dining room. Father had another silent giggle as an image of a lead sprang into his mind again. He saw himself as a somewhat larger animal than the Pekingese, perhaps looking down his nose in a superior way at their excitable yapping.

"Mind your head, Father," Mrs Hazelmere warned in her booming voice. Her warning had come too late; Father Aloysius was already nursing a bruised scalp; he had failed to stoop low enough and had caught his head on the door lintel.

"Oh, you poor, poor lamb." Mrs Hazelmere fussed as the priest ruefully rubbed his forehead, mentally chiding himself for his daydreaming. The Pekingese erupted into a further cacophony of barking before being banished to the kitchen.

"Dear me, what a noise. Now, you poor thing, perhaps a sherry will help. You mustn't mind my two little friends here. They are quite harmless, second in the order of my loves, only to the church and the memory of dear Mr Hazelmere, of course, you must understand, Father." The priest was to get used to being called just plain Father instead of his full name. Mrs Hazelmere was obviously a great talker, he decided, gratefully accepting a large schooner of sherry. He was correct. He also made a mental note that perhaps even his throbbing head, as painful as it was, was preferable to Mrs Hazelmere's yapping dogs or her fussing fingers round his forehead. He was about to reopen his reflections on what sort of a dog he might be when he decided that daydreaming had already got him into enough trouble, and it was time that he listened to the conversation politely.

If Father Aloysius had been correct in surmising that Mrs Hazelmere was a great talker, then Miss Farrow was equally correct in asserting that Mrs Hazelmere was a wonderful cook. Father hadn't had such a good meal in ages. He enjoyed, too, listening to the two ladies chatter, wondering at their fund of local gossip. Occasionally, he was obliged to join in.

"Father, we understand you were quite a hit at the youth club." boomed Mrs Hazelmere, piling Father's plate high with roast potatoes.

"Oh," the priest replied demurely, wondering in what aspect he had been a hit and with whom.

"Even cut that monster Sid Trevinian down to size. You must be awfully strong," went on Mrs Hazelmere, moving the potatoes over slightly on the plate in order to have room for the cabbage and Yorkshire puddings.

"There!" she exclaimed triumphantly, handing Father his plate, "Traditional English Sunday roast."

"Thank you, thank you, this looks wonderful. As Mr Trevinian himself observed, Mrs Hazelmere, I did have God on my side, but even with his help, all that huffing and puffing left me quite worn out and weak. This plateful should restore me to full fitness, I'm sure."

Mrs Hazelmere giggled, "Now, Father, don't tease; if God helped you defeat Mr Trevinian in an arm wrestle, then he probably helped me too in my cooking, so let's just thank him and get on with it, shall we." She paused to put salt on her meal.

"Father, please, will you say grace."

The priest bowed his head, "Heavenly Father, we give thanks for this food and those who have provided it. May we never forget...." At this moment, the kitchen door burst open, and the Pekingese came charging across the highly polished boards of the dining room floor. Howling and yapping with great excitement, they careened, slipping and sliding into the all-enveloping folds of Father's heavy black cassock and proceeded to snap and snarl at the black cloth. Resisting the temptation to think of leads or to cuff the two little dogs away, Father stoically completed the grace "those who do not have enough to eat." The priest paused before looking up and added.

"Speaking of which, when did your delightful little dogs last have a good meal because they now seem determined to eat me from the toes up?"

"Shoo, shoo," Mrs Hazelmere had leapt from her place and was busy disentangling her little lions from the folds of Father's cassock.

"Oh, Father, how you exaggerate, now you two, what do you think you are doing? Get away at once." Brandishing her napkin, the lady of the house chased her two furry friends, yapping back to the sitting room. "Father, I'm so terribly sorry. What can you think of me and my two little dears? Here, please have a glass of wine." Father, who was gingerly rubbing his ankle and thanking the good God for the thickness of his cassock, which had saved him from the worst of the nips and bites, prayed, albeit silently, for a lead and asked God for forgiveness for what he truly felt about the two dogs. He also made a mental note that he was not a Pekingese. At the same time, he accepted a glass of wine. Thankfully, from the priest's point of view, there were no further interruptions from the dogs, and feeling a little frayed at either end, he was able to get on with the delicious food in front of him and also concentrate on what he was saying when he had to say something. The combination of the large sherry and the wine was taking its toll on his tongue control. Father Aloysius was not used to taking alcohol. The priest's contribution to the conversation came over the sweet, creamy trifle liberally laced with brandy. A flushed Mrs Hazelmere, conscious that she and Enid Farrow had dominated the table talk, turned to Father Aloysius and, fixing him with her smile, asked him to tell them something about himself.

"Father, Father, what are we on about all this time, dear me, Enid, poor Father has had to put up with our gossip long enough, it's time we learnt about him. Tell us, Father, all about yourself."

"Myself?" Hastily, Father gathered his somewhat befuddled thoughts, "Myself, well, what do you want to know?"

"Where do you come from? Your family and, and how in heaven's name did you come to be here?" Mrs Hazelmere leaned across the table towards him to offer some more trifle.

"No, please, the trifle is delicious, and I've had a wonderful meal, but enough is as good as a feast, more than enough would spoil it. As for me, it's a long story," Father warned.

"Well, we have time, Father, we have time, coffee, Enid? Mrs Hazelmere left the table to fetch the coffee tray.

"That was a lovely meal, Harriet. I'd love a coffee," replied the house-keeper.

"Usual? Father, how do you like yours? Mrs Hazelmere poured the coffee for Miss Farrow and held the pot poised for the priest.

"Not too strong, thank you." said father, hoping he would be offered the sugar to put in his cup himself. He was.

"Well, you must realise that I was born on the continent where coffee originated, Arabica coffee, that is, which I believe came first from Ethiopia."

"And sugar? Asked Mrs Hazelmere innocently. Father was relieved that Miss Farrow had chosen that moment to help clear the table - the nuances of Mrs Hazelmere's question were lost on her.

"Of course, sugar cane is grown widely in Africa. We used to be given sticks of it as a treat when I was at school. We used to chew on it. That sweet juice trickling down my chin was like heaven, but where it comes from, I'm not sure," Father replied.

"You asked about family," Father considered it prudent to change the subject, "I was born in Karamoja in Northern Uganda. I am a member of the Karamajong. My father was a wandering nomad, a pastoralist. He kept flocks of cattle and goats. My mother, too, I suppose. She died in childbirth when I was very young, and one of my sisters and another of my father's wives brought me up."

"That was tough; you must have been very sad," interjected Mrs Hazelmere.

"No, at least I don't remember. You see, I was very young, and we were part of an extended family. Our families were different. My father was, of course, not a Christian; very few Karamajong were. As was the custom, he had a number of wives, I was, I suppose, not short of mothers, but I don't remember much about it, a lot has happened since. I do remember looking after the animals. And I had a special calf that was mine, and I used to take it into our home at night. I remember our home. It was tiny, so small, not much bigger than," Father looked about him for something to compare his home with, "It was less than half the size of this room and not nearly as high, of course. Many houses in Africa are like yours, Mrs Hazelmere, thatched, but ours was different; it was made of skins so we could take it to bits easily and move to another place. We were always on the move in search of grass and water. I remember," Father paused, his eyes grew misty, and he seemed to gaze across the years, not seeing Mrs Hazelmere's quaint cottage dining room, with its beams, brasses, and china but searching instead some African horizon, a smudge of blue hills shimmering in the heat haze, way across a dusty plain, the yellow barked fever trees that grew along the water course with those weaver bird nests, that hung down from the high branches. The thorn bush boma, his father's cattle, and his father standing so proud and tall with his favourite bull.

"Yes, Father Aloysius," prompted Mrs Hazelmere. The priest's mind jolted back to the present.

"You must understand it was very different," he said. "And it was a long time ago, but I remember the smell of dust and dung, and the bleating of the goats when they scented water, and the deep lowing of the cattle and the thwack of the men's sticks as they herded the stock along, and their cries as they shouted to each other and their favourite beasts. I remember the call of the coucal and the hornbill, the din of the bird song in the early morning, and the deep grunts and occasional roars of lions at night. We used to get lions round our boma, and the crickets, oh, the crickets! You can't imagine the noise of the crickets at dusk. I remember the warm taste of milk fresh from the udder; it was especially good in the morning. Then there was the smell of wood smoke, the acrid stink of it in your nose and eyes when you first stooped low and entered the hut; it used to make my eyes water. In the early morning, when we got up, there was that cool fresh smell of the dew on the grass and the spiders' webs, so many, I remember so well that silver sheen of many, many spider webs all laid out like a carpet on the grass. And the sunsets, those fiery red sunsets. I remember my father..." Aloysius paused, conscious perhaps that he was rambling a bit, the sherry and the wine were talking, he surmised. "I'm sorry," he said, "I must be boring you."

"No, not a bit," Miss Farrow reassured him. "Tell us about your father."

"My father was tall, so tall, and thin and strong. He could walk all day, all day under the sun, without a pause, what a walker. He was a great story teller; He used to tell us stories at night. He used to sit crouched by the embers of the fire and tell us stories, Long, long stories, the tribal legends that were, I suppose, our people's history. He would talk and talk, and we'd fall asleep."

"Is he still alive?" asked Mrs Hazelmere.

"No." Father replied shortly and then, matter of factly, added, "He was killed in a raid." Father Aloysius did not tell them about those memories of being woken in the first light of dawn by the crack of rifle fire, the pandemonium of thundering hooves, and the screams of the women and children and the bleating of the goats. He had escaped in the wild confusion and hidden in a hole that had been dug by a hyena in the base of a tall white ant's nest. The awful smell of the scavenger had made him retch, but nobody had found him. They found all the others. He did not tell them how he lay there trembling in fright, his thighs wet with his own urine, until the sounds of the departing raiders and his father's cattle and goats had faded into the distance. He did not tell them how later, when the hot sun was high in the sky, he was parched with thirst, and he had crawled out of that stinking hole to go and find them, bodies broken and twisted and lying in pools of blood. He did not mention the vultures. They had been circling high overhead and had descended to feast on the corpses ... and the flies, the incessant buzzing of the flies. Father raised his left hand to his forehead and then gently drummed his long fingers on the table top. "That is how I became a Christian." He explained. "You see, the raiders killed everyone else in my family. I was found. The only one left alive. I was adopted by some missionaries. Catholic Fathers rescued me and sent me to a school. There, I learnt about God and Jesus, and I became a Christian. Later, I was sent to a seminary in Ireland, and I became a priest," said father simply.

"Fascinating, but what an awful thing, losing your family that way, I'm sorry, so sorry. Would you like more coffee?" asked Mrs Hazelmere. Father had more coffee.

"Didn't you go back to Africa, Father? Mind you, I wouldn't have blamed you if you hadn't."

Father Aloysius was conscious of Miss Farrow's sympathetic gaze. Perhaps he should not have mentioned his father, but then they had asked, and it was the European way, he supposed. No one would have mentioned it in his tribe; it was not their custom to speak of the dead. Despite all the years of education and his apparent Westernisation, Father Aloysius still found there were times when his old tribal self, his African self, jolted against his current self, his white dog-collared priesthood, and caused him to wonder about the clashes in customs and values that had been part of his life, part of his growing up and adapting, part of his change. In a way, although he acknowledged he had grown, he did not like to think of it as growth because that implied that his father had been in some way inferior; he thought of it as change. It was better, more comfortable to think of it that way. The threads of a previous conversation that day came back to him, the same but different, different but the same. *Hey, hold up, Father, this is getting a bit deep,* he thought. I*t's time* *to lighten up. After all, it's Sunday dinner time, not a philosophical debate.* He grinned.

"Oh yes," said Father Aloysius. "Of course, I went back, but not to my home. I was sent to be a teacher at a school in Zimbabwe."

"I see," Mrs Hazelmere sipped her coffee, "Did you enjoy it there?"

"Yes," replied Father Aloysius, "I enjoyed the teaching, and I also got involved in politics."

"Politics!" echoed Mrs Hazelmere, raising her eyebrows.

"Yes, I was quite active politically. Unfortunately, at times, I wasn't completely discreet. You know a little I expect about the issue of land there and how certain farmers are being evicted from their farms."

"Yes," the two ladies replied together.

"It's a very complex matter, of course," explained Father Aloysius. "But it was my view that the Government was being hypocritical in its support for the squatters' invasions of this certain farmer's land and that the whole thing was not in the best interests of the country. In fact, it could be economically disastrous. I was suggesting that there were better ways of land reform."

"I see," said Mrs Hazelmere. "And what happened."

"Well," shrugged Father Aloysius, "The government does not like people who are foolish enough to disagree with it. I had an accident." The priest did not divulge he had been badly beaten up and that he had ended up where all who disagree with the powers that be ended up, in prison and that there he had been tortured, or that the bishop of Plymouth was visiting a friend of his, and they had visited the prison. He did not tell them how his bishop and the bishop of Plymouth had agitated for his release, and when eventually they got the President to agree, they had decided that it would be better for all concerned if he left Zimbabwe. He just told them his bishop had decided it was safer for him to leave the country.

"You poor thing, an accident, but why here?" asked Mrs Hazelmere. "It's not that you are not very welcome, Father, but it just seems, it seems a long way. You could have gone to another part of Africa."

"Coincidence, happy coincidence," replied Father. "the bishop who had helped get me out of prison had just been on holiday in Zimbabwe. He had connections there. It was just a fortunate coincidence."

"And a very happy coincidence, too," exclaimed Miss Farrow. "Now, Harriet, we must be helping you with the dishes and then getting along, or I'll never get my Sunday visiting done before evening, Angelus."

"And I must take my little dears for a walk," said Mrs Hazelmere and went to release

Min and Muffet. There was another cacophony of yapping as the two dogs charged about the little room, leaping up at Father and wagging their tails in a frenzy of excitement.

"Tell me, Mrs Hazelmere," asked Father apropos of nothing, "Do you have a lead for your dogs?"

"Of course, Father, of course, but not for indoors." Mrs Hazelmere couldn't help hiding her surprise. Father noted the slight tone of annoyance in her reply to his question. Her dogs were a sensitive area; his thoughts of leads had got him into trouble again!

Perhaps it was the fresh air or the combination of the fresh air and all that food and the sherry and wine that made Father Aloysius feel rather light-headed as he followed Miss Farrow down to the water front. The steep steps seemed to wobble a bit as he made his way, slightly over-carefully, down them. He was glad when they got to the flat paving of the wharf. The tide was out. Boats higher up near the bridge were all stranded on mud banks. Further out towards the sea, where the ruins of the old fort perched on a jutting cliff and the water was deeper and the estuary wider, a whole fleet of boats of all sorts and sizes rode at their moorings. On one, an old boat, clinker-built and bright with fresh varnish, an old man was working. A dog, a large black animal, sat by the tiller in the stern, patiently watching his master repairing a fender.

"Excuse me, Miss Farrow, do you see that dog out there on the boat? What kind of a dog is it?"

Miss Farrow looked out to where the priest was pointing, "Ah yes, that's Joe Walsh's Labrador. Joe is a regular here. He loves his sailing. They say he is a good sailor. Loves his dog too."

"Labrador," repeated Father. "Are all Labradors black?

"All black Labradors are black," said Miss Farrow, "There are golden Labradors too."

"I see," said Father Aloysius, "So there are two types of Labrador, black ones and golden ones."

"No, there are black ones, golden ones, and reddish ones; the black ones are more common, I think," said Miss Farrow.

Father Aloysius grinned, the same but different. Perhaps he thought to himself, I'm a Labrador, a common black Labrador. A common black Labrador on Miss Farrow's lead. His foot caught on a piece of uneven paving. He stumbled, bumped into a waterside bench, and before he knew it, he was teetering on the edge of the wharf. A hand caught his arm, steadying him. He turned and looked down. It was Anna, Anna whom he had met at the youth club. Her big blue eyes looked up into his face. She smiled. "Whoops-a-daisy," she said. "Careful."

"Thank you, "stammered the priest, drawing back from the edge of the wharf.

"I'm sorry, I tripped." Once again, dreaming about leads had nearly been his undoing.

"You nearly had a swim," said Miss Farrow. Why don't you sit down here and enjoy the sun and the boats and talk to Anna while I go and visit Mrs Fitzroy? She finds it difficult to cope with more than one visitor at a time. I always call on Sunday afternoon, so she is expecting me. If you are still here when I've done, we'll go back up the hill together. If not, then I'll assume you've made your own way back to the presbytery."

"Thank you," said Father, "A few minutes sitting in the sun sounds good," He sank gratefully onto the green bench. Anna sat down at the other end. For a moment, they sat in silence. Father Aloysius studied the boats. Anna studied the priest. The sun shone down on them both. It warmed Father Aloysius's broad back, and it warmed Anna's bear-brown legs. The boats seemed to blur and swim in the priest's vision; his eyelids grew heavy and then closed. His chin sagged. In a moment, he was asleep. The girl smiled, gazed out for a time at the boats, and then back at the priest. His breathing was gentle and even; his long black lashes lay lightly on the brown curve of his cheek. There were six little scars there, three on either cheek, small oval indentations that shone a darker brown than the smooth surface they dimpled. She wondered what they signified. Perhaps one day, she'd ask him. Idly, she reached out and plucked a long-stemmed sea pink from where it sprouted in a crack in the pavement. She held the flower under the priest's nose and rotated it slowly in her fingertips, allowing it to tickle the top of his lips and the bridge of his nose between his nostrils. Father sneezed and awoke with a start.

"Wakey wakey, sleepy head," chided Anna.

"I'm sorry," Father shook his head.

Anna's fingers rested for a moment lightly on his arm, "You fell asleep on me, what a way to treat the lady who saved you from drowning." she teased.

"I'm sorry, it must be the sun."

"The drink more like it," said Anna poking the priest in the midriff.

"Drink?" queried Father, mildly shying away from her prodding.

"Yes," said the girl, shaking her finger at him, "You've been drinking." The priest was silent, his impassive face completely immobile as he gazed out across the estuary.

"Have you been drinking?" prompted the girl.

"Yes," confessed the priest simply.

"I see," there was admonishment in the girl's tone.

"We had lunch with Mrs Hazelmere, I had a sherry and one glass of wine."

"A sherry and a glass of wine, is that all?" Snorted the girl in mock derision.

"Yes. That's all. I'm not used to alcohol. I very rarely drink, except, of course, at Mass, and then I take only a sip," explained the priest in his defence.

"Obviously! I only wish it took that much to make me happy."

"What makes you happy?" Father Aloysius asked, hoping to change the direction of the conversation.

"Well, a lot lot more than one sherry and a glass of wine," said the girl with a giggle,

"Usually five or six beers and," she broke off in mid-sentence.

"And?" Father prompted.

"And mind your own business." retorted the girl sharply. "This is not a confession, and if it is, it's yours, not mine."

"All right, I confess," said the priest with a feigned sigh. "And what's to be my punishment? Am I to be dragged vomiting round the streets of Pondreath and end up having bad eggs thrown at me in the stocks?"

Anna giggled again. This priest obviously had a sense of humour. She poked him for a second time playfully. "No, silly." She paused, smiling at him, "You're fun, you know."

Father Aloysius glanced at the girl quizzically and shrugged.

"Don't worry," Anna said, serious all of a sudden, "Your secret's safe with me."

"That's a relief," said Father.

"There is a condition, of course,"

"Oh."

"You tell me what you were dreaming about just now."

Father Aloysius grinned and flexed his long arms, "Do you like Labradors?" he asked.

"Anna shrugged, "I like black Labradors, I'm not so keen on the gold or the red ones. They somehow don't look quite right. Why?"

Father Aloysius's grin broadened. "You like the black Labradors," he asked for reassurance.

"Yes."

"I dreamt I was a black Labrador."

"Silly," Anna, her eyes sparkling with laughter, punched the priest playfully on the arm. There was a screech of breaks behind them and the honk of a car horn. Anna leapt to her feet. Father turned. Two bronzed, bare-chested youths sat imperiously in their brightly painted wide-wheeled beach buggies. It had no roof; instead, a clutter of surf boards was fastened to its roll bars.

The young men beckoned to Anna and gave the priest one of those long, anonymous, dark glasses stares.

"Surfs calling must fly," said the girl, patting the priest lightly on both cheeks with the palms of her hands. "See you, and just you be careful climbing that hill, walk in a straight line, we don't want anyone else in on our secret!" With a gay wave, she was gone, her long sun-bleached hair streaming out behind her as the buggie shot off up the wharf and disappeared round the corner of the customs house.

Father Aloysius sighed. Mr Evans certainly had a beautiful daughter. He leant back on the back of the bench and closed his eyes. There was time for one more dream of leads and Labradors before he had to climb the hill and return to the presbytery.

Chapter Five

As with the butterfly, adversity is necessary to build character in people.

Larry learnt about the robbery from his uncle. The lorry was just one of five vehicles that had been broken into that night. The others had all been in various car parks along the coast. Radios, CDs, and personal effects had been taken. Anything it seemed with a re-saleable value. Larry had got up early. After the youth club debacle, he wanted to avoid his uncle, but he hadn't been early enough. Sid was already at the table in the kitchen when Larry came down for his breakfast. As he quietly went about getting his bowl of cornflakes, Larry felt his uncle's eyes on him. It was not pleasant. What was he thinking? Surely he couldn't know? The big man rapped his spoon on the table to get Larry's attention. The sudden sound startled him. He tried to control his surprise, but his hands were shaking. He spilt the milk. "Where were you last night?" his uncle growled. Larry felt his heart skip a beat. His uncle couldn't possibly know, but why was he asking questions? Was it just that he was peeved about the beating he had had at arm wrestling, or did he suspect something, and if so, what?"

"You mean after the club?"

"When else would I mean stupid? Now, don't you play funny games with me, boy, just answer my questions, where?" The big man had raised his voice to shout.

"Ow, shut up, will you? Some of us are trying to sleep," it was his aunt yelling from upstairs. Charlotte had been out at the pub until closing time and was suffering from one of her morning headaches. Sid's neck bulged red, and he ground his teeth. He crashed a huge fist on the table in his rage.

"Shut up yourself, you old cow!" then, turning to glower at Larry, he demanded, "Well?"

"Home. After the club, I came home," stammered Larry, his heart sinking inside him as he said the words.

"Straight home?" insisted Sid.

"Almost. Anna and I had words first."

"Words?"

"Yes, we had a row. I.. I.. I was sticking up for you about the wrestling," stammered Larry.

"That stuck up, little madam... and after your words?" Sid sneered.

"I just walked about a bit, I suppose."

"Didn't find yourself walking about in the car park by any chance, did you?"

"Can't you two be quiet? Philippa's trying to sleep." Charlotte had got up and was leaning over the banisters. Her face was blotchy, and her hair in a tangled mess.

Sid crashed both hands down onto the table. The milk bottle bounced off onto the floor and smashed.

"Shut up, get up, or just get back to bed!" he yelled back at his wife.

Larry leapt to the sink to get a cloth and began to clear up the mess, grateful for the distraction. He hoped there would be another bottle of milk in the fridge for his cornflakes. Charlotte made a rude gesture at her husband and sulked off back into the bedroom.

Gingerly, Larry picked up the broken glass, dropping it on top of the rubbish in the already full waste bin, he shook his head and replied to his uncle's question.

"No, I was nowhere near the car park." He was glad he could tell the truth. "Why?" he asked his uncle.

"Why," grunted his uncle, "Why, because some snotty-nosed little brats were messing about with Arthur's wagon?"

"How do you know?" asked Larry, hoping his question sounded casual and that his voice would not betray his sudden anxiety. His uncle had been in the pub until late that night, and surely it hadn't been on the news or anything like that.

"Arthur told me, nosy. He found they had broken into his motor when we got out of the pub last night. Then the old Bill phoned, special see, wanted to warn me, to ask me to keep a look out." Larry sat down and pulled his bowl of cornflakes away from the edge of the table towards him.

"Look out where?" The mention of the police only increased Larry's fears.

"Junk shops, car boots, that sort of thing," said Sid, nodding at his cereal, "So you tell that silly little sister of yours next time one of her mates takes her to the car boot at Pendon Bay of a Sunday she ought to keep her eyes peeled."

It was at that moment that Philippa had come in. She had blushed a self-conscious red when she had heard Sid talking about her, but the big man gave no hint that he was aware that he might have hurt her. He often referred to his niece in a derogatory manner. She would have loved to have replied in the same vein, but she was frightened of her huge uncle and his uncertain temper. More than once, he had cuffed her round the ear and set her head spinning, and she had seen him take his belt to Larry.

"How would she, or we, or anyone know? I mean, they are not likely to have stolen written all over them, are they," asked Larry.

"You don't have to know, just suspect, leave the knowing to the old Bill." The big man pushed his chair back with a grunt and leaned back on two legs.

"So what do we do if we suspect?" asked Larry.

Big Sid let his chair thump back onto all four legs, "Tell the Old Bill, of course, no, no, wait a minute, don't tell the Old Bill nothing, you tell me, and I'll tell the Bill. The less you have to do with Old Bill, the better, and anyway, if I give him the wink, he feels I'm on his side, and I like to think he thinks he owes me, if you get my meaning."

Larry helped himself to cornflakes and passed them to his sister. She had fetched another milk bottle from the fridge, but Larry hardly noticed. His mind was full of what he had seen the night before, and he wondered whether he should mention it.

He munched his cereals and decided that perhaps it would be better now if he didn't.

Sid was certain to ask why he hadn't mentioned it before and might even turn more nasty than he was already. Nor could he mention it to the police, for if Sid were to find out, he would be certain to feel Larry had betrayed him. He did not have long to ruminate over his dilemma, for Sid was smacking the table top with his huge hand again and pointing at Larry.

"Where did you get that leather from? Car boot wasn't it? Bet you a dollar to a dime it was nicked."

"Unlikely," asserted Larry, "There was a whole rail of them."

"Really!" sneered the big man," And what's to say they weren't all nicked?"

"Nothing, but…"

"But nothing," interrupted Sid. "Just you be careful what you buy, you could be had for handling stolen property. Anyway, how much did you pay for it?"

"Fifteen pounds," Larry replied hesitantly.

"Fifteen nicker!" exploded his uncle. "Fifteen, where did you get that from, for heaven's sake?"

"I earned it."

"Earned it!" snorted the Big man, "How?"

"That last bike I did up, I sold it for for," he almost told Sid that he had sold the bike for thirty pounds, but then he realised his blunder and hesitated.

"For what?" demanded Sid.

"For the jacket," muttered Larry lamely.

"Well, if you are earning that sort of money, you can start paying housekeeping.

It's time your aunt stopped acting like a charity shop and got a few bob back for her pains."

"But, but our dad pays you," protested Larry.

"Your dad does, does he? How do you know what your dad does? Anyway, that reminds me, I had a word with him the other day. Sent his best he did, asked if you were well."

"When is he coming to see us, please?" asked Philippa. She could not completely disguise the hope in her voice.

"See you! Busy man, your dad, but I guess he'll be down one of these days in the not-too-distant future, so you'd better smarten yourself up, my girl, and as for you, lad, I'd start putting by a little of that, the money you make flogging duff bikes to the poor and unsuspecting. You might need it if he comes down, you'd want to give him a nice surprise present or a night out on the Ship, now wouldn't you?"

Larry just nodded and, gathering up his cornflakes bowl, quickly ran it under the tap at the sink and slipped out before his uncle had any more questions about jackets and the money he made selling bikes. Philippa shovelled in another big spoonful of cornflakes and got up to follow Larry out.

"And where do you think you're going?" growled Sid, beckoning her back with one thick nicotine-stained finger. Philippa shrugged and returned to her place.

"Finish your mouthful, finish your meal, and then get up. Manners!" Sid admonished.

"No manners, kids these days, no manners at all. Charlotte, Charlotte," Sid yelled up the stairs to his wife. "Charlotte, do you hear me? Shake a leg, time you was up."

"Now, what's the matter?" his wife grumbled, sticking her head over the banisters.

"I've got to be off. Need some lunch."

"Get it yourself."

Sid's neck bulged red again. He swore. "Get down here, woman, or else! I've got to sort my gear, going to be away two days; might even be a week. Got to get off, so hurry."

Charlotte muttered her own string of obscenities under her breath and then, gathering her tattered dressing gown about her, flounced down the stairs, "Thank goodness for that, we might get some peace for a change."

"Peace," retorted her husband, "Pieces more like it." He stomped off up the stairs to get his clothes packed.

"And what do you think you're sitting dreaming about?" Charlotte flung at Philippa as she clattered about in the fridge.

"When is my dad coming?" asked the girl, picking at her fingers absently and staring across the room.

"Dad? What gave you the idea he was coming?"

"Uncle said he'd heard from him, said, said....."

"Said what? For heaven's sake, stop mumbling and speak up."

"Oh, nothing." Philippa's shoulders sagged, and she wiped a tear from her eye with the back of her hand.

"Oh, for heaven's sake, stop snivelling and get yourself sorted for school. Time your father did come to sort you out, time he sent me some more money too. Don't know how he expects to keep all you lot on the pittance he sends me."

With a little moan, Philippa stuck her fingers in her ears and fled up the stairs. She slammed the door of her bedroom and, throwing herself down on the bed, burst into tears. It was Larry who found her some half an hour later. Sid had already left, and his aunt had gone down to the shop to buy some cigarettes. He slipped quietly into the room. He sat down on the edge of the bed and gently put his hand on her shoulder.

"Here," he whispered, "I've got you some lunch. Get up. It's time you were off to school."

Philippa groaned, "School, what are you doing here? You should be at work."

"Change of plan," Larry explained. "We've got a job to do out at Saltley, and Mike's going to pick me up on the way through. Now you just dry your eyes and get sorted, you mustn't let them see you cry."

Philippa rolled over onto her back. She looked up at her brother. Their eyes met. She felt a warm glow of affection flood her face. He had always looked out for her, and when life really seemed bleak, he was there quietly, reaching out to do what her dad should be doing.

"Larry, when is dad coming?" she asked plaintively.

"Soon, I guess," Larry lied. "So you'd better be getting yourself off to school because that's exactly where he'd expect to find you."

"Oh, you!" exclaimed the girl, and scrambling to her feet, she planted a wet kiss on his cheek as she passed him on her way to the bathroom. "Larry, do us a favour?"

"What?"

"Lend us your jacket."

"My jacket. Aw, what do you want that for?"

"It's cool. Go on, lend it to me, just for today."

"Oh, all right," Larry conceded, "Just for today. But mind you, look after it."

"Promise." A car horn honked outside. Larry bounded down the stairs.

"See you," he called back to his sister and ran down the path to the car waiting by the kerb. She ran to her window to watch him. "Thanks, Larry," she whispered to herself as she slipped into the black jacket. Its weight felt reassuring as she settled it round her shoulders. "Thanks, Larry." She whispered, rubbing her cheek on the smooth leather, "Thanks." It was too big for her, but she didn't care.

For Philippa, the day seemed to improve from the moment she put the jacket on.

Her walk to school was not a time of the day that normally gave her much pleasure, but this morning, she revelled in every step as she met her colleagues on the way and showed off Larry's jacket to them. She wore it at both break times and lunchtime, and she was wearing it whistling merrily when she left the school at the end of the day.

She was with her usual group of friends, and they stopped off at the swings on the corner of the field. It was a pleasant afternoon, and the girls enjoyed having turns on the swings and chasing each other about. Philippa grew hot. She made the fatal mistake of taking her coat off and leaving it on the back of the bench. There it had remained when the girls drifted away down the path, joking and laughing together as they made their way back to their respective homes.

Philippa was helping Aunt Charlotte peel potatoes for tea when Larry arrived home.

He had had a good day, too, and greeted his sister cheerily as he came in the door.

"Hey, ho girls, what's for tea then? Great..... chips. Now look who's getting her pretty fingers all slimy with peelings, if it isn't that lovely little lady of high fashion Miss Philippa T. herself. How's the leather look gone down in big metropolis?"

Leather, Larry's coat, Philippa's mind jolted back to the bench. She had left the coat on the bench, oh no, her heart sank, she'd better run up there quickly at once.

"Sorry, aunty, I've got to pop out for a mo, urgent," she said as she hastily wiped the potato peelings from her fingers and bolted for the door. Before either Charlotte or Larry could say anything, she was out of the front door and half way down the path.

Larry was the first to realise the implications of his sister's panicked departure, his coat, it was his coat, she must have left it somewhere.

"I'll kill her," he muttered, and he, too, charged out of the house and went racing after his sister up the road. Charlotte stood bemused, shaking her head. Here she was trying to make the children a good tea, and what did they do, abandon her: well, they'd have to get their own. She dried her hands and, gathering her coat from the back of the door, locked up the house and headed off down the hill to the pub. Larry caught his sister up at the bend by the ally.

"What have you done with it? Where have you left it?" he demanded, reaching out to catch her arm as she dived into the ally. Philippa shook his hand off and turned to remonstrate with him,

"Don't," she protested, "I know exactly where it …." At that moment, she collided heavily with Father Aloysius. Father Aloysius helped Philippa to her feet.

"My word, young lady, you certainly are in a big hurry. What's the trouble?" The priest ruefully rubbed his chin.

"Oh Mr, Mr…." Stammered the girl breathlessly

"Father Aloysius," suggested the priest mildly.

"Father Aloysius, I'm so sorry. It it's a coat, Larry's coat. You haven't seen a black leather coat, have you?"

"Where do you think you left it?"

"Yes, where?" interjected Larry, who was not in the least bit pleased to see the priest,

"If it's gone, heaven help you!"

"Don't worry, Larry, I'm sure we'll find it. It's up at the bench by the swings, I think.

You must have passed them. Was there a coat there? Was there?" There was desperation in the young girl's voice.

"I didn't see one, but there were…." Larry pushed past them and hurried up the path.

"Come on," he grunted, pulling his sister along behind. "We've no time to stand here gabbling If that jacket's not there!" He left his threat unsaid, but both Philippa and the priest sensed his anger. The girl turned to give Father Aloysius a pleading glance as her brother dragged her up the path. The priest shook his head and shrugged. He mouthed.

"Don't worry," as he followed.

The coat was not on the bench. Hastily, they cast about looking for it, the girl frantically scrabbling about in the litter bin. Larry impatiently pulled her out of it.

"Don't be such a silly ass," he spluttered, "It won't be there, someone must have walked off with it! Now, what do we do?"

Father Aloysius was gazing up the path past the school. "There were some lads that passed me," he suggested tentatively, "One of them was wearing a black jacket."

"There you see," Larry turned on his sister, his hand raised, "You…"

"Larry," Father Aloysius's voice was gentle. "If we, if we hurry, I'm sure we can catch them up." Taking Philippa's hand, he hurried on up the path. They strode along past the school. At the monument at the top of the hill, they paused to catch their breath, gazing down the paths that led away along the cliff tops. There, some distance away, below them were three figures. One was wearing a black jacket.

"There," said the priest, pointing, "I'll catch them, you follow." Hastily, he undid the buttons at the front of his cassock and, hitching it up to reveal his long black legs, he tucked the garment into his shorts. With a grin, he set off, bounding down the slope. Larry and Philippa followed as fast as they could, but they were soon left well behind.

The three youths were caught completely unawares by Father Aloysius's sudden appearance among them; they had paused on a grassy patch, close-cropped by sheep that fell away steeply to a sheer cliff. They were watching the surfers below them, friends of theirs, when Father Aloysius's cassock, by now untucked from his shorts and flying out either side of him like huge black wings, came bounding down the steep path to land with one final long leap right in front of the three of them.

"What the ……..." the tallest of the youths swore and took a step back. "If it isn't bat man gone black."

Father Aloysius stood panting in the bracken, blocking the path. The index finger of his right hand touched the bridge of his nose and stroked down over his lips and chin. He turned his face to the sea and gathered himself.

"Excuse me, I'm sorry to interrupt your walk," the priest said in a quiet, controlled, civil way, "My friend has lost his black jacket and, and I was wondering whether by any chance you had found it and…"

"…… off," retorted the curly-headed boy who was wearing the jacket. "How'd you know it's yours? You can't just walk up to people and ask them for their clothes, darkie."

"Na," interjected the tallest boy, "I mean, my mate left his shorts down on the rocks the other day and went for a swim in the buff, sorry n----r, naked," the youth sneered when he saw Father was puzzled at the expression. "Anyway, when he gets out, the shorts were gone. They were brown like yours; in fact, I think you had better hand over those shorts so we can have a look." At that moment, Larry arrived with his sister in tow. Father Aloysius's hand stroked his chin again. He looked up at Larry. Ignoring the boy's reference to his shorts, he said quietly.

"Well, Larry, does this look like your jacket?" There was a long, studied silence. Larry looked at the curly-headed boy with the jacket on. All three youths stared at Larry. In their cold, hard stares, they defied him to answer.

He felt the hostility of their eyes bore into him, gradually turning to derision as the moments lengthened and he failed to answer. He licked his lips. It was his sister who stepped forward and, pointing, replied quietly,

"It is, it is, there's my hankie sticking out the pocket."

"Yes," said Larry, "It looks like mine." Father Aloysius sighed and reached out his hand towards the curly-headed youth.

"Well," he said flatly, his eyes were hard and blank.

The youth looked away and then swore. He shrugged and took the jacket off. Then suddenly, he whirled it over his head, "Black…….." he mouthed, "You can go and fetch it from the bottom," he threw it high out across the cliff. Father Aloysius's reactions were instant and cat-like; he leapt high into the air and caught a passing sleeve, pulling the jacket down to him as he landed. Crouching, he looked long and hard at the youth. "Thank you," he said quietly. The expression in his black eyes remained blank.

Slowly, he walked over to Larry and handed him the coat. "Go," he signalled with his chin. "I'll be with you in a minute." He turned back. Larry paused a moment, looking at the priest and the three youths.

"Come on, you heard what he said," His sister tugged at his sleeve. Larry turned away up the slope. Father Aloysius walked slowly up to the tallest of the youths.

His eyes, still blank and black, narrowed slightly. A gust of wind from the sea caught his cassock and sent it flapping across his legs.

"What did you call me?" his voice was low, almost a whisper. The youth's face contorted into a sneer.

"N----r," he spat. Hardly had the words come out of his mouth than he was flat on his back, thrown by a deft piece of foot work and a firm shove on the chest from the priest. The priest stood above his protagonist, his sandalled foot on the youth's chest, just below his throat. His eyes were no longer blank and black. Instead, they sparked fury as they swept to the faces of all three young men, taking each one in turn in an awful glare. His blood pounded in his ears. Somewhere deep inside him, he heard the crack of a rifle, the distressed bleating of goats, and then there was the strong smell of blood. It filled his nostrils. His ears were full of the awful buzzing of the flies. There was a distant clang. It was the clang of a bell on the red buoy out in the bay, but to Father Aloysius, it was the clang of the Mission bell. The bell that, more than any other sound, reminded him of the Mission and those good, kind men who had rescued him after the cattle raid had wiped out his family. Just as suddenly as the feeling of wild rage had swept over him, so too, it passed. Slowly, he released his foot from the prone boy's chest.

"Get," he said, the anger in his voice was edged with menace. "If you ever call me that again, I'll ...." He did not complete the threat. The tall youth got up, dusting the grass off his clothes, his head hung on his chest. He would not look at the menacing figure who confronted him. Slowly, all three of Father Aloysius's detractors left, slinking off along the cliff top.

Larry, on the path some way up the hill, looked down. The priest turned way from the youths and bounded up the slope towards him. Larry had seen everything.

Chapter Six

Create your daily routines, they create your future.

Randy Gage

The days passed. Father Aloysius learnt a whole new set of routines. At times, he was tempted to think that that was what life was all about: routines. Father Aloysius paused in his striding along the cliff path. The tide was coming in. He could discern its surge around the rocks of Trenvannas point. Even the sea had its routine. As always, when Father Aloysius walked. He thought. Today, he was thinking about routines. In Africa, the routines had been different. The sun had more regular habits for a start, at least in the area near the equator where he had been born it had. There, it's getting up, and it's retiring behind the hills to bed, which was pretty predictable. They happened at the same time each day if you had a watch, that is. Between six and six-thirty, morning and evening were the times for those with watches. Father recalled with a wry smile his years in a society where there were no watches or clocks and where time and routine were very much governed by the sun and the seasons; the daily getting up and going to bed were set by the sun's regular rhythm, its rising saw the cows taken out to pasture, its setting saw them being driven home. It was the seasons that provided the variety in the nomadic life he and his family had lived: the rainy seasons, when the water courses flowed, and the wells were full, they were a time of green grass and rich pastures close to water, when the stock grew fat, and the milk was rich. Then came the months of the long dry when the hot sun gradually sucked the moisture out of the land and burnt the grass to a yellow-brown. The water courses ceased to run, and as the water in the wells sank lower and lower, the need to move in search of pasture and water became the imperative. Nature, its daily sun-governed rhythms, and its seasonal cycles provided the pulse that he had lived his life to, and time seemed to stretch out longer somehow, and its passing seemed less important than here in the West. He had no real record of his birthday, and his father certainly had had no idea of his age in years. And then, Father Aloysius recalled, came the bell. In itself, it was not a completely revolutionary piece of technology entering his life. Some of his father's cattle had bells; his lead cows and his best bulls had wooden bells thonged round their necks. They had wooden clappers, too, that clacked and told you where your animals were when you drove them through thick scrub. But the bell at the Catholic Mission he had been taken to as a young starving orphan, too shocked with terror to speak for days, that bell was metal and regular.

At first, it had jarred on his ears and frightened him, but he gradually got used to it. It chimed at set times throughout the day. It clanged you awake in the morning; it called you to morning worship; its chime at noon signalled a further time for prayer and food; in the evening, it told you the day's work was done and called you to Angelus before sending you to supper and bed. Father had found himself in a completely different society with a very different concept of time. Eventually, there in that mission station way out in the wilds of the northern frontier region of Karamoja, he had learnt to speak again, then to speak their language, the language of the priests, and to speak also the language of the time, and now it was the clock that drove his routines and set the pulse for the day. The sun, of course, had its say, but here in this Western place, the sun had a closer marriage to the seasons, or so it seemed to him, for its rising and setting, although regular, were not at the same time each day and over his first month in Pondreath had been very different.

The sun had got up earlier and earlier and gone to bed later and later. All this was not new to Aloysius, he had lived a variety of African time, he had lived Irish time, and now he was living English time, but it was something he did not cease to be amazed at, and on occasions like this, it provided him with food for thought. What had prompted this thought was the need to examine his own routines.

Here in Pondreath, his routines were largely governed by devotions both public and private, by pastoral visiting, and by his one voluntary commitment, the youth club. The church and the congregation were small. It was unusual for such a small village to have a Catholic Church. That it did was due entirely to a very wealthy benefactor, Lady Chardingley, who had provided both the finance and the energy to re-establish a Catholic Church in the area in the nineteenth century. Lord Chardingley had not shared his wife's faith nor had his children, and so when she had died, the little church had been left bereft of her energy and leadership but not fortunately bereft of financial support. She had left a substantial legacy to be used solely by the church. The money, more remarkably, had been sensibly invested, and its earnings still paid for the upkeep of the building and the services of a priest, and so St. Prodrick's had struggled on. Its priests, with the exception of the first incumbent, had been, to a man, retired clerics in the autumn of their lives. Its congregation, drawn from a wide area of scattered farming hamlets and fishing villages, had never been large and, over the years, had gradually dwindled to a few faithful souls. Its last priest, Father Hamish O' Sullivan, had been in his late seventies when he had arrived in the parish and had lived on, saintly in his personal devotions and increasingly absent-minded and mumbling in his public services, until the age of ninety-six, by which time he required, and indeed received, more pastoral visiting than he had ever given the people of his flock. Being a reclusive man by nature, he had preferred to minister to his people through prayer than through being at their bedsides. All who visited him, however, were in agreement that they left his presence better for having seen him such was his saintly demeanour.

Father Aloysius was, needles to say, very different. He was young. His genetic pool had cast him in the mould of a man full of vigour and stamina. If his father could only have seen him that evening on the cliff top striding out with league-long strides, he would have been proud of his son's ability to walk effortlessly for hours and would no doubt have regaled him with stories of his own feats of travelling through the bush. Father Aloysius was a man with an appetite for action, and it required a great deal of action to satisfy his considerable energies.

The priest was an early riser. In Africa, as a child, he had been used to getting up at the first crack of dawn. Here in England, he kept up the habit. Often, his first prayers of the day were said facing the rising sun. He enjoyed, too, his early morning run. It was on his early runs, with their pauses for prayers facing the rising sun, that Father Aloysius brought his family to God. In the silence of his mind, he recalled their faces; he did not think of their names, only he remembered their faces. Each one he laid before God in prayer, asking for the salvation of their souls. They had been heathens, he knew; they had died in sin, and their ends had been too ghastly for him to recall, but God loved him, of that, he was certain, and surely the good God had loved them too. Even in their ignorance of God, they were still in the shadow of his love, and so Father Aloysius trusted that their souls would find eternal rest, whatever that might mean. His prayers were then for those he had a ministerial concern for, young and old, infirm as well fit in body, but perhaps showing behaviours that caused concern or who were embroiled in relationship issues. Father Aloysius would then return to the presbytery content he had started the day well. On his return run, he would often think through the day ahead, planning it in his mind.

Father Aloysius's official start to the day came with Miss Farrow at the church when they said the morning prayers together. The priest was punctilious about saying the office in the church. He always made it his business to arrive early, well before the office, in order to prepare himself. It was a habit he had learnt from his Irish contemporaries. There were occasions, of course, when he left it rather late to appear, but that was only when the circumstances were such that it was unavoidable. Further, he let his congregation know that they were welcome to join the service. So far, none had, but he lived in hope; hope was the very nature of his calling, hope for the salvation of his own soul by the grace and love of God, and hope for the souls of those to whom he preached the Gospel. Father Aloysius was. among other things, a hopeful man. His public devotions complete, he would sally out around the town and the nearby countryside on his pastoral work. He had quickly realised that his flock in Pondreath were few and that there were others further afield he should be visiting. While a weekly visit to the hospital in Miss Farrow's old car was acceptable and, indeed, part of her routine, any further use of the car for pastoral work would become, he realised, a burdensome expense. There were the relics of an old bicycle at the presbytery. It had been left by a previous incumbent and had lain, discarded, and rusting behind the garage of the presbytery for a summer.

Then Miss Farrow had found it and rescued it from the brambles that were threatening to strangle it. She had put it in the garage, squeezed up at the end with the boxes of old hymn books that she could not as yet bring herself to throw away. There, it had continued its period of neglect, but at least it was in the dry. Father Aloysius was not mechanically minded, but Larry was. Larry was the youth club's expert when it came to bicycles. It would never have occurred to Sid that Larry and Philippa had long since grown out of the children's bikes that they had had in the happy days before their parents had been divorced and gone their separate ways and that they might need new ones. Charlotte, if she had thought about it, certainly would not have found the money to purchase such things, even though the weekly contribution that the children's father sent her, had it been carefully managed and regular savings made, would have covered the expense in time. It was Mr Evans, the headteacher at the school who, knowing Larry to be of practical rather than academic bent, had arranged a visit to Falmouth scrap yard. There, they had rescued a whole assortment of bits of bicycles. His headteacher had lent him some tools. From these, Larry had built a pair of very serviceable machines, one for himself and one for his sister. From that time on, Larry was a regular visitor to Falmouth refuse tips. He would persuade his friends in the club to get their parents to give him a lift there when they were going shopping. Larry would collect as many bicycles and bike bits as there were or as he could manage. If the kind benefactor who had given him a lift could not fit them in their car on their return journey, he would bring them back on the local bus. These he built into serviceable bicycles for his friends. He sold them for a moderate price and so got himself the pocket money that Charlotte would not give him. Duncan Evans also arranged for him to spend some of the long summer holidays working at a bicycle shop in Truro. It was owned by a former pupil of his. Larry proved to be a quick learner and was soon considered reliable enough to join the shop's mechanic in repairing bicycles for customers. It was Larry who came to Father Aloysius's help as he struggled to get the old Raleigh roadworthy again. Larry had revised his opinion of the priest since the incident involving his jacket. His estimation of the priest went up leaps and bounds when he heard that Father Aloysius had been in trouble with the bishop over the affair. The priest had felt it necessary to make arrangements for a special confession with the bishop. Miss Farrow had taken him all the way to Pendon Bay in her little car, but when she had learnt that Aloysius was inclined to feel ashamed about the way he had behaved, she had just smiled and shaken her head. It was not long before Father Aloysius could be seen pedalling furiously round the narrow Cornish lanes, his black cassock flying streaming out behind him as he sped down the steep hills, desperately working up as much speed as possible to help him on the even steeper uphill gradients. To

Father Aloysius, the up hills always did seem to be steeper than the down hills. The priest did not confine his visiting entirely to those of the Catholic faith. He had quickly come to realise that the Rev. Burns had a far larger flock than his and had vaguely wondered if he might help his Anglican counterpart in his visiting. Father Aloysius had not been left wondering idly for long. The Rev. Burns was the second person in Pondreath to invite him and Miss Farrow to a meal. The two men had met on the quay. By happy coincidence, they had both been on a visiting mission to elderly folk who happened to live next door to each other. They had left at the same time and had virtually bumped into each other. The Rev. Burns had spent some time in Africa and was keen to learn more about his Catholic counterpart. He had asked Father Aloysius and Miss Farrow to come to the Rectory for a meal. During the course of a very pleasant evening, Father Aloysius had learnt that Mrs Burns had been one of the caring ladies who had ministered to his predecessor, Father O' Sullivan, when he was suffering his last long illness. They had talked a little on ecumenical matters. The Burns were very keen that the churches should work closely together. Father Aloysius had thanked Mrs Burns and her husband for caring for Father O' Sullivan and had asked if there might be any way he could repay their kindness. The Anglican priest had thought for a long moment and then had suggested that the two men might be able to work out a visiting plan whereby they helped each other with pastoral visits to the sick and the old, but first, he had warned sagely the advice of the bishops should be sought. This was done. After some discussion as to what the visiting might involve and issues on the giving of the Eucharist to the sick, Father Aloysius had received the blessing of the Catholic bishop of Cornwall to work with the Rev. Burns on pastoral visits. The two men had worked out a plan for visiting the old and the sick and the people in the hospital. Father Aloysius soon found himself gradually getting to meet and know the people of Pondreath. The people of Pondreath were gradually getting to meet and to know Father Aloysius. At first, they did not know quite what to make of him. He was seen as somewhat of a novelty, being black and a priest. They were unused to having a person of another colour live in their village and being a somewhat insular community; they had many of the prejudices that people who have a strong sense of their own identity share towards strangers. At best, they saw him as being different, not one of them, not like a proper Cornish-man with a close affinity to the sea and a heritage that went back beyond the Celts. He had never stood on the deck of a fishing boat in a wild westerly gale or taken his lamp and his pick to descend into the bowels of the earth to wrest his living from the raw rock; he never even had a skinful of cider and staggered home singing the Trelawny Ballard. Not, of course, that many of the people of Pondreath had ever done any of these things, but of such was their heritage, and he was different, and so he wasn't entirely to be trusted. At worst, some were blatantly antagonistic. He was a 'Black' and an immigrant who had no business to be in Cornwall. There were too many immigrants in England already, and now one had come across the Tamar. Their prejudice showed itself in the way their children called him names as he walked past their homes or in the way they just ignored him, for most of the older folk were too polite to express their feelings towards him openly. For some, the combination of his being a priest and black was a challenge; they found it difficult to understand that a person from Africa could be so educated or could have some spiritual authority. Father Aloysius had met all these prejudices before, in many forms. Was he not of the Karamajong, a tribe despised and feared by the other tribes of Uganda, and if the truth be told, he had been called far worse names than Chocolate Drop. Father Aloysius was not immune to being hurt by prejudice, but he had come to learn, on the whole, to manage his feelings and to smile. It was an old Catholic priest who had once told him, "Smile, they don't know what you're thinking."

To Father Aloysius, smiling came easily, and so when children called after him "Chocolate Drop," he grinned and waved, and the people of Pondreath wondered at his cheerfulness. They wondered too at his energy as he strode about their streets and cycled the highways and byways or ran along their cliff tops. There were, of course, many who welcomed him openly, who confronted their own initial feelings of prejudice and came to terms with them, who looked for the best in him and found so much to admire that they soon respected him and liked him. The rector of St. Jude's and the headteacher of the little Primary School were two such folk, Miss Farrow was another, as was Mrs Hazelmere. His house keeper, Miss Farrow, was a deeply spiritual woman, and she and Mrs Hazelmere were good friends. The two ladies had been the backbone of the little church of St. Prodrick's for years. Miss Farrow and often Mrs Hazelmere, too, were the first to join Father Aloysius in his daily prayers in the church both in the morning and the evening. It was Miss Farrow who, when she saw how keen the new priest was to say his offices in the church, took to ringing the bell for morning and evening prayers. The people of Pondreath were at first surprised at this development, but they came to know Father Aloysius as a man of prayer, and that prayer was part of his routines. They came to know him too, as a man with a hugely cheerful grin who was greatly caring not only of the old and the sick whom he visited regularly in their homes and hospital but caring of all he met. They came to appreciate his wit and, to the few who heard him preach, his wisdom too. At the youth club, which met on a Friday evening, Father Aloysius was welcomed with open arms by Mr and Mrs Tarrant and the gang. He had a way with people, especially with children. He was, as Anna had put it so aptly, fun. The children looked forward to Friday evenings, and he did, too. It was his easily recognisable empathy with children that had prompted The Rev. Burns to suggest to Duncan Evans that Father might be able to help him out at the school. Duncan Evans was getting to know Father Aloysius, and the more he saw of him, the more he liked him. Ever since that first day when Father Aloysius, newly arrived in Pondreath, had visited him when he was in hospital having his tests, he had known somehow that Father Aloysius was, for him, in some strange way, special. Duncan Evans was a communist. He was not just an arm chair communist; he was a passionately active communist, a waver of the red flag at rallies, a disher-out of pamphlets, an impassioned speaker at meetings, a fully paid-up member of the party. To the headteacher, the Conservative Party and The Church were the two great enemies of the people. The Conservatives represented the old guard aristocrats, privilege and power held by the few for their own greedy ends and handed on down the generations by a corrupt and flawed system, and the Church was the bastion of the Conservative party. He was an atheist, but he was not content with his belief that there was no GOD; he believed that the Church was responsible for suppressing the masses and that, although Jesus Christ was in his own way a socialist, none the less he had been responsible for one of the greatest injustices in history, the subjection of the common man to demeaning serfdom. Why, then, had he taken so to Father Aloysius? Perhaps it was because he recognised in the quiet, unassuming manner that Father Aloysius showed to him in that hospital some of the qualities that he, as a person, most aspired to, the qualities of honesty, integrity, loyalty, and complete fairness. Duncan Evans was not a well man. The scan had revealed a growth in his left lung. He was going to have to undergo surgery and perhaps further treatment, too. Next to his wife, his daughter, music, football, and the party, the headteacher loved his school. He had been the principal for the last twenty years. He was a gifted teacher and, over that long time, had gradually built the school up into one of the very best in the county. His little orchestra and his choir were the pride of the village; he used to take them to Falmouth to the Music Festival there, and they were hailed as the best in the county. His football team invariably did well in the league and had won the cup for the last three years. His results were good, not that that was what counted with him, for what counted was the fact that his children did the best they could and that they were recognised for their own individual worth. His great gift with children was finding out what they were good at and using that to develop their self-confidence and respect for themselves. To hear Jane Griffiths play her flute was a treat that brought tears to the eyes. It was her headteacher who had given her her first flute and who had nurtured her into one of the finest players the County Director for music had ever heard. Edmund Tarrant, whose father and mother ran the youth club, was now a practising doctor in Bristol. It was Duncan who had gone to the library and got him his first books on anatomy and physiology and who had arranged for him to see an operation at the Falmouth hospital. The people of Pondreath had at first been concerned by his political affiliations, but they had quickly come to recognise their children loved him, and down the years, he had won their trust, respect, and indeed their admiration. Duncan was concerned about his school and what would happen over the period of his operation. Mrs Hardcourt was his regular stand-in. She was reliable, and the children knew her well; she was good with the music and would keep that side of things going well; it was just the games and the football that she could not cope with. Father Aloysius was a teacher; perhaps he could help with the games. Duncan Evans had thought long and hard about the Reverend Burn's suggestion. Despite their opposing political and religious views, the headteacher and the vicar of St. Jude's got on well together. They both played bridge, and, more importantly, they both had a sense of humour. When he had first arrived from Cardiff to take up his post in Pondreath, Duncan Evans had realised that he had been fortunate to get the job. He had the common sense to know, too, that his parents would find his politics difficult. He could not and would not take a religious assembly. And so he had astutely asked the local rector to do it for him, and in this way, he had got to know the Rev. Burns. The Rev. Burns took his assemblies in the school. The two men had known each other for years, and the Welshman had come to respect The Reverend Burn's judgement. However, having a cleric taking assemblies was one thing; taking football was quite another, and it would also mean there would be two clergymen in the school! The schoolmaster mulled it over in his mind. Who else was there? Nobody, he concluded. He had consulted his chairman of Governors, Mr Hedges. They had agreed to ask Father Aloysius to become involved in the school, hence Father Aloysius's concern about his routines. He would have to adapt his routines, but he welcomed the opportunity to be involved and smiled to himself as he recalled Duncan Evan's instructions: 'You'll be taking gymnastics and games mind not Religious Education. I don't want any Bible bashing, I don't want any swearing either, not even if we are losing at football. Mind, heaven help you if we do, you'd be into serious praying if that happens!'

The priest looked forward to starting to teach again. As a school master in Zimbabwe at an all-boys school, he had been a popular teacher. While many of his colleagues used the stick to enforce discipline, Father Aloysius relied on his personality and his humour to engage his pupils. He was, too, caring and concerned about getting to know them as individuals. They found him a person they could trust, and so they were able to confide in him and ask his advice when things were not going well for them. Then, there was his prowess at football and running. He had a rare combination of speed and stamina. For this, he was much admired.

Father Aloysius stretched and, bending, touched his toes. He liked to pause at this spot to do his exercises. The grass was soft and spongy, and the view was breathtaking. He had just completed his callisthenics and was taking one last lingering look across the bay when, out of the corner of his eye, he noticed a figure on the beach way below him. His keen eyesight discerned it was Anna. She was wandering along the shore, kicking at the seaweed that strung along the tide line. There was a girl whose behaviour puzzled the priest. Her routines had certainly gone awry. She was a bright girl and should be at college studying, but she'd dropped out to join a group of 'surfies' who hung about in Pendon Bay and Newquay. She had taken to spending days away from home and would return worn out and bedraggled to sleep and eat and try to beg money from her parents. To Mr and Mrs Evans, it was a nightmare they were learning to live with.

Their bright blue-eyed daughter, who had always done so well at school, had suddenly got in with the wrong set. Mr Evans, in his pride, would talk to no one about it and kept his anxiety and his anger, for the most part, bottled up inside himself, releasing it in fearsome tirades against the girl when his frustration and irritation finally got the better of him. His rows with his daughter did not help. His wife, Louisa Evans, sought to keep the peace between father and daughter and looked for advice to learn how to help her child. She had even asked Father Aloysius to help. Anna turned up at the youth club on the odd occasion, and Mrs Evans sensed that her daughter respected the priest.

The opportunity to speak with the girl had not yet arisen. Anna disappeared from view under the cliff only to re-emerge a few moments later with two youths.

They stood seemingly talking for a while and then, together, turned and wandered back along the beach. Suddenly, another figure appeared round the headland and came striding towards the trio. It was big, Sid Trevinian. His size and his gait made him unmistakable.

Father Aloysius took a deep intake of breath and sank to his knees so as not to be visible against the skyline. Peering over the edge of the cliff, he watched. The youths and the big man met. There was a brief exchange. It seemed that Mr Trevinian handed a small package to one of the boys in return for something. Father could not see what it was. The backs of the boys obscured his view. Then abruptly, Sid turned and strode back along the beach to disappear round the headland. The youths turned, too, in the opposite direction. They soon were lost to sight as they passed under the lee of the cliff.

Father shook his head. It was time he found an opportunity to talk to that girl.

Chapter Seven

Make beautiful the moment.

It was a grey day. A fine drizzle fell, drenching the grass and making the tarred roads gleam grey. Father Aloysius was in the graveyard; high on the slope of a hill, it overlooked the town. He'd ridden up in the rain, slipping on the wet surfaces as he had ground his way up the steep inclines and round the twisting bends. He was hot and panting when he finally reached the lych gate to the town's burial plot. He parked his bicycle in the shelter of the lych gate roof and shook the raindrops from his hair. Wiping the drips off his nose with a damp handkerchief, he undid the box that was strapped to the back carrier of his bicycle and took out the trowel and the tray of pansies. Mrs Towzer had given him careful instructions as to how to find the grave. It was a little way down the hill, on the end of a row under an oak. Father Aloysius followed the gravel path that ran between the serried ranks of stones, and then, breaking left, he crossed the grass towards the oak. It was just as Mrs Towzer had said, under the tree. Father was thankful for its shelter. He read the inscription out loud to himself.

Frederick Towzer 1914 - 1995 United In Christ. So few words for so much done and so many years, thought the priest, and yet the words were good ones, words of comfort and hope. He looked up at the grey sky, suddenly remembering his father.

They had never told him what had happened to the bodies after the vultures had had their fill. Perhaps the hyenas had had them, as they had the other old Karamajong he had seen die as a child, their bodies unceremoniously dumped outside the boma for the scavengers to dispose of. Frederick Towzer had been a warrior, too, a warrior of the sea. Mrs Towzer had proudly shown Father Aloysius his medals. He had served in the Atlantic convoys protecting the merchant ships as they ran the gauntlet of the submarines. England's life line with America, Mrs Towzer had called it. Mr Towzer had had a ship sunk under him and had survived, one of the few, the very few. He'd served on to the end of the war and then had come back to Pondreath to his wife and daughter. Mrs Towzer's eyes had gleamed wet with tears as she had described their reunion to Father Aloysius. She was a regular on Father Aloysius's visiting list. The treatment on her veins had gone well, and they were healing, but she found walking difficult and, so the priest had come to tend to her husband's grave for her.

"We would have been married fifty-seven years today," she had explained as Father Aloysius had taken the tray of pansies from her to strap to the carrier of his bike. She had been a widow all these long years, Father Aloysius reflected, a wonderfully loyal widow. Then a quite different thought struck him: Mr Towzer had been a warrior; his father had been a warrior too, perhaps in the heaven for warriors, they would meet, and perhaps even now, they looked down on him as he knelt at this graveside, turning the soil with the trowel and carefully releasing the pansies from the box, painstakingly shaking out the roots in preparation for planting.

The priest sensed the girl was there before he heard her; he smelt the wetness of her leather boots before his ears picked up the soft sound of her breathing. She had toiled up from the village, following the footpath to the graveyard, and was still catching her breath from the climb.

"Father Aloysius," her whisper was so soft as to barely audible. The priest had sensed it was her; her voice had confirmed it. He wondered why she had come; he wondered too at his own reaction. Her presence gendered a feeling of excitement. He separated a pansy from its neighbour and, without turning, reached back to hand it to her.

"Please hold this for me," he said. Her slim fingers took the delicate plant from his. For a second, their fingers touched. The message of their emotions seemed to flow between them, for in that brief moment, she sensed his melancholy and, too, his excitement; he, for his part, felt a wistful sadness in her presence. She watched as he placed the delicate plants in the holes he had prepared for them, arranging them in a circular pattern with a cross in the middle.

"So gentle and yet so strong," she said. "This is a sad place, but why are you sad today?"

He turned to look up at her. She was dressed in a thick woollen jumper that, being wet, hung heavily about her, her hair was damp and bedraggled. She looked wan, and there were great dark rings under her eyes.

"I was thinking of my father." He replied, "And why are you sad here in this sometimes sad place." he asked in his turn.

She shrugged her slim shoulders and bit her lip, "I, I don't know," she said lamely and then added, "My grandmother is buried here. My dad wanted to scatter her ashes at sea, but she had put in her will that she wanted to be buried in a graveyard where the family would be able to find her resting place, so she's here, just down there." The girl pointed to the bottom of the graveyard, where the newer stones signified the latest burials. "I like the pattern you've made." The priest patted the soil down, smoothing it round his floral decoration. "You take such care," she observed, "Why?"

It was the priest's turn to shrug. "Make beautiful the moment," he replied, "For it may not come again. Mr Towzer was a warrior, he deserves my respect."

"Make beautiful the moment," the girl echoed. "I like that, it sounds like a poem. Was your father a warrior?"

"Yes."

"Is he dead?"

"Yes." The priest looked out across the hillside. His ears filled with the crack of rifle fire and his nostrils with the stench of blood.

"Where is he buried?" the girl asked. She reached out her hand and placed it gently on his shoulder.

"I don't know that he ever was." The priest replied. There was a long silence.

Gently, she stroked his shoulder. Slowly, he got to his feet. Brushing the soil of his cassock, he gathered the trowel and pansy box.

"I'm so sorry." She whispered. The priest felt himself flushing; no one had ever said anything like that in that particular way to him before. His heart was suddenly thumping in his chest. He was experiencing emotions he had never felt before. Instinctively, he reached out a hand and touched her cheek. A great sigh shook his body. He felt a deep longing to take her in his arms. Instead, he bent to pick up the pansy box from where he had dropped it at her feet, and turning to her, he asked gently, almost tenderly,

"Please show me your grandmother's grave."

The couple stood in front of the stone side by side. Gladys Evans had died four years before. The stone was a simple one bearing only her name and dates. The plot was unadorned and over grown with grass that reached above the inscription. As if moved by the same force, the priest and the girl knelt together and pulled away the grass, plucking the plot level and pulling out the weeds that grew at the base of the stone. Their hands touched again, and Anna looked into his eyes, her blue eyes wide and smiling, and said with a wistful shake of her head.

"So strong and so gentle." He laughed and turned away. He moved to the end of the grave and kept his eyes averted for fear of betraying his emotions. The light drizzle that had threatened to soak them ceased, and a watery sun broke through the grey. They stood to admire their handiwork. The girl slipped her hand in his and leaning against his side. "Thank you, Mr Strong and Gentle."

Father Aloysius looked down into her face and said, "Thank you, Miss beautiful blue eyes," Then he slipped away from her and, turning, led the way back to the lych gate.

She watched as he busied himself with his bicycle.

"How is your father?" he asked as he strapped the box back on the carrier.

"My father?" she queried. The priest was surprised by the change in the mood that the question generated. Without waiting for his reply, she said strongly, "Horrid! My father is horrid."

"Horrid, I don't think so, bad-tempered on occasion, maybe, but that is understandable in the circumstances. Have you had another row?"

"Another row, when do we ever stop having rows? But what's that got to do with you? Is this another confession session?"

Father Aloysius shrugged." No, I merely asked after your father's health?" he said, "But it seems clear that it is more than his health that is a problem. Why don't you two get on? Suddenly, the girl slumped down onto the lych gate bench and started to cry.

Once again, the priest felt the great urge to take her into his arms. Instead, he stood quietly by his bicycle, watching and waiting. Eventually, he prompted gently.

"Your father is not a well man."

"I know," Anna sobbed.

"Your mother is worried, worried about him and worried about you."

The girl nodded her head and wiped her nose on her sleeve.

"I know, I know, I know, but you, you don't have to stand there all sanctimonious in your silly black gown. You don't know what it's like. You haven't a clue, have you? You've never ridden a wave in your life. You don't know what it is, what it is to be wild and free and a child of the surf. You haven't a clue, have you?"

"No," the priest agreed," And I don't suppose your mum and dad have either."

"Too true, they don't." the girl said, the bitterness clear in her voice.

"So why are you here, blue-eyed child of the surf?" the priest asked quietly.

"I don't know," the girl shrugged listlessly. "I just saw you coming up the hill and decided to follow."

"Well," said the priest, "I'm going down now. If you ever want to talk, you know where I am. Give my love to your father and tell your mum I'll be round tomorrow for my lesson."

"Lesson?" queried the girl.

"Yes, I'm teaching her about the rosary. She is going to show me how to make bread." The priest replied. He swung into the saddle and peddled off down the hill.

The girl watched him go and then sank back onto the lych gate bench and sobbed until she could sob no more.

Chapter Eight

Treat others with respect and they will respect you.

Father Aloysius returned from the graveyard to see Mrs Towzer and to report on the planting of the pansies. He drew the pattern of the planting for her, and she was thrilled. His reward was her joy, but he also enjoyed a huge cup of steaming tea with heaps of sugar and a large slice of chocolate cake. She would have given him more and was all for drying out his clothes for him, but Father Aloysius insisted that he had other calls to make, and eventually, having promised to return directly to the presbytery to put on a dry cassock, he was allowed to leave. Having done as he was told and changed into dry clothes, Father Aloysius's next visit was to the home of Mr and Mrs Hughes, where he helped Mr Hughes with the painting of one of his skylights. Mr Hughes was a perfectionist and would not trust anyone else to do his home decorating. However, his legs were not what they once were, and he was waiting for a hip replacement. He found ladders increasingly difficult, and the top skylight in his hall way was a little too high for him. Father Aloysius, being grateful that the Hughes family had returned to the fold and were now regulars at the Sunday service, had volunteered to help. He did not realise what he was letting himself in for. Painting was a new venture for him. He was not very good at it and seemed to get paint everywhere, including a patch on his hair. With Mr Hughes directing operations, Father Aloysius got the job done, but Mrs Hughes was too tactful to say whether he had got it done well or not.

Father Aloysius spent that afternoon in school. He was in his third week as a teacher. He taught Physical Education and games. He also took the football club after school.

Father Aloysius had been looking forward to returning to teaching, even if it was only sport. However, he initially found that teaching in a primary school in England was very different from his expectations. The children did not treat him with the respect he had been used to from his students in Africa. They were used to seeing him at the youth club, where he was treated as a friend. His first lesson was with the top class. It was a mixed class of year five and year six children. Their attitude left him disillusioned and dismayed. The children had been disobedient and cheeky. They talked when he was talking to them; they played the fool on the apparatus and screamed and shouted out to each other as they swung on the ropes. As the lesson progressed, he found it increasingly difficult to keep any semblance of order.

His voice went hoarse, he was tense with anxiety and anger, he found himself sweating with fright, and by the end of the lesson, he was shaken and exhausted. The worst offender had been young Philippa, or Flip, as she insisted on being called.

Flip had had a bad start to the day. Her aunt had a hangover and was in a belligerent mood, Big Sid was late for work and was chasing everyone about. There was very little in the kitchen cupboard, and Big Sid was furious. He took the last of the cheese from the fridge and the only packet of crisps left for her packed lunch.

"And what am I supposed to have?" Charlotte had complained when he had rifled the larder. Sid had lost his temper, and there had been an awful row with Sid threatening to do violence to everyone in sight. He could not find his boots and screamed for Larry. Fortunately for the boy, he had left very early that morning to attend his 'work experience' job at the garage in Pendon Bay. When Larry failed to answer, he flew at Charlotte. At first, Charlotte had given as good as she got; she had a vile tongue, and the language she used was not tempered in any way in recognition that Philippa was in the room, but when her husband threatened to hit her, she clammed up.

She was frightened of his huge hand. Sid, when thoroughly riled, had a nasty temper, and she had learnt to read the signs of his rising anger. Instead, she had directed her spleen on the young girl, and Philippa could do nothing right. Desperately, the girl had searched the kitchen cupboard for something for her packed lunch; there was very little, and in the end, she had to settle for bread with sugar sprinkled inside it. Charlotte even snapped at her for spilling the sugar. She had left the house with tears brimming in her eyes.

At school, Philippa had been in a dream and had been admonished by Miss Hardcourt. She turned sullen, and the day had gone from bad to worse. The final indignity came when Father Aloysius turned up to take the class for gymnastics. In her haste to leave the house, she had forgotten her gym kit. This was not an uncommon occurrence. Usually, she was told off and given jobs to do instead of having to attend the lesson. She was not keen on gymnastics. In fact, she had grown to prefer the jobs to the lessons. They were fairly trivial but not unpleasant, and she was unsupervised. She did not have to work hard at them. Usually, she escaped at the end of the day, before anyone had the time to check up on how much she had done. Father Aloysius, however, insisted that she attend the lesson. He hunted out a kit for her from the lost property. The shorts were grubby and slightly too large, and the shirt too small; she had sulkily tried to refuse to wear them, but the priest had insisted, and halfway through the ensuing argument, Miss Hardcourt had come in and had lent her authority to the situation. Time had passed, the rest of the class had already gone to the hall, and when Father Aloysius walked in, the boys were fooling about with a ball, and one of the girls was in floods of tears, having been hit by the ball in the face. Father Aloysius had called the class to order and had to tell them off. Mandy had been sent off to Mrs Fenton, the school secretary. It had been a bad start. Things were to get worse. Philippa had sulked all the way to the hall. She had wandered off to the back and was obviously doing as little as possible to participate in the warm-up activities. When Father Aloysius asked her to put more effort into her exercise, she sulkily answered back that she was trying. She then proceeded to call out and make silly noises. Father Aloysius was completely unprepared for this and was at a loss as to how to respond. After helping her retrieve her brother's jacket, he would have expected her to show her gratitude by supporting him in his efforts to impose some discipline on the class. She thought that she had a special relationship with the priest and that she would be able to get her own way with him. Both were wrong in their expectations. Father Aloysius called her over to talk to her, but she had refused to come. With mounting feelings of anger and inadequacy, he crossed the hall to her. The class had stopped working and started to chatter. Father Aloysius asked them to stop and to sit up straight in silence, but when he turned his back on them, they had immediately restarted, and two of the boys had moved their positions to be near to each other. Father Aloysius endeavoured to talk firmly with Philippa, but she hung her head and turned away form him, and then when he turned round to the other children, she had made a rude gesture behind his back. There were suppressed giggles from the rest of the class. Father Aloysius's feelings of inadequacy heightened; he did not want to send the girl out of the lesson, for that would be a sign of his failure. What would Miss Hardcourt think? He had already had words with Philippa. What other action was there left to him? What other punishments could he use? Father Aloysius chose to ignore her and to go on instead to apparatus work. This was a mistake. He had never used the apparatus in the hall before and did not know how to put it out. The class had already sensed his difficulties but, instead of being helpful, had become increasingly silly. The mood of the lesson had been set, and to rescue it now would have taken a more experienced teacher of gymnastics than Father Aloysius was. He found himself desperately rushing from one piece of apparatus to another, checking it for safety while the class who were supposed to be sitting quietly grew more and more unruly. When he had finally arranged them into groups and had got them going on their tasks, a shambles had ensued. On the ropes, the boys emulated Tarzan and made wild yells. A box was knocked over with a great clatter, and children swapped from group to group as they wished. In despair, Father Aloysius called for order, demanding that the children come and sit in front of him, his voice had grown hoarse, and his mouth was dry; he felt the perspiration tricking down the backs of his legs, and his words came stumbling from his mouth.

"What is the matter with you children?" The priest demanded. "I refuse to put up with this disgraceful behaviour. You will return to your classroom now and sit in your places in silence." Finally cowed by his evident anger, the children had filed out. Father's final humiliation was the return of Miss Hardcourt to find the children in their places with Father Aloysius striding about the room glowering. He felt as if he wanted the ground to open up and swallow him. He was, however, grateful for her help in supervising the class changing and for the sympathetic way she listened to him later. When sitting quietly on their own in the classroom, Father Aloysius had blurted out his feelings of being a complete failure. She had helped him analyse the lesson, and they had worked out a strategy to sort out the problem. Strict sanctions were drawn up. Lesson plans were reviewed. Mrs Hardcourt had smiled reassuringly, "Don't worry, Father, you'll win them over. You are already doing great work with them at the youth club. That, of course, may be part of the problem. You are their friend there; here, you are a teacher; it's a different role. You understand that, but they don't yet. They will."

"Thank you," said Father, "You make it sound as if there is some hope for me,"

"Heavens, yes," responded Mrs Hardcourt with a sympathetic smile. "You'll be fine. There isn't a teacher alive who hasn't been put through the mill from time to time. As for Philippa, she is a tough one; it's the family. She comes from a broken home, and it's been a bad break, but she is a nice girl at heart. She has a bit of her mother in her despite her Trevinian looks. Her mother was a sweet woman. What made her run off with that Glaswegian and leave her children, I'll never know. I can understand her leaving her husband, he's a Trevinian, need I say more, but to leave her children was not like her. I guess she felt trapped. She was not well. Cornwall can be like that for those who fall in bad times. There is nowhere to hide in these little villages. Either you stay and brazen it out, or you go. She went. Larry has had his difficulties, but with Mr Evan's help, he has coped better than his sister. Mr Evans was wonderful with him. Philippa has always been more difficult. Nought as queer as folk," concluded Mrs Hardcourt, "But," she added, "Don't you worry about her. We'll look around and see if we can't find something decent for her to wear at Gymnastics and Games, and I'll have a chat with her."

The class had to stay in at break time to show Father Aloysius how the apparatus was put out and returned. It was Mr. Evans who came up with the clothes for Philippa. When he had heard of the problem from Mrs Hardcourt, who visited him every day in the evening after school, he got his wife to look out some of his daughter's old clothes.

There was a smart turquoise leotard and a netball outfit that Anna hadn't worn since she left primary school all those years ago. It was about time they got rid of a bit of their clutter. Wisely, he suggested that it should be the priest who gave the clothes to Philippa Trevinian. It also gave him an excuse to invite the priest to tea.

Father Aloysius had paid a regular weekly visit to the school master's home ever since the visiting plan he operated in conjunction with the Rev. Burns had been set up. It was on one of these visits that Mrs Evans had shared her anxieties about her daughter Anna with the cleric. Strangely, Anna had never been at home when the priest called. Father Aloysius was not due to visit the Evans' home for a few days. The invitation to tea coming so soon after his frightful experiences with the school children had filled the priest with dread. Was he being called to the headmaster's study for a telling-off? He felt he had let the headteacher down. Fortunately, he had a chance to redeem himself in a manner of speaking the next day following his debacle. He had to take two other classes for gymnastics and the football club for the after-school session. The lessons and the football club had gone well. In his first gymnastics lesson given to the middle class of the school, Father Aloysius had an opportunity to show off his own athleticism. One of the girls had attempted a handstand. She had kicked up into the balance a number of times but had not been able to get to a vertical position. She had asked Father Aloysius to support her. The priest was faced with a dilemma; he had never supported a girl before. He felt embarrassed and reluctant before the idea that he should demonstrate struck him. He used to be a good hand-walker at the Mission school the priests had sent him to as a boy.

"I'll show you," he had suggested. "First of all, it's important to feel the handstand in your fingers," He bent double and spread his fingers on the hall floor, "Your arms should be shoulder-width apart. I like to spread my fingers a little. You kick up into the vertical," Father demonstrated; it took him two attempts to get there, but on his second attempt, he got a good balance and held it. The class clapped. Father grinned as he dropped lightly back onto his feet.

"If you want to come out of it, you just push down with your fingers," he explained.

"If you kick up too hard, it's your fingers that push down when you feel yourself over balancing." He added.

"Show us again, please," the girl had asked. Father had obliged, and this time, he had walked. He walked the length of the hall. The class had all followed him. "Wow," exclaimed Tina, the little girl who had asked for Father Aloysius's help, as the priest flushed from being upside down and dropped out of the balance, "You're a star!"

"Again, please, again, again, again," the children had chanted. The priest had held up his hands and had shaken his head.

"No, no, enough is enough; anyway, it's your turn now." Father Aloysius went on to show them how they could support each other. He chose a boy to demonstrate with.

The lesson had been a good one, and Father Aloysius had felt his confidence in himself return. His next lesson was with the infant class. He was relaxed and fun with the little ones, and they enjoyed being taught by him.

The football club followed on straight after school. The children changed on the back porch, a long-covered veranda. Father Aloysius sent the children out to the field while he reported to Mrs Hardcourt. She had smiled reassuringly at him as he put his head round her door and gave her the thumbs-up sign.

"I know, I know, the children in Class Two have been telling me all about your hand-walk, twice the length of the hall I hear," she had winked at the priest. Father Aloysius had blushed with delight.

"Not quite," he'd said, "But it went a lot better. Thank you for your help."

The old teacher had just smiled, "It was a pleasure. Go and enjoy your football. Have fun."

Father Aloysius had. When he arrived on the field, the children were all kicking balls about. One of the boys was showing off his juggling skills. Father Aloysius had stood and watched for a moment. He gave the boy a clap.

"Very good," he'd said. At that moment, a ball had come hurtling towards him. It had been kicked by Kevin, one of the boys who had given him trouble the day before. Father Aloysius caught the ball easily on his chest. It dropped to his knee, and he had proceeded to flick it from foot to foot, foot to knee, knee to foot, foot to knee, knee to knee, knee to the head, and then as it dropped down to his left foot, he'd propelled it straight back at the boy. Kevin, along with the rest of the group, were walking towards Father Aloysius. The unexpected return caught Kevin hard in the middle of his stomach; he bent double-winded.

"Nice one, Kevin!" teased Michael, who had dropped his own ball when Father had started juggling his. Father had gone over to the lad and had put his hand on his shoulder and patted his back.

"Here," he had instructed, "Stretch up, breathe in and bend over, breathe out, and repeat, You'll have to learn to catch the ball on your chest." Kevin, turning away in a sulk, had opened his mouth to retort with an abusive obscenity, but the priest's hand had turned him back. Kevin had caught the gleam in Father Aloysius's eyes. In that moment when their eyes met, Kevin had known that he would not trouble the priest again and get away with it. He had shaken his head, swallowing back the swear word he'd rubbed his chest.

"That's better, son," said Father Aloysius with a grin, "That's a lot better." The club, boys and girls, had crowded round him. "Now in football," the priest continued, starting his first session with the club, "In football, good football that is, it's the ball that does the talking. Here, I know," he continued. "We are only interested in good football, the best, the very best football, so let's get on with it." The ball did a lot of talking that afternoon. Father Aloysius did a little, and every child had listened to him. They had ended up with a game. It was fun. It was a weary but happy bunch of footballers who returned with Father Aloysius to get changed after the session. They had all walked with him, crowding close and asking him about his own footballing days.

"Long gone, long gone, man," he'd laughed modestly and had peeled away from the group to put the balls away tidily. None the less, there was an anxious tingle in Father Aloysius's stomach when he had pushed the door bell of the Evans' home that evening after Angelus. He need not have worried. He was given a warm welcome by Mrs Evans.

"I'm so glad you have been able to come," she'd said, "He's not had such a good day and he needs cheering up,"

Father Aloysius handed her a jar of the jam he had brought with him. "I'm sorry, what's been the trouble?" he'd asked.

"Oh, Father," Mrs Evans smiled her appreciation at his gift, "You shouldn't have," and then, in a softer voice, she had added, "He's in quite a bit of discomfort, you know. He's there, sitting up in the lounge, go in." She'd ushered the priest through the door.

Father Aloysius had smiled cheerfully as he greeted the sick schoolmaster, but he'd noted the tension in the headteacher's hands as they gripped the arms of his chair and the deep furrows in his forehead. He'd appreciated all the more the quiet dignity of the welcome he had received, knowing that it took self-control and courage for the schoolmaster to smile back at him so warmly and to reach out his hand to the priest.

"Thank you, Father. I'm so glad you could come. I'm sorry I can't get up, wretched tubes everywhere," he'd said, indicating the blanket draped from his waist to his feet that hid a tube to an oxygen cylinder.

"Please sit down." He'd pointed to a chair. Father Aloysius had noted the shake in the hand held out to show him which chair to use. Gratefully, he'd sat down.

"Thank you," the priest had said, "And how are you keeping? I guess you have called me in for a lecture."

The schoolmaster chuckled and winked, "Of course," he'd said, and then quickly he'd added, "Wearing out the floor of the hall with all your hand-walking. Whatever next?"

Father Aloysius had felt his anxiety draining away; the schoolmaster was joking. He'd grinned and, stretching out his arms, had flexed his fingers.

"News certainly travels fast."

"Marjorie comes in to report every day after school," Mr Evans had explained.

"She tells me the children think you are a marvel at gymnastics and that the football went well, too. In fact, young Kevin Acres is reported to have said it was the best football training he has ever had."

"That's generous of him," Father Aloysius had conceded. I'm afraid he was a bit of trouble on Monday when I took his class for gymnastics, but I'm glad that the football seems to have gone well."

"Trouble," The schoolmaster had grunted. "He's a young blood, he's just showing off, only to be expected. They'll all try it on at first, but you'll sort them. I hear Miss Trevinian was also a little difficult." The priest had just nodded. "She's a poor one that," Mr Evans had gone on, "Needs all the love and care she can get, certainly doesn't get it at home. Here we've put some things together for her, an old gym slip of Anna's. Be cheerful with her that'd be my advice. She doesn't have much to be cheerful about bless her, and if you are kind to her, she'll respond. You'll see."

Father Aloysius had taken the clothes. He had wanted then to talk about Anna, but the school master had had enough. Mrs Evans had brought in the tea. They had spent a little more time together, and then the priest had quietly slipped away.

Father Aloysius had given the clothes to Philippa Trevinian the next day. The gift had surprised the girl, but she was delighted. The schoolmaster had been right.

There was a change in their relationship from then on, and Philippa had worn her new gym slip to the next lesson. She had, on the whole, worked well, too, although there were still times when she could be difficult. Indeed, the whole class could. Father Aloysius struggled on being determined that he would stamp his authority on the class. There had been further times of confrontation, and Father had even had to punish some of the more persistent offenders. Turning up with paint in his hair had, in a strange way, helped him. He had been helping Mr Hughes with giving his window a second coat. The class had predictably burst out laughing when he had entered the room. He had been at a loss to see what they were laughing about.

He felt the anger and embarrassment rising inside him, but he'd smiled and had got on with supervising the changing. It was Philippa who had come to his aid and told him what the mirth was all about. Father's smile had grown to a laugh, and he'd explained his attempts at helping Mr Hughes with the painting. Philippa had immediately leapt to his defence and had insisted that the class be quiet and that they behave.

"Father Aloysius has been helping, and it's not fair to laugh at him." She had told the class in a strident voice. "It's your granddad he's been helping, Kevin, so you'd better be especially good, hadn't you!" The class had responded to her appeal, and he had had one of his better lessons with them. At the end of it, Kevin had come up to him to thank him for his care for his grandfather. Father Aloysius had felt deeply touched.

Chapter Nine

The rose is without 'why'
It blooms because it blooms.

Johann Angelus Silesia

That evening, Father Aloysius was early in his pew in the church for Angelus. He sat quietly in the cool, dim light, reviewing the day, his fingers gently toying with his rosary. His eyes fixed on the cross above the altar, the twisted figure of the Christ, and the nails and thorns heightened his feeling of emotional turmoil. His time in the graveyard with Anna had brought to a head feelings he had never experienced in quite such a way before. Carefully he examined them. He was a priest, a celibate, his life given to GOD, the GOD who loved him so well, The GOD whom he loved. Those sinewy arms outstretched, those hands open, open yes to the nails but surely open to him too, that head so bowed down with the terrible crown of thorns. Each thorn a symbol of the world's great suffering, his suffering even. His eyes feasted on the figure of the Christ he loved. He longed to reach out, to take that crown of thorns, to ease that pain, to wear, if necessary, the crown himself, although he knew he was not worthy to do so. He longed to take that poor suffering figure into his arms and to bury his own head against its warm chest and to shield it from the world and all its woes and misery. To shield himself too from the pain of being human, the pain of longing, of loving, and of knowing no end to the suffering. Oh, how his heart ached with his love.

And what of Anna? She was a young girl of seventeen, possibly eighteen. A girl who was, by her parent's request, one of his flock, a girl who was clearly vulnerable, in the grips of some dilemma that she had not the willpower yet to overcome or perhaps even the insight to see. A pretty girl with the most beautiful eyes he had ever seen.

Today, he'd felt those eyes on him, filled with sadness. Today, he'd felt her touch, and it had moved him; it had awakened in him the same longing he had for the Christ, the same huge ache to take her into his arms and to bury his head in her bosom. The same hunger to embrace her woes for her and to shield her from her worries. Carefully, he examined his feelings, acknowledging them and owning up to them. Then, his eyes still on Christ, he examined his actions. What had he done apart from that briefest touch of her face to make him feel guilty, he wondered. Had he not turned away from her when she would have leant on him, had he not left her weeping, when for all the world his natural inclination was to have comforted her, when he had so wanted to comfort her.

"Oh GOD," the priest reflected silently. "GOD forgive me and protect me from myself." He buried his head in his arms and knelt there, bowed down onto the hard wood of the priest's stall.

The bell tolled the time for evening prayer. Anna slipped quickly into the pew at the back of the church. She saw the priest kneeling there, his head buried in his arms, and she wondered why. The girl sat perfectly silent and still. The priest slowly raised his head. There was a whispering in the porch where Miss Farrow had been ringing the bell. Two ladies came quietly in, Miss Farrow and Mrs Hazelmere. They crossed themselves as they took their places in the right-hand pew at the front. Anna noticed their heads were covered. Both wore head scarves. Miss Farrow's was an austere grey, and Mrs Hazelmere's was a deep red wine colour to match her shoes. Father Aloysius stood up to welcome his flock. He did not at that moment see Anna. In his mind, he resolved to take his worries to the bishop at his next confession. In the meantime, he would have been on his guard with the young girl. He would have to keep himself in tight control and try to avoid being alone with her. Little did he realise how soon that resolve would be tested.

The last chants of the 'Hail Marys' intoned Father Aloysius, who slipped his Rosary beads into his pocket and stood up, smiling at the two ladies who made up his faithful congregation each evening. "Thank you ladies. GOD go with you," he said.

"And with you," was their reply. It was not part of the liturgy of the evening prayer, but he found it a fitting way to acknowledge their loyal contribution, and they responded. It was then he saw Anna, her pale face so perfectly still and staring out of the shadows of the back of the church as she sat as if frozen, entranced. His heart skipped a beat inside him. The two ladies saw the girl as they walked back down the aisle, but she did not acknowledge their smiles or Miss Farrow's whispers.

"Good evening, Anna."

Father Aloysius heard them pause on the porch for their customary conversation there.

On previous occasions, he had wondered at what on earth they could find fresh to talk about each evening and had concluded it was one of those gifts women had, that of being able to talk at any time, anywhere. Tonight, he was grateful for it and hoped they would not leave him alone with the pale-faced creature that sat between him and the door. Anna reached out her hand.

"Father Aloysius," her voice was barely a whisper, but in its cadence was all the emotional charge of an appeal. The priest stopped short of her outstretched arm.

He looked down at the pale face. His heart pounded so violently under his cassock that he was sure she could hear it, but his reply was gentle and controlled.

"Anna, you here? What can I do for you?" He heard himself speak the words and could hardly believe it was his voice, so modulated and reserved he sounded, while in his mind, there was this awful scream, "Why, why are you doing this to me? Can't you just leave me alone? The heartache is just too much to bear."

"Please, Father," she said, "I need to speak with you."

"Yes," replied the priest, softly, then more loudly he called to Miss Farrow.

"Miss Farrow, I may be some time, please wait," He sat down in the pew opposite the girl. She had looked startled when he had called after Miss Farrow but gradually recovered her composure.

"You must think I'm awful," she said, wringing her hands. The girl was clearly in a very agitated state. "Saying such terrible things about my father. I, I, it's just we don't get on that well, we'd had a row, you were right, again." The priest folded his hands in his lap and stared down the aisle to the altar. Christ hung there, head bowed; the evening light caught the polished wood of his shoulder. Father Aloysius ran his tongue round his mouth, wetting his lips. His mouth felt dry, and he feared his voice would rasp in his throat and betray his emotions.

"I don't think you are awful at all, far from it, but more important, my child," the title sounded strange. Anna was on the brink of womanhood, but he used it purposely. It would be the priest who counselled this girl; it was the priest she had come to see, "but more important," Father Aloysius continued, "GOD won't think so either."

"How, how do you know? How can you be sure?" like the priest, the girl was looking at the Christ as if seeing him for the first time. Her startled eyes took in the carving's pathetic pose, pinned to bits of wood by three nails, it was all so grotesque, so horribly ugly. How could that, that broken beastly thing there, have any input into her feelings, her longings, her pain? Pain, she acknowledged with a deep sob, yes pain, they both had that. She looked across at Father Aloysius, the tears streamed down her face.

The priest took a handkerchief from the deep recess of his cassock pocket, he reached out across the aisle, being careful not to let their fingers touch, he handed it to her.

What could he say to this young girl that would help her understand how could he explain his feelings about GOD? The GOD that was as much a part of himself, the GOD within him, as the figure on the cross, the GOD that was part of all creation, that was in her as well as him, that looked out at him from every pair of human eyes, whether they realised it or not, how could he explain his own certainty, at times it was true too that it was a doubtful certainty, about GOD, how could he explain. Like her, he had asked the same questions: how could you be sure, and yet he was sure, at this moment in time, he was sure, and he wanted her to be sure, too.

"How can I be sure?" the priest repeated the girl's question, "I don't know, it's an individual thing, it's a matter of faith, I guess, and faith comes to each of us in different ways. To me, it came gradually, I suppose, over time, from the loving hands of the good priests who had found me and rescued me when I was wandering alone, a little boy.

I'd been orphaned, a little boy alone in the bush. I had no water and no food, and they found me.

They gave me life. They gave me love and taught me about GOD'S love, and slowly, I came to learn and to have faith in GOD."

"How terrible!" the girl interjected, "You poor thing," she reached out her hand towards him, but he shifted away and, holding up his own hand, said quietly.

"Don't feel sorry for me, little one. It was all a long time ago. GOD has taken care of me, and now it is your father we must think of." The rebuff, if it was one, for he had merely shifted in his pew, was ameliorated by the gentle tone of his voice and his endearment of little one, which was better than my child. The girl, for all her emotional agitation, still retained a measure of her sense of humour. She returned her hand to her lap and, wiping her nose with his handkerchief, said quietly.

"Yes. Yes, you are so right. I must stop thinking about myself and start thinking about him."

"How much do you know about your father's illness?" The priest asked, keen to capitalise on this change of thought.

"I know he's seriously ill." The girl replied.

"Yes," said Father Aloysius, "He is seriously ill and in a lot of pain, that will make him difficult at times, and so we all have to be very understanding. There is, too, another thing." The priest paused, wondering whether this was the time to talk of her father's mortality.

"Go on," the girl reassured him gently, "I know it's dangerous."

Father Aloysius sighed. "Yes, it's more than dangerous, Anna," he used her name for the first time since greeting her. He needed her to know he respected her as a person.

"This could be his last struggle, his last chapter."

"I know that too," the girl choked back a sob and dabbed her eyes again with the handkerchief.

"We need to make it as good as we can. And then there is your mum, we need to support her."

"Yes," the girl was crying again freely now, the tears streamed down her face, her breath came in sobs. "I know, I know, I'm going home and, and I'll be good, I promise." She got up and stood by his pew for a moment. Their eyes met, his dark and full of compassion, hers full of tears. She gave him a little smile as she handed back his handkerchief.

"Thank you," she whispered and fled crying to the door.

Miss Farrow was waiting there in the gloom. She reached out her hand and touched Anna on the shoulder. The distraught girl flung her arms about the housekeeper's neck and gave way to pent-up emotion. Gently, the housekeeper held her, stroking her hair and murmuring soft words of comfort. Over the girl's shoulder, she signalled to Mrs Hazelmere to fetch her car. "Don't worry, my child, Mrs Hazelmere, and I will see you home safely."

In the church, Father Aloysius sat perfectly still, his eyes on the Christ. His palms felt damp. His heart was pounding as he struggled to concentrate solely on the gruesome figure and to banish the girl from his mind.

Chapter Ten

*There are people
in the world so hungry that God
cannot appear to them except in the
form of bread.*

-Mahatma Gandhi

Mrs Evans's hands were white with flour. "Here," she said to the priest.

"It's on the table," she pointed with her chin. "It's the recipe for bread you want, Anna knocked it up on the computer for me, for you rather. Father, I can't thank you enough for what you have done for that girl and for us, for that matter. I was beginning to despair. Ever since she came back here with Miss Farrow and Mrs Hazelmere, bless them, she has been a changed girl, almost like her old self again. Mind you, she was in quite a state. You must have given her a good talking to. But she needed it, no doubt.

She even went back to college. At first, they were pretty reluctant to have her, can't blame them myself. Fortunately, Duncan's friendly with the principal. Anyway, she's back on sufferance. Any silliness and that's her lot. So far, she has been very good, gone every day, even working at home." Mrs Evans wiped the flour from her hands and took some scales from the kitchen cupboard.

"Here," she said, busily gathering the ingredients for the bread, "There is an apron behind the larder door. She has been so much better with her dad, too,"

Father Aloysius smiled, "How is he?" he asked.

"So so," Mrs Evans giggled at Father Aloysius's attempts to tie his apron behind his back.

"Here, let me help you, He's going through a better patch. The nurse should be here soon. She helps me get him up most days, but she had to change her routine today. She's coming in a bit later. We'll all have coffee together. He'll be wanting to show you his latest project for the school. Now, we must get cracking if we are to get this bread made." Mrs Evans showed Father Aloysius how to mix the ingredients.

"I'm afraid I'm still a mixture of Imperial and Metric when it comes to measures. For bread, I weigh in pounds," explained the housewife as she directed the priest to pour a pound and a half of stoneground flour into the mixing bowl. "Now you need half a pound of that granary flour in with it, and then we have the baking powder, and we need yeast. Mustn't forget the salt."

Father Aloysius glanced at the recipe.

"Shall I put the kettle on?" he asked.

"Well done, Father, quite right. We need the hot water now to help dissolve the treacle.

We just measure out half a pint of hot, then when the treacle's dissolved, we put in half a pint of cold. I use black treacle instead of sugar. I find it gives the bread a good flavour.

The water needs to be tepid for the yeast to work really well." The operation was duly completed by Father Aloysius. Mrs Evans eyed the measuring jug critically.

"The water needs to be just right," she explained, "Too much and your loaf is too wet, too little, and the mixture is too dry. Now we put the liquids in the large mixing bowl under the beater, we then give the flour a little stir before adding them to the water.

That's it, get the yeast and the salt mixed in." encouraged the cook. Father Aloysius quietly made a mental note that, like Miss Farrow, Mrs Evans was a thorough lady.

He carefully poured the flour into the mixing bowl.

"Good," encouraged the cook, "Now we put on the dough hook , but not too fast, mind, or we will have flour all over the ceiling."

Father Aloysius cautiously turned the knob. Nothing happened. Mrs Evans laughed and flicked the switch on the wall. The mixer sprang to life, and they nearly did have flour on the ceiling. Fortunately, Mrs Evans was able to switch the mixer down. She patted Father on the head.

"Hold your horses, not too fast to begin with," she instructed.

"In Africa, we say hurry, hurry, has no blessing," said Father Aloysius, watching the mixture whirl round and round.

Mrs Evans giggled, "In Africa, I guess many things are different. I think that will do.

Now, we take the dough out of the mixer, return it to its original bowl, and leave it on the boiler to rise. I usually put a tea towel over it that helps the rising operation. Now, we can have a little break for three-quarters of an hour or so while the yeast does its business. Let's get the kettle on again for coffee; the nurse should be here in a moment." They had their coffee and a cream cake in the lounge, where Mr Evans sat propped up in his great chair. The schoolmaster was in a cheerful mood. He hailed the priest with a grin.

"So you've pinched one of the wife's aprons, have you, Father Aloysius? Not quite ready for the naked chef yet, then?" He teased. The priest noted that the patient's hands held a portfolio of plans on his lap, were still shaky and, if anything, looked thinner and paler than he remembered them from his last visit, but Mr Evans sounded strong and positive. He was full of enthusiasm as he shared the plans with the priest.

"Here," explained the schoolmaster, "We have a huge field. It's one of the good things the village forefathers did when they brought the land for the school playing fields, they over provided. Now we have two good-sized football pitches, the cricket square in the middle, even with a wide apron round there is lots left over after we have made provision for sport. We want to make that grass area a more varied environment, so, for example, here in this corner, well away from the nearest houses and the road, we could have a pond. We would bank up the soil we dig out from the hollow along here and extend this bank with more soil. Behind the bank, here we could plant trees so we would have a little wood there. That would provide not only a whole new habitat but also act as a windbreak for the fields."

"What about your athletics track?" asked Father Aloysius, "Where does that go?

"Good point, chef. You must have a track for the pancake race," teased the schoolmaster. "Our track, one hundred metres straight, goes along here, and right round the edge, and through the wood here, you would have a wide chip bark path for a cross country. You could use the banks as well,"

"Sounds good," agreed the priest.

"Now here, I've seen this really great idea in a magazine for what they call a chequerboard garden. You use paving to create a garden area, each child has a square the size of a paving block for its garden. They are not too large, so they are not daunting for children, and they are surrounded by paving so they can walk round them even in the wet without getting their feet too muddy. Here, look," he held up a magazine and pointed to some photographs, "This school here has one, and it's bigger than our school, every child has a garden."

"Every child," exclaimed the priest, "That must take some maintenance."

"Yes, but apparently, it works, you involve families, mums and dads, and even grandparents. When Mum comes in a few minutes early to collect her child from school, she visits the garden; they have gardening days, usually at the weekend when gangs of people from tots in nappies to grandparents come to work on the grounds.

The idea is the community is involved in its own school, each child has ownership of a bit of real estate, they care for their school, and there is no vandalism."

"I suppose you could have recreational things, like swings, as well," suggested Father Aloysius.

"Certainly, a play area with bark chips could go here. That would make it in good view of the school as well as being very visible from the road. That way, there is less risk of damage being done to the equipment after school hours. You could have all sorts of climbing equipment. That would cater to the boys. When we were kids, we all climbed trees. Now, children are discouraged from climbing them, but they still need to climb and to develop those arm muscles."

"You are talking a long-term development,"

"Exactly so, what a discerning man you are, Father Aloysius. I guess next, you are going to tell me that perhaps I am not the man for the job." Father Aloysius shook his head vigorously, but the schoolmaster continued with a gentle smile. "Don't worry. I know the future is unlikely to be very long term for me, but....." The headteacher's voice trailed off.

"But..." Father Aloysius prompted.

"Well," said the schoolmaster, visibly gathering himself, "There are two elements to this project, one is, as you have so correctly suggested - time, the other is leadership, and that is where you come in."

"Me?" queried the cleric.

"Yes, you have the time. You are likely to be here a while yet if my conversation with the bishop is anything to go by, and you have the leadership skills necessary for the job, too."

"But," protested Father Aloysius, "You can't be serious. I know nothing about grounds development and not much more about gardening, certainly gardening in this country, and anyway, apart from not being qualified in terms of knowledge, I doubt if I have either of the other advantages you so glibly assume I have."

"I see, so you are just going to dismiss it out of hand, are you?"

"No, I didn't say that. I, I, I just think there might be someone else better qualified for the task."

"Possibly, but you are the man on the spot, and you are the one being called."

"Called?"

"Of course, you shouldn't find that so outrageous. Isn't your Bible full of people who were called?

"Like?" Father Aloysius was stalling for time.

"Well, let's start at the beginning, shall we? What about Abraham, then there was Jacob and Joseph, and what about Moses, and if that's not enough, you could add Gideon, and while we are in the mood, dear old Jonah, and that's just the Old Testament?

Now, when we come to the New Testament, you could mention one or two disciples, but first, of course, must come to Mary, and in case you should think I'm labouring a point, why don't we end with Paul?"

"And they told me you were a communist," said Father Aloysius, shaking his head in mock disbelief.

"Surely, but like any good communist, I have made it my business to know what the opposition believes, which, of course, is only partly true. I did, you must remember, have a good Welsh Baptist upbringing."

"So where does that leave me?" Father Aloysius, with a growing sense of anxiety, realised that the wily schoolmaster had carefully engineered the situation so that he would find it difficult to say no.

"You've been called." said the schoolmaster emphatically. "Now, you could try doing a Jonah, but I wouldn't fancy the belly of a whale bit, and so if I were you, I'd just agree with good grace."

"You're wrong about one thing, Mr Red," said Father Aloysius, determined to go down fighting, "There are more than two necessary ingredients that are essential to the success of this project."

"Doubtless, but I'd better give you the satisfaction of elaborating, or you might renege on me, so what else does the project need?"

"Vision, my friend, vision, and that's where you come in or already have come."

"Very flattering, I'm sure, so with my vision and your formidable energy and commitment, I guess we could be a good team."

Father Aloysius just nodded.

"Bread calling," it was Mrs Evans who brought Father Aloysius back to earth from his reverie.

"You'd better go," suggested the schoolmaster. "The boss is calling." Father grinned. He bent over and squeezed the schoolmaster's hand.

"I'll be back." He said quietly and slipped out into the kitchen.

Chapter Eleven

Education is a shared commitment between dedicated teachers motivated students and enthusiastic parents with high expectations.

Father Aloysius took his first loaf of bread to his first P.T.F.A. meeting. He had been invited by the school's Parent, Teacher, and Friends Association to talk about the grounds project. He was a little nervous about the meeting. He had taught the children of some of the parents on the committee and wondered how they would receive him.

He need not have worried. They were a cheerful lot, ably led by Mrs Gibbs, their chairperson. She was a practical, down-to-earth lady with great energy and enthusiasm.

Mrs Hardcourt was there representing the school staff. Father Aloysius was glad of her gentle, reassuring smile of welcome as he came into the staff room. The secretary, Mrs Fenton, too, greatly impressed the priest. Mrs Lancing, a mother of one of the children he taught, was quiet and unassuming, but she was not afraid to speak her mind and clearly had strong environmental views. She had been the one who had welcomed him and who had found him a seat while she hunted out some butter and jam and then presented Mrs Gibbs with the challenge of cutting and distributing the loaf. Duncan Evans, too, had obviously prepared the ground well, for when Father Aloysius laid out the sketch plan he had drawn up with the headteacher's help, they responded knowledgeably.

"This is obviously Duncan's dream," said Mrs Gibbs as she examined the plans.

"But how long is he to be with us to see his dreams take fruition, I wonder?"

Father Aloysius's gaze was on the floor. He rubbed his forehead with his long fingers and then looked up.

"Duncan is not likely to be with us for long. That is why I am anxious to get something started fairly soon." Mrs Hardcourt nodded her head in agreement.

"We could start planting the trees this autumn. Each child in the school could plant a tree," suggested Mrs Lancing.

"I'm sure we could get the support of the parish council, and then, of course, there is always the garden trusts," added Mr Newton.

"Fine," Mrs Gibbs responded. "But we ought to do something before the autumn."

"The pond," Father Aloysius said quietly.

"Yes," agreed Mrs Gibbs. "We could probably go ahead on that early in the next half of term. If we have a few weeks of dry, Joe can bring his digger in, and it won't make too much of a mess of the field. We'll be able to bank some of the soil before the tree planting. It would have to be before Joe gets into harvest, but in some ways, the sooner, the better."

"I think we'd better have two sub-committees," suggested Mrs Lancing, "I'd be happy to be on both. That way, I could pass on the ideas of one committee to another."

"Great, so who is for the pond?" she glanced about the staff room.

"If it means I can squeeze a new pair of wellies out of Ian, I'd be more than willing. My ones leak," said Mrs Father. Mr Grey and Mrs Zanby both raised their hands to indicate agreement to join the pond committee.

"Well, that's one committee sorted. Now, Mrs Hazelmere, surely you are going to join the tree lot?"

"Yes, I somehow knew you'd say that," chuckled the lady on Mrs Zanby's right,

"I'm sure Clive will give us a hand with the parish council." Mrs Hazelmere's husband was on the parish council.

Mrs Gibbs nodded, "Wonderful, the pond committee and the tree committee sorted. Now, what about fundraising?"

"Ah," said Father quietly, "Duncan has volunteered to write off to all sorts of people for grants; he's got a list of people to approach, which is good. It will help us, and it will also make him feel part of the project. One of his great challenges is not only coping with the illness but also gradually coming to terms with handing on the school. It's best if it's a gradual letting go, both for the school and for him. All this is part of that process."

"Hmm.... I hadn't looked at it like that," said Mrs Gibbs. "Very wise, you'll keep an eye on him, won't you, Father?"

"Of course."

"Now, that sort of fundraising will take a little time to come through," added Mrs Gibbs.

"How about holding a half-term disco, make it a celebration for getting the tests out of the way, it could also be a fundraiser," suggested Mrs Hardcourt.

"If we involve the Tarrants and the youth club, we will widen the involvement in the project. If the older children have some stake in the project, they are less likely to vandalise it later on. They would appreciate being part of the dance."

"Excellent. I agree the broader the base of involvement, the more likely will be our long-term success. How's your dancing, Father Aloysius?"

"Dancing?"

"Yes, rock and roll, or is ballroom more your thing, Father?"

"Well, as a matter of fact, I came from the dusty plains. Our people dance, of course, but I'm not sure the bishop would approve if I did too much of that." Father Aloysius chuckled.

"But will you help out, Father? Will you help out?"

"Certainly, of course, I'll hand out the squash, something safe like that." Again, the priest giggled. Mrs Gibbs smiled and went on to organise the third committee to deal with the dance. Father Aloysius sat listening quietly. His mind had slipped back across the miles and down the years to when he was young. There had been a gathering of his people down by the Inera River, where the yellow fever trees grew tall and spread their shady branches wide. There was an initiation ceremony for the young men who were old enough to become warriors. First, the elders and later the whole tribe had danced, leaping high into the air and stamping their rhythms out on the sun-scorched ground until the dust flew in clouds and the rocky outcrops along the far bank of the river threw back the echoes of their wild cries. Later, they lit fires and roasted a bullock. When they had feasted their fill, they danced again in the firelight under the stars. Their bodies gleaming with sweat as they cavorted on and on into the night until they were exhausted and had crept away to sleep. He did not think the bishop would approve.

"Well, that's that," said Mrs Gibbs, winding up the meeting. "Thank you one and all. Father, you're looking rather wistful. Are you all right?"

"Me, ah yes, perfectly, thank you," replied the priest, gathering himself again.

"A penny for your thoughts?" asked Mrs Gibbs.

"Me, ah well, I was just thinking, thinking about the type of dancing that is common in Karamoja," the priest replied with a gentle smile.

"Well, Father Aloysius," said Mrs Gibbs, placing her hand on his arm, "If the dancing is as good as your bread, then it will be excellent, thank you."

The priest left to a chorus of grateful thanks.

Chapter Twelve

Dance is an act,
paint your dream and follow it.

Father Aloysius, of course, had heard about disco dances, but he had never actually been to one. It was all a new experience for him. The flashing lights and blaring music, the clever patter of the D.J. slurring his words down the microphone, and the dancers, eyes aglow with excitement, bouncing and bobbing to the music, had him mesmerised. Safe behind the drinks counter, he watched in amazement. It was the girls performing intricate group dances who seemed to be enjoying the evening the most. Some of the boys were good performers, but there were others who lacked the coordination and discipline to achieve the same level of performance. While groups of girls danced together, the boys were more inclined to dance solo, and many of the younger boys were content to race about the floor, darting in and out of the toilet to wet their hair and comb it into little quiffs that stuck up from their foreheads like a series of spikes. The P.T.F.A. had organised a good number of adults to support the evening, and so the ambitions of the more excitable younger boys to cause mayhem were easily contained. Father Aloysius remained behind the refreshment table dispensing drinks, his feet that tapped to the music safely hidden. Several of the girls asked him to dance, but he quietly smiled and shook his head. Halfway through the evening, Anna and Larry arrived. Anna, her hair gleaming and eyes shining, was in an effervescent mood. She and Larry danced. Two lithe figures move in fluent harmony to the music. Soon, all eyes were on them. Larry, dressed in black, Anna in a red shirt and light blue slacks, swirled and whirled about the floor to some sixties jive, everyone clapped to the rhythm.

"Go, Larry, go, go, Larry, go," the call instigated by the D.J. was quickly taken up. Father Aloysius watched, entranced. Anna seemed to sense his eyes on her. She waved and blew him a kiss.

The priest felt himself flush with embarrassment. He turned away. There at the back door, Big Sid Trevinian had just slipped into the hall, followed by three other figures. That part of the hall was in partial darkness, and whilst Father Aloysius had no trouble in recognising Big Sid, whose huge bulk was momentarily lit up by a flashing strobe, the other figures following so quickly, hard on his heels, were less easy to recognise, but there was something familiar about them that rang momentary alarm bells in the cleric's mind. Just then, the music reached its climax, and his gaze returned to the dancers. Larry lifted Anna high into the air and then, placing her daintily on her feet, bowed low in front of her on one knee. Everyone applauded wildly. Anna raised her partner to his feet, and they turned and came over to the table. Father Aloysius felt his pulse suddenly start to race, but he smiled broadly and, endeavouring not to let his hand shake, poured out two orange drinks.

"Congratulations, you looked very good," he said, fastening his eyes on Larry. Larry grinned, clearly pleased, and gratefully accepted the drink. Anna put a long forefinger on the third black button of Father Aloysius's cassock. "Your turn now, Father," she said demurely. The priest felt himself flushing with embarrassment again, he almost spilt the drink he thrust at her.

" I'm sorry I, I, I have to be here to look after the drinks."

"Ooooh, you!" exclaimed the girl, pouting, "Look, we'll help you, and then we can take it in turns so you can dance, won't we, Larry?" Anna gave Larry a meaningful stare as she slipped behind the drinks table to stand beside the priest, but at that moment, Rachel appeared to drag Larry onto the floor. Anna was clearly disconcerted. Desperately, she looked about for someone to act as relief on the drinks table, but then suddenly, they were enveloped by a hoard of thirsty customers. She and Father Aloysius found themselves very busy dispensing refreshments. If Anna was displeased by the way things had turned out, Father Aloysius was even more disconcerted to have the young girl beside him, her arm inadvertently brushing his thigh and their hands touching as they hurried to pour the required drinks. As the last of the drinkers turned away, the D.J. put on a particularly catchy piece of music. Anna jigged on the spot, and even Father Aloysius could not prevent his feet from tapping to the beat. Suddenly, Anna clapped her hands above her head and, pointing gleefully at him, cried, "There, you can't stop yourself, you do really want to dance, don't you!"

"Ye. No. Oh, you." said Father Aloysius, feigning crossness. "You know I can't dance."

"For heaven's sake, why not?" demanded the girl, her eyes flashing. "Aren't I good enough for you, or are you afraid I might, I might…"

"Shush," interrupted the priest. "It's not that, and you know it. It's just that priests, well, priests don't dance. It's, it's just no, not, well, you know, it's just not politic.

"Not politics! Well, if you won't stoop to soil your feet on the floor with me, I'll find someone who will!" The girl flounced off round the table and slipped away through the dancers towards the back of the hall to reappear a little while later with a tall, faired, haired youth in tow. She glowered at Father Aloysius. The priest then knew who had slipped into the hall behind big Sid a little earlier. Unconsciously, his left hand stroked his chin. He deliberately avoided looking at the dancers from that moment on. Instead, his eyes roved along the darkened back of the hall where Big Sid lounged, leaning against the back wall. It was the conga that was Father Aloysius's undoing. When Anna saw that the priest was ignoring her, she determined to try another tack. She slipped away from the tall Trevor to the D.J. and arranged for the conga to be announced. As the dance gathered momentum and more and more people joined the line, she caught Philippa, who was passing her by the arm.

"Hey, get off, will you," protested the younger girl.

"Wait," hissed Anna, "Now, listen, I bet you a pound you can't get the priest to join the line." Philippa immediately skipped off to take up the challenge.

"Father, Father, come on, you must join the snake," she insisted as she danced up to him.

"But I ...."

"No! No excuses, come on," The girl pulled Father Aloysius by the sleeve away from the drinks table and onto the floor. "There," she said triumphantly. "Even Mrs Hardcourt is dancing. Here, grab hold of my waist, and we'll join in the conga." For a moment, Father Aloysius hesitated, then Mrs Hardcourt waved cheerfully, and he shrugged, grinned, and joined the dance. For a brief time, he was the end of the snake, then suddenly, he was aware of other hands on his hips and a voice that came from behind his left shoulder.

"Hi, Father Aloysius. I knew I'd get you to dance with me in the end."

"No, no," laughed the priest as the dancers snaked round the hall, "No way, you can't call this dancing anyway. I must get...." He did not get a chance to complete the sentence. The conga snake stopped suddenly, and Anna, whether it was intentional or not, Father had no way of knowing, cannoned into him, and he felt her arms about him and her body pressed close to his back. He stood still, aware of a whole flood of different sensations, a mixture of excitement he had never experienced in quite the same way before and, once again, embarrassment. Father Aloysius had no experience of being held in that way, and although he was no stranger to desire, his desires had been manageable in that they had been part of a fantasy world, sublimated by rigorous self-discipline. He had managed his thoughts by concentrating on planning acts of kindness. Now he was being held by a girl whom he did not understand but to whom he recognised he felt strongly attracted, his desire was there, and she was holding him, so too, for the third time that evening, there came feelings of embarrassment and confusion. Father Aloysius was not used to being the subject of female manipulation, he was used to being in control and in a sense dictating the emotional climate for others rather than having them dictate it to him. He glanced down at her hands, the hands that held him, small, strong yet delicate with firm tapering fingers. His desire was to take those fingers and kiss them, but instead, he gently prised them from his chest and, stepping away from her, apologised.

"I'm so very sorry, I I...

"Why are you sorry, silly? It wasn't your fault. Anyway," she said archly, "I ..."

Father Aloysius turned away. "I must get back to the drinks." At that moment, Philippa rushed up and caught him by the sleeve.

"Father, Father, come quickly," she whispered urgently and dragged him away from the line.

"What's the matter?" asked the priest in hushed tones.

"It's Sid," the girl mouthed the words at him and held her finger in front of her lips to indicate the need for silence. They made their way to a rear door at the dark end of the hall. The door led into another room, a school cloakroom with lockers for shoes and facilities for hanging coats. The cloakroom was without lights but was illuminated by an outside lamp in the playground. The door they had crept to was slightly ajar.

Philippa, releasing the priest's sleeve, leaned forward to peer through the crack. Then withdrawing, she indicated for Father Aloysius to look for himself. The priest bent forward and looked into the cloakroom. Big Sid had his back to the door. Two of the youths who had been party to the taking of Larry's jacket were leaning on the coat stands. Sid bent over he seemed to take something from a small bag that he had at his feet. Father Aloysius could not be sure, but it seemed he handed something to the taller of the boys. He felt the hairs on the back of his head start to tingle.

Philippa tugged at his sleeve. He looked round. The girl's pale face stared up at him.

"Drugs," she mouthed. The priest put his head back at the crack. The tall youth who had earlier been dancing with Anna had turned to his companion. They appeared to be in some consultation, but in the dimness of the light, it was hard for Father Aloysius to see exactly what was going on. He shook his head and shrugged, indicating to his companion that he could not really see anything. He straightened up and turned to the young girl, stepping away from the door as he did. His mind was racing. What had he just seen?

At that moment, Anna, who had been talking to the D.J., spied on him.

"Father Aloysius," she called as she hurried over, "So that is where you disappeared to. I wanted to get Tony a drink, but you seem to have run out of orange, and he can't stand Ribena."

Father Aloysius's heart sank. Her intervention would certainly have disturbed Sid and the boys. He hastily stepped further away from the door.

"I think they have some spare bottles in the cloakroom," he said and was surprised at how calm his voice sounded.

"No, no, Silly, not the cloakroom. What on earth would they be storing drinks there for?" Anna's strong denial came somewhat as a surprise to the priest. "It will be the staff room," she said as she pushed past him to the cloakroom door. She entered the cloakroom with a clatter, switching on the lights. Father Aloysius did not follow her, but he stood still to listen, eager to hear what might transpire.

"Sid, Garry, what on earth are you up to? You know you can't smoke in the building."

Anna's voice sounded somehow rather contrived. "Have you seen any orange squash here?" she asked. Sid's reply was lost in a blast of music as the D. J. turned on the next track, but moments later, the big man appeared at the door. Father Aloysius turned and wandered aimlessly towards the D.J. He was conscious of Sid's eyes on his back. It was not a pleasant sensation.

"I'm so sorry," he apologised to the D.J. "We are looking for the squash, you will get a drink as soon as we can find it." He managed to glance in the direction of the cloakroom. Big Sid stood there, filling the door frame. He was staring hard at the priest.

They eventually found the spare squash in the kitchen, and Tony the D.J. got his drink.

Father Aloysius remained behind the refreshment table for the rest of the evening. Anna pointedly did not talk to him again. She spent a little time dancing with the tall youth before the pair of them disappeared. Larry was clearly displeased, but he stayed to the end dancing with Rachel. Father Aloysius was left to ponder the situation. What exactly was Anna up to? Was her behaviour with the tall youth to spite Larry, or was it to spite him, he wondered. Just what had Sid and those boys been up to in the cloakroom, and why had Sid stared at him so fixedly for so long? In between serving the thirsty dancers, he mulled these questions over in his mind but, for all his wondering, came to no fixed conclusions. The rest of the evening passed without incident.

Much later, when the disco was over and all the dancers had left, Mrs Gibbs brought round tea for those who had remained to clear up. She and the Tarrants were enthusiastic about the evening. The D.J. had been good and had kept the dancers bouncing and bobbing to the end. In his wind-up farewells, he had even managed to talk a little about conservation and how the money raised by the disco was to be spent.

"Larry managed to tear himself away from Rachel and asked me to dance," Mrs Tarrant had beamed as she paused in her mopping to sip her tea and then had added with a sigh of relief that they had had a really good evening, no one had been sick, there had been no fights and no broken windows.

"Great!" agreed Mrs Gibbs. "And I think we have made quite a bit of money for the grounds project. Well done, Father Aloysius. You are obviously an accomplished barman, but what about a dancer?"

The priest rubbed his chin ruefully, "I think I'll stick to the squash," he grinned quietly and slipped off with a brush to the cloakroom. The room was used for the children's coats and bags and was set up specifically for the purpose of metal benching and stands that housed wire lockers for shoes and boots and hooks for coats and bags. Father Aloysius picked up a coat that had been left behind in the end-of-term rush and abandoned on the floor. He estimated where Sid might have been standing. There, on top of one of the scratched metal benches, was a pile of cigarette ash.

Chapter Thirteen

*Stories have to be told or they die
and when they die we can't remember who we are
or why we are here.*

Sue Monk Kidd

That half-term school break was a busy time for Father Aloysius. True, the school had broken up, so he was not concerned with lessons and all that involved, but there was his little flock to minister to, the home visits, and the youth club holiday scheme to help with, too, as well as the pond project to plan. It was the club and the visiting that took his time. Visiting took Miss Farrow's time, too, for she had her little round of regular people she cared for. Often, the two of them would go together. They were a good pair. Miss Farrow, bright, bustling, and eager, with an ever practical eye, would be the one to take the little parcel of home-made scones or cupcakes. She too would be the one who could deal with the washing or turning a bed, the one to see the need for something to be done about the pot plants or the pet that was proving too much, the one to alert the district nurse and the surgery for the need for attention to be given to old Mr Lovell's bronchitis or Mrs Towser's ulcer on her shin. The priest would take his little case for administering the Mass at home with him and would quietly hear confession before giving the sacrament. For most, he was just a cheerful face and someone else to chat to. Often then, he would slip away, leaving Mrs Farrow to dispense her cakes and further share the time of day with their host while he hurried up the hill to help with the holiday club. There, he would find himself helping Mrs Tarrant and her happy band of mothers get through a hectic three hours of fun activities with fifteen or more of the younger children in the village. There were art activities, a variety of construction toys, books, board games, and even two computers. The hall was set up with mats, giant bean bags, and a small climbing frame. On fine days, the children had their break out on the playground and had the use of trikes, scooters, and a variety of wheeled wooden tractors and carts. Father Aloysius enjoyed helping with the art activities, especially if there was painting. The children's work was always so fresh and spontaneous; he loved listening to the imaginative way they talked about their work. The priest sometimes contributed his own pictures. They were usually of animals, African animals, and he would make up a story to go with the picture. Father Aloysius was in great demand as a storyteller. The children always had a quiet time after their lunch, they ate packed lunches. The quiet time was story time, and they would all curl up on cushions on the carpet, and one of the adults would read a story. Father Aloysius usually made his own stories up, and sometimes, he did it with the help of one of his pictures.

He was a learner of the computers. A very serious little boy called Trevor was his tutor. He had a lesson every day, and each day, he learnt something new. In return, Father Aloysius would organise a ball game for Trevor and his friends in the hall. The construction toys always amazed the priest. As with the art, the making of something usually involves a story.

"Father, where on earth did you learn to tell such marvellous stories?" asked Mrs Tarrant one day after a particularly long and rewarding session with some of the children using the Lego box. The priest had just smiled and shrugged his shoulders. "All right then, what sort of toys did you have when you were young?" asked the supervisor, determined to get an answer from the priest. Again, Father Aloysius smiled. "Well." he replied, "We had bits of wood, and we used to make our own weapons, throwing sticks and bows and arrows and catapults, but I didn't really have toys until I was rescued by the priests and brought up on the mission station. There, we used to get old tins and make them into wheeled vehicles with bits of wire and wood. We usually got jam tins from the kitchen. I seem to remember that the jam was plum. They had a bright label with Kenya Canners Nairobi on them. Tins had a big recycling value up there on the Mission Station; none were ever thrown away. They could be made into cups and bowls and all sorts. When we could get them, we made them into toys. I had this great jeep. I used an offcut from a building truss, a big oblong bit of wood that I painted bright blue. The wheels were four tins. They were nice and wide. The axles were bits of wire. I used to drag it about on a length of sisal string. I was so proud of it. I used to pretend I was the District Commissioner in his Land Rover. I made quite a few vehicles for my friends, too, but that jeep was the only toy I really owned. We used to recycle a lot of things. I remember my first shoes were made out of a car tyre. They lasted forever. The tops were made from the outer tube, and the treads were the sole. Sometimes, the tops were made out of the inner tube because they were softer. We used the inner tubes too for our catapults and sometimes even to make beds. The frame was a rectangle of poles made of tree branches. Stretched across were strips of inner tube. Tins and jars and things like that had a great second-hand value. I'm sorry I seem to have gone on a bit."

"No, it's good to hear how others live," said Mrs Tarrant. "Here in Cornwall, we don't think of ourselves as well off, but compared with your childhood, our children are so lucky, they don't realise it. Rescued by the priests, you said, Father, how was that?" asked Mrs Tarrant, glad she had managed to get Father Aloysius talking at last and determined to make the most of it while he was in the flow as it were. This time, the priest smiled again but shook his head,

"Perhaps another time, it's a long story, and I've promised to visit Duncan Evans. Miss Farrow will be there, and she will be waiting for me."

"Give him our love, won't you," said Mrs Watson, one of the young mothers who had come to collect her son Michael. "Come on, young Michael. It's time we were off and let these good folk get on with their business." She gathered her son to her and started putting on his coat.

"Mum, can we go by the shop?" the little boy asked as his mother struggled to get his arm properly into the sleeve.

"Heavens now what? Never content that's your trouble. You ought to have been listening to Father Aloysius here. He had to make his own toys out of scraps and throw-aways and I bet he wasn't always whining for something more, were you, Father? I bet you were pretty content with what you had, simple as it was."

"Content, I'm not sure about that," replied the priest. "Certainly, we never asked to go to the shops; they were over fifty miles away, but as for content, I guess we were always looking for bigger and better tins."

"Ah, go on," laughed the young mother, picking up her son's lunch box from where it had fallen while she had struggled with the coat. "Tell me, Father, I bet even though you didn't have much, you were happy."

"Well, Father, did you have a happy childhood?" asked Mrs Tarrant. There was a pause. Father Aloysius stood still a moment, looking across the room. In his ears, he could hear wild cries, the sharp crack of the whips, and the guns, the guns, the guns and the flies, the buzzing flies. The priest took a deep breath and smiled, "Yes, yes, mostly I was very happy. I had much to thank God for, you see."

"There, Michael," Mrs Watson glowed triumphantly, "You must learn to be happy with what you've got; things, more and more things won't make you happy. Good afternoon, Father. Thank you, Mrs T. Michael. What do you say to Mrs Tarrant?"

"Thank you, Mrs T," the young boy lisped, and everyone laughed. Father Aloysius tousled the boy's hair and grinned. Michael looked up at him and grinned back.

"Father Aloysius, were you ever naughty?" he asked. Again, the priest laughed.

"What's this confession? Yes, of course, young Michael, but that's another story. Now you look after your mum. Take her straight home, and don't let her buy too many tins at the shop." It was a happy group that went their separate ways after the Kiddies' Club that day.

Chapter Fourteen

*In failing to confess
I would only hide you from
myself, not myself from you.*

-St. Augustine

Duncan Evans was depressed. He sat in his chair gazing out through the French doors to the view beyond the garden over across the moors. He loved the moors; he loved the wide skies and the distant rolling hills and the ever-changing patterns of the clouds rolling in from the sea to cast their shadows over the slopes, bleak yet beautiful. There was a timelessness about the landscape and a certain untamed, rugged wildness. What little evidence there was of man's efforts to tame the countryside had a feeling of antiquity about it too, the brown crumbling chimney of a long abandoned tin mine and the walled fields, their stone surrounds broken only where a rutted cart track wound its way up the hill were all ancient relics of a bygone age, they had been there years, decades-long in the time of their slowly decaying old age. The view was his solace, but today, it could not soothe his worry. It was Anna; she had left home again. It had been the night of the dance. She had gone to the dance with Larry. He had collected her from the house. The headteacher had been pleased to see him. They had enjoyed a little light banter together.

"Now, you be sure to bring Anna back safe," he had said. Larry didn't. At the dance, it seems she had fallen in with her old set, the surfers from Pendon Bay. She had gone off with them and had not been home since.

Miss Farrow was with Mrs Evans when the priest arrived. They were talking in a concerned manner.

"Oh, Father, I am so glad you have come, you must help us."

"Of course, but what's the matter?" "It's Anna, she's gone again, off with that gang from Pendon Bay. We are worried sick, and poor Duncan.... he just sits there staring out over the moors. He won't eat, and he hardly says anything."

"Can I see him?"

"Yes, yes, please do. You may be able to cheer him up. We have just made tea. Would you like some? We'll bring it in."

"That would be great." Mrs Evans opened the lounge door and ushered the two visitors in.

"Duncan darling, you have two friends come to see you, it's Father Aloysius and Miss Farrow." The headteacher sat with his back to the door. If he heard his wife, he gave no sign of it, he just sat still, gazing into the distance. The priest walked quietly across the room. He stood for a moment, looking down at his friend. Then he reached out his hand and took Duncan's hand in his.

"Hello, Head, how are you?" he asked, squeezing the pale, thin hand he held. Duncan Evans looked up. His face was drawn, his mouth a hard gash, turned down. His eyes looked tired. The headteacher coughed and looked away.

"Been better." The voice was hardly audible.

"It's Anna, isn't it?" queried the priest.

The headteacher just nodded and then, after a long pause, said, "You got her back before."

"She'll come back," the priest tried to sound reassuring. "I'll, I'll go and see her."

"Thank you." the voice was just a whisper. At that moment, his wife came bustling into the room with Miss Farrow. Between them, they brought the tea trolley over to where Duncan sat.

"Well, well, isn't this nice? Here's Miss Farrow come to see you too, and we've got the tea. I know Father Aloysius must be thirsty, he's been helping at the holiday club."

"Yes," said the priest, "And Mrs Watson and Mrs Tarrant send their love."

There was a flicker of a smile in the headteacher's eyes. "So you've been busy with the little ones." His voice was slightly stronger.

"Yes, it's fun. Young Trevor Harding is helping me with the computers. He's an excellent teacher, but I fear I'm not his star pupil."

"Computers, eh? Yes, young Trevor is a bright boy. He'll soon have you putting your sermons on the internet."

"Heaven forbid!" exclaimed the priest.

"Doubt if heaven will do anything about it." The pale head nodded, and the grim, moody face smiled.

"Now, now dear," admonished his wife, "Here, where would you like your tea?"

The headteacher took the cup in a somewhat shaky hand. He sipped sparingly.

"So, what else have you been up to?"

"Oh, visiting mostly."

"Scrounging tea off old ladies, eh."

"Duncan, please," Mrs Evans tried to make her voice sound severe, "You know visiting is a very important part of a priest's work."

"It's all right, Mrs Evans. It's good to see Duncan hasn't lost his edge. Actually, Duncan, it's usually me giving out the drinks."

"Oh, of course, communion after confession, so not only are you scrounging tea, but your cleaning up on all the local scandal and gossip. I don't know, it's all right for some."

"Duncan, really, you're impossible. I don't know why Father Aloysius has come to see you, I really don't," Mrs Evans chided.

"Why the priest should come visiting the devil? Well, yes, I suppose you have a point, but you know what they say better, the devil, you know. Anyway, Father Aloysius, what about your confession? Surely you have to confess, too?"

"Yes. As a matter of fact, I've got an appointment with the bishop on Thursday. I make my confession to him."

"Confession to a bishop, my, you must have some really 'A' plus sins. Well, well, Miss Farrow, what is it that Father Aloysius will be confessing, eh?"

"Hopefully that, he makes my coffee too weak, and he takes too much sugar," came the instant response from Miss Farrow.

"Ah yes," said the headteacher sardonically, "Pretty serious stuff."

"Tea, Father?" asked Mrs Evans. The priest was looking out across the moors, searching the view her husband had been so absorbed in only moments before. He seemed preoccupied, too.

"Thank you." Then, turning to the headteacher, he nodded his head. The serious look on his face softened into a shy smile, "I suspect there will be a lot more than just coffee and tea to confess about."

"Then let me know if you need any help with the penance," quipped his friend. The priest just smiled and said his farewells, but there was no smile on his face as he made his way back to the presbytery; it had been replaced by a worried frown. There were two things on his mind, both concerned his friend. What was he going to say to the bishop, and how was he going to persuade his friend's daughter to return? He needed to resolve his feelings for Anna.... and that was urgent. He could not visit the Evans' house again until he had done so. It was not just that terrible feeling of guilt that he had felt as he had stood beside his friend, but for Anna's sake, too, he must ensure that his relations with her were completely honourable. His bedside prayers that night had been long and earnest.

The next day, Father Aloysius made his confession to the bishop. Miss Farrow had taken him to Pendon Bay. She needed to do some shopping, and she had a date with a friend. The bishop was there on a visit and had suggested it might be a good idea for the priest to visit him there as he was short of time. Normally, he would have preferred to visit Father Aloysius in his own parish. He regularly visited the clergy in his diocese. These visits were primarily to offer them support, but they also included an opportunity to make their confession. Of course, he could have made it an expectation that they visit him. However, it made more sense for him to see them in their parishes. It gave him an opportunity to see them on their home turf and to get a feel for the parish they served.

The bishop listened patiently while Father Aloysius, quietly, humbly, talked about Anna and his feelings for her; he talked about the youths she was involved with and his feelings towards them, and his dilemma. How was he to serve his friend Duncan Evans best? What should he do?

"Father Aloysius," the bishop cautioned quietly, "You are clearly worried about your relations with your friend's daughter, but it would seem to me these feelings are still but feelings. Am I correct? Can you assure me that you have divulged all?"

"Yes, bishop. You are correct. I have endeavoured to keep my relationship with Anna Evans totally what you would expect of a priest."

"Thank you, that is reassuring. I am sorry to have to ask you these things, but as your bishop, I have a duty of care not only to you but to all those to whom you minister. All of us who have taken the vows of celibacy are prone to temptation. Some sadly fall, and when they do, that brings the Church as a whole into disrepute, and very sadly, often, they are not the only ones to suffer. The person they are involved with suffers too. We are all prone to feelings, Father Aloysius, they are not a sin in themselves; it is what we do about them that matters, that is our test. You'll remember we discussed what you felt about the racist abuse you received. Remind me what the strategies we had for dealing with it were?"

The priest's hands were held, fingers touching in the attitude of prayer. Gently, he tapped his fingers together three times, "We decided firstly, we should pray. We should pray for the strength to turn the other cheek, to look beyond the insult to the heart of the offender, and to recognise in that person, despite their prejudice, there was a soul that is loved by God. We should try as Jesus did on the cross to forgive and to love them as one of God's children. That should be our personal response to the hurt in us. We do have a public duty, too.

Secondly, we should learn to see the red lights, to see the situations that have the potential for encouraging that sort of thing, and to avoid them if possible. We should de-escalate confrontational situations and be sensible. We should cultivate a keen sense of humour, for humour allows us to look at ourselves with humility and at others with laughter. Laughter is the best medicine, they say.

Thirdly, we should make our own position quite clear. This is the public duty we referred to earlier. Racist abuse is wrong. It is punishable under the law. We should never take the law into our own hands, but we should not be shy of referring to the law to combat racist abuse." Father Aloysius inclined his head to indicate that he had finished.

"Very good, Father Aloysius. Now, with regards to Anna - pray, pray for the strength to love her as Christ would have done, to love her as one of God's children, and pray for the strength to remain true to your vows made to God and the Church, vows of poverty, chastity, and obedience. The bar is high, some would say too high, but with help from the Almighty, you can succeed.

Secondly, see the red lights. Avoid all situations where temptation might present itself. And in that respect, it would seem to me you have done well so far. There will inevitably be times when being alone with someone, such as Anna, can't be avoided, then you have to be especially on your guard, which brings me to my third point, which is you have to make it make it clear where you stand. Make it clear to her that as a priest, you have vowed to eschew the pursuit of wealth, to eschew carnal desires and to remain chaste, and to put yourself in a position of obedience to God at all times. The strategies for dealing with the two temptations seem to be very similar, do they not?" queried the bishop quietly.

"Yes, yes, they do." agreed the priest. "What of my penance?"

"Penance?" queried the bishop, "I'm not sure you deserve a penance. However, in order to keep you on the straight and narrow, as it were, I am going to ask you to read the letter of St. Paul to the Ephesians with special reference to Chapter five, and I am going to ask you to tell me if you ever get inappropriate thoughts. Often, these things creep up on you, and if you entertain them, you are already taking a step down a slippery slope. Recognising the signs early is the best way to see you don't fall into a grievous sin."

"Is that all?"

"If you meditate on that chapter, that should suffice."

"Thank you, bishop, you have been a great help."

"No, Father Aloysius, it is I who should be thanking you, and indeed, I do thank you for all the good work you have done in Pondreath. May the good Lord continue to bless your many labours there and, as the prayer says, lead you not into temptation. Incidentally, that is a prayer you could also pray for me, your bishop."

"You have been very understanding, I am grateful, and certainly now, when I say the Lord's own prayer, I will be thinking of you as well as myself."

Miss Farrow was waiting in the foyer of the church. She smiled warmly as the priest came through the door. "Well, Father, how have you got on? I hope you have a suitable penance to do for making my coffee so weak and for taking so much sugar."

"Oh, Miss Farrow, how terrible I forgot completely to confess either of those sins."

"What!" exclaimed Miss Farrow in mock horror. You'll have to go back inside at once." She took him by the arm and led him out of the front door and down the steps to the drive where her car stood. As he accompanied her, the priest was filled with a sense of great relief. He had made his confession. Now, he must follow the bishop's advice. It was not going to be easy, but he owed it to his friend to make sure he did.

Chapter Fifteen

The gifts of caring, attention
affection, appreciation, and love
are some of the most precious
gifts you can give and they don't
cost you anything.

-Deepak Chopra

The squat was a semi-derelict old fisherman's cottage tucked in the lee of an old boatyard at the end of the quay. Father Aloysius had heard stories about it from several of the folk he visited in Pondreath, and Larry had been able to confirm that that was where the surfies hung out. Father Aloysius had found his way there easily enough. He had his directions from a friendly policeman who had raised his eyebrows mildly when Father Aloysius had approached him in the High Street and had asked where the place was to be found.

"Just listen for the music," he'd advised, and when it's too loud to hear yourself speak, then you're there. If, by some miracle, they've got it turned down too low for you to hear, it's the house almost at the end of the quay. It used to be white and has no front door, and if the refuse lorry ever gets there, there is always too much rubbish for it to take it all away."

"Obviously, the posh end of town." Father had replied.

"Yes, and I am surprised you got an invite." quipped the policeman.

"Oh, us sinners like to stick together," re-joined the priest. He had then gone on to explain the purpose of the visit and how he'd hoped to persuade Anna to return home with him.

Sergeant Graves had wished him every success. "We visit the place from time to time. They are a mixed bunch, and I guess your girl won't be the first or the last to cause her parents worry. Good luck."

Father Aloysius and Miss Farrow picked their way round the piles of driftwood and boxes of rubbish that strewed the quay to the gaping front door of the cottage. There was no music.

"Anyone at home?" The front door was open. Father Aloysius called out as he approached. He could hear voices, but there was no reply. He knocked and then entered. To his surprise, he walked straight into Big Sid Trevinian. Sid's huge bulk filled the entrance to a room beyond. He was obviously deep in conversation with someone in the other room, but it was impossible to look round him to see who it might be.

"What the …… do you want?" Sid swore, his face dark with anger, he glowered at the priest.

"I've come to see Anna. Is she here?" asked Father Aloysius.

"No." It was one of the lads who the priest had seen at the disco who spoke, his voice echoed Sid's hostility. Father Aloysius sensed he was not telling the truth but, for a moment, was at a loss as to how to pursue the matter. He was conscious Miss Farrow was waiting outside. Perhaps he had better tell her this visit might take longer than expected. His housekeeper was gazing up at the gulls wheeling about high above the harbour.

"Everything alright?" she queried.

"In a manner of speaking, but this might take some time."

"All right. I'm due to meet a friend, I don't want to be late."

"Fine. You go."

"We will be in the cafe, in the High Street, on the right, next to the bookshop." The priest nodded, and Miss Farrow departed. He watched her go.

"Hallo," The voice came from behind him. The priest turned. The girl stood in the doorway, dripping. Her black wet suit clung to her slim frame, and her thin brown legs and arms protruding from its worn ends were goose-fleshed with cold, but her smile was warm and friendly.

"You must be Father Aloysius," the girl said shyly, squeezing water from her long, dark hair.

"Yes, yes, I am, and I'm looking for Anna. Can you tell me where I can find her?"

"Anna," the girl called, "Anna."

"I told you," the boy who was just visible beyond Sid Trevinian spoke angrily, "She's not here."

"Don't be silly, Simon," said the girl. She beckoned the priest to follow. She entered the house.

Sid was still standing, blocking the door. The girl pushed past him. Father Aloysius made to follow her, but Sid put out his arm and took hold of the door frame in one heavy hand, barring the way. For a moment, their eyes locked, and then the big man entered the room. Seizing his opportunity, the priest followed.

"Anna, Anna, it's Father Aloysius, he's come to see you." The girl addressed a person seemingly at the other end of the room. There was a groan. It was Anna. She was surrounded by the clutter of clothes and bedding, crouching on a mattress. Despite her tan, her face looked pale, and there were great dark rings under her eyes. She plucked distractedly at the fringe of an Afghan coat.

"If you've come to ask me to go back to.." her voice was low and hoarse, it trailed away to a whisper.

Father broke in hastily. He sensed that if he was to get anywhere with her, he must make it clear that it was her he valued, as well as her father. "No, I just came to see you. I wanted to thank you for the recipe for the bread. I've brought you some."

"Bread. Huh!" Sid's voice was garrulous. "I bet you didn't think to bring the wine!" he grunted sardonically.

"No, I'm sorry, no wine, but I did bring jam." He reached out the bag in his hand towards Anna. She scrambled to her feet and, ignoring the big man who was standing glowering down at her, crossed the room. She was dressed in a T-shirt that was far too big for her. It came down to her knees. Coming towards her visitor, her bare feet pattering on the stone flags, the girl took the bag and reached into it with one hand. She took out the loaf.

"That's kind of you, thank you," her hand reached forward, and her slim fingers took hold of one of the buttons of his cassock. She turned it gently. Her blue eyes looked up at him through dishevelled wisps of fair hair. "Look, um, we can't talk here, why don't you wait for me down by the Sea Wall? I'll get some things on."

"Now wait a minute, young lady, no one goes anywhere until I'm paid," growled Sid.

"Paid, what for? Anyway, I told you I haven't got any money." There was a hint of defiance in Anna's voice, but Father Aloysius sensed behind it there was a note of desperation, too.

"No one leaves until I'm paid," reiterated Sid.

Father Aloysius held up a hand. "How much?" he asked.

"Twenty pounds," demanded Sid.

"Twenty, come on, Sid," it was the girl in the wet suit who spoke, "That's absolute robbery."

"Twenty or." Sid did not complete his threat. Father Aloysius had slipped his hand into the pocket of his cassock and had taken out a slightly crumpled note, money he had been saving to pay for a meal with his housekeeper on her day out. He held it out to Sid.

The big man grinned and closed one large fist round the money, crumbling it into a ball. He grunted with satisfaction.

"May I ask what it's for?" enquired the priest.

"Cornflakes." Sid turned. He gave Father Aloysius a long, cold stare and then stamped out of the house. Father Aloysius shrugged.

"Milk extra," he said mildly and followed Sid outside. "Mr Trevinian," he called after the big man who was striding off round the corner. He knew he should not ask it. He knew it was not a wise thing to ask, but he knew he would ask it all the same.

"What?" Sid paused and half turned towards the priest.

"Are you dealing in drugs?" Father Aloysius's voice was even and steady, but his heart was racing. The big man just snorted, his blue bloodshot eyes narrowing slightly.

"It's none of your business what I do, so if you want some good advice, very good advice, stay away!"

"If it is drugs you're selling to the kids, it's a matter for the police," replied Father evenly.

"Who'll tell em?" sneered Sid.

"I will."

"You do, and you're dead!" Sid spat and, thrusting his hands deep into his pockets, strode away.

"And that's without milk or sugar," said the priest quietly.

Father Aloysius, too, strode off down the quay but in the opposite direction. He stood for a long moment, looking out across the clear blue bay. The tide was slipping out, leaving banks of clean, shiny, wet sand, uninhabited as yet by any member of the bucket and spade holiday hoards. It was clear of any footprints save the few faint marks left by a pair of oystercatchers that had scurried along its fringes. Above, across the paler blue of the sky, a line of fluffy white clouds marched like some troop of revellers off to a fair, all tucks and billows.

"My GOD, how beautiful is your creation," murmured the priest, "And how beastly are some of the creatures that inhabit it." He sighed and turned to face the cottage. Anna came eventually, closely followed by Simon, who seemed to be remonstrating with her. The dark-haired girl whose name Father Aloysius had yet to learn seemed to be remonstrating with Simon, and behind came four others, another girl and the three youths. Father knew them from the incident with Larry's jacket. There was a protracted argument, and then suddenly, Anna broke away and hurried over to where the priest waited patiently. As she came, he noted the agitation in her face. The task of getting her home was not going to be easy. She stood for a moment, silent as he was, gazing out over the waters. He felt the emotional tension in her, from the tautness of her body line to the hardness of her breathing.

"Well," she said, nudging his arm. He remained still. "Well, why did you come?"

"To see you, of course," said Father quietly, "And to make my confession."

Confession?" Her voice was sharp. A wisp of her blond hair blew across his face.

"Yes, I've been to make my confession to the bishop. Normally, he would have come to Pondreath, but he is very busy, and fortunately, Miss Farrow wanted to do some shopping here, so I agreed to come with her and save him time."

"To the bishop," her voice was full of incredulity. "I bet that didn't take long."

Father Aloysius smiled and, waving her hair from his face, replied, "The bishop was very understanding and listened patiently for a long time."

"Uh, I don't think!"

"Anyway, how are you?" asked the priest, who was at a loss for anything else to say and was desperately thinking as to how best to talk to Anna about her father.

"Fine," there was a flatness to her voice, which made her sound anything but fine, "Fine, just fine."

It was the priest's turn to grunt. He repeated his question. "How are you?"

"All right, all right, I'm hungover and drugged to the eyeballs, but so what, you don't care?"

"I'm sorry." Father Aloysius was suddenly aware that this conversation might be getting him slightly out of his depth, and he wondered where Miss Farrow was. The red lights were flashing in his mind, and he was very conscious of his all too recent conversation with the bishop.

"Sorry, you've got nothing to be sorry for. After all, you've just been to confession, absolutely lily-white you, anyway you're supposed to sound disapproving." chided Anna.

"Well, yes, disapproving," Father Aloysius put a mock severity into his voice, "Disapproving, of course. I don't know what the younger generation is coming to! This sort of thing certainly didn't go on in my day." He stole a quick glance at Anna and saw, to his relief, a trace of a smile cross her face. "Don't be silly, girl," he said, reverting to his normal voice. If I criticised you and came over all disapproving, you'd knock my head off or run a mile, and that wouldn't be very productive. Besides, I mean what I say, I'm sorry. I mean, you're obviously not feeling very well; you seem to be out of sorts with your friends and to put it in the modern jargon, but only mildly, you seem to have got yourself a heavy dose of attitude."

"You!" She punched him on the arm and then flounced away from him, "Still, you can't tell me you care."

"No, of course, I don't care. I mean, I just baked you the best loaf ever! I put my soul in mortal jeopardy by adding a pot of Miss Farrow's delicious jam without telling her. I ignore the advice of the bishop, and then, to cap it all, I give you this," the priest, fishing his hand into his pocket, took out his rosary. It was a slightly bigger one than many people used. The beads were wooden and black, and the Christ, a gaunt metal figure, hung on a wooden cross. He had been given it by one of the priests at the mission when he was a boy. He had treasured it ever since. It was a mark of his desperation to achieve some rapport with Anna that he offered it as a gift to her now.

"Your prayer beads, but you need these."

"Hardly, at least I know the prayers well enough without having to use a rosary. I ought to by now." The girl took the beads and gently ran them through her long fingers, feeling them with her fingertips, her head bowed shyly.

"Thank you. But I ..." her voice trailed away.

"Don't worry," his voice was deep and reassuring, "I could teach you to use them. Some people use drugs to help them get through the day. Some people pray. I pray it's a lot more effective, cheaper, too."

The girl shuddered, and her grip on the beads momentarily tightened as she tensed.

"I suppose you've done an in-depth comparison." Anna's reply was tinged with bitterness: "Personal experience?" She shrugged, and, looking up at him through narrowed eyes, she asked, "What do you know about drugs, Father?"

It was the priest's turn to hang his head. Feeling foolish and inadequate, he stammered his reply, "Nothing, I ...."

The girl reached out a hand and plucked at the long sleeve of his cassock. She held the beads up with her other hand. The sun gleamed on the silver chain and twisted figure.

"They're lovely. Where did you get these beads, Father?" she asked.

"I was given them by one of the priests at the Mission station where I grew up."

"You mentioned your father once," the girl prompted, "Did he live there?"

"No. He was…, it's a long story,"

"I'd like to hear it."

The priest sighed heavily, "Someday, someday when we have time." He shrugged, "I was an orphan on the Mission Station. The priests rescued me. I had nothing. They gave me that rosary. For a long time, it was the only thing I owned."

"It's precious." The girl had been gazing at him intently. Her eyes returned to the beads; she stroked them again gently.

"Well…"

"Precious," the girl affirmed firmly, and then she looked up at him with a piercing flash of her blue eyes. I'm so sorry about you being an orphan." She stepped closer to him, reached up with one hand, and gently touched the scars on his right cheek.

"One day, you'll tell me," the tears welled in her eyes. Then, abruptly, she turned away. "Thank you for this," she said, holding up the beads and looking at them. "It's lovely and very precious. Bye." She flashed him one last glance and then turned and ran back to the cottage. She clutched the beads firmly in her left hand.

Father Aloysius shook his head as if to clear it. His fists clenched as he fought to regain some emotional stability. He raised his eyes to the sky in a silent prayer for strength and then slowly walked back past the cottage to the road to look for Miss Farrow. He had failed to get the girl to agree to return to her family; he felt wretched. 'You can't help your feelings,' the bishop had said, 'It's what you do about them.' What was he to do about his feelings and about Anna? He was at a loss to think. All he could do was pray.

It took the priest some time to find his housekeeper. Miss Farrow had met an old friend, and they were sitting talking over a cup of tea. The table was on the pavement. It was Miss Farrow who saw Father Aloysius first. She waved to him and called him over.

"Father, Father, come and meet Hilda." Miss Farrow organised the priest a seat.

He shook Hilda's hand and sat gratefully down. "Hilda is a great gardener," Miss Farrow continued, "She'll be able to help you with your plans for the school grounds.

I'm sure, won't you, Hilda?" Like all good gardeners, Hilda was quick to agree to share her expertise. They talked about gardens over tea for some time. Miss Farrow sensed the priest was feeling somewhat subdued. At an appropriate pause in the plant conversation, she leaned over and asked quietly.

"Everything go alright at the cottage?"

Father Aloysius shrugged and waved his hands in the air in an enigmatic gesture.

"I see," she paused a moment and then, patting the priest's arm, reassuringly murmured, "Don't worry too much. GOD works in mysterious ways. The priest just smiled.

A little while later, tea and talk done, the priest and the housekeeper had returned to the car. Miss Farrow was driving. She had to proceed with caution down the road, the pavements were crowded with holiday makers and shoppers often spilled out onto the street. Down on the front, they halted to make a right-hand turn across the traffic into a lane that would take them up the hill and out of the town. Suddenly, there was a banging on the back window. Startled, both priest and housekeeper turned as best they could in their seats. It was Anna.

"Wait," her scream was hoarse. She bounded round the side of the car and tugged at the rear door handle. The door opened, and she tumbled in, dragging a bulging cloth bag after her. "Are you going to Pondreath? She asked breathlessly.

"Yes," replied the priest and the housekeeper in unison. The priest was a little relieved to be going straight back now that he had given away his lunch money.

"Please, can I come?"

The couple in the front of the car glanced at each other. Miss Farrow nodded.

"Of course, it will be a pleasure," said Father Aloysius.

"I told you," said Miss Farrow.

The priest looked puzzled. "Told me?"

"God moves in a mysterious way," the housekeeper said quietly.

On the back seat, the girl had curled up into a ball. Her head was buried in the folds of her bag. She sobbed. Father Aloysius decided it would be best to leave her alone. God was at work.

Chapter Sixteen

*Truly accepting love,
forgiveness and healing
is often
much harder than giving it.*

-Henri J.M. Nouwen

Mrs Evans sat on the end of her daughter's bed. "Feeling better then?" she asked. The headteacher's wife had never lost her Welsh lilt.

"Yes, thank you." Anna sipped the tea her mother had brought her.

"That's nice, thank you, Mum." Then she slipped out of bed and crossed the room to where her clothes were lying in a muddle on the floor. She extracted a pair of flared jeans from the pile and, slipping her hand and into the pocket, withdrew a rosary.

"What's that then, pet?" asked Mrs Evans.

"Beads, Father Aloysius gave them to me," Anna drew back her curtains and looked out over the garden. A steady rain was falling from a dark grey sky. "Ugh!" She shivered and slipped back into her bed.

"Looks like a rosary to me."

"It is. Father Aloysius was given it when he was a boy. Did you know he was an orphan, Mum?"

"No, pet, can't say that I did."

"His dad must have died. He doesn't like talking about his dad or his family. He was bought up by Roman Catholic missionaries. One of the Fathers gave him this. That's how he became a priest."

"I see, looks like it's broken." Mrs Evans reached out her hand. Anna hung the beads over it.

"That pig," Anna spat the word out through her clenched teeth, "Simon broke it. I'd gone back to them. Don't ask me why. I must have been out of my mind with Dad in the state he is in... you having to cope on your own. It was a sudden impulse, and I gave in to it. I am so sorry. So very sorry." The girl looked distraught.

"Well, love, let's not dwell on that. You're back, and that's the most important thing. We are so relieved and grateful, grateful to you and to Father Aloysius. Your dad had a word with him. He promised he would get you back. I don't know what changed your mind or what Father said, I just know you're back. I don't care about the whys or the what and whatever, I am just grateful and especially grateful it being half term you didn't miss any college."

Anna sniffed and wiped he nose with a tissue, "Oh, don't. Don't be grateful to me. I don't deserve it. Father Aloysius is the one to thank. All I can say to you is sorry, so very sorry, and mean it."

"We all make mistakes, love. We just need to learn from them."

"I will, I'll do my best, Father Aloysius found me. I don't know how. I think he'd come to ask me to return home, but he didn't ask me. He probably thought I'd refuse, so instead, he gave me this. It's very precious to him, you know."

"I see," her mother was gazing at the twisted metal figure on the crucifix.

"Oh, Mum," exclaimed the girl leaning forward to share her Mother's examination of the Christ figure, "That's what I found myself doing. When I got back to them, Simon, he's a surfer, he started to have a go at me. He snatched the Rosary off me and started whirling it about his head. He was manic! He was calling me all these names and swearing and shouting at the top of his voice. I tried to get the beads off him, but he just hit me! I went sprawling. Then I started to scream at him to give it back to me, and so he broke it, he deliberately broke it, and then he threw it back in my face. It hit me here," The girl indicated her forehead with her fingers and shuddered. "Then it landed, it landed on my lap. I picked it up, and I found myself looking at the figure and then looking round me, at Simon and the room and everything else there. And it suddenly seemed so horrible, so dirty and horrible." The girl paused and, reaching forward, touched the cross where it lay on her mother's palm with the tips of the fingers of her right hand. She took a deep breath and continued, "It was then I decided to come home."

"Thank God you did, but I have to ask...." Louisa paused. For a moment, she wondered about the wisdom of questioning her daughter, but she needed to know. She needed to know if her daughter was prepared to confide in her honestly.

"Tell me, do your friends take drugs?" Anna's mother prompted gently.

"No!" Anna covered he face with her hands and sobbed. "Yes," she whispered.

"And do you?"

"No, no, not now, I promise." Anna reached out her hand to her Mother. "I promise." She was crying silently, the tears coursing down her face. Her mother reached out her arms and hugged her daughter to her.

"So you did take drugs?"

"Yes," this was said so softly that Louisa hardly heard it. Anna had buried her head in her pillow, sobbing.

"There, there, my love," Her mother soothed softly, stroking the girl's fine blond hair.

"Shush, you're home, you're safe here. Don't worry, love. The main thing is you're home," gradually, the tears ceased. "Here," Mrs Evans reached out to the box on the bedside cabinet and handed her daughter another tissue.

"Thanks," Anna's voice was a whisper. She dabbed at her face. Soon, the tissue was soggy. It was replaced by a second. Anna smiled wanly, "Thanks, Mum."

"Where do they get these drugs from?"

"Oh Mum I can't say. It's too dangerous, and, Mum, I never used illegal drugs."

"I see."

"And Mum, I owe Father Aloysius twenty pounds."

"Twenty pounds, what for?"

"He bought the last lot." Anna sniffed.

"What, Father Aloysius bought you drugs?"

"No, no, he just paid for them, and they weren't for me." the girl's hands flew to her face again.

"Oh no, Mum, you mustn't tell, Mum, you mustn't! Please say you won't! Father Aloysius didn't know what the money was for."

The girl shook her head, "No, no, you mustn't," her fingers plucked at the duvet cover.

"You ......"

Louisa just nodded.

"And now?" queried Mrs Evans.

"No, not, now," the girl paused. "Please, may I have the Rosary?" Anna took the beads carefully from her Mother's outstretched hand and, holding the cross up in front of her, said, "Now I want to stay at home, to be with Daddy and you and, and when I picked up this cross after Simon had thrown it at me somehow I suddenly started to see things differently. I saw the mess there and the mess I was in, and I saw Daddy. In my mind, I saw Daddy, and I knew I wanted to be home."

"Oh Anna, I'm so pleased, so very pleased." Her mother leaned over to give her daughter a kiss. "You don't know how relieved I am and your dad is, too. I'm so pleased for him."

"Mum," Anna paused, "Dad's very ill, isn't he? I mean, very, very ill?"

Her mother got up from the end of the bed and walked to the window. She stood there silently for a moment, looking out at the rain. She slowly nodded her head.

"Yes," she said simply, "Yes, he's very ill."

"Mum, he's dying, isn't he?" she slipped out of the bed.

Mrs Evans turned and, with a sob, came to her daughter. They met on the carpet between the bed and the window. It was Anna's turn to be the comforter.

Chapter Seventeen

*Vision
is the ability to see potential
in what others overlook.*

-Rick Warren

The initial planning session for the environmental day and the digging of the pond had taken much of an afternoon and early evening. At first, it was just Duncan Evans briefing Father Aloysius. Later, Anna joined, and later still Larry. It had gone well, and in particular, it had been a good evening. Duncan was having one of his better days. Anna had come back that day from college with top grades for one of her assignments, and Duncan was beaming with delight. Anna, too, had seemed happy and relaxed with her father as she went about helping her mother get tea. Father and daughter had smiled at each other often, and when she had fetched the tea time refreshments, she had tousled his hair and had given him a kiss on his forehead.

"This is not just about putting in a pond," the headteacher explained as he looked at his plans, "It's about developing community spirit. In Africa, I guess most places have a strong sense of identity and community spirit," the headteacher had surmised.

"Africa's a big place," Father Aloysius had laughingly replied, "But I suppose you're right. At least it's been true of the rural communities I've known."

"Rural, yes, I guess that's part of it. Here in Cornwall, the farming and fishing communities and, in the past, the mining communities have always been pretty close. Towns are full of strangers, and you have to work hard to create communities there. Schools are little communities, but you need to create a strong partnership between the local community and the school. Parents are the key," the headteacher explained. "At our school, we've always encouraged parents to be part of the place, it's amazing the difference it can make. There is so much expertise out there among the parent body, and parents all want to do things for their children. They need to do things for their children. Don't worry," the headteacher had been keen to reassure the priest,

"You'll get plenty of helpers, you just have to organise them and provide cheerful, positive leadership." The priest wasn't too sure about the leadership and the organisation, but he was doing his best to smile. He was still smiling as he walked home that night. Duncan had been very thorough in explaining his plans for the day. He felt more reassured about the task ahead. Yes, it has been a good evening.

There were to be several more such evenings in the lead-up to the actual day. They did not involve Duncan Evans but were for the school and the Parent Teacher and Friends Association. Both Larry and Father were involved. To achieve a good outcome for what the headmaster had envisaged needed much attention to detail and careful planning. As to how successful they had been would only be apparent on the day, but as Duncan had emphasised, preparation is everything. The committee had certainly done their very best on that front.

Father Aloysius was sweating and happy to be so. It was all for a good cause, but digging didn't come naturally to him, he had discovered. He had gone at it too hard at the start. It was old Bill who had put him right. He had ambled over and put a steadying hand on Father's shoulder.

"Hey lad, slow up, steady, steady, at that rate, you'll be flaked flat in minutes or have us all gaping through a hole to Australia, steady on, here, let me show you." The big Cornish man had placed his spade with a certain slow deliberation just where he wanted to dig out the next section of the trench. Then, placing one large boot on the rim of the spade, he leaned his weight on it, shoving the blade through the turf and deep into the soil. With a grunt, he withdrew his implement and repeated the operation four times, then with a big grin of satisfaction, heaved out a heavy clod of clay and placed it neatly on the bank that was building up behind the trench.

"There, see slow and steady, but it gets the job done quicker for all that."

"I see, thank you," said the priest, and then, by way of explanation as to the inadequacy of his technique, he added, "I'm not really used to spades."

"I see, don't you use them in Africa?"

"Yes, but it's more common for people digging a plot for maize or vegetables to use a jembe." The priest's reply evoked a lot of questioning expressions from the four other men in his pond-digging party, who had all stopped work to listen.

"A J Jem, what on earth's that?" Bill had taken his cap off and was scratching his head."

"Jembe, it's more like a pick, only the blade is flat and wider, and it's not as heavy as a pick," the priest explained. You use it in the same way as you use a pick."

"So a jembe is all arms and back, where with a spade, you use your legs and weight. I can see why you needed some tips on using your spade. A jembe is a totally different rhythm. So that's where you get your arm strength from."

Farther Aloysius shook his head. "Actually, mostly it's the women who do the fieldwork, not the men, and anyway, I am a Karamajong, and they are pastoralists."

"The women!" exclaimed Bill, "The women, can you credit it, mind you, if you think about it, it's not such a bad idea for all that."

Father Aloysius, like the others, was leaning on his spade. He gazed across the playing fields, past the school, to the cliffs and the bay, but his mind was far away. In his mind's eye, he saw a line of women. Their bright shukas gathered up high on their thighs. They were digging, swinging their hoes in unison, and as they dug, they sang, and they dug to the rhythm of the song. The high-pitched voices echoed through the priest's mind. There was a leader, the woman, at the end of the line. She led the refrain, the others followed, repeating her words. One girl had a baby on her back. The priest sighed and, with a grin, turned back to the ditch and his spade. As he dug, he continued to speak. "As I said, my people were pastoralists, we kept animals. Where I grew up, it's too dry and hot for most crops. In some areas, it is true the people are being encouraged to give up their nomadic lifestyle and to plant crops like millet and vegetables, but the frequent failure of the seasonal rains makes this difficult. I never grew anything, we were always on the move, searching for grazing for our cattle and goats, so I never planted any seeds or harvested anything I had planted." Father Aloysius did not admit to never having used a jembe...

In his travels round Africa, he had seen people of other tribes digging their plots. He had come to admire the way the women worked together, heaving up great clods of soil with their hand hoes and breaking down the clods into a tilth for the sowing of the maize. He loved to hear them sing. He sang now as he worked, it was a pastoralist's song his father had sung to his cattle as he herded them through the bush.

Every so often, the priest paused to look about him. It was a happy scene. A whole host of people had responded to the appeal put out by the Parent Teacher and Friends Association for help with the pond project. First, Joe had brought his digger in to scoop out a shallow depression. Now came the task of the lining of the hole and the construction of the surrounds. Some sixty people had turned up at the school that morning. Mrs Hardcourt and Mrs Lancing, along with Father Aloysius, had welcomed children from every class, parents, older brothers and sisters, past pupils, and even grandparents, and a baby had come along. All, except the baby, were armed with their spades, trowels, and an assortment of barrows, forks, rakes, and other gardening implements. Now, they were all hard at work on a variety of projects.

A working party was barrowing in the sand to be spread and raked evenly in a layer on the bottom of the hollow that would be the pond. Another party, led by Clive Janner, was busy constructing a grassed bank that would go two-thirds of the way round the pond. They were using soil and turfs that had been taken from the hole for the pond. Joe had found some old plastic piping. This was being cut into lengths and buried in the bank to provide havens for toads or frogs. Others were digging holes for the fence and painting the posts with wood preserver. A huge piece of black plastic liner was spread out on the field. It was being cut to size. Mrs Gibbs and Mrs Hazelmere had measured it out carefully and were helping a group of older children with the task. A big garden centre had donated the liner. It had been one of Duncan's letters that had persuaded them to support the school. Beside the liner were rolls of old carpets. Duncan had written to all the parents in his newsletter asking for carpet scraps. A group of younger children was having fun rolling each other up in it, with much screeching and laughter. Over in the school playground, Larry, with Anna and Philippa as his assistants, laboured away banging at some timber constructing a dipping platform.

It was not long before the trench round the pond was completed, and Father Aloysius was grinning at all and sundry and organising the carpet to be rescued from the children and dragged across to be placed on top of the sand in the pond. Next came the liner, its edges had to be tucked into the trench, and then the trench was filled in again. In the middle of this operation, the ladies arrived with trays of coffee, tea, and squash and plates piled with crispy bacon butties.

"Tell me, Father Aloysius," it was Bill again, "I can see the point of the plastic, although I would have thought it would be better to use the natural clay and mix it with straw and puddle it to make it waterproof like they did in the old days but what's all this sand and carpet for?"

"We have to make it nice and soft, it will mean the liner is less likely to be punctured."

"But I thought the idea of a pond was to have plants and things?" queried Bill, determined to have the last word.

"It is," replied the priest.

"Well, how do you plant anything on this black plastic thing then?"

"We don't. There is another layer we have to put down, and that's clay," explained Father Aloysius.

"So we go to all this sweat to dig out a hole, just to fill it up again! I don't know, I really don't." Bill winked at Mrs Hazelmere and scratched the stubble on his chin,

"Mind you, that was a nice bacon butty that was, Mrs Hazelmere, I'll give you that."

"You're welcome," Mrs Hazelmere smiled with pleasure as she collected up the mugs.

"So Father Aloysius, I'll ask you another thing then: do they have these liner things in Africa then? I bet they don't."

"No," agreed the priest, "I never saw one, but I never saw a bacon butty there either. Mind you, that's not to say there has never been a pond made with a liner anywhere in Africa or a bacon butty, for that matter."

He turned and went to fetch a barrow full of soil. Gently, he shovelled it onto the liner. The gang was soon at work again.

After that, Father Aloysius was everywhere, he worked with the fencers, easing posts into holes and tapping them down with a sledge, his brow gleaming with perspiration. He helped heave the dipping platform over from the school with a whole laughing gang of children and watched over them, placing it carefully on its base. He and Anna assisted Larry in finally fixing it in place and screwing it down. It was a joy to see the transformation in the girl. 'God moves in mysterious ways.' Miss Farrow was so right.

He joined Mrs Hardcourt and Mrs Fathers and her gardening gang raking at a patch of finely tilthed soil where they planned to sow wild flowers. He helped the men line the pond with clay, and everywhere he went, he grinned. This was the community spirit that Duncan had talked about when he had called round to the headteacher's house to plan the day. The priest wasn't too sure about the leadership part of the exercise, but he had done his best, and certainly, people seemed to be enjoying it, as had he. Gradually, the tasks were completed, and Father Aloysius was there, still grinning, to thank people as they drifted happily away.

Later, much later that evening, in the soft summer twilight, Father Aloysius, Joe, Anna, and Larry stood on the bank above the pond and surveyed the day's work.

"Looks a bit of a mess now," observed Joe, "But you wait, give us a bit of rain, and she'll soon fill up, then we can put the plants in, and this will be the spot then, this will."

"You've been a marvel, Joe, and you, Larry and Anna, thank you," said the priest, yawning and stretching weary arms above his head. "You, everyone, they have all been marvellous."

"Yeah," agreed Joe. "It's been a good day. There will be a lot of folks that will sleep well tonight, but they'll be satisfied folk. Thank you, Father Aloysius."

"Yes, thank you, Father," Anna was smiling up at him. "Dad will be thrilled. Why don't you come home with us and tell him how we've got on? He'll be anxious to hear." The priest hesitated. "Please, Larry's coming, but Dad would love to see you too."

Father shrugged and smiled back at the girl. "That's kind of you, if you're sure, I'd love to," he replied. The group all shook hands and, taking one last look at the scene, departed. Joe ambled off to load up the last of his wheelbarrows into the back of his truck. The priest, with Anna and Larry, hurried away to the schoolmaster's house.

On the way, Father Aloysius took a detour to call in at the presbytery. He needed a shower, and he also needed to make his peace with Miss Farrow for being out on yet another evening.

His housekeeper had long since adapted herself to suit the energetic and sometimes erratic ways of the young priest. His predecessor had very seldom gone out after dark, and she had found herself somewhat tied to the presbytery. She had quickly found that

Father Aloysius's lifestyle meant that she was often free in the evening and so could go out herself. She welcomed this, and when Father Aloysius was out on an evening engagement, she would slip away to her sister's home above the shop, down on the way to the quay. Miss Farrow had a small flat above their garage and store room. Mr Fowler, her brother-in-law, kept a grocer's-cum-newsagent's shop and Post Office. He and his wife were always busy but never too busy to welcome an extra pair of hands to help check stock or to do the ironing or some other domestic chore. Sometimes, when Father Aloysius had had a last-minute invitation out to eat, and she had already prepared his meal, Miss Farrow even took the priest's food down with her. Her two nephews had huge appetites, and the housekeeper hated any sort of waste, and if they didn't need the meal, there was always someone about the shop who did. She always checked with Father Aloysius first but had never known him to refuse. This evening, she had made him a cottage pie. The smell of it greeted Father as he strode in the front door.

"Halloo, Father," called the housekeeper from the kitchen, "My, you've been busy, you must be worn out. Do you want to eat now while I run you a nice hot bath, or do you want to bath first and eat later?"

"Oh, Miss F, you are a saint. That smells just too delicious, but because I'm such a sinner, I'm going to have to ask you to excuse me tonight. I've got to grab a quick shower and dash off to see Mr Evans to report on the day."

"Shower, you'd be better off with a long soak after all that digging and such, but I guess if you've got to dash, you've got to dash, and it will be good to see Mr Evans and to tell him that the day went well?"

"Yes," beamed the priest, "You were all wonderful, and everyone really enjoyed the bacon butties you ladies made, thank you. Now I must dash for that shower if you'll excuse me. It's going to have to be instant, vertical soak tonight, I'm afraid."

"What about your cottage pie, Father? Shall I put it in the microwave for when you get back?"

"Oh, Miss F., it smells wonderful, but that would just make me fat. Will you excuse me, please? I'm sure your nephews like cottage pie."

"Huh, they'd eat anything that lot. Well, if you're sure, Father, it would be a pity to waste it."

"Certainly would," said the priest, diving into the shower room with a clean cassock over his arm. "Give them all my regards down at the shop, won't you, and please thank that good brother-in-law of yours for the bacon."

"How do you know I'm going there?" queried Miss Farrow as the priest disappeared into the bathroom. Father Aloysius saved his reply until he emerged steaming from the shower.

"Oh, sorry," he teased, "Where did you say you're going? Was it the cinema or was it the pub? I didn't know you fed the publican cottage pie as well as those hungry nephews of yours."

"Away with you," said Miss Farrow in mock severity. Doing her best to suppress her smile, she ushered the priest out of the front door. "Here," she said, thrusting a jar of homemade red current jelly into the priest's hand, "Give Mrs Evans that, I think they will like it." She watched his tall figure stride off down the street and chuckled quietly to herself, "Always one for a laugh, Father Aloysius!" She soliloquised.

Chapter Eighteen

*A well-developed
sense of humour is the pole that adds
balance to your steps as you walk the
the tightrope of life*

-William Arthur Ward

As for Father Aloysius, he grinned all the way to the schoolmaster's house. He was still grinning when Anna opened the front door. She was still in the day's work clothes, jeans, and a red blouse. "My, we are shining, bright, and smiling," she greeted him archly.

"And late, I'm sorry," replied the priest, and holding out the red currant jelly, he added.

"With the compliments of the saintly Miss Farrow."

"Oh, thank you," replied the girl, responding to the priest's big grin with a smile of her own. "Dad loves this. Come through, he's already eaten, I'm afraid, but we can have our food with him while we talk." Anna led the priest into the lounge. Father Aloysius sniffed the air as he followed her. He thought he could distinctly smell cottage pie. His grin broadened even further.

Duncan was sitting in his usual chair, a rug pulled over his knees. On the table beside him were plans of the School Ground's Development Scheme. Father Aloysius thought his face looked thinner and even more strained than when he had last seen him. The voice, too, that greeted him was soft and hoarse. He had looked so much better when they had met to plan this day. Now, well, now was another day, a different day in lots of ways.

"Ah, Father Aloysius, I'm glad you could come; from the look of my daughter, you have been working everyone pretty hard."

"Certainly, they all worked very well," replied the priest, "but they needed no encouragement from me. Everyone pulled their weight magnificently, and we got a lot done. Here, let me show you." Father Aloysius reached forward his hands for the map.

"Here," he said, kneeling down by the headteacher. "Here is where Bill dug the hole."

The priest was conscious of Duncan's hand on his, he felt a gentle squeeze. He looked up.

"Excuse me interrupting," Duncan coughed as if to clear his voice, but he still continued in a hoarse whisper, "We ought to keep a list of all the people who have helped. I'll want to write to thank them."

"But," Father Aloysius was about to protest. Again, the hand squeezed his. This time, the voice was firmer.

"No, I'll write; it's the least I can do. It's important, you know, its part of the overall strategy. When you involve people in voluntary work, the least you can do is thank them. That way, they feel valued and involved. The more involved they'll feel, the more committed they become to the common cause. You know, Father Aloysius, what I like about you, apart from the fact that you are obviously not a member of the Conservative party, what I like about you is you have the right kind of philosophies. In fact, I'd go far as to say we share the right kind of philosophies." Father Aloysius smiled.

"I don't understand Duncan. I didn't know you believed in sin, salvation, and the risen Lord Jesus Christ."

"No, no, no," it was Duncan's turn to smile. "Of course, I don't mean that, although the sin bit has a lot to do with the Conservative party, I'll grant you, what I mean is we both believe in being inclusive and in thanking people."

"Yes, you will be aware of the parable of the Ten Lepers, and certainly Christ was all-inclusive when it came to those who believed or were even in need," replied the priest.

"Ten Lepers, Jesus healed them. I know, and only one thanked him, and he was a Samaritan and certainly not a member of the Conservative Party," chuckled the headteacher.

Father Aloysius sighed and shook his head in mock disbelief.

"No, the point is, Father, you always thank people. I've noticed it. You are really good at thanking." Father Aloysius was about to protest, but the headteacher continued, "Now, don't interrupt, all my educational career, I've said thank you, and I've made sure, too, my school had a strong thank you culture. And you know what? It's paid dividends. You'd be surprised at the number of people who have become quite deeply involved in the school just because I'd taken the trouble to write to them to say a 'Thank you' for something. I remember….."

At this point, the headteacher was overcome with a coughing fit. Father Aloysius stroked his hand and, getting to his feet, looked about for a glass of water,

"Now then, 'Mr Headteacher,' sir, calm down," he gently patted his friend's back. "Would you like……"

"Dad, shush, there there then," Anna had come hurrying in. She knelt in front of her father and, taking his hands in hers, raised them to her lips.

"You're getting over-excited. You mustn't go on so, or Father Aloysius will have to have his meal in the kitchen. He's making you talk too much," Duncan Evans had a wicked gleam in his eye despite the coughing-induced pain that obviously racked his body.

"Not Aloysius, not Aloysius at all, it's those damned Conservatives."

"Oh, you!" the girl remonstrated with her father shaking her finger in his face. "Now, just behave. I'll get you some water."

"Thank you, my love," The headteacher winked at the priest. Father Aloysius just held his own finger to his lips.

"Shush, you heard what the lady said. Just behave." A few moments later, Anna returned with a glass of water.

"Here you are then, my pet," she held the glass to her father's lips, but he took it from her hands. The girl touched the top of her father's grey head with her lips, "Alright, you hold it, and I'll go and bring Father Aloysius his supper. Father," she turned her head to the priest, "Just see he doesn't spill it please, or choke himself, I won't be a second I'll fetch you your food, you must be famished. Here Larry," she called as she hurried towards the kitchen door, "Fetch us some chairs please so we can all sit with Dad and eat our supper."

The four of them, Louisa Evans, Larry, Anna, and the priest, sat in a semicircle in front of the headteacher. They ate their meal on their laps. Duncan was full of questions, and they talked while they ate. The cottage pie was piping hot and served with carrots and beans.

"One day," observed Duncan with a wry smile, "One day, those carrots and beans won't be the Spar varieties. They'll come from your own school vegetable patch."

"Sounds good to me, not that there is anything wrong with these," replied the priest.

"Yes, but there is nothing like homegrown. Once you know, we used to grow nearly all our own vegetables. Nothing like it," the headteacher stretched his arms out in front of him and flexed his fingers.

"Yes," snorted his daughter, "And half the time, they were addled with carrot fly or chewed at by slugs."

"Ah, but they still had the taste," asserted Duncan, "nothing like homegrown, picked freshly from the garden and straight into the pot and then onto the plate for taste, and no air miles involved either. When you think of the distance some things travel before they get to our plates these days, it's scandalous. No wonder we are grappling with global warming!"

"I don't think every scientist would agree with you over the Global warming bit," his daughter replied, determined to make her case for the clean, even easy-to-cook carrots that came from the Spar.

"No, but ..." it was Larry who spoke this time somewhat hesitantly.

"Yes, lad, don't be shy, then speak up," urged the headteacher.

"Well, you can't say carrots grown in California and frozen and flown all the way over here are going to taste better than ones grown in your own patch."

Anna smiled at him and touched his arm affectionately. "I'll remind you of that next time you go buying crisps from Ned's place," she said archly.

"But that's not the point," again Larry paused.

"Yes?" Duncan encouraged him with a smile.

"The point is this: you're trying to teach kids to appreciate food, homegrown food."

"Precisely Larry, what's the key issue facing the earners and voters of tomorrow?

Conservation, of course, sustainability of global resources, justice, and food for all. We all need to learn we only have one planet, and we have to look after it.

Children who never get earth under their fingernails, who haven't grown anything in their lives, will have no idea about what it takes to produce food, let alone have any of the basic concepts necessary to understand the issues of conservation."

"Everything's so instant these days," added his wife. "You can even go shopping on the net. Youngsters growing up with computers need something else in their learning to balance the instant idea. To grow carrots, you have to plan ahead, do the groundwork, till the soil, plant the seed, and wait." Father Aloysius nodded in agreement.

"Yes, wait," continued the headteacher, "And dare I say it, Father Aloysius, pray, pray, and pray that the rain will come and water your crop. Pray that the sun will shine to ripen it and that the bugs and beasties won't have the lot before you enjoy so much as a nibble, let alone a mouthful. I bet you did a lot of growing of your own food along with the praying back in Africa, Father Aloysius." The headteacher had quietly waited for his opportunity to bring the priest into the conservation.

"To tell you the truth," said the cleric, putting his fork down onto his plate," Where I grew up, it was too dry to grow much, and we were always on the move, so I never got the opportunity to sow anything let alone harvest it."

"What on earth did you eat? You're not going to tell me there was a Tesco behind every ant hill," teased Anna.

"Quite right, or almost quite right, we had lots of ant hills, but not one Tesco's," Father Aloysius rubbed his forefinger over his nose and round his chin. "No Tesco and no carrots either."

In his mind, he could hear the bleating of goats and the groans of the cattle as they were prodded to their feet and the snorting they made when they scented water. His fingers itched to feel the udder of his own cow. He ran his hand over his brow.

"We were pastoralists, wandering nomads; we had our goats, a few donkeys, some had camels, but we all had our cattle. We wandered from place to place in search of grass and water."

"And what did you eat?" asked Larry.

"Oh, we had milk, a lot of milk, milk was mixed with cows' blood. We had meat, and of course, there was maize or millet and beans, but we traded that, we didn't grow it."

"But I bet you knew where the milk came from," said Mrs Evans.

"Blood, ugh, how did you get the blood? I mean, that must have meant killing a lot of animals?"

Father Aloysius smiled, "Yes, we knew about milk. When I was born, I was given a calf, a calf to grow up with me, a calf I had to look after, not at first, of course, but when I was big enough, a calf, I got to learn to milk. Yes, we had to learn to be good stockmen. My father was a very skilled stockman, he taught me. As for blood, we bled our cows from a vein in the neck. The blood was collected in a calabash and stirred. Milk was added. You drank the mixture. It was very nutritious, the cow was fine, and the wound soon healed. Of course, you couldn't use the same animal every day. That's why we needed to have big herds of cattle." Father Aloysius's gaze went to the window. There was a faraway look in his eye.

"You must miss him." Anna's voice was soft and gentle. Her hand rested on the sleeve of his cassock.

"Sometimes," It was all the priest would allow himself to reply. He turned his attention to his plate. He sensed that the headteacher was getting tired, and he did not want to prolong his visit. He helped him fold up the map and gather the plans together and then, when he had eaten his apple crumble, quietly excused himself.

Mrs Evans saw him to the door. "Thank you, Father, it was good of you to come, and please don't mind his politics and his comments about religion, he can be a bit of a tease."

The priest smiled and shook his head, "Don't worry, It's a privilege, I respect him for his integrity. He's determined to be involved to the…" Father Aloysius stopped himself in mid-sentence.

"Don't worry, Father; we know this is the last chapter. You are right he is a fighter, and it will be to the last. We just have to make it a good one, and that's why we are so grateful to you."

Father Aloysius saw Anna appearing behind her mother. He raised a warning finger to his lips, "Thank you again for the cottage pie, delicious, and the crumble, of course. Good night," he turned to go.

Anna pushed past her mother, "Bye, Father," she called after his retreating back, "And thank you."

The priest half turned and gave her a little wave of acknowledgement and then hurried away. Anna gazed wistfully after him before returning to the house. Louisa Evans took her daughter's hand, "He's a good man." Anna's head was bowed; she looked up at her mother and smiled.

"Yes, a very good man."

There was a sudden clap of thunder. The wind, moments before hardly noticeable, had suddenly picked up. It brought the rain.

"Oh dear, I do hope Father doesn't get too wet." Anna had already disappeared and was searching for a torch. She reappeared with one and also two umbrellas.

Anna hurried down the road, calling after the priest. The wind kept catching her umbrella. She was panting heavily when she caught up with the cleric.

"I hope you are not too wet already," She gasped. She handed him the umbrella.

"Why, how thoughtful of you, thank you, thank you so much."

"No, it's us who should be thanking you for all you are doing for Dad. It's made such a difference to him having this project, and you've helped Mum too." A gust of wind threatened to blow their umbrellas inside out.

"Whoa, good isn't it? But you must be getting back, and there is no need to thank me; your Dad has helped me and your Mum. They are very special people," said the priest, grappling with his umbrella.

"Good? How do you mean? The two umbrellas clashed as Anna leaned towards him.

"The pond, it's filling the pond." Father Aloysius stepped back a pace.

"I see, yes, anyway."

"We must both be getting home," interjected the priest. "Good night, and thank you." He turned and strode off into the dark. For a second time that evening, Anna stood wistfully watching him disappear. Then, with a sigh, she turned and whispered to herself, "You're a good man," she too turned for home.

The priest hurried down the hill, rejoicing in the rain and the odour of newly wet soil after a long dry season. The scent of it brought back many memories of the long, dry months and sometimes years he had experienced growing up as a boy in a land that was prone to droughts. There, that first rainfall was always a cause for much rejoicing. He and his young brothers and sisters would dance wildly, cavorting about in the puddles. Of course, the rains brought their own challenges. The rivers, dry for much of the year, suddenly became torrents. Bridges were washed away, and the dirt roads became very slippery. The biggest hazards were the mosquitoes and the dreaded malaria. The disease was the scourge of Africa. Few there were who in a lifetime could claim they had never had a bout of the disease, and the mortality rate, especially among children, was high. As he crossed the bridge, he reflected that by all accounts, Pondreath had had its challenges with floods, too, and the bridge he strode over was a replacement for another much older one that had been washed away in one such flood. Wearily, he made his way up past to shop to the presbytery. He was grateful for the umbrella; it had kept him from being completely soaked. It had been a long day but a good one. The bishop would be pleased. He was getting better at managing to control his emotions regarding Anna. But what about his maker, who knew his every inmost thought? What would the verdict of the figure on the cross be? It had been good to spend time with Anna's father. He was clearly failing but was determined to keep battling, and his insisting on writing letters to thank all the participants in the pond project was so typical of him. It was a huge challenge to be asked to take on this - Duncan's last project. He prayed quietly that he would be worthy of it.

Chapter Nineteen

*One's best success
comes after their greatest disappointments.*

-Henry Board Beecher

Father Aloysius surfaced with an involuntary cry of delight, shaking his head and wiping his face as he lunged to his feet in the surf, and then turning, he strode with the retreating wave back towards the breakers. The priest was not a good swimmer; never until now having lived anywhere near the ocean, he had had little opportunity to learn to swim. He had woken even earlier than usual and reluctant to wait, tossing and turning for the alarm to go off he had donned his shorts, singlet, and trainers and had quietly slipped out of the house and set off for his customary early morning run. Instead of following his usual route up out of the town past the school to the cliffs, he had, on a whim, turned downhill. The previous day's pond digging had left him a little stiff. Yes, he was fit, his regular runs and his cycling saw to that, but the long labours with shovel and spade and all the heaving and humping of barrows of sand and stacks of fence posts had used his muscular frame in ways he was not used to, hence his stiffness. He had let his long-legged strides take him down through the lanes to the quay and then out along the path to the beach. Noticing the tide was coming in, he had slipped off his trainers and, tying them together by their laces, had hung them round his neck. He had set off barefoot down the beach. The sand was firm, and he bounded along with a feeling of joyous freedom at being barefoot one more. While water had been scarce where he grew up, being barefoot certainly wasn't, for much of his early childhood, he was a barefoot boy, and it was good to have the feeling of the sand between his toes again. It being earlier than usual, he had time on his side, and he headed for the distant headland. As he approached the towering cliffs, he saw how the sea had worn a cave in the rock face. Hot and breathing heavily from his exertions, he paused to catch his breath at the entrance. He peered into the damp darkness. There was a shallow channel leading into the cave. The rippled sand was something he had never seen before. He wondered at the power of the sea and the action of the waves as they carved out holes in the cliff face and left rippled patterns in the sand. Sensing that time was moving on, he had glanced at his watch, and seeing that there was time to spare, he had made to enter the cave when another thought struck. How about a swim, he probably still had time. He had turned away from the cave and hurried up the beach to where it was clear from the flotsam and jetsam of seaweed, driftwood, and water-borne rubbish. He reached a safe spot to deposit his watch and trainers. He left them by a rock, and having taken note of the place, he set off to frolic in the waves. His second attempt at body surfing was not quite as successful as his first. He mistimed his headlong launch and was left behind by the rushing waters. He was tempted to go back for a third try, but then his sense of the need to be heading back led him out of the water and back to his belongings.

The return run was a mixture of joy and satisfaction at having discovered a new pleasure, accompanied by a feeling of anger at the amount of rubbish strewn along the tide line. Why, why, why, he wondered, was the human species so feckless and so seemingly oblivious to the way they were trashing their beautiful planet? Father Aloysius paused on the steps that led down to the beach to dust the sand off his feet before putting on his trainers. The litter bin at the end of the path to the village was overflowing. He felt guilty for ignoring it, but he needed to be getting on. He set off at a fast pace, shortening his stride but redoubling his effort when he got to the lanes, he laboured up the steep slopes. He was nearing the top when a voice calling out from behind him caused him to pause and turn. It was Titch on his early morning round delivering papers.

"Father, Father!" he shouted. "Have you seen the pond?"

"No, why?" the priest replied between pants.

"Best look," and Titch, who was also in a hurry, disappeared down a narrow ally to continue shoving the daily paper through letter boxes. Father Aloysius glanced at his watch as he set off again for the presbytery. He might just have time, if he skipped breakfast, to get to the pond before he was due to take Morning Prayer, after which he had to get to the school to attend the morning assembly. As he ran, he wondered as to what Titch was telling him and was filled with foreboding.

Commander Nesbitt was standing by the gate in the fence that surrounded the pond. He turned as Father approached and shook his head. "Morning, Father," he greeted the panting priest, "You're not going to like this." Father Aloysius's worst fears were realised when he saw the pond. The previous night's rain had left a goodly sized puddle in the bottom of the hollowed-out basin, but half submerged, there was a litter bin. Some of its contents floated about on the water. There was litter scattered everywhere."

"Oh," he exclaimed, "Visitors. Just the kind we didn't want."

"Vandals more like it. Makes your blood boil after all the work you have done."

"You too, you were part of it," responded the priest.

"We all need to do our bit, and as a governor, I have a responsibility to the school. As for you, well, you and Mr Evans and Larry have done a great job getting us all, nearly all, to get together, and it's a wonderful project, but don't worry, this is just a blip. We won't let the Vandals win."

"But how? Now I must be off. I take morning prayer in church in fifteen minutes." The priest turned to go.

"And then? The commander's question caused the priest to pause.

"Assembly at the school, I have to thank the children for all their hard work, what do I say about this?"

The commander smiled, "Yes, and from what I hear, you are very good at that. You just have to thank them and praise them, then share the challenges ahead. We have all worked together to accomplish the first bit, a tremendous community effort, but that is not the end, perhaps an even bigger task lies ahead: completing it and maintaining it. If you're free after the assembly, we could meet for a coffee in the staff room and a chat about the details of how to respond."

"Thanks, and thanks for your wise words. I'll meet you at the school. The priest hurried away.

It was a rush, but Father Aloysius got to Prayers on time and to the school assembly. It was a challenge, but he coped. Both Mrs Hardcourt and the commander were fulsome in their praise for the way he had handled the issue, and the children were both proud and disappointed in equal measure as they filed back to their classrooms. The headteacher, the school governor, and the priest retired to the staffroom. Mrs Hardcourt made the coffee, and Commander Nesbitt found some plates in a cupboard and produced three brown paper packets.

"Breakfast, Father Aloysius," he announced, "We have got some serious thinking to do, and you have had a busy morning, not good to go to battle on an empty stomach, you know; can't have you keeling over from lack of food, tuck in." Father Aloysius needed no second invitation; he was hungry.

"Thank you," he said gratefully as he helped himself to a large currant bun.

"Now, what do you think our best course of action might be?" The commander asked Miss Hardcourt. She thought for a moment. "Well, I guess we will just have to tell the police for a start."

"Good, and you might mention there are some footprints in the mud on the edge of the pond. Now, before the children go home, we need to advise them to stay away from the pond. The police might possibly visit today before the children go home, which would be helpful, but I don't think it's likely, and it certainly won't be a priority. If they don't, we can tape it off. We don't want the children touching things and compromising the evidence. I have already taken some pictures of the site as a record. Then you, I believe, have a list of the volunteers. We need to warn them to stay away, too. If you give me a copy of the list, I can do that. We appreciate you are always very busy, but if you and Mrs Fenton can manage to fit it into today's schedule, you could send a letter home. It could be a bit along the lines of Father Aloysius's assembly: praise and thanks and then the bad news, followed by an outline of our action plan. We have, for example, told the police, and we could mention that we have reported that there are footprints in the mud round the pond. That will get around, and it might deter our unwelcome visitors from a second go at the pond. We can appeal for help. Someone might have seen something, but somehow, I don't think we will get much useful information, and we may never get to the bottom of it. But while it would be great to see justice done, we must put our energies into completing the project and not be side-tracked by recriminations. Then we can wait a day or so, so people can see the damage and I will organise a small working party to clear the place up. I'll write up the project in the village magazine along the same lines as your letter and Father's assembly. The word will get about, and that hopefully will be all the deterrent we need for the near future. It could have been a lot worse, and I suspect our visitors, who don't have a very well-developed sense of social responsibility, will also not have a very well-developed idea of how to sustain more damage without being caught. They will get bored with it. Softly, softly, keep vigilant, but don't overreact I think is the best policy for now, but what say you, Father Aloysius?

"The Gospel of St. Matthew chapter five," The priest replied, referring to the teachings of Jesus in the Sermon on the Mount, "Yes, I guess you are right. Thank you for your wise words." He made a mental note to make his presence felt at the school gate at the end of the school day and make his early runs past the pond.

The commander turned to Miss Hardcourt for her approval. She was quick to agree.

"One more thing," added the commander. "I have some night vision binoculars. If I hear anything, or more likely if my dog indicates she hears anything, I can use them to give the area a once over. Father Aloysius, the last cake? I'm sure you have deserved it."

Father Aloysius was more than glad to oblige.

"How can I refuse? Thank you. I suspect I will have to add gluttony to my list of shortcomings when I next make my confession to the bishop, but we don't want to waste anything, do we?" Father Aloysius carefully placed the last cake in the paper bag it had come in.

Miss Hardcourt stood up. "Well, that didn't take too long, thank you both of you. I suspect putting our action plan into place will take a lot longer, so we had better get cracking. The sooner we get this sorted, the happier I'll be."

"I guess that goes for us all," the Commander concurred, picking up his walking stick, "Well, Father, off we go, lots to be done." Miss Hardcourt was already halfway through the door. The two men followed. Outside on the path, they shook hands. "I'll be in touch when I feel it's time to clean out that rubbish. Meanwhile, you know where to find me if you need me," volunteered the commander, and the two men went their separate ways. Father Aloysius looked at his watch. It was only half past ten. He felt he had done a day's work already. He opened the brown paper bag to take out the cake, and then, with a sigh, he closed it.

"I know who would really love this," he muttered to himself, and he set off to the presbytery. It was not long before he was proved to be right. The delight on Miss Farrow's face when he offered her the bun more than made up for any misgivings he might have had at giving away his well-deserved treat. The priest excused himself and retired to his room. He sat down at his desk intending to make a start on the next Sunday's sermon, but his thoughts were full of other things, and he found it difficult to concentrate. He took off his shoes and lay down on the bed. Moments later, he was asleep. It was the phone that woke him. Miss Farrow took the call. It was Mrs Evans who said her husband had been taken off to hospital in an ambulance. She had phoned just in case Father Aloysius was planning a visit. Duncan had gone to the hospital. Was this the last paragraph of the last chapter? He had so wanted his mentor to be able to see the environmental area and not just the photographs.

Louisa Evans had prepared herself for the inevitability of her husband's decline. She had hoped that he might just slip away in the night, but it was not to be. Fortunately, she had also anticipated that he might have to return to the hospital. Three bags stood by the front door. A bag each for her and Anna and one they had packed together for Duncan. Since returning from her last slip back into her old ways, Anna had made a determined effort to be a caring, loving daughter. Louisa was grateful, but one thing played on her mind. It was the whole business of drugs. Drugs could be addictive; she did not know what her daughter had been taking. Fortunately, it seemed she was coping with any cravings and side effects of her experiment by using them. Perhaps there were no particular side effects to the type of drug she took. Then, there was the whole business of the law. Surely, it was her duty to report what Anna had told her to the police. True, Anna had implored her to say nothing, but did that mean she was breaking the law herself by not exposing the truth to the authorities? She tried to rationalise her behaviour and to put it to the back of her mind, but it was always there, a nagging fear and a doubt in the wisdom of her silence. However hard she determined to ignore it, it was always there. She could not bear to think of the possible consequences of the police being informed. Her husband was overjoyed at having his daughter back. She was clearly playing her part in a way that was touching to see. Until recently, the pair had been at loggerheads with each other. Now, it was clear there had been a reconciliation. Louisa had not shared her conversation with her husband, nor did she tell him of her worries. Telling the police would bring disgrace and shame to the whole family. It would make whatever time Duncan had left of life a nightmare of recriminations. She just could not risk that. It was her duty and indeed that of her daughter to do their very utmost to ensure Duncan Evans died in peace. She resolved to do nothing until it was all over. Then, she might be able to review the situation and, together with her daughter, decide to do the right thing by the law.

Her husband had daily visits from the nurse. She came to monitor his pain and to do her best to alleviate it. In the end, it was her recommendation that Duncan should be admitted to a hospital where they could manage the pain better. Duncan was a stoic, brave patient, but he was clearly suffering. Louisa had hid her disappointment and had complied.

Chapter Twenty

Malice will always find a target to aim at.

Father Aloysius was glad he had opted not to wear his cassock on his cycle ride to the hospital. It was by far the longest journey that he had attempted on the old bike. The route was hilly, and with the wind, he found progress was slower than he had hoped. There was another reason, too, he reflected, as he peddled hard up a steep incline: Miss Farrow had insisted that he wear a helmet. Where she had got it from, he did not know, but insistent she was and pleased he was too to be wearing trousers and not his normal clerical garb; a cassock and a helmet would have made him look ridiculous. He was not normally self-conscious about his appearance, and he mentally chided himself on this sign of vanity. Cycling, he had discovered, allowed him time to think. And on this journey, he had plenty of time for reflection and self-examination. His posting to a small Cornish seaside town had exposed him to a whole new set of challenges and, of course, opportunities. Nothing in his previous experience had prepared him for the situation he now found himself in. He had to learn on the job and to adapt, and this meant invariably that he was changing. Change was nothing new for the Africans. The change from being a child of the bush, herding his father's cows and goats, to being a mission boy and then a priest, with all that that involved, had been huge changes, but he had never really taken the time to reflect on how those changes were affecting him. In his daily prayers, he now included a prayer that he be helped to be more grounded and more secure in his faith. The words 'lead us not into temptation' had become particularly resonant.

Father Aloysius had decided to cycle to the hospital to see his friend partly because of his teaching schedule, which meant the bus was not a good option. The bus service was infrequent and not wholly reliable in its timing at stops. It did not fit in with visiting hours, and he needed to be flexible. Mrs Evans spent as much time as possible at her husband's side, and any visit he made would have to be sensitive to her husband's condition. Evenings could have been an option. True, he had had a number of evening engagements since his friend had been admitted, but he could have joined Miss Farrow, who had arranged to visit each evening, but he had been reluctant to do so. Miss Farrow was determined to visit each evening because Anna needed to see her father. The priest was conscious of the bishop's advice. 'Lead us not into temptation,' perhaps in this case, it meant recognising the red lights and taking heed of them.

A crossroads loomed ahead. A large white articulated lorry was approaching, but it was some distance away. In any case, it was his right of way. Apart from that, there were no other vehicles. Cornish roads can be notoriously narrow, and Miss Farrow had warned him that cars often sped far too quickly down the twisting lanes. She had strongly reiterated that he should take great care as often hedges and even stone walls edged the road, and verges were narrow. There was little passing space and often hardly any room to take avoiding action. Father Aloysius had been fortunate. Although a number of cars had passed him, the drivers had all been very courteous and had given him a wide birth. He had tried to reciprocate by keeping as close to the verge as possible when he heard a car approaching, and on a number of occasions, he had pulled over onto the verge and stopped to let cars pass when the lanes had been particularly narrow. Each time he did this, he got an appreciative response from the driver, either a cheery wave or a honk of a horn or even an acknowledgement signalled by a flash of the brake lights or indicators. Father Aloysius shot a quick glance at the signposts as he peddled past. He still had five miles to go. He hugged the verge and listened out for the lorry in case it was coming up behind him. He was some distance from the crossroads when he heard the grinding of gears and hissing of breaks. He surmised that the vehicle had reached the junction. Which way would it turn, he wondered?

It was not long before he had an answer. He was aware of the faint noise of an engine. He pulled over to the verge. The edge of the road was worn and uneven; a large pothole loomed, and some sixth sense caused him to swerve to the left into the grass instead of the right into the road. At that very moment, the lorry swept past, barely missing him. He felt its drag and wobbled. His front wheel hit a rock, and he was flung head-first over the handlebars towards the stone wall. His helmet crashed down onto the gravel as he slid to a halt, his ears were full of the roar of an engine accelerating. A piece of gravel thrown up by a rear wheel rattled against the helmet. It had all happened in a fraction of a second. He raised his head, watching the lorry as it sped away. He was too dazed to read any number plate, but he did note the colour of the writing on the tailgate, although he had no time to read it. It was red, and it began with a large capital P. He pushed himself to his knees, his eyes still fixed on the lorry, he shook his head in disbelief, not wanting to give credence to the thoughts that were filling his mind. The driver had made no effort to warn him of his approach or pull out at all. Was he deliberately trying to knock him off his bike? Even worse, was he trying to kill him? Father Aloysius's eyes narrowed, and he stroked his chin with his left hand. A trickle of blood flowed down from his graze to his sleeve. The lorry disappeared round the bend.

"Well, that was a near thing. Thank God for the pothole!" and, as an afterthought, added, "And for the helmet. Well done, Miss Farrow. You saved my skull from a big dent, and as for you, my friend," he shook the index finger of his right hand pointing down the road, "This cat has more than one life and should we ever meet you may find reason to regret that."

The priest wiped his palms on the grass and, reaching out his left hand to steady himself against the wall, rose a little gingerly to his feet. His left knee hurt. Noting the hole in his trouser leg, he took a handkerchief from a pocket and, rolling up his trousers, examined his knee. With the aid of some saliva on his handkerchief, he cleaned up this graze, removing all the grit. He then rolled his left trouser leg even higher up his thigh. He did not want the graze sticking to the inside of his trousers. Next, with the back of his hands, he wiped himself down. Lastly, he removed his helmet and ran the tips of his fingers over his skull. Thanks to the helmet, his skull felt intact. Having assessed his bodily damage, he turned his attention to the bicycle. The handlebars had twisted round, but that was easily rectified. Glancing both ways up and down the road, he pushed it out onto the tarmac and set off. He had to do his best to ignore the discomfort of the grazes on his palms as he gripped the handlebars. Restoring his peddling rhythm was not easy, as he constantly had to pull up his trousers, but he persevered.

An hour later, he was at the hospital and locking his bicycle up to the stand provided. His first call was to the visitors' toilets to conduct a second examination of his injuries and to give his wounds a proper wash. He tied his handkerchief round his knee, restoring the left trouser leg to its normal length, and then, with a final glance at himself in the mirror, set off to find Duncan Evans.

The Enquiries desk directed him to the ward. It was on the second floor. He ignored the lift and took the stairs. There was a water dispenser by the nurses' desk. He helped himself to several cups before enquiring as to where he might find his friend. Duncan had a room of his own. The door was ajar. He knocked gently and entered. Mrs Evans was getting up from her chair by the bed. Father held up a hand to indicate there was no need for her to get up. He inadvertently exposed his grazed palm. She noticed immediately her concern showed on her face. Father held a finger to his lips and shook his head. Duncan, propped up by pillows, was laying eyes closed. He was hooked up with tubes to a drip on a stand. He had headphones on and was clearly listening to some music.

"He's been sleeping on and off all morning, and I've arranged for Miss Farrow to bring Anna to see him. It's not that long until they will be here, and then it will be quite a squash. I think I had better wake him." She touched her husband's arm. He stirred, and his eyes opened.

"Huh, it's you, is it, and I was in the middle of a good dream. Anyway, you're far too early to be offering the last rites. "His friend had clearly not lost his sharp wit and was in full control of his senses, surmised the priest. He smiled and approached the bed.

"No, I've come to ask your advice, but if I had known you were dreaming, then…"

"Advice? I am a bit passed giving advice, especially to a priest."

"It's not as a priest I am asking but as a teacher."

"I see. Well, I did once have some expertise in that area, but" Duncan Evans had turned his head away and was gazing out to the world beyond the window. He turned back and looked up at the priest. "So what's happened? No, let me guess, is it something to do with the pond? Perhaps you have had some visitors."

The priest nodded, "Oh, you know, you've already been told. I…"

"No," interrupted the headteacher, "Just a guess, an informed guess, I grant you. We have lived in Pondreath a long time, and you get to know the people; all part of the job, so let's see if I am as lucky with my second guess. You have decided on a gently, gently response to the visitors. In other words, you are following the advice given in the Gospel of Matthew chapter five, am I right?

Father Aloysius chuckled, "Yes, and it never ceases to amaze me that knowing your current religious views, you know your Bible very well."

"Oh," The headteacher nodded in response, "As I said before, it always helps to know the opposition. If there is any merit in my knowing the so-called good book chapter and verse, the credit must go to our Baptist minister and our Sunday schoolmistress. She made sure we knew our Bibles, chapter and verse."

"So what made you change your allegiance?"

"Ah, a long story, university, I guess. I did a history degree, and my tutor, who taught what they called modern history, was an ardent communist, but it wasn't really that which changed me. I just found I couldn't believe in a supposedly loving God, creator of the Universe, who would allow the conditions that I saw in my village to exist." The headteacher paused clearly talking was an effort. He took a deep breath as if to gather strength. When he spoke again, it was softer, as if he knew he needed to conserve his energy. "The poverty was atrocious. Mines were closing. There was nothing else, and unemployment was a challenge. My Sunday school teacher probably could have given me an answer, but I never got to ask her. She died totally unnecessarily from pneumonia, probably as a result of the shocking living conditions, but I digress, and worse, I'm giving too much information to the opposition, so tell me exactly what's happened?"

Louisa Evans stood up and indicated that Father Aloysius should sit.

"But what about you? I can't take your chair, I'll fetch another," the priest protested.

"No, please, I need a coffee; it will be good for you two to have a natter on your own. I'll nip down to the café. I expect you could do with one, too, after your exertions.

"Exertions?" queried her husband.

"Yes, Father came on his bicycle."

"You cycled all the way from Pondreath! It will be the Tour de France next; he'll be needing more than coffee. Better get him a bun or something," the patient coughed.

"Yes, of course, that's exactly what I intended, now that's enough from you. Father, please sit down and rest your legs. "With that, she slipped away.

Father Aloysius was grateful for the seat. He did not want to tire the headteacher with a long tale full of woe, but he was conscious too that his friend would be keen to hear all about the project and what had occurred. It was important that he was allowed to feel he could still contribute. Quietly, he outlined what had happened and what had been done about it.

The headteacher lay for a moment in thought before speaking. He chose his words carefully. "So you think the dastardly deed was done in the night or very early morning? That night, it rained, but not all night. The rain had cleared well before dawn. The damage was discovered early, which all points to the probability that this was not just an opportunist prank by some youngsters out for a bit of fun but that it was done deliberately by someone who was prepared to put up with a bit of wetting or be up very early, which begs the next questions, who and why?"

"Yes, precisely who, and why, or why and who?" muttered the priest, looking intently at his friend.

There was a long pause before the headteacher spoke again. "We are a small community. Despite all the visitors that come streaming down to Cornwall in the summer, we are a pretty insular lot, some may have taken a dislike to you. You must be aware that not all people in England take kindly to people they assume to be immigrants.

"Yes, I'm no stranger to that. I guess prejudice is a universal human failing. In my homeland, Uganda, my tribe, the Karamajong, was looked down on by others who considered us to be backward and uncivilised. What I need to know is who might be responsible and what to do about it?" The priest was gazing out of the window at the wide-reaching sky. There were dark clouds gathering in the distance. He stroked his chin, and his eyes narrowed. There was another extended pause before the headteacher spoke again. His voice had become almost a whisper. The priest looked down at the floor. Perhaps this was all too much, he was tiring his friend.

"It could be any number of people, it could be more than one person, and maybe we will never know for certain." Duncan stirred on his pillows and turned to face Father Aloysius and smiled; he reached out his hand and put it on the priest's arm, "Don't let it worry you too much. I was new in the town once, so I have some idea of what it is like. I have probably had a part in making you high profile by getting you involved in the school, and another thing, it may not be just you that people resent; it could be the both of us, which brings us to what to do about it. Not much, certainly don't change what you are doing, which is doing your job to the best of your ability, building a community, a caring, kind community."

"Building the Kingdom of God," Father Aloysius nodded.

"Yes, I guess you could put it that way. I have never thought of doing good in that way before, which goes to prove you are never too old to learn something new." The headteacher gave the priest's arm a squeeze and, turning his face to the ceiling, he closed his eyes. It was Father Aloysius's turn to reach out his hand and gently place it on that of his friend. The headteacher's eyes remained closed, but he smiled.

That is how Mrs Evans found them. "I am sorry to have been so long, there was a queue for the coffee machine. I wonder if you could clear a space on Duncan's table for me." Father Aloysius hastened to oblige. She placed the small tray she was carrying on the table and handed the priest his cardboard coffee mug and a paper bag.

"Thank you, but what's this?

"Oh, just a little nibble to give you a bit of energy for your return trip, and I am sorry to say it, but you shouldn't be too long. It looks as if we will get some rain. What have you two been up to? Have you had a good chat?"

The priest was about to reply when her husband opened his eyes.

"Yes, dear, we did, and it's done me the world of good," he said in a strong voice, "I've even learned something new." He winked at Father Aloysius.

"Good, I'm glad, and what might that be?" queried his wife.

"Oh, that every deed of care and kindness is building the Kingdom of God," came the retort, and after a pause, "Pity, I don't think Karl Marx said it, but I like that, makes sense, don't you think?"

Louisa Evans turned to the priest.

"Well, you do seem to have done Duncan a lot of good."

"I assure you he has been even more helpful to me, and thank you so much for the coffee and the bun. It's very kind of you."

"Just another brick in the Kingdom of God," volunteered the patient, and they all laughed.

Father Aloysius was enjoying his coffee and Chelsea bun when a nurse arrived. He assumed wrongly that she had come to see the headteacher. She had come at the request of Louisa Evans to see him and to put some plasters on his grazes. Feeling embarrassed, the priest had protested that he was fine.

"I think you are outnumbered, my friend. Best do as you're told, just think of it as another brick," advised the headteacher as he lay back on his pillows to let the nurse do her routine checks on his blood pressure, heart rate, and temperature while his visitor finished his coffee and bun. Father Aloysius was still chuckling silently to himself when he said his farewells and followed the nurse out to get plasters put on his palms and knees.

Most of the ride home proved to be uneventful. His thoughts as he peddled revolved mostly round his good friend and his sense of humour. It was something he needed to cultivate: a sense of humour. He surmised that different cultures seemed to have their own brand of humour and that in England, what made people laugh was far more varied than he remembered was the case with his people in his tribal homeland. Here, it could be crude and rude but also sophisticated and nuanced. We are all the same but different, like dogs, he reflected. He wondered what black Labradors felt was funny and whether humans were the only species with the capacity for humour. He chuckled to himself as he recalled that afternoon with Anna on the quay after his lunch with Mrs Hazelmere. Perhaps he did have more of a sense of humour than he had credited himself with.

With some two miles to go, the rain caught up with him. It was heavy, and he was soon soaked to the skin. There was nothing to be done but peddle stoically on. In his homeland, rain was a huge blessing. He recalled once again the joy people felt at the first downpour of the rainy season and that wonderful smell that the sun-parched earth exuded when those first showers came. Within days, it seemed the bleached grass would be sprouting green, and for a time, the countryside would be lush and verdant. Elders of his tribe still wedded to the old ways, would use the rainy seasons as a way of marking the passing of time. He would now be over thirty rainy seasons old, he guessed. The time of the raid on his manyatta was the time of the long drought.

The steep hill down into the town forced Father Aloysius to abandon his memories of Africa and to concentrate. The road surface was now more slippery, and he had to apply his brakes with care. Then, once the descent had been successfully accomplished, he crossed the bridge over the river and climbed up the steep and narrow lanes past the church to the presbytery. He was panting as he pulled up at the front door. The bike went into the garage. He left the helmet there, too. He did not want Miss Farrow noticing the scratches. Fortunately, she was too concerned over his wet state to notice his plasters. He was cold and shivering. She handed him a freshly laundered towel and sent him off to have a hot shower. She had just time to brew him a large mug of tea before she set off to take Anna to the hospital. Normally, she would already have been at the hospital at the time Father Aloysius returned, but she had made an arrangement with Anna to leave later so that she could be home when he returned. The priest was grateful for her care, but he was also relieved to hear her departure and pleased to be able to sort himself out on his own before taking evening prayer. He also needed to go over his sermon in preparation for his services the next day. Preaching a ten-minute sermon was quite a challenge. He had developed a new routine for preparing his homilies. He would read the scriptures set for the day a fortnight before. This allowed him time to reflect on their significance and on how they might relate to life in the twenty-first century. On the Monday of the week he was due to preach, he would do a detailed study of the passages using a number of different commentaries. By Wednesday, he was ready to write his sermon. This gave him three days to commit it to memory. As with teaching, preparation was the key to success.

He found the better prepared he was, the more confident and relaxed he was. Being relaxed and confident was particularly important when it came to teaching. It seemed to be infectious; when he was relaxed and positive, the children seemed to respond better. It all helped to create a good learning environment.

Miss Farrow returned from the hospital in good time for Angelus. Father Aloysius was already at the church. It was still raining hard. He stood at the door to welcome his small but faithful congregation and to help with the umbrellas.

"I hear you cycled to the hospital today, Father. How is our Duncan?" enquired Mrs Hazelmere.

"In good spirits, and he is being well cared for."

"Did you enjoy your ride? Lots of hills to climb, but then you are young and fit."

"Yes, I did enjoy the ride, even though I got quite a soaking."

"Ah, so you were caught by this rain, not so nice, but it will help fill up the pond. Every cloud has a silver lining, I guess."

"Yes, it's always good if you can see a silver lining. Thank you, Mrs Hazelmere."

It was still raining when Father Aloysius finally got to lock up the church and return to the rectory. "Every cloud has a silver lining," he reflected with a smile.

Chapter Twenty-One

*Many receive advice,
only the wise profit from it*

-Harper Lee

Father Aloysius had three new attendees to morning Mass that Sunday. The first to arrive was the commander. After the rain of the previous day and night, the day had dawned bright; and the sky was clear blue, and everything looked fresh. The commander strode across the field swinging his stick; there was a spring in his step and a determination in his strides. Father Aloysius, as was his wont, was standing at the door of the church greeting people as they arrived. He had spotted the commander when he was some distance away but had thought he was probably off on a walk, perhaps to get a Sunday paper. His attention was diverted by Mrs Hazelmere, who always had one or two seemingly pressing matters to talk to him about. When he next looked up, the commander was at the church door.

"Don't look so surprised." The commander was smiling broadly, and he held out his hand. "However, I do have to admit it's many years since I have been in this church. Before Betty passed on, we were regulars at Church Parade down the hill, but I don't suppose that counts to you."

The priest laughed as he shook the commander's hand. "By your own admittance, it's been a long time, and so perhaps we'll excuse you being way out of date, at least in this parish. You see, the Rev. Burns and I are good friends, we share a visiting rota. True, we have yet to worship in each other's churches, but I am sure that is only a question of time, and in my opinion, at least worship at St Jude's is just as valid as worship here. I mean, surely it's a matter of common sense; if you believe God is everywhere, then he can be worshipped anywhere." To this, the commander was obliged to concur.

"Thank you. I had never thought of it like that. Anyway, I hear you preach a good sermon, so I have decided to come here today. It's not so far to walk."

The other two visitors were late. Mrs Evans and Anna had slipped in quietly and had chosen a seat at the back, near the door. Father Aloysius did not notice their arrival, and it was not until it came to the sermon and he was about to preach that he saw them. He had placed his watch with his papers on the little stand on the pulpit provided for such purposes and had looked up. He found himself looking directly at Anna. The pause was involuntary, as was the churning feeling in the pit of his stomach. It was only for a moment but seemed an age; it was her smile that made the difference. She nodded her head, and he relaxed and smiled back, then turning towards the altar, hoping that no one had noticed his surprise, he fixed his eyes on the cross and commenced with the opening prayer.

"Gracious, ever-loving God, inspire us with your Spirit that we may learn from your word and be inspired to build your Kingdom of love in our hearts and in this place." The sermon was based on Matthew thirteen and was about mustard seed, and yeast, pearls, and fishermen's nets, and hidden treasure and about the people of Pondreath, and as he spoke the words, he looked down at those from Pondreath who had graced the pews of St. Prodricks that morning. He looked at each separate person, and they looked back at him, and he spoke of love and grace in such a way that they made a difference to their understanding of their worlds and of the Kingdom of Heaven. When he came to Anna, she nodded, and they both smiled.

After the Mass, as people left and he spoke to each of them, they all thanked him for his sermon; some even told him how good they thought it was. To these, he smiled and just pointed to the heavens and said modestly.

"To God be the Glory." When it was the commander's turn to shake his hand and to have a word of affirmation, Father Aloysius received an unexpected reply: "Psalm 155, if my memory serves me right."

"It certainly does," said the priest, and then, almost as an afterthought, he added, "I wonder if could I have some words with you sometime? I need some advice."

"Of course, come to lunch, twelve-thirty," and without pausing for a reply, the commander strode away and headed off up the hill for home.

Father Aloysius was concerned to be punctual and to be on time for lunch, which he surmised was important to Commander Nesbitt, and so he set off in good time from the rectory to climb the hill to keep his lunch date. He nearly didn't make it. On the way, he had to pass the new school pond and environmental area. There, he met Mr and Mrs Hughes, carefully studying a bird dabbling about on the far edge of the pond. Mrs Hughes held her finger to her lips to indicate that silence was required; the priest confined his greeting to a nod and joined them in their bird-watching. Mr Hughes handed him his binoculars. It took him a little time to adjust the lenses to suit his vision, but once he had achieved a suitable focus, he was amazed at the clarity the binoculars gave him and had to suppress a strong inclination to exclaim his surprise out loud. The bird had the long legs and beak of a wader. The feathers of its folded wings were a dark brown, but its belly was a lighter shade, almost a sandy brown. It stood about eight inches tall. Mr Hughes had taken a notebook from his coat pocket. He had scribbled a few words in it and held it up for the priest to read. Buff - Breasted Sandpiper, rare. Last seen by me in 1994 October 14th. Father Aloysius nodded his appreciation and returned the notebook. Mr Hughes scribbled again. Well done, digging this pond. Important for birds. He gave the cleric a mime pat on the back. Father Aloysius smiled his thanks and glanced at his watch to check the time. Five to twelve, he mouthed hasty thanks and slipped away. Restraining himself from breaking into an immediate run for fear of disturbing the bird, he broke into a gallop as soon as he had judged it was safe to do so. With seconds to spare, he clattered up the steps to the front door and rang the bell. The commander must have been waiting in anticipation just inside because the door opened immediately.

"Ah, here you are, well done, I observed you down at the pond looking at something and thought you might not make it on time, I clearly underestimated your long legs, well done. We have something in common, you and I, in that we both have housekeepers. Mrs Trimmer is very punctilious about getting off, especially on the Sabbath, so I am grateful you made it on the dot. Interesting bird?

"Buff – Breasted Sandpiper, rare apparently," replied the priest, grasping the commander's outstretched hand. The shake was firm, just as he expected it would be.

"Yes, yes, very rare, at least in these parts. I last saw one sometime in the nineties. It was with Mr Hughes. We used to do quite a lot of bird-watching together. He's an expert, you know."

"Evidently," Father agreed. "It was October 4[th,] 1994. That's what he wrote in his notebook.

"Gosh, 1994, his memory is as sharp as a pin for these things, not quite so good when it comes to playing bridge. He introduced me to bird watching. I taught them both bridge. Don't suppose you play bridge." It was a statement, not a question, but nonetheless, Father Aloysius agreed that he did not, bridge and most other card games were unfamiliar territory for him. Judging from the lunch, roast beef with a good selection of vegetables, followed by cheese and biscuits, Mrs Trimmer was an excellent cook. The commander was not keen on sweets, and to his surprise, the Naval man also declared himself to be only a moderate drinker of alcohol, and so he was offered squash or water to drink. Father had water and, remembering his lunch with Mrs Hazlemere did so with gratitude, the effects of that lunch and the alcohol consumed were not to be repeated. Halfway through the meal, the cook came in to announce it was time for her to leave. Taking his cue from the commander, the priest rose to his feet when she entered. It was an opportunity for him to express his gratitude to her, which he did warmly. He was rewarded with a beaming smile.

"Oh, the commander likes his food. He's not fussy, but he just appreciates good food," she said as she left. "Have a good afternoon. I'll see you tomorrow, Sir, and I've left your supper in the fridge." The commander gave her a smart salute, and she left.

"Lovely lady," he said and nodded as if to emphasize the point. She was so good to me when my wife died, couldn't have coped without her."

"I also am indebted to Miss Farrow," Father Aloysius replied.

"She has made my settling here possible; I also would have been lost without her."

The two men chatted amicably until the first course was complete. The commander then suggested that they clear the table and then retire to the library for cheese and biscuits and a cup of coffee, and there, Father Aloysius could share what was on his mind. Father Aloysius helped clear the table and did the washing of the plates, leaving the commander to dry them and put them away, between laying up a tray with a selection of cheeses and two different kinds of biscuits, and a percolator of coffee, two mugs and the milk. "Sugar?" he enquired as an afterthought.

The library was a grand room panelled from floor to ceiling with tall glass-fronted bookshelves on three sides. Between the two windows, some well-seasoned ash logs burnt merrily in the fireplace, and sprawled out in front of the fire was a large golden retriever. It stirred as the men entered. "Don't worry about her," the commander said reassuringly, "She senses you are a friend, highly intelligent dogs, retrievers, good guard dogs too."

Father Aloysius settled gratefully into the deep leather armchair. He enjoyed the coffee, tried two of the three cheeses on offer, and, feeling distinctly drowsy, was about to fall asleep when the commander broached the subject of concern that had resulted in the priest being invited for lunch. "Now, what's on your mind, my good friend?" The commander asked.

There was a pause, then leaning forward in his chair and reaching his hands out towards the fire before rubbing his forehead with both hands and making a steeple with his fingers, the priest sighed, then quietly, in a matter-of-a-fact way related the incident of the lorry when he was cycling to the hospital and how he had later found the lorry parked on the quay just down from the bridge and having made enquiries as to whose lorry it was had learnt it belonged to a local haulage firm. The driver was Sid Trevinian. Sid was in the pub. The priest had been staring into the fire while he related his story. He now turned to the commander. "Now the question is, what do I do about it?"

It was the commander's turn to pause. Then, after a moment's thought, he replied with a shrug, "For the moment, nothing. You were alone on the road, there were no witnesses. Proving that there was any intent on Mr Trevinian's part in your near miss would be difficult, if not impossible. Mr Trevenian is a rum character, to be sure, but I am sorry to say I doubt if many people would agree with your suspicion, and that's all it is: a suspicion that he deliberately wanted to mow you down. Cornish people are loyal to their own, and you might just turn some folk against you. You'll have to watch your back, but I'd bide my time if I were you and see what happens next."

"You don't think I should at least confront him? The priest queried.

"No," I don't was the firm reply. By all reports, he has got a short fuse, if you understand what that means, and he might resort to violence, and if not that, he would certainly get to work spreading vitriol about you and turn people against you. Tell the bishop by all means, but bide your time and see what transpires, is my advice. But if anything does happen, please don't hesitate to tell me."

Father Aloysius thanked the commander. The two men chatted for a while. The commander was keen to know how Father Aloysius had become a priest. Father Aloysius always found this difficult. Being as a matter of fact and as brief as he possibly could, he explained the massacre of his family and how the Catholic mission Fathers had rescued him and nursed him out of his state of shock, had taught him to speak again, and then had taught him to speak their language and had sent him to school and later to the seminary. Father Aloysius suddenly noticed the time on the large clock on the mantle shelf. He had Angelus to take and some pastoral visits still to do. The priest thanked the commander profusely and left to do his duties. Miss Farrow was already ringing the church bell.

Chapter Twenty-Two

*In the Confrontation
between the stream and the rock, the stream
always wins, not through strength
but through persistence.*

-The Buddha

Father Aloysius's visiting list included people on both sides of the river. For reasons of timing, he could not simply visit all the folk on the North side of the river and then crossing the bridge to visit those on the South. Instead, he had, during the course of his pastoral work, to cross the bridge several times. The bridge was made of iron and was all struts, beams, and girders. There was a plaque on the South side. He had passed it many times but had never read it. He was about to pass it by again when he noticed that his shoelace had come undone. He paused to tie it and, in doing so, noticed the name Towzer. As Mrs Towzer was on his visiting list for that afternoon, his curiosity was aroused. The bridge was a replacement for the old Victorian structure made of brick that was itself a replacement for a wooden bridge. The former had been badly damaged in a terrible flood that had inundated the village in 1958. The iron structure had raised the height of the bridge above the river by a metre, hence the ramps at either end. Fredrick Towzer was named as one in a list of twelve benefactors who put up the money. He decided to visit Mrs Towzer last. She liked a chat, and he sometimes found getting away a challenge, which could mean he left too late to see others he wanted to see. His decision was justified. Mrs Towzer, like many whose lifelong partner had passed away, found living on her own could be a lonely business, and she welcomed the chance to have, as she put it, a good natter. She also made very nice scones. She was happy to share her memories of that terrible flood of 1958. From her, he not only learnt that it was indeed her husband who had made a generous donation towards the erecting of a new bridge but also about a later flood in the seventies that had led to the bridge being reinforced with girders underneath. These Mrs Towzer explained while they strengthened the bridge, could lead to logs being snagged under the bridge when the river was in spate. However, the river had to be very high for that to happen, and fortunately, that was rare. It fact, it had only happened twice in the last fifteen years. It was almost dusk when the priest was finally able to extricate himself, but in truth, he had enjoyed the chat and had certainly relished the scones and the tea.

As the priest walked back down the quay towards the bridge to get to the road that led up the hill to the rectory, he paused to gaze for a moment at the spectacular clouds - pink in the setting sun. Having spent his early childhood out in the wilds and even as a young boy herding his father's cattle and goats, he had learnt to read the sky. Many a time, he had found himself heading back to the boma from the watering hole in the dusk, driving his father's flocks before him with the sun setting over the thorn scrub and had been enthralled by its beauty. In Africa, near the equator, twilights were short.

Here in Cornwall, depending on the time of year and the weather, they seemed to be longer. He wondered how long he had before nightfall. He was mouthing a silent word of praise to his God for the beauty of his universe when a sudden commotion broke out on the other side of the river. Father Aloysius turned just in time to see Sid Trevinian walk round the front of his lorry and aim a hefty kick at a little dog that was lifting his leg on the front wheel of the lorry. The Pekinese yelped in pain and limped off towards its owner, followed by a stream of curses. The dog's owner was Mrs Hazelmere. She was taking her two pets for their customary evening walk before shutting up the house and retiring to the lounge to sit in front of the fire. Her charges were both on leads, but this one had escaped and had scampered off, ignoring all its owner's strident efforts to call it back. Mrs Hazelmere was incensed and hurrying forward, dragging her other dog with her and scooping the escapee into her arms while at the same time berating Sid.

"You horrid monster, how dare you kick my dog? Who do you think you are? That's absolutely despicable." Sid was unimpressed and unrepentant; he shrugged his shoulders and raised two fingers to the irate lady. It was then that Father Aloysius decided he must intervene. He ran hastily forward and crossed the bridge. The pair had squared up and were both expressing their dislike of each other as loudly as they could. Sid, seeing the priest approaching again, made another crude gesture at Mrs Hazelmere and, turning on his heel, disappeared round the front of his lorry. Father Aloysius heard the cab door open, and then bang shut. Sid reappeared moments later at the tail of his lorry. He strode off to the pub. In his hand was a brown paper bag.

Father Aloysius's initial feelings of disgust and concern were now laced with suspicion and anger. He resisted the temptation to chase after the lorry driver and, controlling his feelings, tried to bring some calm into the situation for Mrs Hazelmere. This was made more difficult by the reaction of the dogs, who took to yapping at him. With gentle soothing, they quietened, and he was able to take Mrs Hazelmere by the arm and accompany her back to her cottage. The old lady was more riled than shaken by the incident and threatened to call the police. However, no sooner had she opened her front door and ushered the dogs inside than they started to yap at the priest, making any further conversation difficult. He decided to settle for wishing her a good night and turned away, and she hastily shut her door.

With the anger still burning inside him, he turned towards the bridge to make his way home. Suddenly, he stopped. Was he going to let Sid Trevinian get away with this last shocking behaviour scot-free? Surely, someone ought to hold the man to account. He turned towards the pub. The red lights were flashing full-on in his mind, but he ignored them. A visit to the pub was long overdue. He would just go in for a drink and see what sort of a place it was and what reaction his appearance in clerical garb might provoke. There could be no harm in that. Taking a deep breath, he turned the door handle and went in. He did not have to wait long for a reaction. The pub was busy. The lorry driver was sitting with three friends in their customary place near the door. When it opened, he turned to look to see who was entering.

"Good God!" Big Sid exclaimed as the priest passed him. "If it isn't the - - n----r." Sid seldom said anything without expletives. The anger and tension inside that Father Aloysius already felt almost reached boiling point and showed clearly in his face. He paused in mid-stride before exhaling audibly and heading for the bar. Conversation in the pub had suddenly died. He was greeted with a curt "Yes?" by the publican. Father Aloysius was acutely aware that all eyes were on him and that every word he said would be heard by all. With the red lights flashing again in his mind as he reached inside his cassock for his wallet, he forced himself to smile politely.

"I would be grateful if you could serve me with a J2O, please," he requested. There was a burst of derisive laughter from Sid.

"- - orange squash. - - n----r can't even drink something decent!" He got a black look from the publican, but his face showed no emotion as he looked back at the priest.

"That will be three pounds seventy-five," he said flatly. "Ice?"

"No thanks," replied Father as he put the money on the bar and took the drink. He had a sip before calmly turning and heading straight for the table where Sid and his friends sat. Forcing himself to smile and to make every action slow and deliberate, he pulled up a stool and sat directly opposite the man who had insulted him. He was conscious that all eyes were on him. There was a collective murmur of surprise from those watching as Father Aloysius raised his glass to Sid and, then, in a quiet but clear voice referencing one of the expletives that had heralded his entrance, stated calmly.

"For your information, I am legitimately born."

Sid let out a derisive grunt, but his expression changed dramatically as the priest went on to ask, "I wonder, do you make a habit of kicking old ladies' dogs and also trying to run down cyclists in your lorry, and incidentally, what's in that brown paper bag you brought in here drugs?"

Sid's blue eyes narrowed, his neck muscles bulged, and his face grew puce with rage. He slammed his glass down on the table and suddenly, with a roar of rage, lunged forward in an attempt to strike the priest. There was a collective gasp from all watching. Father Aloysius had been anticipating a reaction and, with a drink in hand, had slid backwards off his stool and had stood up. The table was overturned; glasses smashed on the stone flags, and beer flew, but Sid's huge fist sailed harmlessly past the priest's face; he overbalanced and was in danger of falling over the table but was prevented by quick action from his friends, who grabbed his jacket and pulled him back.

Father Aloysius had another sip of his drink, "Pity about the beer and the glasses." He was conscious of a presence at his side. He glanced sideways. It was the publican who told him curtly to leave.

Suppressing the rising feelings of fear that had suddenly threatened to make him shake and feigning nonchalance as if nothing had happened, the priest turned and made his way to the bar. Downing his drink, he smiled at the publican's wife, Nancy, whose face was a picture of anxiety and wonder. He took a ten-pound note from his wallet and put it on the bar.

"A small contribution for the glasses," he said and then added, "Good evening and thank you," before turning to head for the door. The publican's wife hastily reached over the bar and took his sleeve. He turned back. She pointed to a side door at the end of the bar. "Not the front door, go that way!" she mouthed quietly. "It leads to the street and will be safer."

Father Aloysius shrugged, "I'll go the way I came in I'm not a runner," He appeared ice-calm but was far from it.

"No." Nancy's voice was full of urgency. "Please, we don't want any trouble here. Please, that way."

The priest smiled reassuringly at her and, uttering another word of thanks, complied. He found himself in a side alley. To his left, it led to the quay. To his right, it led up, rising steeply towards another street higher up the hill that ran parallel to the quay. He turned right. The hill would be in his favour; he would climb it far quicker than Sid or his friends should they try to pursue him. In this premonition, he was correct. No sooner had Frank the publican righted the table than Sid, indicating that his friends should accompany him, headed for the door.

"Don't worry, we'll get that – n----r," he shouted back as he left, crashing his way out and upsetting the umbrella stand. The four men spilled out onto the quay; they looked right, and they looked left. Father Aloysius was nowhere to be seen.

"The alley," Sid shouted, "and led the way round the front of the pub to the alley. By this time, Father Aloysius, sprinting upwards, had reached the top, and Sid had just caught sight of him turning into the road. He swore and followed. The alley was narrow. The pursuers had to proceed in single file, and Sid, the slowest by far, was at the front. He was panting heavily when he reached the top. Father Aloysius had disappeared. The big man swore.

"Let's split up," suggested one of his companions, who was also a driver for the haulage firm Sid worked for, "He turned right, Ned and I will chase after him. Nigel can keep an eye on this street, and you, Sid, go back to the quay and see he doesn't double back and go for the bridge."

Between gasps for air, Sid grunted a reply, "Alright, but phone me if you get him, and I'll ...." the last words were left unsaid. His friends were already on their way, leaving Sid to walk back. He was in no condition to run. The street at the top of the alley twisted and turned and led to the main road. This dropped down through the town and ended up on the quay by the bridge. Father Aloysius had disappeared right, and Sid's henchman from the haulage firm was correct to anticipate that the priest might double back and seek to drop down to the bridge and to cross over in order to get home to the presbytery, for that is just what he did, diving into the first ally that led downhill that he came across. With giant strides, he sped down to where the alley forked. He took the left-hand fork. It was a dead end. He was faced with a white wall. If he tried to scale it, he would lose time, and he did not know what lay beyond. Besides, it was getting increasingly gloomy. He retraced his steps and, taking the right-hand fork, he dashed down to the quay. Meanwhile, on the road above, his two pursuers had also reached the alley. They peered down it. It was empty. They turned to go on down the road when Nigel changed his mind.

"Wait, I think we should split up." After a moment's hesitation, his companion agreed. He entered the alley, leaving Nigel to continue on. The pause had cost them time. The priest had already reached the right-hand fork as Jim, Sid's lorry driver friend, entered the alley, and Jim made the same mistake as the priest. He took the left-hand fork and, on reaching the wall, had to retrace his steps.

As Sid got to the end of the alley by the pub, Father Aloysius emerged from the alley further down the quay. Sid swore. The priest would cross the bridge before them and disappear. It would soon be dark. Desperately, he scanned the quay on the opposite side of the river. With a roar of satisfaction, he saw his brother Mick leaving his fishing boat and pausing to light up a cigarette before heading for his cottage. With much frantic waving of arms and bellowing, he managed to attract his attention.

"The bridge, the bridge, stop that - - -priest."

Father Aloysius heard Sid's cries, and glancing across the river as he ran, he saw Mick, cigarette in hand, heading for the bridge to intercept him. A moment later, Mick was obscured from view by a line of vans parked along the edge of the far quay. The priest knew he would reach the end of the bridge well before Mick, but could he risk crossing the quay and heading up the hill to the presbytery? No, he decided. On reaching the ramp that led off the bridge, he turned left and dropped down onto the river bank. Reaching up, he grasped the lip of the bridge's main beam that spanned the river and, stepping out from the quay, pulled himself along. It was a desperate manoeuvre, but if he could get as far as the reinforcement beam under the bridge, he could swing onto it and hide under the bridge. He made it with moments to spare. With his heart pounding and his face pressed against the cold metal, he hung on and prayed for dark.

Mick, on finding the bridge empty, cast about looking under the vehicles and upturned boats. His brother had reached the bridge and was crossing it. Father Aloysius listened to the footfall overhead, he had become aware that a part of his cassock was hanging down below the beam. He dared not move. What if one of his pursuers should look under the bridge and see it? All would be lost. In the event, when Mick's searching round vehicles and boats had proved fruitless, and he did cast a cursory glance under the bridge, but in the gathering gloom, he failed to see the priest and mistook the cassock for an old piece of rag, a bit of flotsam, a remnant left by the last time the river was in spate.

Father Aloysius breathed more freely when he heard all five men above him discussing their next move. Darkness had fallen, and now, apart from four street lights, two at either end of the bridge, the only light came from the half moon and the stars above and chinks in curtains or at windows where there were no curtains, which were but few. Father Aloysius strained to hear what was being said. The confab continued for some time. Sid wanted to proceed up the hill to the presbytery. The others, Mick apart, were keener to return to their beer at the pub. Eventually, it was agreed that Sid and one other should broach the lion in his den and proceed to the presbytery. Mick would stay put to keep an eye on the quay and the bridge. The remaining two would return to their ale.

This led Father Aloysius to conclude that he was safe for the time being but that he was going to have plenty of time for reflection. It was time to count his blessings. Thanking God for loose shoelaces and Mrs Towzer, he decided it should be at the top of his to-do list, but he realised too that remaining where he was for long was untenable. Not only was it precarious, but it was growing increasingly uncomfortable and cold, and so it was with a huge sense of relief he heard Mick talking to a lady, who from the conversation appeared to be his wife. She had left her cottage to find him and sent him on an errand to the pub to get her a packet of cigarettes. She took over his watch but was enticed away by a friend who lived further down the quay.

Extricating himself from the beam was even harder than getting onto it. He was cold and had started to stiffen up. Reaching out round the edge of the beam, his groping hand found a strut that allowed him a better grip than the lip of the cross beam. Gingerly, he turned himself onto his back and, taking a firm hold of the strut, he slipped off his perch. For a moment, he hung there by one hand. Desperately, he reached up with his left hand and found the lip and, leaving the strut, moved along towards the quay. He was conscious that he was probably now visible, but he was grateful for light nonetheless. It allowed him to snatch a glance sideways. He inched himself towards safety and, breathing heavily, dropped onto the river bank. He was shielded from the eyes of the ladies by a parked van. He heaved himself up onto the quay and, bent low, crept round the front of the van. The ladies were some distance away and were deep in conversation. Quickly, he moved past the bridge and away on down the quay. Once past the bridge and away from the street lights, he could proceed with greater speed, but he still needed to walk carefully for fear of tripping over an unseen obstacle in the dark. At the end of the quay and the line of cottages, a path led down to the beach. He followed it. The sea beckoned. The tide was out, but the sand, still wet, was firm, he'd made it, he had escaped. This was familiar territory. It was where he often ended up on his early morning run. Ten minutes away, down the sands, another path zig-zagged its way up to the top of the bluff, the hill, and Commander Nesbitt's house. For a moment, he relished a feeling of elation, but then, thinking about his friend, the commander, he recalled his friend's advice. The commander had cautioned him not to provoke a confrontation, and that was exactly what he had done. Ignoring all the red lights that had flashed in his mind warning him not to, he had deliberately entered the pub. Do nothing had been his friend's advice, and what had he done, he had goaded the big man. Yes, of course, there was all that provocation, but what about turning the other cheek; what would his bishop have expected of him, and now, he would be the talk of the village, and not only that, people would be taking sides. Where did that leave him and his role as a priest? Where did that leave the church? Elation had been replaced by shame. What would he say at his next confession? And what about Sid. Where was he and his friends now?

Sid, at that moment, was at the presbytery. On their arrival, they noted the lights were on. Sid had battered at the door with his big fist. Startled by the noise, Miss Farrow had answered the door. Sid was somewhat taken aback to see her.

"How can I help? Miss Farrow asked.

Sid had looked down at his feet and then, clearing his throat, had asked if Father Aloysius was at home. On hearing that he was not, he was about to turn to leave when Miss Farrow explained that the priest was out doing his Sunday visiting and that he should be back soon. She invited the men in to wait. The three men were ushered into the kitchen. Miss Farrow offered them a cup of tea, which Sid roughly declined. They sat in silence for a short while, but not being a patient man and feeling very uncomfortable just sitting in the presbytery kitchen, Sid suddenly got up and mumbled, "Can't stay," and the three men stomped out, leaving the front door open they headed for the pub. Miss Farrow closed it with a feeling of some relief. Then, writing a note for Father Aloysius to tell him his supper was in the fridge, she turned out the lights and, locking the front door behind her, hurried off down the lane to her sister's place above the shop. Her sister was married to Ben Fowler, and they owned Pondreath's only shop. Miss Farrow had a small flat above the garage. They always shared the Sunday evening meal together.

Chapter Twenty-Three

*Offering Sanctuary
is a revolutionary act; it expresses love
when others offer scorn and hate.*

Diane Kalen- Sukra

It was a somewhat dishevelled priest who stood on the porch of The Gables, hesitating to ring the bell, such were his feelings and misgivings about what had occurred since he was last at this very door not many hours before. Commander Nesbitt had eaten the light supper left by his housekeeper and was sitting reading in front of the fire in his library. His dog lay sprawled out at his feet. Both were startled by the bell.

"Who on earth can that be?" the Commander addressed his dog. If he was surprised to see Father Aloysius when he opened the door, he did not show it.

"Father Aloysius, how nice to see you, do come in." The Priest smiled sheepishly and apologised for disturbing the household. The welcome was warm, and the commander seemed oblivious to his condition. Father Aloysius bent down to take off his sandals. "No, no, don't worry about that, a little sand won't ruin the carpet. The dog and I were on the beach earlier, lovely long walk, eh boy?" The Commander bent down and patted his companion fondly on the head. "How was Angelus?"

"Fine, thank you," replied the Priest, who, having taken off his sandals, was dusting the sand off his feet. He followed the Commander through to the library. The Commander was about to sit down when a thought suddenly came to him.

"I've eaten, have you?

"No, but don't worry, I.."

"Nonsense, young man, you seem to have been getting about a bit since lunch. You are probably famished, it won't take a moment to fix up some soup. Bread and cheese do? No doubt you'll have tea, and yes, yes, I know you take sugar!" Father Aloysius grinned.

Had the Commander been talking to Mrs Hazelmere, he wondered, and yes, he did take sugar. "On a tray in the library suit you?" Having directed the cleric to the library, the Commander busied himself in the kitchen. It was not long before he returned with a tray loaded with slices of bread and butter and a selection of cheeses. There was also a bowl full of figs and dates. He found his guest standing in front of the fire. "Please sit down."

"I've come to make a confession," explained the priest as he sank into the large leather-covered chair.

"First things first, young man," the Commander responded, placing the tray on a table beside his guest. "Eat first, and then we can come to the penitent bit. Excuse me a moment; I'll just get myself a drink and a bit of cake each. You tuck in." Father Aloysius was only too happy to comply, and the food made him feel a whole lot better, as did the fire. He had not realised how cold and hungry he had become. The meal completed, the two men cleared the dishes before returning to the library.

"I've been foolish, very foolish," The Commander listened attentively as Father Aloysius, leaning forward in his chair, went on to relate the events of the last few hours. When he had completed his sorry account, he sank back in his chair. The Commander got up and put another log on the fire, then, returning to his chair, smiled at the cleric.

His next words were not what Father Aloysius expected.

"I have to say I am not surprised at all, all rather predictable. The Commander crossed the floor to a bookshelf. Opening the glass door, he took a book out. "When you left this afternoon, I did a little research. I have this old book on Uganda. As for Mr Trevinian, he acted entirely in character, what you see is what you get. You, well, I wouldn't go as far as to say you acted entirely in character. However, as I have said, I am not surprised. You see, you come from the Karamajong tribe, a tribe of warriors; knowing that, I guess I can conclude you acted under stress as a Karamajong warrior would. However, now we come to the important bit, and I am going to revise my earlier advice here.

I know you have no proof, especially about the drugs, but it would do no harm to mention the drug's suspicion to the police. But first, I would check with the Bishop when you make your next confession, and if you want a reference, look no further. One more thing, you don't need to feel ashamed. I would say you were a little ill-advised, but you did not shirk what you saw as your duty, and you were brave. Just watch your back."

Father Aloysius let out a deep sigh, "Thank you." He said.

"And last but not least, the bed's already made up in the spare room, and you're staying here tonight, so I suggest a good hot bath and off to bed with you. We will talk about the immediate consequences of this evening's events tomorrow over breakfast. For now, the important thing is to have a good night and not to dwell on what has happened. In my experience, a night's sleep helps put things into a better perspective, and we will be in a more informed position to manage what needs to be done or not done in the immediate future after sleeping on it. Father Aloysius suddenly felt very weary. He did not argue. Having sorted the Priest some pyjamas and a toothbrush, the Commander gave Miss Farrow a ring to warn her not to expect the cleric until after breakfast. From her, he leant of the two visitors to the Presbytery. He decided to keep that news to himself. It could wait until the morning, no sense in sharing it before then. He wanted the Priest to have a good night's sleep. He did, however, tell his friend that he had phoned Miss Farrow and that all was well.

Both men were up early the next morning, but Father Aloysius was the earliest by some time. He did not have his running clothes or trainers, but he still felt he needed his early morning run, so he made do with the clerical dress he had had on the evening before, without, of course, his cassock. He slipped out the back door, leaving it unlocked. The morning was crisp. He was stiff from his exertions of the day before.

He knew breakfast was likely to take time as there were things to talk about, so he did not take his usual route down to the beach but confined himself to the roads and ran only to the cairn on the top of the bluff. On his return, he found Commander Nesbitt busy in the kitchen. The two men exchanged greetings, and then Father Aloysius slipped off upstairs for a shower and a shave. An enticing smell of fried bacon greeted him as he descended the stairs. They ate in the kitchen. Father Aloysius was not used to having a cooked breakfast, but he relished this one and enjoyed his porridge followed by two eggs with bacon, a sausage, baked beans, and mushrooms, and then a slice of toast and marmalade all washed down with three cups of coffee. It was by far the biggest breakfast he had ever been given, and he enjoyed it immensely. While the priest ate, the Commander talked.

"Thinking about yesterday, it's hard to predict what the consequences might be. It probably depends on how effective the gossip grapevine is and what version of events gets put about, and we must remember, too, that you are the only one who knows the whole story, Mr Trevinian will know most of a slightly different version, but all the others will know a lot less. The bit that will get the most airing is, of course, the confrontation in the pub, and I suspect most of the gossip mongers will be from the big Trevinian camp. However, every version of what happened will have a different slant depending on who is telling it, and you might even have a few supporters given all that," the Commander continued buttering himself a piece of toast and adding a thick dollop of marmalade, "I still feel my advice of last night stands, just carry on your own cheerful way as if nothing has happened, keep to your usual routines, act normally. Just watch your back. You will no doubt have dealings with the Trevinian children, and as with the rest of that family, Sid included, take them as you find them, try not to provoke, resist reacting to any silly jibes, and act as if nothing has happened. In the colloquial jargon of the younger generation, play it cool, but just watch your back. Tell the Bishop to report that Mr Trivinian and a friend called at the Presbytery yesterday, but otherwise, just be the normal you. The normal, you have won a lot of friends in this community, trust in the God you believe in, and continue to serve him in serving the community as you have been doing, and it will all work out for the best. Now I've waffled on long enough, what can I do to help?"

Father Aloysius wiped his mouth with his napkin. "Thank you a thousand times. Thank you not only for taking me in and treating me like a king but also for your sound advice. If I had taken it in the first place, I would not be in this situation, but it is what it is, and so I have a second chance to heed your wise words and to play it cool. He smiled at his friend.

"Good man, good man," the Commander responded.

"However, I am concerned that Miss Farrow had to deal with Mr Trevinian," the Priest added, "I should have found some way to warn her that he was on his way, but I was so concerned about my need to escape that I didn't think of it. Another big error of judgement. Did she say what happened?"

"You needn't worry on that score. If you had found a way to warn her, she probably would have been nervous, but as it was, she handled the visit remarkably well, she invited the two men in and even offered them a cup of tea while they waited. They, of course, refused, and they didn't stay long. When I phoned, she was on the point of locking up and going home."

"Ah, bless her, but I will mention the visit when I phone the police. As for how can you help me, what can I say?" Continued the priest, "You have done so much already. I guess if I show signs of straying from being normal, you ought to prod me back again, but otherwise, otherwise just play it cool will be my mantra."

Grinning broadly, the two men shook hands.

There was a sound of the front door being opened. "That will be Mrs Trimmer," hardly had the words left the Commander's mouth when Mrs Trimmer came in.

"Good morning, all," she greeted the two men. Nice to see you, Father Aloysius. I heard you were here. I hope you have had a good breakfast."

"Wonderful, thank you, breakfast, lunch, and dinner all rolled into one, all delicious," responded the cleric."

"Good, I am pleased. I hear you had quite an exciting time yesterday evening," observed the housekeeper.

Father Aloysius shrugged his shoulders. "Yes, you might say that," wondering at the speed the grapevine seemed to be working. "Now, perhaps you'll excuse me. I have a busy day ahead, and I ought to get cracking."

"Oh really, anything special going on?" queried Mrs Trimmer.

"No, nothing special, the usual Monday things, Just the normal round, but thank you for asking," He hoped that the housekeeper didn't notice the nod and the wink he made in the Commander's direction as he turned and left the room. Shortly after this, the Priest said his farewells and thanks to the Commander on the porch and proceeded down the hill to face another normal Monday in Pondreath.

"Play it cool, you lucky man," he repeated to himself.

Chapter Twenty-Four

*You are free to Choose, but you are not
free to alter the consequences.*

-Ezra Taft Benson

Father Aloysius hurried down to the Presbytery. He wanted to thank Miss Farrow, and he needed to change into clean clothes before taking Angelus. His housekeeper greeted him warmly, and while grateful herself for his thanks, she made little of the incident and was just pleased that he had not returned to find the two men there. She had already heard about the goings on at the pub and was gradually piecing the events together in her mind.

"I gather there was a little excitement at the public house," she observed and then asked for his cassock. The Commander had done his best to clean Father Aloysius's cassock, but Miss Farrow decided she ought to try to improve on his efforts. Having served the previous incumbent for many years, she knew a thing or two about restoring clerical garb to a presentable, if not pristine, condition. Father Aloysius shrugged and handed over his soiled cassock.

"Yes," he concurred, "I suppose you could say that. I might have been a little foolish and have provoked a situation that got a little out of hand, and I am very sorry you ended up having to open the door to two of the participants in the excitement. May I say you handled the situation remarkably well. Thank you."

"To quote you, Father, 'To God be the glory.' Those two gentlemen were not the only visitors to the Presbytery while you have been away."

"Oh really, who else? The priest was both surprised and puzzled. He was even more surprised at his housekeeper's reply.

"It was the police."

"The police! Just when was this?"

"Reading between the lines, they had taken a call from Mrs Hazelmere about the incident involving her dogs and had decided to make a number of early morning calls.

One apparently was to Mrs Hazelmere, and from her, they went to the Trevinian house.

Mr Trevinian had already left for work, so they went to the lorry depot and saw him there. From what I can tell, Mr Athelton, the manager, agreed to put Big Sid on a long-distance job, so he will be away for a few days. I suppose they think that him being away will give time for the dust to settle, so to speak, and everyone will be calmer for it. Anyway after that they came here to see you. I told them you had stayed the night with the Commander but would be back soon and that you would be getting ready to take Angelus. I asked them if they wanted to attend, but they said they had other calls to make but would return to catch you after the service."

"I see," and even as he said the words, the priest was wondering what the police would ask him and what he should divulge to them, especially on the sensitive matter of the drugs. Perhaps he concluded, as he didn't see any at all, he would not say anything. However, there was no time to dwell on the matter. The Angelus bell was ringing. Miss Farrow held out his cassock for him to put on and then, excusing herself hurried off to the church. Father Aloysius glanced at his watch. With four minutes to go, he had time to stand quietly by the window for a brief moment, to say a prayer, and to calm himself. Normally, he would have been at the church sometime before the service, but on this day, the situation of the night before had determined that it would be different.

With a minute to spare, Father Aloysius entered the Church. He was taken aback by the number of people in the church, three or four times the usual number. As he entered, they turned in their pews and spontaneously burst into applause. He stopped in mid-stride, rooted to the spot, confused and feeling not a little embarrassed. He did not know how to respond. As he took in the faces of those who had assembled, he wondered at the nature of how much of an impact his arrival in this little seaside village had made.

Mrs Hazelmere, of course, and Miss Farrow, other staunch regulars like Mr and Mrs Hughes, but then there were those among them the Tarrants from the Youth club, Miss Farrow's brother and his wife from the shop, The Commander and his housekeeper, Mrs Trimmer, the Rev Burns and his wife from St. Jude's and Mrs Towzer that he would not normally have thought would express their loyalty to him by attending a service. The biggest surprise of all, Mrs Evans, Anna, and Larry, he was almost overcome with feelings of overwhelming joy. He raised both hands, fingers spread, and smiled. Then, bowing his head in gratitude, he walked slowly down the aisle to the Priest's stall. He opened his prayer book and turned to face the congregation.

"In the name of the Father and of the son and of the Holy Spirit, welcome to this our act of devotion and prayer. I must say the Holy Spirit has, it seems, been working overtime. I have to confess you are a far bigger congregation than normal, and I certainly was not expecting as many, but praise be to God you have come, and you are very welcome. I see we are quite an ecumenical group of people, so, in respect of this and the fact that you are all busy people, we will confine our prayers this morning to saying the Angelus; this will be followed by the Lord's Prayer. Then, there will be a time of silence for you to use for your own prayers. Finally, I will ask The Rev. Burns to join me in saying a blessing. You will all probably know the backstory of this church far better than I do, but just a word about the liturgy here: our benefactor Lady Chardingley, whose generous legacy still maintains this church, decreed that the Church should follow the ancient monastic tradition that the Angelus bell should be rung three times a day, morning, afternoon and evening and that prayers should be said morning and evening each day. You will find the Angelus on page four of our prayer books. You are invited to join in the responses. Father Aloysius glanced round the congregation to ensure everyone had sight of a prayer book, and after inviting his flock to kneel, he turned towards the altar and launched into the old, long, familiar words of the Angelus.

Father Aloysius was conscious that not a few in the church that morning would have never said the Angelus prayer before, and he wondered self-consciously how they might be feeling. Certainly, The Lord's Prayer was more familiar territory, but when it came to the time for silent prayer, the priest found himself surprised at how unprepared he felt to face his maker and pray. He was stirred by a mixture of emotions: gratitude, guilt, fear, and anxiety as to how others, one such being the bishop, might react to the events that had brought him here on his knees in a church full of his friends. Their presence made him feel very humble. He gave God thanks, he gave thanks for them all, then after confessing his misgivings about the way he had acted, he addressed his fears and turned his thoughts to Sid Trevinian and his friends. They needed his prayers, too. As he prayed for Sid, he asked his God's forgiveness once again for provoking the man and determined to avoid confrontations in the future. Feeling a little more composed, he rose to his feet to bring the time of silent prayer to an end. Quietly, he walked down the aisle and gently touched his Anglican counterpart on the arm, signalling it was time for them both to say the blessing. The two men, side by side, approached the altar steps and, after bowing, turned to face the congregation. Father Aloysius faced the Rev. Burns and smiled, and, addressing the congregation, he announced.

"Good friends, thank you, thank you from the bottom of my heart for being here today. You don't know how much your coming means to me, so thank you, a million times thank you. Now let us conclude our time of prayer with the grace together before the Rev. Burns, and I give the Blessing." Not everyone knew the grace, but with a strong lead from Miss Farrow and Mrs Hazelmere, there were enough voices to give an adequate response. The two clerics, in unison, gave the Blessing and then turned to face the altar for a final time. As he stood there gazing up at the crucifix, Father Aloysius was conscious of a great feeling of relief. He whispered his thanks to his companion, and the two men shook hands before facing the congregation.

Just as they were about to descend the steps, Mrs Hazelmere left her pew and came to the front. Holding up her hands, she declared in a strident voice,

"Father Aloysius, thank you for a lovely service, and I am sure I speak for all here when I say you have made the start of this day rather special. But before you go about your duties and we all depart to our own busy days of activity, I just want to say a very big thank you to you for being such a perfect gentleman yesterday. One of my favourite hymns is that one by Sydney Carter, based on the parable of the Good Samaritan, you know, the one 'Cross over the Road.' I'm sure all of you know it, and I see some present who will no doubt have sung it in Assembly in our excellent village school just up the road." There was a general murmuring of recognition. "Good, I thought you'd recognise it, but don't worry, I am not going to ask you to sing it now. I just want to say, Father, you not only crossed over a road but a river too to come to my aid yesterday, and so on behalf of my two little dogs and myself, as a small token of my gratitude, I'd just like to present you with this." Bustling back to where Miss Farrow had just emerged from, reaching down under the pew to retrieve a large tin, she grasped it with both hands and then, holding it high for all to see, presented it to the Priest.

It was Father Aloysius's turn to hold the tin aloft, "Well, what a surprise, thank you. A lovely tin, but I wonder what it can it hold?"

"Open and see," was the firm retort.

Father Aloysius complied. It was a large fruit cake. After further expressions of surprise and gratitude, the priest insisted that nothing would give him greater pleasure than to share the cake there and then. Miss Farrow was despatched to fetch some paper napkins, a plate, and a large knife. The cake was shared while Father Aloysius made it his business to greet each of his supporters and to shake them firmly by the hand. His gratitude was heartfelt and obvious to all present. As his friends slipped away, Father Aloysius ruefully reflected that when he had woken up earlier that morning, he could not have possibly imagined that the first consequences of his actions of the previous day would be a record congregation and a magnificent cake.

There was a Police car parked outside the Presbytery when Father Aloysius left the church. As he approached, two police officers got out. It was Sergeant Graves and a police lady Father Aloysius had not seen before. The interview was brief. They took a statement from him and advised him, much as Commander Nesbitt had done, not to get into any provocative situations, but if anything untoward happened, he was to call them, and they would deal with it; it was their job. When he was asked if he wanted them to take up the matter of racist language with Mr Trevinian, Father Aloysius just shook his head.

"I've heard it all before, and to be truthful, we all have our prejudices. For me to want you to press charges would be hypocritical. I come from Uganda. There, my tribe is looked down on. We are regarded as savages, and then in our own tribe, there are clans, and each clan thinks it's better than the others. It's all a question of difference. Difference leads to prejudice, and prejudice can have far-reaching consequences. Greed, ambition, and prejudice can lead to wars and to persecution. Addressing our prejudices is the duty of us all, me included. I guess education is the only way to deal with that."

"Umm," responded Sergeant Graves, "Very magnanimous of you. Racism, as you know, is prohibited by law, but in this case, you are probably right. It's possibly wise not to be too fussy. But if it continues or if there are any other threats of violence, you must, I must stress, tell us." The priest had concurred and had left it at that. Both parties were, in fact, relieved by their mutual decision. For Sergeant Graves, he was conscious of the fact that the force had enough to do without adding to their workload. He was of the opinion that far too much was expected of the Police; they could not be expected to cure all of society's ills. For Father Aloysius, there was the thought of how pressing charges might affect his relations with the Trevinian children and also possibly, by implication, Anna. He wondered if a better way was to actively seek reconciliation with his protagonist. He resolved to look for opportunities to work in that direction.

Later that day, Father Aloysius faced his second challenge. He was scheduled to take P.E. and football at the school. The priest was more than a little concerned about how he was going to cope with young Philippa. It was almost certain that she would have heard the gossip about his confrontation with her uncle. How would she react, he wondered. As it was, his worries proved unfounded. She was absent, and the school secretary, anticipating his concern, had informed him when he signed in at the school office.

There was no mention of Father Aloysius's adventures of the previous evening in the class. In fact, the children were exceptionally compliant and seemed to be going out of their way to be polite and helpful. Was this a consequence of what they had heard on the grapevine, he wondered. If it was, he was grateful; he was expecting the worst, but the opposite had happened.

Having returned the children to their classroom, the Priest slipped into the staff room for a cup of tea before taking the After School football club. There was a full three-quarters of an hour before the end of the school day, and rather than go back to the Presbytery, he remained in the school and spent the time in the staffroom or the library where he could review his lesson, prepare for the next one, and spend time working on getting ready for the Assembly he would take the next day. He was deep in thought when the caretaker came in.

"Afternoon, Father. It's started to rain; it is too late to cancel football. You'd be better off in the hall," he remarked and then promptly left. Again, there had been no mention of the goings on of the evening before. Father Aloysius was beginning to suspect that his concerns over the ability of the village grapevine to spread gossip had been totally unfounded. Perhaps no one knew after all. The football club over the Priest dismissed the children from the veranda where they normally changed. Inevitably, there were stragglers. Kevin was one of them. It was he who broke the embargo.

"Father, is it true that you had a big bust-up with Philippa's uncle yesterday?"

Father Aloysius was busy stuffing footballs into a big net bag. He straightened slowly and spent a long moment gazing out across the field. His concerns had not been completely unfounded after all. Turning to the boy, he shook his head and, with a gentle smile, said, "No comment,"

"Oh come on, Father, tell, we won't say anything to anyone. You can trust us three," the boy pleaded. The boys watched, waiting while he finished the clearing up of the balls and then paced deliberately head down to the end of the veranda and back. He stopped when he got to the boys.

"No comment," he said, shaking his head, "Now it's stopped raining, and it's time you were all off home for your teas. Have a good evening."

The boys picked up their bags and started to shuffle off when Kevin decided to have one last try. "Father, we heard that Big Sid took a kick at one of Mrs Hazelmere's dogs and that you had words with him, and you mentioned drugs."

Father Aloysius sighed, "Look, I'll say one thing and one thing only, and that will be the end of the matter. Sometimes, and this is true of everyone, we say and do things without thinking of the consequences. We ignore the red lights that tell us to stop and act foolishly, and I am guilty just as much as everyone on these matters now, good night." Without waiting for a reply, he picked up the bags of balls and bibs and, turning, strode off to return them to the P.E. shed.

Kevin shrugged, "Good night, Father," he called. His companions echoed his greeting. They left muttering among themselves. The Priest heard them and smiled. When Father Aloysius had safely put everything neatly away, he emerged from the shed to see the boys had gone. "Well," he muttered to himself, "The cat is out of the bag after all. Perhaps my next assembly will be about red lights and consequences and playing it cool!"

Chapter Twenty-Five

You never know
How strong you are until being strong is
the only choice you have.

-Bob Marley

Father Aloysius pulled his bicycle out of the shed and glanced at the sky. It was a grey day. Over to the West, the clouds were building. It would be good to get his visit done early, he decided. A phone was ringing. The sound came from the Presbytery. He lent his bike against the shed door and hurried to answer it. He was reaching out to lift the receiver when it went dead. The Priest sighed and wondered who might be ringing. He was about to turn away when it rang again. It was Miss Farrow.

"Praise the Lord you are still there, Father. I've just had a call from Mrs Evans. She is at the hospital with her husband. She wants me to take Anna to see her Father."

"I see. Is Duncan slipping away?

"Failing yes, I sense he is. I think you ought to come." There was an urgency in Miss Farrow's voice.

"Right, I'll come straight away to the shop?"

"No, I'm down on the quay."

"Give me two minutes," responded Father Aloysius, reaching for the key to the front door of the Presbytery and taking it hastily from his cassock pocket. He was as good as his word. He ran with giant strides down the steep hill, his cassock billowing about his legs. As he burst out onto the quay, Miss Farrow started the car. Wondering where Anna might be, the Priest fastened his seat belt. Anticipating his question, Miss Farrow released the hand break, and they were on their way.

"Well done, and if you are wondering about Anna, she is with a friend. She stayed the night. The Farm is about three miles from here, hence the need to get going. I've phoned so Anna should be ready when we arrive. The thing is, there is a storm forecast, and the road to the farm has two fords. Sometimes, they become impassable." Even as she spoke, there was a sudden gust of wind, and with it, the rain started to fall. Father Aloysius took his rosary beads from his pocket. Miss Farrow clearly knew the road well. She was driving as fast as she could, concentrating intensely on the road. The wipers were barely going fast enough to keep the windscreen clear. She heard the click of the priest's beads as he intoned his silent prayers.

"Good," she said, adding, "I sense we are going to need all the prayers we can make."

The first ford was fine. They shot through the shallow water.

"One down, one to go, just keep praying." The car slithered round a sharp bend. Father Aloysius's fingers tightened on the beads, and he continued to pray. There was a fork in the road with a signpost, but they were going too fast to read it. Miss Farrow, gripping the wheel tightly with both hands, with a flick of her head that was designed as a way of pointing with her chin, explained that the turn-off they had just passed was the way they would take to the hospital, which meant they would not have to cross both fords twice.

They descended a steep hill. At the second ford, the stream was clearly rising; the water was deeper, and they splashed through it in a cloud of spray.

"Two down, one to go," muttered Miss Farrow.

Anna was ready for them. As Father Aloysius got out of the car to hold the door open for her, she dashed out from the shelter of the porch. He took her case from her and ushered her into the front seat. The car was already moving as he bundled himself into the back.

The rain was now a deluge. The wipers had difficulty in keeping the windscreen clear. The car was steaming up on the inside, too. Anna adjusted the airflow intake to direct it onto the screen, and it gradually cleared. Despite the restricted visibility, Miss Farrow had hardly slowed at all. They sped down the hill to the river. Water was rushing through the ford. Miss Farrow slammed on her brakes and came to a slithering stop.

"Just as I feared, it's rising by the second." she banged the steering with both hands in her frustration. Father Aloysius leapt out of the back of the car and strode into the river. The water lapped round his calves with such a force that it almost unbalanced him. Miss Farrow wound down her window.

"It's a risk, I know, but we have got to get across, Father, be ready to push." The car inched slowly forward. Father Aloysius splashed after it with both palms on the boot just below the rear windscreen.

"Go, keep going, please God, keep going," he prayed aloud as he pushed, leaning his weight into the vehicle's forward progress. They had reached the middle; there was hope. Perhaps his prayers would be answered. Then, suddenly, the engine spluttered and stalled. With a cry of desperate frustration, the Priest, head down, arms extended, put all his weight into his pushing. He had to keep the car going forward. Miss Farrow kept gunning the engine. The Priest heard a door slam, and there was Anna beside him. Slowly, their combined efforts got the vehicle to the far bank, but there, the slope out was against them. Father Aloysius glanced at the girl; she was soaked.

Through her matted hair, he saw her flash him a smile. Gritting his teeth, he exerted all his strength. Battling with every ounce of their energy, they kept the car going ever so slowly up the slope. At last, the rear wheels were clear of the water. Miss Farrow was about to stop gunning the engine in order to reach for the handbrake when the engine coughed and spluttered into life. The vehicle seemed to leap forward, leaving Anna and Priest sprawling, their feet still in the rushing water. With a cry of joy, Miss Farrow eased her foot down on the accelerator, and the vehicle, coughing and spluttering, moved jerkily up the hill. The Priest pushed himself to his feet and, reaching out to help Anna, he echoed Miss Farrow's shout of triumph with a roar.

"We did it, we did it!" Anna gasped. She squeezed the Priest's helping hand and then, letting go, raised her fists to the heavens in a gesture of defiance. Panting from their exertions, the two watched the car make its erratic progress up the hill. Twice, their hearts were in their mouths when the engine seemed to be threatening to die, but twice, it recovered and eventually disappeared round a corner. Miss Farrow dared not stop until she reached the top of the hill. There was a loud clap of thunder. The two bedraggled passengers turned to face each other.

"Well done, it's follow my leader time, I guess," Father Aloysius set off running up the hill with Anna doing her best to keep up. The girl was exhausted, she was panting heavily, and her legs felt like jelly. Gulping in the air, she staggered on with desperate determination. The Priest glanced behind him, he sensed she was about to collapse. He hurried back to her and took her by the hand. They rounded the corner. There was the car. Encouraged, they redoubled their efforts. To Miss Farrow, it seemed an age before they finally made it. At last, there was Father Aloysius opening the front door for Anna; she ignored it and, opening the rear door, crawled into the back seat. Father Aloysius was about to occupy the front seat when, in a shaking voice, she called for him to join her. He did and was rewarded with a grateful smile before she, leaning against him, rested her head on his shoulder and then took his hand in hers.

"Please," she whispered, "Let's go."

On the ridge, they were exposed to the full force of the gale. The road was flanked with stone walls that served as hedges, and these afforded some protection, but where there were gateways or gaps where the walls had collapsed, the car received a mighty buffeting. Miss Farrow had to modify her speed and be ever ready to compensate for a sideways lurch. A further distraction came from flying debris. The nightmare of their journey was further compounded when rounding a corner, they were suddenly faced by a fallen tree. For a second time, Miss Farrow had to slam on the brakes, and once again, it was Father Aloysius who leapt out to deal with the obstruction to their progress.

"Wait," he shouted to Anna, "I'll call if I need you." He slammed the door behind him. Fortunately, the tree proved to be a sapling. Its trunk had snapped. Had it been uprooted, it might have caused more of a problem, but Father Aloysius was able to heave it round far enough to leave a sufficient gap for the car to get by. He waved Miss Farrow forward and waited until the car was safely through before he got back in. Anna pressed something into his hand. It was his cross, the cross he had given her.

"Thank you," he whispered, and taking her hand in his, he added, "We'll share it."

Chapter Twenty-Six

*In the end, it's not
the years of your life that count. It's the life in your years.*

-Abraham Lincoln

Anna was exhausted. She shivered and found it difficult to stop her teeth chattering. Miss Farrow had the heater turned up high. She hoped the warmth would help dry out her companions' sopping wet clothes. It did a little, although the priest's heavy cassock and his double dousing had made the process for him much slower. Gradually, the warmth helped bring relief from the cold, but the weariness remained. Leaning against the priest gave her comfort. She dozed. For Miss Farrow and the cleric, the drive seemed to go on for an eternity. That the roads were empty of vehicles was a blessing. At last, with a great feeling of relief, they arrived and drew up under the hospital awning outside the entrance. Father Aloysius had gently nudged Anna awake.

"We are there," he whispered softly, and then, in a louder voice, said, "You go in. We'll park the car and then join you."

Anna shook herself; turning to the priest, she said.

"Please don't be long," and then touching Miss Farrow on the shoulder, she added, "Thank you so much, you were just amazing, getting us here safely despite the terrible conditions, thank you and you too, Father, thank you." She hurried off.

"Well done, Miss Farrow, "Father Aloysius added his praise to that of the grateful girl, "Well done, and thank you, mission accomplished despite everything the elements could do to stop us."

"To quote a certain person not a mile away, 'To God be the glory,' but thank you too. Without you, we would still be stuck at that Ford. I am just so glad you could come. It was a team effort. I spotted an empty space just over there, so I suggest you get out here in the dry, it's my turn for a taste of the rain. I'll park the car, and I'll join you at the desk. I don't know about you, but I am desperate for the toilet."

"If you're sure, but just let me get the case from the boot."

Anna paused at the desk just long enough to check whether or not her father had been moved since the last time she had visited him a few days before. He hadn't. Completely oblivious of her dishevelled state and the looks she was getting from passing staff, she hurried off down the corridors to the lifts. At the entrance to the wards, she stopped at the dispenser by the door to apply the disinfectant to her hands. There was a nurse with a trolley who looked at her somewhat quizzically.

"Excuse me, can I help you?" she said. "You do know you are out of visiting hours." The latter was a statement, not a question.

"I'm Anna, Anna Evans. My dad's here, Mr Evans."

"Ah, I see," the nurse's demeanour changed immediately, and she quietly led Anna to the door of her father's room. It was closed. She opened it and whispered.

"Mrs Evans, your daughter's here," then, turning to Anna, she said, "If you need anything, just come to the desk and ask," Anna nodded.

"Thanks." There was a scraping of a chair being moved and the clacking of shoes on tiles, and Mrs Evans appeared. If she was in any way surprised at her daughter's appearance, she did not show it. Mother and daughter embraced.

"Mum, Mum how is he?" Anna asked.

"Thank you for coming, love. He's been looking forward to seeing you, um, when you go in, just smile."

"Father Aloysius is here too, he's with Miss Farrow. They are just parking the car."

"Good, I'm so glad you made it. It must have been quite a drive."

Anna just nodded and taking her cue from her mother's calm demeanour she followed her into the room and prepared herself to smile. Her father was lying on his back propped up by pillows, his eyes closed. His hair had been brushed. He was white but otherwise looked completely at peace. Prompted by her mother she sat on the chair by the bed and leant towards him. His hands pale and so very thin were resting on the blanket. She noticed his nails had been cut. She placed her left hand on his and addressed him in a soft voice.

"Hello, Dad, it's me, Anna."

"Anna, my darling," his eyes opened, his voice was so soft as to be barely audible, "Thank you for coming." He smiled up at her. It was all she could do to stop herself from crying and she so wanted to hug him. Instead she gave him the best smile she could muster.

"Dad I love you." His eyes lit up and he almost chuckled.

"And I love you." he said in a voice that was more Welsh than she had heard for a long time "And now just a word, that Larry is a good boy, give him my best won't you." He was still smiling as his eyes closed. For a moment she thought he had passed on but a very slight squeeze of her hand proved otherwise. She sat gazing at him fondly, typical Dad still thinking about what might be best for her, his statement was a coded message to her. Larry would be so pleased to hear that he had thought of him, but his main concern was obviously for her.

"Yes, Dad," she replied gently, "Larry is a good boy, and he thinks the world of you." Her father's eyes flicked open for a second; his reply took her by surprise.

"He thinks a lot of you too."

Anna felt herself blushing as she laughed to herself, typical Dad, determined to have the last word to the very end. Typical Dad always thinking of others. Her father had slipped back into a semi-conscious state. Her mother was sitting in the other chair in the room, her eyes were closed. She looked weary. Anna wondered how much sleep she had had having spent the previous day and much of the night by her husband's side. A doctor came quietly into the room, she smiled at Anna.

"You must be Mr Evans' daughter," she said quietly. "It's been a long vigil. Your father certainly is a battler, bless him.

"Is he, is ---?"

"Yes, he's slipping away, bless him. He's comfortable, and he's in no pain, a very brave man and a real gentleman."

"Thank you. I'm so glad I got here."

"If you don't mind me saying so, you look as if you have been in a battle yourself, the storm?"

"Yes," Anna suddenly felt very drained.

"You are welcome to use the shower on the ward. I'll get the nurse to put some towels out on the chair in the corridor."

"Thank you, that's kind. You, you you can't tell when can you? The girl asked hesitantly.

"No, dear, you just have to let nature take its course; it could be any moment, it could take a while, but he is at peace bless him."

"Yes, thank you so much," the tears were welling up in Anna's eyes. The doctor took some tissues from the box on the bedside table and handed them to her. Anna wiped her eyes. "I'm sorry." She got to her feet, her mother had woken up. There was a knock on the door, it was Father Aloysius. The doctor excused herself and having greeted the priest left.

"Oh, Father Aloysius, I wondered whether you'd come. He's still with us," Mrs Evans said, "He has just spoken to Anna." she led him to the bedside and, taking the priest's hand, placed it on that of her husband.

"Duncan, it's Father Aloysius." There was a long pause, then just as they were wondering whether he would regain consciousness Duncan Evans opened his eyes.

"Ah you Father, good," the words were mouthed more than said, "I'm glad you've come. I want you to take my funeral."

"Of course, it will be a privilege,"

Duncan Evans raised his eyes to the ceiling as if to indicate his disagreement with the word privilege. The priest, sensing the need for Mrs Evans to be at her husband's side stepped back. She took his place.

"God bless, Jesus loves you," said the priest quietly.

"We all love you," added his wife.

"Yes," he smiled. His eyes closed. Those were his last words.

"He's gone," Mrs Evans stepped forward and kissed her husband's brow. The priest stepped forward and as he gazed down at the man who had been such a good friend to him. He was conscious that in his ministry to the dying he ought to be guided by a religious liturgy, but he resisted the urge to use it. He had mentioned Jesus that was enough, now he needed to respect the views of the man who lay before him so instead of launching into the old familiar words of prayers that had been ingrained into his memory over the years he simply reached out to Mrs Evans and Anna and taking each by the hand quietly prayed.

"Well done brave traveller, well done and thank you. We all leave a legacy when it is our time to go. Thank you for yours, a truly rich legacy of love, of respect, of courage and of wisdom, thank you. You have fought a long battle now you are at peace, well done, well done brave traveller rest well, rest in peace."

It was Mrs Evans who added the word Amen. Anna echoed it. Then, prompted by a mutual need, they all embraced in a collective hug. It would be just the first of the many expressions of grief that, with the emotions of the situation they would find themselves in, would lead to an overwhelming need to seek physical comfort from others. It was significant in being shared by all three, and its memory would be important to each in its own way. The priest was the first to relax his arms. Anna was the last as she clung to him, her face buried hard against his chest, finally, with a little sniff and a mumble.

"Thank you," she let go. Father Aloysius heaved a huge sigh, then quietly went out, closing the door behind him, leaving mother and daughter alone with their grief.

Miss Farrow had been waiting patiently in the corridor. She had not long returned from a foray to find a coffee machine and had wrapped three cups in her coat to keep them warm. She proffered one to Father Aloysius.

"I've not long brought these I hope it's not gone cold." The priest took a sip. It was still warm.

"Thank you it's just what I need right now." He sighed and shook his head.

"How was it?" his housekeeper asked.

Father Aloysius sucked in air and exhaled. "Very peaceful," then added, "They are not all that way." As he said it he suddenly found himself thinking of his father, the gun shots, the flies and the smell of blood.

Chapter Twenty-Seven

*A person's most useful asset
is not a head full of knowledge, but a heart full of love,
and a hand willing to help others.*

It was late when Larry got the text. Anna was brief in the extreme. It just said 'Dad's died.' For a long moment he just sat there on his bed staring at his phone. Then leaping to his feet he smacked his palm hard on the door, before doing the same with both hands on his head. He swore. Fortunately his aunt despite the wind and rain was still out at the pub but Philippa heard him and called out from her bedroom next door, "God what a din, what's up with you?"

"Nothing," then thinking better of it, added, "Old Evans is dead."

"What!" Philippa in her pyjamas rushed into his room, "How do you know? Larry just held up his phone and just said "Anna."

"Let me see." demanded his sister. Larry showed her.

His sister swore. "I can't believe it. Poor Anna. Have you replied?"

"No, it's only just come."

"So?"

"So," her brother returned to his bed and sitting down wrote a reply. "So, so sorry. Anything I can do? love Larry." He pressed the sent button.

"Let me see."

"No, mind your own business, it's gone anyway." His sister throwing Larry's clothes on the floor flumped onto his chair. The two started to share memories of their former headmaster. A reply came from Anna. Larry read it out, it merely said 'Just tell everyone.'

"Everyone!" his sister exclaimed, "What does that mean?"

"It means," explained Larry with exaggerated mock patience, "for us to tell all our mates and to get them to tell everyone else they know."

"Yes, I guess." His sister replied. Larry started to text his friends. The two talked for some time. They were finally interrupted by the return of their aunt. Philippa crept off to bed. When he had sent texts to all the people he could, Larry too, went to bed. It was a long time after that before Larry finally fell asleep. He'd been thinking about what he should do.

The storm blew itself out sometime round midnight. Larry despite his late night was up early. The shop opened at seven. Larry was there. To his disappointment the buckets where they kept the flowers were empty. Mr Fowler, always cheerful and ready to help a prospective customer, told him that he was far too early and there would be flowers later after the morning's delivery. "Come about eleven," he said, "There should be some by then, but even that's a bit early to go courting," he teased and winked at Larry.

"It's nothing to do with courting. Wish it was," Larry responded and went on to explain that Mr Evans had died, and that was why he really wanted the flowers, for Mrs Evans.

"And Anna?" prompted the shopkeeper.

"Yes, and Anna," Larry was conscious that he was blushing.

"Dear me, poor Duncan. He has been ill for a long time, I guess it was only to be expected. So is this public knowledge then that your old headmaster has died?"

"In a way, yes. I got a text from the hospital last night. Anna told me to spread the news, I guess you could help with that please."

"Of course, now that I know it can be shared."

"Thanks I'll be back later." Hardly had he stepped through the door when he remembered he had also wanted a card. Returning to the shop he went to the card display. He was pleased to find that there was a choice of two. He decided to buy one of each and to give one to Mrs Hazelmere. Perhaps she would look more favourably on his request for her to help him make a cake for Mrs Evans and Anna. There was a queue of people buying their daily paper, true to his word Mr Fowler was sharing the news of the death of the headteacher of the village's primary school. When he saw Larry join the queue holding the cards he waved him away, "You can pay for those later when you come for the flowers," he said.

Larry wandered down to the quay and crossed the bridge. He looked for lights in the windows of Mrs Hazelmere's cottage. There were none. He sat on a bench and took a pen from the pocket of his leather jacket. He needed some paper. He wanted to write a rough draft of what he might put on the card for Mrs Evans and Anna. There was a bin nearby. He scrabbled about in it and found a brown paper bag. He smoothed out the creases and set to work. 'Dear Mrs Evans and Anna, thank you, Anna, for your text, what sad, sad news. We feel very upset, but it must be much worse for you.' perhaps so much would be better, he crossed out the last few words of his draft and wrote, 'so much worse for you.'

"Mr Evans was such a wonderful man, the best headmaster ever. He was so kind to me and Philippa. It wasn't as if we were favourites. He had no favourites He was kind to everyone. He just took time to understand you. He helped me into mending bikes. I owe him so much.' Larry paused in his writing and considered how best to end. He drummed his fingers on his forehead. He couldn't say too much there wouldn't be room. After more thought and mutterings of different endings to himself he wrote 'If there is anything we can do to help please, please tell us. We'd like to help, anything just ask. Yours with our love' love, was love too much? No no, he did love Mr Evans. In so many ways he had taken the place of his father when his mother had left. Yes love it would be. He signed off with 'with our love Larry and Pippa'. He was reading his draft through to himself when he heard his name being called.

It was Mrs Hazelmere. She was standing at the door of her cottage.

"Larry," she called out are you all right?

"Yes, yes I'm OK but"

"Come," interrupted Mrs Hazelmere it would be better we talked inside." Larry got up and crossed the quay and followed Mrs Hazelmere into the hall. There was a lot of barking from dogs in another room. "Shut the door please I don't want the dogs to get out." I saw you though the kitchen window and wondered if you needed anything."

"Well, I wanted to talk to you, I, I..."

"Yes?"

"Mr Evans has died."

"Oh no, oh dear, dear dear me poor Louisa, how terrible, when?

"I got a text from Anna last night."

"I see, and how can I help?"

"Well, I thought I'd like to make them a cake and have it done in time for them when they get back from the hospital. Mr Evans was so good to me. He was a dad to me."

"Yes I see, I suppose they were there during that terrible storm." Larry nodded. "It's a lovely thought, and I take it you would like me to help."

"Yes please."

"Fine, I'd be glad to, we could make it here, would that be a help."

"Very much. Thank you," Larry went on to explain how he had called a shop to buy flowers and his arrangement with Mr Fowler to return after the delivery. He held out a card to Mrs Hazelmere. "There were these cards. I got one for you."

His host took the card with a warm smile, "How very thoughtful of you. Was that what you were doing sitting on the bench, writing a card?"

"Yes, just the draft."

"Well there will be time to write it properly when the cake's in the oven baking, we had better get started right away. The first thing we must do is to decide what sort of a cake you want to make. A fruit cake would be nice but it takes four or five hours to bake, a sponge cake or a chocolate cake can take between twenty and thirty minutes."

"Larry decided on a chocolate cake."

"Now we need to see if we have all the ingredients." Then, as an afterthought, she asked, "Have you had breakfast yet." Larry was about to say yes, he had when something about the way Mrs

Hazelmere was looking at him made him realise she knew that he hadn't.

"No."

"Well if you can wait we'll do all the measuring and mixing first and get the cake baking then we can both have breakfast, alright?" Larry was more than happy to agree; he had not expected to be offered breakfast as well as help with making a cake. Larry had learnt to cook of necessity. He often had to make meals for himself and his sister. However, his skills were limited and certainly didn't stretch to making cakes. He had had no idea that a fruit cake for example could take so long to bake. Mrs Hazelmere proved to be a good teacher and, of course, had all the ingredients and the equipment they needed too. Together, they made a good team. While Mrs Hazelmere was giving time to placate her dogs, he could get on with the tasks she had outlined by measuring out the ingredients of the cake they planned on making, and when she returned, all was ready for the mixing. It did not take them long to mix up the ingredients, put it in a cake tin and have it in the oven. Breakfast was next on the agenda.

"Well," declared the lady of the house, "isn't it fortunate I happened to get a dozen eggs yesterday? Baking does tend to require eggs, but we have plenty and so what about eggs and bacon?" For Larry, for whom a cooked breakfast was something he had often dreamed about but had only experienced on very few occasions, eggs and bacon sounded wonderful, and it was. He expressed his appreciation not only with a plate clean of every scrap but also in telling his host that it was the best breakfast he had ever had despite the fact that he had had to break off eating it to take the cake out of the oven, a proud moment for him.

Later that morning, having written his card and accompanied Mrs Hazelmere taking the dogs for their morning, walk Larry crossed the bridge and climbed the hill to the shop. The delivery had been and he selected a bunch of carnations. He was fishing in his coat pocket for the money when Mr Fowler held up his hand and shook his head.

"On the house," he said.

"But what about the cards?" asked Larry.

"The same, on the house, but you can do something for me."

"Of course, I'd be more than glad to. You have been very kind, thank you. What can I do?"

"You'll no doubt be going round to the house to deliver your flowers yourself. You could take this for me. It's from my wife and I." He reached under the counter and lifted up a basket for fruit with a card on the top.

"Wow, that looks lovely. Mrs Hazelmere and I have made a cake. We'll take it all round now."

"Thank you we'd be obliged, you may have to leave it at the front door, I doubt if they will be back from the hospital yet. My wife got a call from her sister shortly after you left this morning. Miss Farrow didn't think they'd be back until after lunch. Apparently she and Anna stayed at the hospital last night. I suspect there is a lot to do. Mrs Evans' had her car there. When the storm abated enough to drive safely my sister in law and Father Aloysius returned here, but they were too late to have evening prayers so that was cancelled but Father Aloysius was here for the morning prayers today. Louisa and Anna may be back for tea and then they will really appreciate your cake, well done."

It was as Mr Fowler had said it might be. There was no one at home when Mrs Hazelmere and Larry called. The house had a covered porch. They left their gifts there. Mrs Hazelmere gave Larry a lift to his work. Earlier he had sent a text to his work to say he would not be in that morning.

Chapter Twenty-Eight

*The best preparation for tomorrow
is to do your best today.*

H. Jackson Brown Junior

For Mrs Evans and Anna there was much to do following the headteacher's death. It was her husband's wish that his body should be cremated and the ashes scattered from the top of the cliffs at a favourite spot of theirs not far from where they lived. Before he had fallen ill, when he had had a busy day at the school and wanted somewhere to 'blow away the cobwebs,' as he called it, he and his wife would take a walk there in the evening. The wake he suggested should be in the school hall, there being no other large buildings other than the church in Pondreath, apart from which it would be fitting as for so many years the school had been his second home.

Duncan Evans was very well respected in the village; he had many friends. For his widow and his daughter, the kindness of their neighbours and friends, and others too in the community, was a great support to them in their grief. Anna was particularly touched by Larry's card and flowers and was impressed with the way he had gone about getting Mrs Hazelmere to help him make the cake. They had once been such good friends, but she was conscious that as they progressed through secondary school, due largely to her own actions, they had had less contact with each other and had seemed to be drifting apart. While she had been rebelling against the constraints of home and what she saw as a small-minded community, he had remained loyal in spite of the shabby way she had treated him. That evening, she phoned to thank him, and they had a long conversation with Larry, reiterating his gratitude to her father for the way he had helped him through difficult times. Anna had never heard him speak with such confidence or such evident emotion before. When eventually they rang off, she was left with a strong feeling that the Larry she knew, or thought she had known, was not the Larry with whom she had just conversed. Too late, she realised that she had not shared with him the fact that Larry was the subject of one of her father's last wishes. She felt a twinge of guilt; she had not been the friend to him that he had been to her, and by not telling him of her father's wishes, she had failed him yet again.

The last few days, the watching and the waiting, of short sleeps snatched at odd moments between the long hours of wondering when the inevitable would finally happen, and then the drama of the storm, such a contrast to her husband's final last hours and eventual passing had left Mrs Evans both physically and emotionally exhausted, and yet from somewhere she needed to find the energy to cope with the next phase, the laying to rest. Anna too, had been stretched to the limits. For both of them it was Father Aloysius and Larry who were to be the vital supports in helping them make the necessary arrangements.

On the morning of the day after Mr Evans's demise and his return with Miss Farrow from the hospital Father Aloysius had just returned to the presbytery from taking the morning service when he had a phone call from Mrs Evans. She wanted to thank him for all his help on the previous day and for his part in the harrowing journey to get Anna to her father's bedside. She sounded tired.

Father Aloysius replied gently, "It was a great privilege for me to be there with you at such a precious time; if you don't mind me saying so, you sound tired, which is very understandable. Is there anything we can do to help? Would you like a visit?"

"Yes, yes," came the reply. "I think that would be helpful. We could talk about what comes next. Duncan left some instructions, but talking it through would be a help, and I'm sure it would help Anna too." It was agreed that Father Aloysius and Miss Farrow would call the following evening. The priest sat quietly for a moment by the telephone. He needed time to think. First, he must inform Miss Farrow. She would be able to give him some valuable advice. He would also benefit from a talk with Commander Nesbitt and, perhaps too, the Rev. Burns. He ought to visit the school. Perhaps that should be his first duty. He decided to phone before going just in case the timing was not right. His call was answered immediately. The school secretary was clearly glad to hear his voice. There was a hasty consultation with Miss Hardcourt, and, yes, the acting headteacher could see him straight away.

Mrs Evans had wasted no time in phoning the school to give the sad news of her husband's passing the morning after his demise. It was well she had made the call early before the school had opened. Anna's text to Larry and his subsequent texting of some of his friends and his early visit to the shop where Mr Fowler had been informed meant that the news was already circulating the village. Miss Hardcourt had been extremely conscientious in visiting her headteacher when he had been at home. She knew he was a very ill man and when he was taken to hospital, she realised that the end was imminent. She had prepared herself for what she knew was inevitable. Even so, that early call from Mrs Evans had been hard to take. It was a struggle to keep her emotions under control and to appear both calm and sympathetic in expressing her deep sorrow. As she put the receiver down she could not help bursting into tears. Duncan Evans had appointed her to her post as his deputy. He had been a wonderful mentor, and they had become good friends. Now, he was gone. She took a box of tissues from the top drawer of her desk and dried away her tears as she steeled herself to meet the demands of another day and the task of sharing the sad fact that Mr Evans would no longer be returning to the institution he had served so well. She had just time to inform the staff personally before the children arrived, but first, she must phone Mr Nesbitt. He was a trusted friend and could be asked to inform the other governors. The

Rev Burns was due to come in to take the assembly. They would have to do it together, but she needed to warn him as he would possibly be setting off to get to the school shortly. Later, after taking the morning Assembly, she would phone Shire Hall and inform the education authority.

She started with the phone calls, making them as brief as possible. Commander Nesbitt, sensing the urgency in her voice, made his response brief. She caught the Rev. Burns just as he was leaving. He, too, was sympathetic to her request to keep their conversation short. She decided to talk to the staff all together in the staff room. She dispatched her secretary to give them the message. Gathering them all together would inevitably take time. She needed to buy some time and went out onto the playground to speak to the duty teacher. She quietly told her the news and then asked her to hold the children outside until she had told all the others. The staff, as she had hoped, had all responded promptly. She did not have to wait long before they were all accounted for. They, as she had been, had been living in the expectation of the time when such sad tidings would come. They listened attentively. Some had guessed what it might be about while on their way to the staff room. They were all completely professional. It was a sombre group that quietly filed out to their classroom to attend to the morning registration. The Rev. Burns was in the office when she returned. They had a moment to plan how they were going to deliver the assembly. She would open and break the news. The Rev. Burns would then speak briefly about the deceased. On a pastoral note, he would appeal to them all to take care of each other and talk about how good families pulled together at such times supporting each other. Their song for the morning would be 'When I Needed a Neighbour.' by Sydney Carter. He would then lead the school in prayers, leaving Miss Hardcourt to deal with any notices and to dismiss the children.

The assembly had been less difficult than she had imagined it would be. She was glad she had been able to prepare her teachers beforehand. She was very conscious of their support as she shared the news with the children. The Rev. Burns spoke in a most moving way about heroes and the way they inspired others to follow their example. Duncan Evans, he said, had been a true hero for the school, and they all must follow his example and be heroes, too. In his prayers he gave thanks for heroes and prayed that each person in the school would be given the strength to be a hero. There followed the song. That morning, the children, following the lead from their teachers, all sang their hearts out. Miss Hardcourt, in addressing the school, asked the school council to report to her office at lunchtime so that they might consider how best the school could respond to the news. She then told the children that if any of them had worries as a result of the news, then they should share these with an appropriate adult, their teacher, or their parent. And so started a new chapter in the life of Pondreath Primary School.

Miss Hardcourt was in her office with the Rev. Burns when the phone call from Father Aloysius came. The Anglican cleric decided it might be best to wait for his arrival before discussing the implications of what the school community now faced. Father Aloysius sensed a deep sadness in the school he visited that morning. Miss Hardcourt greeted him with a gentle smile.

"Thank you for coming. I'm so glad you could join us. Please have a seat. The Rev Burns and I have just broken the news to the school. We decided to wait until you arrived before discussing how best to guide our little community through these very sad times. I hear you were a great help in the ordeal of getting Anna to the hospital in that horrendous storm. Would you like anything to drink, tea perhaps?" The priest declined, as did the Rev. Burns.

The Rev. Burns, prompted by Miss Hardcourt, prefaced their discussion with a moment of reflection and prayer. The vicar then turned to Father Aloysius for an insight into how the family was faring.

"Father Aloysius, we are conscious that as we meet to discuss what we can do to help the community at this most sad time central to all our thoughts are the family and their needs at this most stressful time. Anything we do must be with them in mind and so we need to be very sensitive. You have been caring for their pastoral needs, and am I right in thinking that you were there at the end? Please tell us how was it and how Mrs Evans and Anna are coping?"

The priest, hands still clasped as for prayer, nodded. So much had happened. He glanced briefly out of the window at a sky full of scudding clouds, then, quietly, in a tone of respectful reverence, shared the peaceful nature of Duncan Evans's passing.

He told them of his friend's last wishes and of what he learnt from Mrs Evans and Anna about the instructions he had left regarding the funeral and that, above all, the headteacher wanted a quiet private cremation and a scattering of ashes from the cliff top. It seemed he did not want a fuss. In this, they faced the challenge of balancing the wishes of the deceased with the needs of the community. Duncan Evans, by nature of his role and the way he performed that role, had been a central figure in the lives of so many of the people in the village. He had come to Pondreath an outsider.

The Cornish have a strong sense of their own identity. They are a proud people. The communities, especially the smaller ones, are close-knit. Outsiders have to work hard to gain acceptance. Duncan Evans had not only done that, he had won their respect, and even their admiration and love. They, too, would need and deserve to be considered in the plans. Like the family, they needed to feel a sense of closure. That might require an opportunity for a public gathering, but how would the family feel and respond to this? It was agreed that Father Aloysius would have a crucial role as a go between for the family and the school. As for the immediate needs of the school, the two clerics agreed to stay and to be a presence in the staff room and on the playground during break and also to return at the end of the school day for the last two remaining days of the week, to be a visible presence at the school gate. Father Aloysius was able to get advice from the Rev. Burns regarding the crematorium and arranging the simple service. He and his wife would both call at the Evans home during the course of the next week. As Father Aloysius left the school, he was hailed by Commander Nesbitt.

He was on his way to the shop to purchase, among other things, a sympathy card; he also wanted to inquire about Father and how he was after the ordeal of the storm and, of course, to talk about the needs of the family. Father Aloysius invited his friend back to the presbytery, where he once again relived the events of the previous two days and also reported on the meeting he had just attended at the school.

The commander was in full accord with the views of the Rev Burns on the need for the community to have something in the way of a ceremony or celebration to give them a sense of closure.

"Duncan was a bit of a living legend in this community. All these small Cornish communities have their oral histories, their communal memory of times past. They all have strong links with the sea and fishing, and most have had their share of tragedies.

They are no strangers to times of public mourning for the loss of one of their own, and it all becomes part of the communal memory, helping to bond the community. Duncan is now a precious memory. He has a place in our history. In his service to the school, while living, he has been instrumental in enhancing that bonding process that will continue for years beyond the grave. Yes, there needs to be some public event. Perhaps it could involve the school, the dedication of a plaque, or something like that. I'll ask the others in the governing body. I know the P.T.F.A. is thinking of doing some fundraising for an outside classroom. Perhaps it could be named after Duncan."

While the two men had been talking, Miss Farrow had been busy in the kitchen preparing a light lunch. In perfect timing with the end of their discussions, she came in to announce lunch was ready and invited the commander to stay for a bowl of soup and some salad and sandwiches. He was only too pleased to accept. Father Aloysius could not but help feeling he had had a good morning, with two instructive and informative meetings, and now he was hosting the commander under his own roof, which would go a small way to repaying him for the very generous hospitality shown to the priest on previous occasions.

Later that afternoon, Father Aloysius was able to tell the Rev. Burns about his fortuitous meeting with the Commander and of his ideas of involving the P.T.F.A. in their project of an outdoor classroom. The lines of communication had been well established. Again, the priest felt a sense of satisfaction.

When the next evening, Father Aloysius kept his appointment with Mrs Evans and Anna, he was both surprised and pleased to find Larry there. They had a tap dripping in the bathroom. It was time it was fixed. She thought of Larry and wondered if he could do it. She phoned. He had just got home from work when he received the call.

His heart skipped a beat when he heard her voice, and he leapt at the opportunity to see her. Gathering his tools, he had gone straight over. He hoped she had a washer. She greeted him at the door with a kiss on the cheek.

"Larry, thank you for coming, and thank you for the cake. It's delicious. You will have to have some."

"Well, as I said on the back of my card, it was Mrs Hazelmere, really. Now I hope you've got a washer."

"Will these do? I went scrabbling around in the garage. I knew Dad had some somewhere, I found these."

Yes, they look like what we need, but we won't know for sure until we get the tap stripped down."

She led him into the bathroom and showed him the tap. "I looked on YouTube how to do it, but then I thought of you and your practical skills, and I thought Larry is the man for the job. I hope you don't mind."

"Of course not. I said on my card, just ask. I'm glad you did, especially if it involves cake. Can I see the YouTube instructions, please? But first, you'd better show me where the main tap is. I'll have to switch the water off, so you'll need to fill the kettle and a few saucepans just in case." Anna showed him where the mains tap was, and after doing as he suggested and filling the kettle and two large saucepans with water, they turned off the water supply, and she fetched her phone and got the YouTube instructions up on the screen. She stepped close to him so they could watch them together. He was very conscious of her proximity. Was it her scent he could smell, or was it something in the bathroom?

"We're expecting Father Aloysius any minute. He coming to talk about the funeral arrangements, not that there is much to discuss. Dad wanted it all to be very private and low-key, just family, which in reality means just Mum and me."

"I see. I hope I won't be in the way. You can leave me to get on with this, and I'll see myself out."

No, of course, you won't be in the way," she reached out and touched his arm, "In fact, you are very welcome to join us. I have had texts from Tina and Will, and Mr and Mrs Tarrant phoned. I suspect you have been telling everyone. Quite a few of his old pupils from way back have been phoning."

"I hope that's OK You did say tell everyone."

"Yes, of course it is. I meant what I said, and it's been lovely for Mum to get the calls from his old pupils, so affirming the community is being so good. It's made all the difference to Mum. When we got home, she was exhausted; we both were, but everyone has been so kind it's made all the difference."

"Good, I'm glad. I was worried for a moment."

"Silly," she teased, and then switching suddenly to a more earnest and serious tone, she added, "Larry, there is something I should have mentioned the other night when I phoned to say thanks for the cake. Dad...." She was interrupted by a ring of the doorbell. "That'll be Father, I'll tell you later." She left to welcome the priest, calling out as she went to answer the door, "We'll be in the lounge. Join us when you've finished, and if you need anything, just shout".

"Fine, "Larry replied, then shaking his head, he muttered to himself, "Careful boy, careful, just control your feelings, can't read too much into...." he left the rest of the sentence unsaid as he turned his attention to the tap and set to work. The YouTube instructions had been most helpful, and it took Larry less time than he had anticipated.

He turned the mains on again and checked the tap. The washer seemed to have done the trick. Feeling rather pleased with himself, he tidied up his tools, wiped the basin down, and went to join in the discussion. The lounge door was closed, but he could hear voices. He knocked gently.

"Come in," both Mrs Evans and Anna called out in unison. Anna got up to meet him.

"How did it go?" She enquired.

"All done. I've switched the water back on and tested it, and it seems fine."

"Oh great, thank you so much. Come and sit down, and I'll fetch you some tea and..." she added in a theatrical voice, "The cake!"

"Welcome, Larry. Come and sit down, and thank you for doing the tap. It's been dripping for ages."

"Glad to be able to help," Larry replied, sitting in the chair next to his host that had been proffered. "I hope you don't mind my being here," he added, looking earnestly at his host.

"Not at all. You'll be able to help us. You know so many of Duncan's former pupils, and I am very grateful to you for spreading the word. I've had several calls, and they have said such nice things about him."

"Good, your husband was a wonderful man, and he was such a help to me. He helped me get into mending bikes. He was like a dad to me."

"Yes, I know, and you've been the same to us," she took her handkerchief from where she had tucked it into her sleeve and dabbed the tears from her eyes. "Everyone has been so kind. I can't begin to tell you what a help it's been."

For Father Aloysius, having Larry there was a boon. His taking the initiative and spreading the word and the response that it had generated all made it easier for the priest to broach the need for some action, some event that would give the village an opportunity to share in the grieving process and to get some sort of closure. But first, they would have to plan the visit to the cremation and then the scattering of the ashes.

The priest had given the matter a lot of thought. He was concerned.

He had risen early that morning, as was his habit, but he had changed his routine. He always visited the pond first to see if there was any evidence of vandalism, which thankfully there had not been, proving that, although the police did not have the resources to investigate the original vandalism, the actions that had been taken had been deterrent enough. Next, he took one of two different routes. The first took him down to the quay and along the path to the beach, where he enjoyed running barefoot on the sand. He returned up the steep steps to the path that led to the headland and then home. The second went the opposite way round. On this particular day at the quay, he had crossed the bridge and made his way up to the top of the town, passing close to where the Evans' lived. He had followed the path along the cliffs. It was a crisp morning, and the sky was clear. The views out to sea and along the coast were breathtaking. As he ran, taking in the majestic sweep of the bay, the soft white sands and the dark hard rock of the cliffs, the wide horizon and the sea with the relentless waves forever marching on towards the beach and tumbling white and frothy against the rocks of the headland, he had imagined Duncan and Louisa Evans walking the path he now followed, and he could well understand why it was one of their favourite walks and why Duncan had chosen these cliffs to be the place where his last remains were to be scattered. It did not take him long to reach the spot where he imagined that the final ritual would take place. He had stopped. Reaching high, he raised his hands to the heavens and prayed, giving thanks for the wonder and beauty of the place and praising his God for creation. He gave thanks, too, for the life of his friend. He had prayed for the day and his own part in it, and for Anna and for her mother, for Larry, for Miss Farrow and the school, and for all for whom Duncan had been such a special person, naming them one by one. He had felt very humbled when Duncan, on his death bed, had charged him with the task of presiding over his last rites. As he had stood there ankle-deep in the wet heather, Father Aloysius had asked his maker to make him worthy of that honour.

It had been later, when he had returned exhilarated, that he had wondered how best to approach his scheduled meeting with Louisa Evans and her daughter. He needed to be well prepared. To that end, Father Aloysius had spent much of the rest of the morning making phone calls. The Rev. Burns had been a great help in giving him his advice, and he had followed this up by phoning the crematorium. They, too, had been most helpful in providing names and telephone numbers of those he might like to contact to arrange for a simple cremation. He had obtained three quotes from three different undertakers who provided such a service. These he had brought with him.

He had also reflected on what he might say both at the crematorium and then on cliff tops when they committed his friend's ashes to the winds.

Anna came in with the tea on a tray. She placed this in front of her mother and returned to the kitchen for the cake and plates. While her mother poured out the tea, Anna cut the cake. It was not lost on

Larry that he was given a particularly large piece. By way of making conversation while they enjoyed their tea, Anna asked the priest how many funerals he had taken. He replied that he did not really know but quite a number.

"Were they mostly in Africa?"

"Yes, I guess the majority were, I suppose, but I have taken quite a number of funeral services here, too."

"They must be very different."

"They can be, but you must remember Africa is a vast continent and that its population is made up of many different people. One tribal group may have very different customs from another, and of course, Africa is changing, and many of the old customs are giving way to different ways of doing things. This has been the case in the country of my birth with the spread of Christianity and the growing influence of Islam in the north."

"Were your parents Christian?"

"No, they were not. Being wandering nomadic pastoralists, they never had the opportunity to hear the Gospel. The part of Africa where I was born was a wild and lawless place, but..." The priest paused; his hesitation was born out of respect for both his friendship with Duncan Evans and out of respect for his father. The present concern was to do the best for Duncan, his family, and the community and not to allow anything to distract him from that. As for his father, well, his father would have believed it was not good to speak of the dead, and he wanted to respect that, too.

"I'm sorry, you told me that you did not know where they were buried, so they didn't have a Christian burial then?

"No," Father Aloysius shook his head."

"So, what was the custom in your tribe?"

Father Aloysius looked down. Slowly, he carefully placed his cup on its saucer and raised his left hand to his head, his long fingers massaged his brow. He sighed. The memories came flooding back, as they always did when his past was the topic of conversation, the sound of gun shots, the cries of terror, the bleating of the goats, the stink of the hyena, and the buzzing of the flies.

"I'm not sure you want, ought, to hear about that now," he looked at Anna, "Maybe some other time," then, changing the subject, he thanked Mrs Evans for his tea and complimented Larry for his part in making the cake.

"I am conscious that these are sensitive times. Perhaps before we start to consider what we need to do to honour a very special and precious person, we might benefit from a moment of silent reflection and think about Duncan Evans, much-loved husband and father, headteacher, mentor, friend, and a hugely respected member of the community." He laid his hands palm up on the table and closed his eyes. In that poignant moment of quiet as they grappled with their own individual emotions, each, in their own way, felt the presence of the man they had lost very close.

The silence was broken by a sob. Louisa Evans quietly reached out to hold her daughter's hand.

"Thank you," Father Aloysius ended the time of reflection. Quietly and methodically, he reported on his morning activities to prepare for this moment and what needed to follow. Now, it would be up to the family to decide.

Mrs Evans put an arm round her daughter's shoulders.

"Thank you, Father, for all you have done. It would seem sensible to choose the undertaker nearest to us to provide a simple cremation. It will be just family, as Duncan wished, that is, Anna and me with you, Father, to guide us. We would like to drape the coffin with the Welsh Flag and have ' O Land of my Fathers' sung in Welsh by the Pendyus Male Voice Choir. I know we haven't got very long, but would it be all right to have some readings?

"I'm sure that would be quite in order," replied the priest. What have you in mind?"

"My husband left some suggested readings in his instructions. He grew up in a mining village. The family was devout Baptists, and he, as a lad, spent a lot of time in the chapel.

He knew his Bible well. Of course, we all know how he changed and came to be a staunch atheist. He has suggested reading from the Old Testament it's that one that is often chosen on such occasions: Ecclesiastes three verses one to eight. We wondered if you could read that for us, Father?"

"Certainly, it would be a privilege; it's a lovely reading."

"Then we'd like Dylan Thomas, Under Milk Wood. Anna and I read it as a party piece just last March on the occasion of his birthday. He was fifty, and we had organised quite a big bash for him, and there were lots of his friends there, some from his childhood days in the valleys. It's sad to think, for many of them, it was the last time they would see him. Anyway, he loved the poem, and it went down very well. We'd like to read it together. It will be a reminder of happy times."

"Perfect, anything else?"

"Well, it's quite a long piece, so we probably better leave it at that. For our second bit of music, we'd like Beethoven's 'Ode to Joy.' Of course, it's far too long to play the whole thing, but we could just have the final chorus. We could go out to that."

"Anna, is there anything you'd like to add or say?"

"No, I don't think so. Mum and I have discussed it. We think Dad would approve."

Choosing that last bit of music was the most difficult bit. Music was so important to Dad. That's why he put such a lot of effort into it at the school. It gave him a great buzz to hear his pupils perform that and sport. Dad lived a life full on; he was a happy person by nature, and he liked his classical music, so what better than 'An ode to joy."

"Well done, that leads us on nicely to the scattering of ashes,"

"Yes," It was Mrs Evans who took the lead again. "Again, private, just you, Father, me, and Anna, and you have taken the trouble to walk the cliffs and probably know the exact spot, or in any case, know what it's like. The view is breathtaking, especially on a fine day. I know we can't guarantee that, but whatever the weather, it's spectacular. There's almost no need for words, we'd like to let nature do the talking. All we need to say is bye-bye."

"Or perhaps au revoir?"

"Yes, for you, Father volunteered Anna, "Dad once told me 'you only get one chance at life, and that's it, that's why it's so important to give it your best shot!"

"That's what he used to say to us," Larry agreed. "When we were representing the school at football, he'd say, 'I don't care who wins, what's important is to give it your best shot.' That's what really matters."

"You can say 'Au revoir' Father, but we'll probably just say bye-bye. Mum, what about that Irish blessing, Father Aloysius might like to say that?" suggested Anna.

"Yes, he could, but we might want to edit the last line. Your dad wouldn't have used the word God, and as you have said, he didn't believe in life after death. Perhaps we could leave out the bit about meeting again and God holding him in his hand and say.

"May the rains fall soft upon your fields, and we will hold your memory in our hearts as long as we live."

"Yes, I could certainly say that if it is your wish. Is that it? We have got the crematorium sorted and the scattering of ashes unless there is anything else?"

"There's one other thing, or perhaps two other things, the time, and both Anna and I would like both to happen sooner rather than later if possible."

"Well, we will do our best. I can make myself available at any time. We can ring up the undertakers and the crematorium tomorrow first thing. That's one thing, what about the other? What's that?"

"Well, Duncan was adamant we should have a wake and that it should be in the school hall."

Anna glanced at the clock on the mantelpiece. "Another job for tomorrow,"

"Yes, phoning the school and deciding on caterers."

"I have a suggestion about that if it's all right to give an idea." Larry suddenly felt very self-conscious but was encouraged by Anna's smile and her mother's quick affirmation that they would be pleased to hear his views.

"I remember when I was at school, and we had that farewell for our old deputy, Mrs Pearce, who had been at the school for ages. The P.T.F.A. got everyone involved in the celebration meal; everyone brought something. It was all laid out on a big table in the hall, and you helped yourself. I seem to remember the school cook did a lot of baking of bread and made lots of cakes. My mother put her name down to make a salad bowl, and she also provided a plate of those little sausages you eat on sticks." Louisa Evans thought for a moment,

"Thank you, Larry, it's an interesting idea. What do you think Anna?"

Anna, eager to support Larry, smiled at him again, "It would mean everyone had a chance to express their thanks to Dad in a practical way. We all like to feel we are helping on occasions like this. It needs coordinating. I'm sure the school cooks would help, and I'm certain Dad would have liked the idea. He was all for the things that brought the community together; that's why he was so interested in your school gardening project, Father."

Louisa Evans turned to the priest, "Well, what do you think, Father Aloysius?"

"Good idea, eating together is always good, and everyone making a contribution would really make it a shared experience."

Father Aloysius had been worried about how he was going to broach the subject of involving the community in a public act of paying tribute to a man many people admired. Now Larry had done it for him. All his worries had proved unfounded. He was able to share with the grieving family the events at the school the previous day and the suggestion that had come from the governing body that perhaps they could launch an appeal for the building of the outside classroom that Duncan and the school P.T.F.A. had been intending to make their next project. It could be named after Duncan.

Having broached the subject, he was relieved when the idea met with warm approval.

"Well," concluded Mrs Evans, "We seem to have covered most things, and now we can move forward. Thank you so much, Father, and thank you, Larry. I don't know about you, Anna, but I am pleased to say I feel a lot better now than I was this morning."

"Yes, Mum. Dad always said, 'a problem shared is a problem halved," With all of Father's work and Larry's suggestions and, of course, the cake, it's all coming together, and people are being so kind and helpful, especially you two." She smiled at both the priest and Larry.

The priest returned to the presbytery content. His hard work and preparation had paid off. Of course, there was a lot to do, but that could wait for another day. For the present, the bishop would be in Truro the next day. He was due to make his next confession.

He would need to prepare. How successful had he been in seeing the red lights and in heeding them, and what would the bishop think of a priest who got involved in pub brawls, he wondered.

Chapter Twenty-Nine

*Leaders inspire
accountability through their ability
to accept responsibility before they
place the blame.*

-Courtney Lynch

Father Aloysius entered the confessional and knelt. He felt he had prepared well and was at ease. The bishop welcomed him and asked God's blessing on this sacrament of penance, to which Father Aloysius replied in the usual way as he bent his head.

"Bless me, Father, for I have sinned. It is now some months since I made my last confession. Then, I confessed my feelings of inappropriate desire, lust towards a vulnerable minor, and my anger when subjected to what I considered to be racial abuse. I was counselled to think of red lights and to use them as a warning sign to help me when I am tempted to sin. I was counselled to avoid situations where I knew I would be vulnerable to temptation, to pray, and to have a sense of humour. In matters regarding my temptation to lust, I consider I have made some progress and have used prayer and the red lights, both of which have helped." He went on to explain that sometimes circumstances made it impossible to avoid situations that increased the possibility of temptation but that he had been able to resist the temptations. He gave examples of such times, one being the storm and the events surrounding the escape from the river at the ford.

He then turned to anger. He had not been entirely successful in using the red lights as a warning and had provoked reactions from others that might have, even should have been avoided. His actions had led to other people being tempted to commit mortal sins. He related the events he had already reported to the bishop regarding Sid Trevinian. All this had taken some time. The bishop, conscious that his priest's knees might be getting sore, invited him to use the chair in the confessional and to sit. It was with relief that the priest sat with clasped hands, waiting in anticipation for the bishop's response.

"Thank you, my son. In many things, you have acquitted yourself well, but tell me, do you think it is time for a move?"

This came as something of a bombshell.

"A move!" it was the last thing Father Aloysius had expected his superior and mentor to suggest. His surprise was clearly evident.

"You sound surprised, it's happened before."

"But, I um..." The priest was at a loss for words. The bishop waited patiently while he ordered his thoughts, "If you mean my move from Zimbabwe, then that was a completely different situation. You can't compare Harare to Cornwall, surely."

"You are right, of course. However, your life was in danger in Harare, but is that not the case now. Hasn't Mr Trevinian threatened to kill you? Death is death, pretty final both in Zimbabwe and here."

"So you would move me for my own protection?"

"Protection, yes, but also to remove you from temptation. If you returned to Africa, and Africa is a big place, so it would not be to Zimbabwe, you would be less likely to face racial abuse....... the Lord's prayer."

"You mean lead us not into temptation and deliver us from evil?"

"Precisely."

"Tell me please, bishop, would you? Do you honestly think you would be able to replace me at St. Prodricks?"

The bishop considered for a moment before replying, "Possibly not, and it would be even more unlikely to find someone with your considerable gifts. However, nothing is impossible for God."

"Yes, well, of course, I would go wherever I am sent, but …"

"But what, be frank, tell me how would you feel?"

"Disappointed, I'd thought I'd done with running away. I think I have made a good stab at settling down in Pondreath, and it's given me great satisfaction, what with the school and the youth club and all the people I visit."

The bishop nodded, "Well, yes, you have certainly done something that very few of our clergy in this diocese have done, and that is you have worked wonders for the youth in your parish. We have also been impressed with the way you've been working with the Rev. Burns on visiting. As you may have gathered, it would be my wish that all of our clergy were more ecumenically minded." The bishop took some sheets of paper from his briefcase and unfolded them.

"Please bear with me. I'd like to read you part of two letters I have had. The first is from a lady, 'Dear bishop, I am writing to you to commend your appointment of Father Aloysius to our parish; he is an excellent priest and has worked wonders for our young people. He preaches well and is very conscientious in his visiting. However, there is another thing that I must mention. Yesterday evening, a person who shall remain nameless took it upon himself to kick one of my dogs. This person is renowned for his boorish behaviour and for his physical strength. Father Aloysius saw the incident and hastened to my aid. He then, in my opinion, acted with considerable courage by going into the public house to confront this bully. I am very grateful to him for coming so fearlessly to my aid.'

The second letter is from a gentleman; he also commends your courage and the fearless way you confronted the assailant of the lady's dogs. He goes on to describe what happened in the public house and how you evaded being hit and escaped the attentions of four perusers who followed you out.

He mentions drugs, ' I think you probably know that like many of our communities, Pendon Bay and probably Pondreath have a drug problem. Father Aloysius, by raising this issue through pointed remarks and questioning, is now at risk from reprisals. I think you ought to know about this. I have advised him to mention his suspicions to the police.' I believe he may have done this already."

"Thank you. I had not realised my friends had written to you. They are generous in their views, and yes, I have informed the police. They have issued a warning, but there being no clear evidence, they can do no more at this point. The gentleman in question is a long-distance lorry driver and has been away from home on some long trips recently. As I understand it, he has only been back briefly at weekends since. Least ways I have not seen him."

"Well, that is for the good. I am not going to ask you to move. In fact, it was never my intention, but I needed to be certain you did not feel it would be desirable, and if in the future you have a change of mind, please don't hesitate to inform me. However, I will say this: you need to take care. Racial slurs will hurt, and you have my sympathies, but you must find a way to ignore them, to turn the other cheek. You don't need me to remind you that our Lord suffered taunts and rejection, too. The lesson of the cross is forgiveness. Easier said than done, I know. Your penance and mine too, on your behalf, is to pray for those who revile you and especially for your would-be assailant. Look for opportunities for reconciliation. That must be our hope, and your duty is to search for them. This must be a daily task, praying for yourself that you may find strength and wisdom. Wisdom to recognise the red lights, and in so doing heed them, and find the strength to resist temptation. Now, last, but by no means least, thank you for all you are doing to build the Kingdom in the place you have been sent. God Bless you." The Bishop then recited the absolution prayer.

Miss Farrow was pleased to see the priest return smiling. She knew he had not been looking forward to his confession. It seemed to have gone well, or at least better than he had expected. He would be better company on the way back to Pondreath. He was.

He even laughed when Miss Farrow narrowly missed going through a red light. She could not understand why, but she was grateful for all that.

Being the housekeeper to a cleric was sometimes not as straightforward as it would seem. Having been appointed by the bishop, she, like Father Aloysius, was accountable to him. There had been occasions when the bishop had phoned her to ask after his priest. He had been concerned for the cleric's welfare, especially in the early days after his appointment. A recent call, however, had surprised her. The bishop had enquired about Father Aloysius's relations with Sid Trevinian and also with Anna Evans.

Regarding the former, she had been able to explain the situation regarding the Trevinian family and felt perfectly at ease in doing so. With Anna, it was different.

She was conscious that Anna was going through a difficult time and that she had gone to Father Aloysius for help. She was conscious, too, that he had felt himself to be vulnerable to her attentions. She was a young and impressionable girl and had found him attractive. For his part, she had observed he had done his best to avoid being alone with her. She was certain in her own mind that he had been completely honourable in all his relationships with both her and all the other ladies he visited. She had at first resented the bishop using her as it seemed to check up on his priest, but having given the matter some thought, she realised the bishop was in an invidious position and was probably right to have made enquiries. She had endeavoured to be frank with him, but it had not been easy. She felt guilty and told the bishop so. He had apologised for having put her in a difficult position but had gently explained his position and his responsibilities. This further helped her see the wisdom of his actions. Being accountable for others was a huge responsibility. She did not envy him.

Chapter Thirty

*Unity is strength
where there is teamwork wonderful
things can be achieved.*

-Mattie Stepanik

The next fortnight was a busy time for Louisa Evans and her daughter. It was an exceptionally busy time for Larry. He had taken it upon himself to help with the planning of the wake. He was greatly assisted in this by the school, by Miss Farrow and the Rev. Burns and his wife, and, of course, by Father Aloysius. The family had expressed a wish that the funeral should be sooner rather than later, so the first priority was to fix a date, arrange for the cremation and the scattering of ashes, and spread the word about the commemorative event of thanksgiving at the school.

Father Aloysius, with Louisa Evans, arranged for the cremation to be on a Thursday early in the morning. Father Aloysius would collect the urn with the ashes the next day, and they would scatter them according to her husband's wishes. That Friday evening after school, they would hold the wake in the school hall.

The Rev. Burns, along with Mrs Evans, composed a short announcement in the local paper and also in the paper that served the Welsh village where Duncan Evans had grown up. Duncan's brother, who still lived in the area, also undertook to spread the word and to arrange for an announcement to be made in the Baptist Church that he and his family had attended in their childhood. Larry, with the help of the school secretary, compiled lists of former pupils. He contacted those he could by phone. He asked them to pass on the message to others whose numbers he did not have. The school put out a letter to all the parents telling them of the date and time of the wake and asking for volunteers to provide food. Larry worked with the P.T.F.A. and the cooks in the kitchen, and the school office kept records of replies.

Father Aloysius changed the routine for his early run. Each day, he made his way to the spot on the coastal walk where the ashes of his friend would be cast to the winds. He would read the passage from Ecclesiastes chapter Three, verses one to eight, and meditate on the passage, a verse a day. It was on the third day when he read, 'A time to kill and a time to heal, a time to break down, and a time to build up,' He was struck by the strangeness of fate. What was he, a child of Africa, doing here gazing out over the sea to a far distant horizon? Why, as a child, the sea had never even entered his imagination. Here, high on the cliffs, he was close to nature, but how different this nature was to the nature of his young days. Born in a primitive hut made of skins, sticks, and dung in a stockade created from the thorn scrub, the grass turned green after the rains but for much of the year was grey-yellow or dull sun-faded brown. There, the natural world was so very different and very close. In fact, he had lived cheek by jowl with sun-scorched earth and the sun-bleached grass that was the fodder for his father's flocks of camels and goats and the donkey and his cows, all of whom he knew intimately. From a young age, it was his job to mind them, to drive them from the stockade in the morning to their grazing grounds and the watering hole in the river. The river that was dry for much of the year but where water could be found by digging down in the sandy bed was so different from the streams and rivers of Cornwall. Yes, water much of the time. No, most of the time was scarce, and now here he was, gazing out over endless stretches, miles upon miles of ocean. The water of those wells was muddy brown, sometimes slimy green; this ocean was so blue, so many shades of blue.

What was this child of Africa doing here reading from a book written centuries ago about a time lost in the mists of the past, in a country he had never visited? Why, as a child, the concept of the country was not yet part of his world. 'A time to kill.' Yes, they had certainly done that.... and there mingling with the sound of the wind and the screeching of the gulls that filled his ears, the sound of the guns, and the cries of the dying and the buzzing of the flies that gathered round the corpse-filled his mind. A time to kill, surely that was not part of God's plan, but then he hadn't known about God then. Then killing was what people did, what warriors did; violent death was never far away. A little bird cheeping in a gorse bush close by caught his attention and brought him back to the present, but only for a moment. Little brown thing, so dull compared with the weaver birds that built great intricate nests in the thorn trees of the acacia scrub of his childhood home. Smiling, he recalled the cry of the hornbills and the chatter of the guinea foul with their bright blue helmeted heads bobbing as they scuttled about in the undergrowth, but all that was a long time ago, many, many miles away, a world away, a time before he had met God at the mission station, and it was their God the God of the white man, that God that had brought him here.

'A time to heal,' well, yes, that maybe was why he was here. He was here to heal or to help in the healing of broken hearts and shattered dreams, to bring hope, and to build for life beyond the present after the healing. Perhaps that was why he was here. A time to heal; in helping to heal others, he was healing himself. God knows he needed it. He was a man whose life seemed to be destined to be dogged by trauma. Each trauma had left its scars. He had had help, help from the priests at the mission in his homeland, help from a psychoanalyst specially trained in dealing with trauma, when after his experiences in prison in Harare, he had been brought back to Dublin, to the seminary where he was trained, where he became a priest. He was a broken wreck, but he had had help. There are traumas so unspeakable that leave such deep wounds that one is left wondering, despite all the help, whether you ever really get over them. Perhaps that was why he was here. He was here to heal and also to be healed, fully healed.

A gust of wind, cold and clutching at his shorts, once again brought him back to the present. He shook himself out of his reverie and ran back, back to be part of the healing and the building.

Immediately after her husband's passing, Louisa Evans was exhausted, numbed by fatigue, but then the reality of her situation, of being a widow, no longer a wife, a cook, a carer, a nurse for the man she had chosen to be her soul mate, that reality began to sink in.

Fortunately, there was so much to be done that she had little time for self-pity, and fortunately, too. The healing began. Larry's diligence in contacting so many of her husband's former pupils brought a flood of cards of condolence through the letter box.

All had heartfelt expressions of gratitude for the part their headteacher had played in their lives. Many of them contained memories. These were a great comfort to her, as, too, were the ministrations of her friends and local community. Everyone had gathered round, and their support made all the difference.

For Anna, there was a growing realisation of the part Larry was playing in their lives.

A number of cards they had received had referenced that they had heard the sad news from Larry. His loyalty and the quiet, tactful way he was working on their behalf made a big impression on her. For her, the healing process was all bound up with the realisation that he cared for her. There was hope.

On the morning of the cremation, Father Aloysius rose an hour before his usual time. He put his cassock on over his running gear and went into the church. In the dark, he knelt before the altar. His prayers were to Mary, Mary who, in the words of the Apostle John, had stood on the slopes of Golgotha near to the cross and had watched her son die, Mary, to whom the angel had come when she was just a slip of a girl to give her the news that she was to be the mother of God's son, "Mary," he whispered the words. "Mary, obedient Mary, called to be the mother of the son of God, called to give birth to love, love such as the world had never known before, love, so pure, so perfect, so forgiving, be with me, be with us today and fill us with that perfect love, and may the soul of Duncan Evans rest in peace."

Peace was the last word of the passage he had been asked to read. "Please, Mary, intercede for us sinners and give to Duncan, give to us your peace." The priest groped for his beads as he sought the support of the old familiar words of the Angelus. Then, making the sign of the cross, he rose and, having hung his cassock up in the vestry, left the church.

In the soft early light of dawn, he made his way down to the bridge to climb up through the village to the coastal path along the top of the cliffs. He was at ease with himself; his mind was at rest as he ran, allowing himself to appreciate, with all his senses, the quiet beauty of a new day. Then he saw them, two figures, dark against the skyline, hurrying along the path ahead of him. They stopped.

They had reached the spot chosen for the dispersal of the ashes. He slowed; should he go on, he wondered. They were facing the sea. One turned, it was Anna; she waved a hand beckoning him on. He joined them, Anna and Larry. No one spoke. Anna took both of her companions by the hand, and they stood still and silent, just gazing out across the ocean to the distant horizon where the sky met the water. There was no need for words, and there were none, not then in the peace of that moment of silent communion with nature nor in the return journey along the path. They walked in file, Father Aloysius at the rear. When they reached the spot where the path met the lane just before the first houses, they stopped, looked at each other, and smiled. Larry raised an arm in salute, and they went their separate ways. Later, much later, they would be able to speak to each other about that moment, and none of them was surprised to learn that each had felt a deep sense of peace.

In that strangely precious moment on the cliff top, they had all drawn strength from each other, a strength that was to support them in their various roles at the crematorium, a strength that allowed Anna to achieve quiet confidence as she greeted Father Aloysius and Miss Farrow and then moments later Larry at the door of the Evans home. Miss Farrow had agreed to act as chauffeur. Larry was to mind the house in their absence and prepare a good breakfast for them when they returned. The sun was shining in a cloudless sky. Anna was almost joyful in her appreciation of the bird song and the filigree glint of dew-wet spider webs draping clumps of grass on the verges.

"Dad would have loved this," she exclaimed as they drove round the bend, and there was the sea and the white-topped waves tumbling and frothing up a deserted beach.

Anna had never attended a crematorium service before, and their visit, scheduled for eight o'clock out of respect for her father's views, was not a service or certainly not a service in conventional terms. Her Grandmother had been a Baptist. She had lived with them for the last year of her life. Her funeral had been a conventional church funeral. That was when Anna was younger, but she still remembered it. She was curious as to what sort of place a crematorium might be. She was surprised to find the building was quite modern and that everything was neat and simple, and ordered. There was an air of dignified solemnity about the place. There were graves, of course, but there were flower beds too, all well attended and neat.

As they followed Father Aloysius through the heavy oak doors, Anna took her mother's hand.

Music started, and the sonorous voices of the Pendyus Male Voice Choir singing 'Land of my Fathers' in Welsh filled the room. There, at the end of the aisle, raised up on a cradle, was the coffin draped in the Welsh flag. She was conscious of a feeling of great pride and glanced at her mother and smiled.

"Dad would have loved this," she mouthed the words. Louisa Evans smiled in reply.

Father Aloysius moved to the side and indicated they should stand in front of the coffin.

They waited, enjoying the music. Louisa sang the words under her breath. As the music closed, Anna found it difficult not to applaud. She had been imagining her father singing along with the choir, too. Yes, he would have been very proud. Father Aloysius had opened his Bible. He licked his lips and looking up directly at the coffin and then at the two ladies he read the chosen passage.

'There is a time for everything and a season for every activity under the heavens; a time to be born and a time to die," He had rehearsed the passage thoroughly and hardly needed to glance at the words, he imagined Duncan Evans to be listening and made every word a tribute to his friend. When he came to the final line, 'a time for war and a time for peace,' he stretched out a hand to touch the coffin and repeated the last three words, 'a time for peace.'

He turned to the ladies and nodded. Inspired by the priest's performance, Anna launched herself into the opening of the poem, with sparkling eyes she relished every syllable of every word, and Louisa in her turn, brought the same enthusiasm to her delivery. They were giving their best to the man they loved. The poem ended. Feeling both elated and exhausted they accepted Father Aloysius's quiet suggestion that they should sit and as they listened to the last chorus of Beethoven's Ode to Joy they held hands. Father Aloysius waited for the final bars to die away before he quietly stood up and went to the dais to press the button to activate the closing of the curtains. In the finality of that last act Anna was overcome with emotion and burying her face in her mother's lap she burst into tears. Father Aloysius gave them a moment then gently touched Anna's shoulder to indicate they should leave. With the tears steaming down their cheeks the two ladies followed the priest out into the sunshine. There they enveloped him in a tearful hug.

"Thank you, Father," it was Louisa who spoke, "Duncan would have been very proud."

"Yes," echoed Anna, and through her sobs, said, "Dad would have been so proud. Thank you, Father, you have been wonderful, just wonderful."

"To God be the glory, for me, it's been a privilege, and you were wonderful too. You lived every word of that poem, and you are so right. I agree Duncan would have been proud, very proud."

Miss Farrow was waiting by the car. She gave them all a hug. She had given some thought to the journey back, and had chosen another of Duncan's favourite pieces of music to play, Nigel Kennedy on the violin playing Beethoven's violin concerto. Anna took the opportunity to text Larry and to warn him to get the eggs in the pan and coffee on. It was a hungry trio who tucked into Larry's meal with gusto and Anna suddenly couldn't stop talking, she kept reciting snatches of Under Milk Wood.

Father Aloysius spent the rest of that day along with Miss Farrow, Larry, and the Rev. Burns preparing the school for the wake the following day. Louisa Evans and the school secretary had previously gathered together from various albums photographs and cuttings from newspapers that covered the duration of Duncan Evans's long tenure as the school's headteacher. These now had to be sorted and mounted for a display. Mrs Pearce the former deputy, now retired, came over from Truro to help with the captions. She had served the school for many years and had a good memory for names. The last display board was for the plans of the proposed outside classroom which would be named after Duncan. Father Aloysius found working alongside the Rev. Burns with Mrs Pearce and the school secretary on mounting this display gave him a better understanding of how the school had developed under Duncan Evans's leadership. Larry, who had taken two days off work, helped Miss Farrow and the cooks in the school kitchen. Meanwhile Anna and her mother spent the time creating a book of memories for guests at the wake to sign. They gathered together all the condolence cards they had received and stuck them in the book.

The next day, the Friday of the scattering of the ashes and the wake, Father Aloysius just as he had done the day before rose early and made his way to the church to prepare himself for the day. Gone was the anxiety of the day before, following his meeting with Anna and Larry on the cliff walk, the crematorium service, such as it was, had given him confidence and he brought his gratitude to his prayers. He wondered whether the young couple would be there again but they were not. Just as the day before, the day promised to be fair and that was further cause for gratitude. Later Miss Farrow drove him to the crematorium to collect the urn of ashes. It was a strange sensation holding the remains of the man who had done so much to help him settle into his ministry in a little Cornish seaside village. He was at pains to treat the urn with a dignified reverence. They arrived back in the village a good hour and a half before the priest was due to meet with Louisa and Anna Evans for the scattering of the ashes. Father Aloysius held the urn safely in his hands. He slipped out of the car and started to walk towards the church intending to place them in front of the altar, but then as he reached the door a thought struck him, perhaps the church was not an appropriate place but where could he put them, surely the presbytery was not ideal either. Then it struck him, the best place to place them for a short stay was the pond, the project so dear to his heart the completion of which had meant so much to him, and that project had been so instrumental in his own challenging period of settling into the parish. Smiling to himself he took the urn over to the garden development area and gently placed it by the pond. He sat down on the bench that had been donated by Commander Nesbitt. It was not long before he was joined by the commander himself.

"It's such a pleasant day, do you mind if I join you?" He asked politely.

"No, of course not."

"Duncan?" the Commander nodded in the direction of the urn.

"Yes, Duncan, dear man."

"As you say, and this was to be his last project, although there is still more to do here and the outside classroom to be built. He was a man of vision, Duncan, and such a good judge of people to help him implement the vision. It took a little time for the Pondreath folk to warm to him, but he was such a genuine person; he had no side to him, everyone was important to him, and he was such a worker, a bit like somebody else I know."

Father Aloysius chose to ignore the compliment. The commander chuckled, "He was modest too, like somebody else I know. I hear the business at the crematorium went well."

"To God be the glory."

The commander just smiled. "That lad Larry has certainly stepped up to the mark hasn't he."

"Yes, remarkable really, considering," Father Aloysius paused.

"Considering his guardians," the commander completed his observation for him.

"Well, it just goes to show that given the right circumstances, nature, combined with the nurture of others, can help redress a balance that is tilted towards the hopeless, and Duncan was very much part of that process."

"Yes, Duncan, the school, the Tarrants and the youth club they have all played their part I guess."

"And you too," observed the commander.

"Now if you'll excuse me I have things to do in the village. It won't be too long before you will need to be off. I hope it goes well and I look forward to this evening. Go well."

"Thank you good friend, thank you. This evening it is." The priest stood up and the two men shook hands. Father Aloysius spent a few more minutes going over the blessing he had been asked to give in his mind before rising again and picking up the precious urn and heading off to the presbytery. There he found a basket that would do very well in the task of carrying the urn down the hill and up along the cliff path. It had been made in his home country.

Down on the quay, as he made for the bridge, Father Aloysius was surprised to see two coaches parked on the other side of the river. They appeared to come from Pendon Bay.

"I wonder what that's about," he said under his breath to himself as he climbed up the road through the village to the Evans' home. He was reaching out to ring the bell when the door opened. Louisa Evans greeted him with a smile. It was a warm afternoon. Both she and Anna wore pretty frocks but had anoraks on, just in case the wind might blow chill once they were on the cliff path. Louisa wore a headscarf.

"Hello, Father, thank you, it was good of you to collect, um to collect Duncan," She smiled again as she referred to her late husband's ashes.

"Miss Farrow kindly drove me to the crematorium."

"Yes, well thank you both, now let's take Duncan on his last walk. He loved this walk.

We walked on our first day here, he had come for the interview and had been appointed. Someone had mentioned this house was for sale. We came up and had a look. It was in a pretty shabby state but it had possibilities. We took a walk along this path and it was the path and the views that made up our mind for us, and we bought the place and we never regretted it. I don't know how many times we walked along these cliffs. Countless, and we never ceased to marvel at the views. Now this will be his last time, bless him." She sighed.

"Yes, this is a very precious time. Duncan's last journey. And may God bless you too,"

"Thank you, Father. Lead on, please."

"I was wondering, would you like to carry the basket?" suggested the priest. It's not heavy."

"Yes, yes," it was Anna who replied, "Please, Mum, Dad would have wanted you to, I'm sure."

"Well, I, yes I suppose so," Louisa Evans took the basket from the priest's outstretched hand. She wiped a tear from her eye as she did so, "Thank you, now perhaps I had better lead and Anna you follow next." The trio with Father Aloysius in the rear set off along the road, past the last houses and then followed the well-worn path. Anna walked with her head high, Louisa conscious of what she was carrying was more careful about where she placed her feet and was more inclined to look down. As they rounded the last bend in the path and broke out onto the moors Anna gave a gasp of astonishment. There some fifteen feet back from the path spread out perhaps an arm's length apart was a long line of people. They stood heads bowed hands clasped in front of them perfectly still and absolutely silent.

"Mum," Anna touched her mother on her shoulder; she had not seen them, "Mum, look!"

Her mother raised he head, "Heavens, heavens above! She exclaimed. After a pause as she examined them more closely, she said in a hushed whisper,

"Your dad's old pupils, oh, oh, how amazing, just amazing! Turning to Anna she shook her head, "Oh dear, your dad would have felt so honoured." Turning back with head held high she led the way without another word towards their destination. Some two hundred yards from where they were to scatter the ashes the line ended. The Rev. Burns, Commander Nesbitt, and Larry turned as they passed. Anna stopped to look back; the long line of former pupils was disappearing down the path heading back to the town.

"Oh, Duncan, what a tribute, they have paid their respects, now they are leaving us alone, amazing." The tears were streaming down Louisa's cheeks, "Just amazing."

"Larry wait, please, "Anna hurried after Larry. He stopped. She put a hand on his shoulder and gazed up into his face. Tight lipped he met her gaze.

"Oh, Larry, Dad would have been so proud. Thank you," She reached up and kissed him on the cheek. He smiled, shrugged, and without a word, turned and left, following the others. Anna watched him go, then, giving the retreating column a little wave, she whispered,

"Thank you, thank you so much." Hurrying back to her mother she threw her arms round her neck and gave her a hug, "Oh Mum, you're right, Dad would be so proud, it was Larry I know it was. Dad was very special to him and now he's organised the best tribute ever."

"Yes, and now Duncan, it's not far, come on," Mrs Evans led the trio off to the designated spot, a little away from the path at the cliff edge.

She lowered the basket to the ground and, turning to Father Aloysius, requested.

"Father, please, will you open the casket for us,"

Father Aloysius had been just as moved by the silent tribute of Duncan Evans' former pupils as his daughter and wife were. With a lump in his throat, he replied in a hoarse voice.

"Of course," gently, reverently he lifted the urn from the basket, and carefully he removed the lid. Holding the urn in one hand he took a large square white cloth from his pocket. He handed it to Anna.

"Spread it out on the ground, please."

She complied. He put his hand into his pocket again and produced a slightly smaller Welsh flag. This was spread on the white square. Finally slowly he raised the urn and gently tipped the ashes out onto the flag. Standing upright he indicated to the two ladies to take a handful of ashes. Then he did the same and holding his arms up high cast the ashes to the winds. Clearing his throat he recited the Irish blessing.

"May the wind be always at your back. May the sun shine warm upon your face; the rains fall soft upon your fields until we meet again, and we will for ever hold your memory in our hearts."

"Good bye Dad," Anna cast her ashes high towards the blue sky.

"Farewell, Duncan darling, my love, farewell. I love you and always will." Louisa was the last to commit her husband's ashes to the elements. The priest then made two bundles of the last of the ashes in the two cloths. He handed those in the flag to the headteacher's wife and the white bundle to his daughter. Anna was the first to cast her bundle out over the cliff face; her mother followed. All three stood silent and still for a long moment, gazing out across the sea. Then, without a word, Louisa led them back down the path. They had a wake to attend.

Duncan Evans had wanted a private cremation and a private scattering of ashes and his wishes had been respected, but he was also a man committed to the community he had served and served so faithfully and well for very many years, long enough to find himself teaching children of former pupils. He had run a happy school. Being very conscious of the importance of the formative years of a child's life he was committed to giving every child in his care an excellent grounding to their education. Among those gathered to pay their silent respects and to stand by the path that morning there were former pupils who had come from far and near. A group had shared a car and had come down from London but there were too, parents of current pupils at his school, villagers who had lived in Pondreath all their lives and who had never left.

They all had one thing in common: they shared fond memories, happy memories of those early years.

Duncan had had three quotes that he was fond of sharing from time to time. The first was, 'To live richly today is the best preparation for tomorrow,' which meant fun. It also meant variety. He was conscious that among his staff, he needed not only dedicated and skilled practitioners but also characters and interesting people with a range of talents. Where he had felt there were gaps in the pool of talents he could draw upon among the staff, he had looked beyond the school to the wider community.

The partnership, child, parents, and teacher was vital in this respect. He never tired of telling the parent body that education was not the sole prerogative or the responsibility of the school. Learning could and should happen anywhere and everywhere. Parents and even grandparents were given easy access to the school and invited into classrooms where he believed they could be a great asset. At first, staff and also among the parents there had been reservations about these ideas, but gradually, all parties came to see the benefits. He used to say.

"When you have only one pair of hands in a class, only two eyes and ears, and thirty or more children of different aptitudes and attitudes, then that is quite a challenge. Extra eyes, ears, and hands are always useful. Teaching and learning should be a team activity, we are all learning together."

He was always looking for ways to stimulate the children and had extended his search for talent into the community. Music, for example, was dear to his heart. He had persuaded a retired secondary school teacher who was a gifted musician to run a choir, which was to become one of the best in the county. The school orchestra was run by a former soldier, a cornet player in a regimental band. He became the conductor, and his wife played a fiddle. Among their circle of friends were other musicians. Duncan persuaded them to join the school orchestra, and so it became the community orchestra, an orchestra of all ages. Duncan was always on the lookout for second-hand instruments and then for people to play them.

The second of Duncan's favourite quotes was 'Excellence is not an act but a habit." A fun school did not mean a school without discipline. His emphasis was on establishing a culture of self-discipline, and of encouraging children to think of others at all times, a culture of respect for others. He gave pupils opportunities to take on responsibilities and have an involvement in the daily running of the school.

The last of his maxims was one he had coined for himself. 'You are only as good as your last lesson.' As a headteacher, he retained a teaching role. He put the same classroom demands and expectations on himself that he had of all his teachers. He was trained as a teacher, and as a teacher, he remained. He was always learning from others and from keeping abreast of developments in the world of education. He was happy to learn from anyone, old experts and young pioneers, anyone with good ideas.

As for the wake, he wanted it to be a party, a party open to all in the village, and he wanted it in the school hall. That is what he got. That Friday afternoon, there were none of the extracurricular activities. The children were all due back with their parents and some with grandparents too at six. The team led by Miss Hardcourt,

Commander Nesbitt, and Larry worked hard to complete all the preparations that had been going on for the whole week. The orchestra and the choir gathered early to prepare for a musical welcome to guests. After that, Anna had compiled a medley of her father's favourite pop songs to be played to help in creating a party atmosphere.

The only thing missing were decorations, but all the food tables were decked with bright tablecloths, and the hall was made to look as festive as possible. The dress code was smart casual. Some of the adjoining classrooms and the staff room had been made ready as places where people could sit. This was in anticipation of a large number attending; the hall would be standing only.

The numbers were large. Larry was glad of Commander Nesbitt's suggestion that they should ask former pupils to bring two drinks, one for themselves and one for someone else. They were more than happy to do so. Some former pupils, at Larry's request, brought their instruments with them; they joined the community orchestra, and others who had sung in the school choir joined the choir. They were early arrivals and had the opportunity to practice beforehand.

Louisa and Anna arrived promptly at six. The hall was already full. Larry met them at the gate. As they entered the school hall, the orchestra heralded their arrival with a welcoming fan fair, which was followed immediately by the choir singing the Welsh National Anthem in English. The party had begun. The choir sang a tribute song.

The words were written by one of the older pupils and sung to a familiar tune: 'Morning has broken.' The Rev. Burns spoke next, words of welcome and then a very moving tribute to Duncan. He then went on to launch the appeal for the outside classroom, the last of what could be called Duncan's projects. Finally, the orchestra played *For He's a Jolly Good Fellow*, and everyone joined in singing the words. Both Louisa Evans and Anna were clearly overwhelmed. Louisa's hands were shaking when she took the microphone from the Rev. Burns.

"Dear, dear good friends, I am speechless. Duncan would have had the words, but all I can say is thank you, thank you so very much. Duncan would have been thrilled. This school was his life, and you all meant so much to him. It's so good to see you all, and you have all been amazingly kind. All you former pupils up on the cliff walk this morning, along with others, that was so very special. Thank you, and thank you, orchestra and choir, and to all who have provided such delicious-looking food. Thank you all, everyone for coming.

Anna and I have felt so affirmed by all your cards and kind words. Your caring for us is not only a great tribute to Duncan but a testimony to this school and to this community. He would not have said this, but I will, God Bless you all, and we thank you from the bottom of our hearts."

There was a moment of quiet, which was broken by a loud whoop by Anna, who was standing with Larry by the bar,

"Let the party begin. God Bless you all."

This was greeted by applause as Anna dragged Larry over to one of the tables of food and, collecting a paper plate, began to help herself to food. Larry signalled that the bar was open and everyone should help themselves from one of the tables of food. And so all Duncan Evans's wishes came to pass.

The wake went on well into the night. For Louisa and Anna, there were so many people to see and to thank. For a lot of Duncan's former pupils, there were old friends, some of whom they hadn't seen for years, to catch up with. Many wanted to talk to their former teachers too, writing in the book of memories and looking at the displays, the pictures of their former headteacher, and all the photographs of happy events over the years, not to mention the plans for the outside classroom. There was plenty of food, and it all had to be eaten, and there was more than enough to drink.

The time slipped by. People gradually left, those with young children first, and then later, much later, those with older pupils and the former pupils. Some of the latter were taken in the coaches back to Pendon Bay, where they had left their cars or had arranged to stay the night before catching trains. Many had family and were spending the weekend in the village.

Some of the latter stayed on to help the team clear up the hall and put the staff room and the classrooms that had been used as seating areas back to right, ready for the Monday. Among them was the school inspector, Mr Smith. He was new to the area and looked on the evening partly as a way of expressing the County's gratitude for Duncan Evans's work as a headteacher but also as an opportunity of getting to know people involved with the school better. Duncan Evans would have been impressed. Louisa, Anna, Larry, and Father Aloysius, along with the caretaker Mrs Corbett and Commander Nesbitt, were the last to leave. As they stood for a moment at the door, waiting for Mrs Corbett to check on all the external doors and to make sure all the windows were shut, their talk was about how successful the evening had been and how much Duncan Evans would have enjoyed the occasion. It had been a village community at its best.

Anna had drawn Larry to one side, taking him to the end of the playground where the new classroom was to be built. She faced him.

"Larry, I don't know how to thank you. You have been a wonderful support and such a friend, and you've worked so hard, getting all those former pupils back and sorting the transport and everything, its been an amazing evening," she was fiddling with the button of his jacket as she spoke, "and much of it has been down to you, thank you, thank you very much." She put her hands on his shoulder and gave him a kiss. Larry sighed and smiled.

"You don't have to thank me, your dad was very good to me. Without him, I'd have been a complete loser, as it is. I know I am not great shakes, but the one thing you can't say is that I am not grateful."

"Oh Larry, don't put yourself down. You have lots going for you. I mean, you're a hard worker, you are good at your job, and this evening shows you are an organiser and a leader too, and to me, you," she looked up into his eyes, "You are very special."

Larry blushed, he took her into his arms, and they kissed. Then, patting her on the bottom as they parted, he stepped back.

"Now your mum has had a big day. You need to be off and to look after her."

"Yes, I guess, but promise you'll come and see me tomorrow, please."

"Um, OK, but do you think your dad would approve?"

"Don't be so silly," Anna punched him playfully on the chest, "Of course, he would, and you know it. Be with us for lunch, and don't be late!" They walked up to join the others just as Mrs Corbett was locking the front door.

That night, both Louisa and Anna, tired though they found sleep difficult. On their return to the house, they both confessed to feeling very weary. However, once in the confines of their own rooms in their own beds, the sleep they yearned for eluded them. After tossing and turning for what seemed an age, Louisa finally decided to get up and make herself a drink. Tip-toeing down to the kitchen, she made herself a mug of cocoa. She took it to the lounge and drew back the curtains. The moon, high in the sky, was on the rise. It will soon be full, she thought as she switched out the light. She sat quietly in the dark by the window, sipping her drink and gazing up at the night sky. Yes, it had been a good day. Her husband would have approved. Larry had been wonderful, Father Aloysius too, especially at the scattering of the ashes, and Anna? She had certainly risen to the occasion. She and Larry seemed to have something going, Anna could do worse, he was certainly much better than that bunch of surfers. Yes, he was younger than she was, but he was so much more mature. Duncan, well, yes, he would approve. He had always seen the best in his pupils, and he had certainly been very perceptive in his opinions of Larry. Father Aloysius and Larry between them seemed to have rescued his daughter from going down a road that could only end badly, very badly, a road to destruction, but thanks to them, she had turned a corner and perhaps started on a journey to a better future. She hoped so. Strange, her father's passing had meant a new beginning for Anna, but what of her own situation.? Well, life was never going to be the same again. The tears she had been battling against all day, all week that she was resisting now suddenly got the better of her. She wept silent, bitter tears.

There was a creak from the stairs. It was Anna. She turned on the light. Louisa sighed, she had not meant to disturb her daughter.

"Mum, what's the matter? Oh, you're crying, you poor thing." Anna hurried over to her mother and, kneeling in front of her, enveloped her in her arms.

"I'm sorry dear, your old mum couldn't sleep, she is just having a good cry."

"It's alright Mum. It's all right to cry, ' a time to weep and a time to laugh,' remember, it's alright to cry. You've been so brave, amazing, and such an example to us all. Now, it's all right to cry. I couldn't sleep either and came down to make myself a drink. Can I make you one?"

"Thank you darling, no, I have one already, a cocoa, I'll make you one."

"No, please, I'll do it, and then, then we both can have a good old blubber together."

Mother and daughter sat side by side, holding hands, Louisa had dried her eyes. As her daughter pulled up a chair next to her, she smiled.

"It's been a good day, perfect really, just as he wished."

"Yes, Mum, perfect."

Mother and daughter sat and quietly shared the day together and gave thanks, and as they shared their special moments, they smiled. There is a time to weep and a time to smile. The moon had journeyed on out of sight. It was well on its way down towards a new horizon. Louisa shook herself and got up.

"Oh, our friend, the Moon has gone on his way. Time we were getting back to bed. Tomorrow is another day. Thank you, darling, you have been such a help. I love you. Goodnight."

"Good night, Mum. I love you too."

Back in her room, Anna tried to sleep, but thoughts surrounding the day kept her awake. Her mother had coped so well, and for her, Larry and Father Aloysius had been such a help. Her parents had always been very close, but it had taken her father's illness and his passing to show her how close and how important her parents were to each other. She now had the responsibility of helping her mother during this time of grief. She thought of her father. He had been so respected in the village. Why had she been such a little headstrong fool and got involved with that crowd of surfers?

It had taken Father Aloysius to bring her back home. Mercifully, just in time to save her father further worry. As she lay there curled up under her duvet, she realised that she was clutching the priest's beads. His gift to her. His precious beads. Perhaps the only really precious thing he had apart from his faith. She examined her relationship with the priest. This was another cause for concern, another thing made her feel guilty.

She found him attractive and had flirted with him; she recalled how she had followed him to the graveyard. He was obviously attracted to her, but he was strong enough to know where to draw the line, and she had known what she was doing was wrong but had continued all the same. And what of Larry? Larry, who had despite the nature of his foster parents, despite the fact that he had been deserted by his parents, despite all those disadvantages, had risen above them to be a decent young man and had proved himself to be such a capable organiser and a leader, what of him? And she who had all the advantages of a good home had spurned him and put him down and had been unkind. Yet he was still loyal to her. It was Anna's turn to cry. She cried herself to sleep.

Chapter Thirty-One

*The robbed
who smiles steals something from
the thief.*

-William Shakespeare

For Father Aloysius it had been a long day full of challenges. He was weary and unusually for him it showed itself in his gait. He trudged up the hill. As he turned the bend and passed the church to his surprise he saw the light was on in the presbytery kitchen. He hurried to the front door wondering why. The door was open and ajar.

With a feeling of mounting anxiety he called out, "Anybody at home?" There was no reply. The place was eerily silent. He strode to the kitchen door. The drawers had been pulled from their places and all their contents were strewn all over the floor. The cupboard doors were open and their contents too were mixed in with pots pans and kitchen utensils. For a moment he stood still in shock. Then shaking his head in disbelief he rushed from room to room, they had all been ransacked. The last room he went to was his bedroom. By this time he expected, even feared it would have been trashed. He was right. With a mounting sense of anger he looked about him. Who possibly could have done this? Why? Was it robbery? What were they looking for? What had been taken?

He bent down to start tidying up, but stopped. This was evidence. He must leave things as they were. He turned and made for the door, he would phone the police.... again he stopped on the landing. It was late. Whoever had been here was long gone. Getting the police out now was pointless. They could come in the morning. He would phone them and tell them he had had visitors and ask them to attend the presbytery in the morning. He would tell them he would lock up and leave things as they were, he'd just tidy his bed.

He needed to go to sleep. He could not face waiting for the police now. They needed their sleep too just as much as he did. The nearest police station was in Pendon Bay.

He called. It was an answer phone and had a recorded message. If his concern was urgent he should phone the police headquarters in Plymouth, if not he could leave a message. He took this advice.

He locked up, checking all doors and windows. Wearily he went up the stairs to the bathroom. He hung his cassock on the hook behind the door. His ablutions completed he retired to the bedroom and changed into his pyjamas. There was an unturned drawer at the place beside the bed where he normally knelt to say his last prayers of the day. Father Aloysius moved down the bed and knelt, his rosary in his hand. Having cancelled the evening prayers in the church he started with the Angelus, then holding his crucifix in front of him he thanked his God for all the blessings of the day. He praised his maker for the way the people of Pondreath had come together to celebrate Duncan Evans's life, the way so many of the headteacher's former pupils had come to pay their respects together in that silent and dignified tribute on the cliff path.

All had been carried out with such sensitivity, and he thanked his maker for the way so many people had attended the wake and responded so generously to the appeal for the outside classroom. He had seen the community at its best and he was greatly impressed. After his prayers of thanks, he went on to examine his conscience. What had he done that he might subsequentially regret, was there anything he had neglected to do that he should have done? What of his feelings for Anna? Had he observed the red lights and resisted the any temptations that he might have felt? Did he have any feeling of envy or even jealousy at the budding relationship the headteacher's daughter seemed to be entering into with Larry? He confessed any misgivings he might have had before he made intercessions for all who mourn and for all the unwell. He prayed for Sid Trevinian and his wife, for Philippa and for the visitors to the presbytery that night. He asked his God to give him a forgiving heart.

At peace with himself he rose slowly, surveyed the room for the last time. He smiled. What chaos, if they had been coming for money they would have had lean pickings.

His wallet was in his cassock pocket. Any spare cash he kept in a box in his bedside cabinet. The drawer was empty. He could not see the box anywhere. Perhaps it was money they were after. Well they would have been disappointed. Before the wake, suspecting he might need money, he had taken a lot of his contingency cash with him. Some he had given to the appeal as his contribution. No doubt all would be revealed over the course of time. He shrugged and slipped into bed. He slept well.

The following day he rose at his normal early hour. Before leaving for his run he hastily wrote a message for Miss Farrow in case he were to be detained and not get back before her. He did not want her to arrive at the presbytery and find it in its present state. It would be a shock and she might start tidying up. All needed to remain in situ for the police to see.

That morning he decided to return to his normal route for his run. He headed up to the top of the hill passing the commander's house and started down the path that led along the cliffs and eventually dropped zig-zagging to the beach. There below figures on the beach caught his eye. Not Sid Trevinian again! Somehow he was not surprised, one was unmistakably Sid Trevinian, the others were youths. He cast his mind back to the occasion he had witnessed a meeting between the lorry driver and Anna with some lads at the same spot.

"Brown parcel time again," he said under his breath. He was correct. Sid handed over a brown paper bag, one of the youths gave him some money in return.

"My money no doubt" surmised the priest. He was tempted to race down to the beach and to apprehend them, but realised they would be long gone before he got there and in any event this was a matter for the police. He decided not to go to the beach but rather to go down to the bridge and through the village to the cliff walk that led to the place where just the previous day his friend Duncan Evans' ashes had been scattered. There he said his first prayers of the day.

Father Aloysius was on his way back to the presbytery when a police car passed him. It stopped. The driver wound down his window.

"Good morning Father, you're up early. We understand you are a popular fellow, visitors last night?" It was Sergeant Graves. Father Aloysius stopped, and leant against the car to catch his breath."This is P.C. Smith," the sergeant said introducing the policewoman sitting in the other front seat. "Sheila Smith, we've got the S.S. on this job." P.C. Smith smiled. It was obviously a joke she was used to.

"Thanks for coming. I hadn't expected you so soon."

"The early bird and all that, we'll see you at the presbytery."

"Sounds like a plan. I'll see you shortly."

Not long after the police arrived Miss Farrow too, appeared. Fortunately Father Aloysius was at the door and could break the news gently. The police did a thorough investigation and took a statement which made reference to what the priest had told them concerning the things he had seen that morning on the beach. While they were doing this Miss Farrow set about putting the kitchen straight and she was able to put on the kettle. She offered the police a drink but they, as was their custom, declined. Their search confirmed that only a relatively small amount of money had been taken and this meant it was not worth their while to get the finger print team out. They were at full stretch and it would take some days for them to be able to get out to Pondreath. Sergeant Graves did commit to paying a visit to Sid Trevinian when he heard about what Father Aloysius had seen on occur on the beach that morning. He had been the one to call on the depot where Sid worked after Mrs Hazelmere had reported on the incident of the fracas involving her dogs. Later Father Aloysius was to learn that Sergeant Graves had indeed called on the Trevinian home and that Sid Trevinian had been in. He apparently had made a fairly convincing show of being shocked when he heard that the presbytery had been ransacked and he also had a reasonably plausible explanation of what was in the brown bag. There was little more the police could do but big Sid knew for better or worse that they would keep their eye on his activities. Miss Farrow feared it might be for the worse. Father Aloysius, conscious of his bishop's advice, hoped not.

While the police had been busy at the presbytery Miss Farrow on Father Aloysius's suggestion had been telephoning the small band of people who normally attended Angelus on a daily basis to warn them that the service would take place later than usual. The news was out and news in Pondreath spread quickly. Mrs Hazelmere after registering her surprise that the police had managed to get to the scene of the crime so early started to consider how she might help. Father Aloysius liked his cake. Had she time to bake one? She decided not but then another thought struck her, perhaps there had been cakes left over after the wake. There had been such a mountain baked, perhaps, just perhaps there might be one left. She hesitated to call Louisa Evans but maybe Mrs Corbett the caretaker would know. Larry, in organising the preparations for the wake had, with the help of the school secretary, made a master list of people's names along with their addresses and contact numbers. He had been careful to obtain their consent for him to have and to share this information and then had distributed the lists to all concerned. Mrs Hazelmere quickly found her list and made a call. As she had hoped there was indeed some food left over that had been left in the school staff room fridge. The caretaker readily agreed to meet Mrs Hazelmere at the school and together they would check whether there was anything like a cake that would be suitable to give to Father Aloysius. To their joy there were two cakes completely untouched and one was a fruit cake, Father Aloysius's favourite. She would take that and over the weekend she would replace it so the school staff would not miss out.

It was but a short walk from the school to the church and Mrs Hazelmere arrived there well before the scheduled time for the service. She decided to call at the presbytery first. It would be better to deliver the cake then and there than take it into the church with her. She arrived just as the police car was about to leave. Mrs Hazelmere always one to grasp every opportunity to make the best out of chance encounters, was able to personally thank them for following up her complaint about Mr Trevinian and the way he had treated one of her dogs. Little did she know that Sergeant Graves was about to visit that very same person once again but about a very different matter. If she had, she might have rejoiced in the happy coincidence that the end results of both incidents involved a cake and Father Aloysius. As it was, the priest was not available to receive his cake, he had returned to the presbytery to change before taking the service of morning prayer and was in the shower. Miss Farrow accepted the cake on his behalf. On entering the church he was relieved to see that the congregation was smaller than usual. He felt reluctant to be the centre of attention. After the service he accepted the commiserations of those who had attended with gratitude. He made light of his misfortunes and refused to speculate as to who might be responsible. He did not want to be drawn into any village gossip and looked for an early opportunity to excuse himself and return to the presbytery. On learning about the cake he expressed his heart felt thanks but made that his excuse for not lingering.

He and Miss Farrow spent much of the rest of the morning completing the clearing up after the burglary. They were interrupted mid morning by a ring on the door bell.

It was Louisa Evans who had come with Anna and Larry to see how he was and to give him some home-baked biscuits. When Louisa explained they had been left over from the wake, he burst out laughing.

"Louisa, thank you, how kind of you to come, come in please. Miss Farrow and I have almost got the place restored to order and a break would be welcome, so let's put the kettle on and share a cup of tea and one of your biscuits." His visitors did not appreciate the reason for his mirth until he offered them a piece of cake to go with the biscuits. Then they were all able to share in his laughter.

"I was wondering why you burst out laughing when I told you that these biscuits were left over from yesterday. Now I understand, Duncan would, I am sure, be very pleased to know that at least you have had a few perks from his funeral."

"He's probably having a good chuckle now."

"Maybe, I'd like to think so and if that is the case then along with his amusement he would also be concerned about you and wonder who on earth would have done such a thing."

"That," replied the priest in an emphatic tone, "Is a matter for conjecture. We may have our suspicions, as do our friends and the police, but without any proof, as I say, it's all conjecture, so perhaps it is better not to speculate but to be thankful and count our blessings that our visitors didn't make a worse mess than they did and that they found little worth stealing. Also, we must be grateful that we, I am fine." Father Aloysius, deliberately changing the subject, added,

"Great cake, I wonder who baked it, I'd like to get the recipe." He was conscious that any speculations might lead to a suggestion that involved Larry's foster parents and that would be embarrassing.

"I may be able to help you there," volunteered Larry, "It looks very like one that Miss Hardcourt made."

"Father," said Anna speaking for first time, "We came not just to find out how you are, and I have to say you are a saint to be so uncomplaining because I can't imagine how you must have felt when you finally got home after a very busy day to be greeted by a big mess.... but we also wanted to say a great big thank you for all you have done for us over the last few weeks. You have just been wonderful, amazingly wonderful and wait," she sensed he was about to interrupt and held up a hand to stop him," And I know you're going to blame it all onto God but I think you need to get a bit of credit as well."

"More than a little," agreed Larry.

Father Aloysius chuckled again, "Well, you know how it is, to God be the glory and it was a team effort, I mean so many people reached out the hand of love. I saw this village in a new light and it was inspiring, a great testimony to your dad and what he meant to the village. For me it was just a privilege, so thank you for allowing me to be part of something so precious to you."

"All right a team effort," conceded Anna, "But teams need leadership and you and Larry were such great leaders," she reached out to touch Larry on the arm as she said this. It was Larry's turn to change the subject.

"Thanks for tea and is there anything we can do to help clear up?"

"No, I don't think so, Miss Farrow, anything?"

"It's kind of you to ask but we are almost done and......"

"There is something, Larry. You might just take a look at my bike. The brakes are a bit sloppy."

"Fine." Larry was glad of the chance to do something for his friend to feel useful.

"I'll get the key to the garage." While the priest went to fetch the garage key Larry wandered outside. He walked slowly over to the front gate, his eyes on the path searching for something, anything that the intruders might have inadvertently dropped. There in the flower bed just to the right of the gate he saw a key, he picked it up, it looked very much like the front door key. He held it in his palm. As Father Aloysius approached he closed his hand over it.

"You've found the garage key, then?"

"Yes, Miss Farrow bless her helped me."

"Swap," Larry held out his hand, the one closed round the key, he smiled at the priest "A key for a key," he opened his hand.

"The front door key where did you find that?"

"Over there in the shrubs by the gate, your visitors must have dropped it. They obviously used it to get in."

"Interesting, they must have found where I hide it, I've been wondering how they got in."

"Hide it, why?"

"Yes, I hide it under that stone by the door. It's a spare. I put it there in case I lock myself out or lock my keys in the house by accident."

"I guess that stone is too obvious a place," Larry was shaking his head. "Why not give it to Miss Farrow's sister to keep safe for you. There is always some one in the shop. Then if you have an accident or lock yourself out its not far away and there is always some one there and if they are out Miss Farrow can get in there and it will be safe for you to collect should you need it."

"Not a bad idea, thank you, I'll have a word with Miss Farrow, thank you." They swapped keys, "Do you mind if I leave you to look at the bike, Miss Farrow may need me to help put things in the right place in my bedroom."

"No go ahead, I think you can trust this friend with this key," Larry winked at Father Aloysius, who grinned and nodded.

"Yes, definitely." The priest headed off to the house, leaving Larry to look at his bicycle. Anna was washing up the tea things. Her mother was sitting quietly at the table where he had left her. He picked up a chair and sat beside her.

"How are you?" Louisa Evans shrugged and the tears welled up in her eyes. "You know how it is," she replied quietly,"Good moments, bad moments, sad moments."

"Yes," The priest paused a moment before commenting. "Yes, we are all different but I do know what it was like for me," and in his mind he could hear the guns and the crack of the whips, the goats bleating and the cries, and then the silence broken only by bird song and the incessant buzzing of flies. "Yes I know, one doesn't ever forget, but time does move on and so will you and with help the pain will ease. I had that help from the priests at the mission." Father Aloysius paused, he silently chided himself for using an old cliché that often wasn't helpful. Louisa nodded and feeling reassured he continued, "You have lost a very precious person, a person who has been there by your side for a very long time and now is no longer there and it's left a big hole. It will take some time for it all to sink in. You've had a very busy time, you did so well with all the arrangements and the formalities and you coped with it all with such self assurance such confidence, the crematorium, the scattering of ashes and the wake. Now all that's done, all you have are the cards and the memories, and that big hole. You are tired and you know you have to rebuild your life again but maybe there doesn't seem to be much point. It's hard and you need help. Don't be afraid to ask, and to talk about how you feel. In my experience you never completely get over it but talking about it can help. So please when you need help ask and I am not suggesting you have to ask me. I am sure there are lots of others who will be there to listen when times are hard."

Thank you, Father, I will, I promise." She smiled at him through her tears. "We must go and leave you to your clearing up."She got up and, taking a tea towel, started drying the tea things. The priest went upstairs. Miss Farrow, diligent and organised as ever, had completed tidying the bathroom and his bedroom. Everything seemed to be in good order. He thanked her and returned to the kitchen. The ladies had finished dealing with the tea things and were ready to go; they had arranged with Larry that he would catch them up and say their farewells. Louisa took both the priest's hands in her own,

"Thank you, Father, from the bottom of my heart. You are a good, good man. You meant a lot to Duncan, especially towards the end, thank you."

"Duncan was very good to me." replied the priest, "He opened so many doors for me getting me involved in the school and the grounds project, I owe him so much so thank you and God bless you." Louisa gave his hands a squeeze and turned away. It was Anna's turn next. The red lights were flashing as taking a step backwards he turned to face her. He gave her a little bow and then holding his hands up, He spoke gently.

"You don't have to thank me, Your father was a wonderful man. It was a huge privilege for me to get to know him, so no, you don't have to thank me again, if anybody needs to say thank you," he clasped his hands and tapped his chest, "it's me." Anna looked up at him, she bit her lip and blinked back the welling tears. Her voice was a horse whisper.

"Oh Mr miracle worker you know you are very special to us, please look after yourself. Promise me you'll take care and stay safe, please, and I will thank you whether you like it or not so thank you, thank you so much." She turned to join her mother and together they set off down the hill. Father Aloysius stood at the gate and watched them disappear round the bend. Time can help with the healing of grief, you can, you will rebuild your life but you never forget, no you never forget the buzzing of the flies.

Father Aloysius sat quietly on the bench by the pond waiting for Commander Nesbitt. The commander had been at morning prayer and had suggested they meet and perhaps go for a walk together. It was a bright day but the temperature had taken a dip and there was a chill wind. He was glad he had taken Miss Farrow's advice and had dressed up well. He had arrived at the pond a little early and so was taking a few moments to reflect on the events of the last week.

It had been the first funeral he had been asked to take in Pondreath. It had certainly been an unusual one. Knowing Duncan Evans' views on all matters of religion he had wondered about why he had been asked to take it. Perhaps the headteacher's upbringing in the Baptist church had at the end meant more to him than he would care to admit and in the dark times of wrestling with his mortality as he lay in hospital at night he had hearkened back to the days of his childhood and had rediscovered belief in an all forgiving God. Somehow Father Aloysius doubted that was the case. Could it be that Duncan in his far reaching wisdom had taken the opportunity to use his death as a means of giving him a challenge, a challenge that would help him grow not only in terms of his abilities, after all a challenge accepted and overcome is a powerful aid to learning, but also in another way altogether. He was mulling this thought over in his mind when his friend arrived.

"Good afternoon Father. Glad to see you have dressed sensibly. This is a chill wind."

"Good afternoon, Commander. Yes, it's not exactly tropical, but no doubt a good walk will help to keep us warm."

Commander Nesbitt indicated the direction they would be going with his stick, and the two men set off side by side.

"Father, I think it's time you dropped the commander bit. After all I've been retired for a long time and I do have a Christian name, people round here seem to like the idea of a naval man living on the top of the hill and that's fine, but sometimes I feel it implies I am of a different class, and quite frankly class is something that has its roots in prejudice and snobbery. One thing I did learn in the Navy was that when it comes to the crunch times in life and things look bleak then we are all pretty much the same and on board ship everybody has a role to play to keep the show afloat and no one is indispensable but everyone is vital, and that being the case, all those in the team are equal in importance. Don't they say we are all equal in the eyes of the Almighty. Anyway the name is Jim."

"Thank you, Jim, my name is Aloysius."

"Aloysius, doesn't that mean warrior? Was that your name in your own tribal language?"

"Yes, in a way." It's a long story. Our manyatta was raided. I was the only survivor. One of the missionary Fathers who found me could speak a little Karamajong. He was French. I was young, a boy, and I was in complete shock. I couldn't speak, I was dumb. I was that way for some time. He tried to ask me my name. I did not reply. He tried to ask me my father's name. As far as I remember all I could whisper was warrior. So he decided to call me Aloysius which as you say, can mean warrior.

"My word, what a story. How old were you when all this happened?"

"To be honest with you I'm not sure, my father, and not just my father, the whole family were totally illiterate. They were wandering pastoralists. Their contact with what in the West is thought of as civilization, was minimal. Life had not changed much for them for generations, so they had a very different concept of time to what we use today. No one had a watch or a clock. The passing of time was measured by the changing seasons, the dry seasons and the wet seasons. As for my age, they told me I was born during a very wet year. The grazing was good. I was, I suppose, an omen of good fortune. I think I was eight or nine, but it could have been twelve. Later, much later, I did look at the Uganda rainfall records just as a matter of curiosity. There were years of significant rainfall and droughts too but the problem was sometimes there were two consecutive wet years. My father was a tall man. I was probably tall for my age group too. At the Mission for the records they decided I was nine."

"Do you remember much about your life before the missionaries found you and I suppose you could say, adopted you?"

"Yes, I do,"

The raid? Father Aloysius sighed. He stopped and turned towards the sea, he gazed out to the far horizon. It was some time before he spoke." I remember the raid. I remember the raid as if it was yesterday."

"I see. Have you ever spoken about it to anyone?"

"A long time ago. At first I could not speak at all and when I could it was a custom of my people that you did not speak about the dead, so for many years I did not tell anyone."

"And then?

"I was sent to study at a secondary school in Moroto. There was a lady teacher there, an English lady. She was working on a translation of the Bible into Karamajong. She was a very kind lady. I helped her with some of the translation work. I told her."

"Did that help, sharing the memory?" Father Aloysius thought for a moment before he answered.

"Yes I suppose it did."

"And you haven't told anyone since?" Father Aloysius sighed.

"Not in the same way, just a few and mostly just a few words. As a Karamajong you don't speak about the dead. I did have help from someone else. That was for another trauma altogether, but he also helped me regarding the raid and my loss."

"Your father?"

"My father and all those in that manyatta, I was the only survivor?"

"This is obviously a very difficult subject for you. Do you mind my asking about it?"

"No, no, you are a friend, a trustworthy friend."

"My whole working life was spent in the Royal Navy. I served on a whole range of ships in places near and far. When you are serving on the front line you experience and see things that most other people thankfully can only read about as articles in the papers, things that shock you to the core, things you will never forget, things that become etched into your memory. This can be very stressful and leave scars that can take years to heal, and for some people this can lead to quite serious mental illness. Some of my time as a senior officer was spent in dealing with post traumatic stress disorder in some of our personnel. No doubt you have heard of that?"

"Yes." Father Aloysius nodded, "Yes, I have."

"May I ask do you have flash backs." Father Aloysius turned to look at his friend, their eyes met.

"It was all a long time ago," he said quietly.

"But?" It was a question. Father Aloysius looked down at the ground for a moment and then raised his head again to meet the commander's questioning gaze.

"If by flashbacks you mean do I hear the sounds and have the images of that day returning to me in my mind, yes, I do."

"Do you get them often?"

"That depends, I suppose, on circumstances."

"Circumstances that trigger the thoughts, interesting. Can I ask what are the triggers?"

"The triggers, well when people question me about my past can be one, another maybe when I am talking to people about death. Come to think of it there were other triggers too, but they were when I was in Africa, they were mostly associated with sounds. Now I guess I don't hear those sounds so much."

"How do you cope with your thoughts."

"I guess I am fortunate in that I have a faith. I don't let myself dwell on them. They may, actually quite often they occur when I am in conversation with someone. Then of course I try not to let it show, and I concentrate on the matter in hand, Sometimes if the opportunity occurs I can pray, I try to make my prayers positive. So as I remember the raid I give thanks for being spared, I commend those who were not spared to the mercy of God and I try to ask for forgiveness for the raiders."

"That all sounds good. Do you ever get them at night, and do they occur in dreams?

"They used to, when I was young, especially in my early days at the Mission, but the Fathers there taught us how to pray, that I think helped. We were taught to kneel down by our beds just before we settled down to sleep. In our prayers we were taught to think back through the day and to give thanks for the good things and to confess and ask for forgiveness for anything that we were conscious of that was wrong. I still do that. When I get into bed, I am at peace in my mind. I usually sleep very well."

"Thank you for sharing all this with me, I hope it hasn't seemed that I have been prying. What you have told me has been reassuring. I am not a psychologist or even a trained councillor but I do have some experience in such matters. I suspect you won't ever forget that day, but you have obviously worked out ways of dealing with it, and indeed have had help to deal with it in your training to be a priest. As I say I am no expert but should you ever think you might need more help then I may be able to recommend others better informed in such matters for you to go to."

"Thank you, Jim, as you say talking to someone else about a matter can help. Talking to you has been a help."

"Good, that's what friends are for. I guess we need to be moving on."

"Forward march, Commander."

"Jim!" insisted Jim Nesbitt.

Father Aloysius saluted, "Forward march, Commander Jim." Both men laughed, then walked on in silence. The path had narrowed, and in places following it involved stepping over or round rocks, and they needed to concentrate where they placed their feet. They were a full two miles further along the cliffs when the commander stopped and pointed with his stick. Hopping about on the rocks below were two large black birds.

"Crows," suggested Father Aloysius.

"No, not crows," the commander replied. "They are ..."

"Rooks then," Father Aloysius had interrupted his friend. A lesser person might have taken offence but the naval man merely gave the priest a quizzical look and then imitating a broad Cornish accent the commander gave his reply.

"They be choughs, which of course are related to rooks, ravens and jackdaws but are the Cornish version. You will see them on the Cornish coat of arms. In the Cornish language they are named Palores, which I am reliably informed means digger. They use that long red beak for digging away at loose soil to find worms and beetles and the like. They have grown increasingly rare in recent times but conservationists are working to re-establish them here in Cornwall."

"I see, thank you. I guess by introducing me to these rare birds you have been helping me along the way towards being integrated in the community."

"Very insightful of you," the commander smiled at his friend. "We'll have to start working on the accent next."

"Arrgh!" Responded the priest.

"Not bad, not bad at all, but what you really need to do is to learn the language."

"I take it you can tutor me?

"I'm afraid not, in the Navy, I did learn to brush up my schoolboy French, and I learnt a bit of Russian and German for that matter, but Cornish, well, so few people can speak it now that there doesn't seem much point. If I were Cornish born and bred, maybe, but I am an interloper just like you."

"Talking of integration, when I was sitting on the bench before you collected me to bring me here, I was thinking about Duncan.

Duncan, as we all know, was not a man of faith. He had other affiliations. However, that didn't stop him from asking me to take his funeral. I was wondering why he had done that; could it be he had had a last-minute change of heart?"

It was the commander's turn to interrupt. "A deathbed conversion, it would have been most uncharacteristic of him; by all accounts, he had had a strict Baptist upbringing but, no,

I think Duncan having a change of heart is very unlikely."

"Why then? Was he thinking more about me, and it was his way of helping me to become more integrated into the community."

"Possibly, in fact, I would say probably, and if that is the case, well, he certainly achieved his aims. Yesterday, you were very high profile and, along with Larry, were instrumental in giving the community a very special evening. Yesterday will live long in the collective memory of the community. The more I think about it, the more plausible it seems. He chose you because he wanted to help you become a real leader in Pondreath. He was a shrewd judge of character and had obviously earmarked you as a potential worker for good in the community."

"God Bless Duncan," the priest looked up at the heavens.

"God bless Duncan," echoed the commander. The two men turned and made their way back to the village. It would soon be time for the evening, Angelus.

Chapter Thirty-Two

*The art of life lies in
a constant readjustment
to our surroundings.*

-Kakuzo Okakura

The weeks slipped by. For the priest the 'Duncan effect,' was very evident in the number of people, some of whom he was not conscious of speaking to before, who stopped him to commiserate over the burglary or to thank him for his part in Duncan Evans's funeral. At the school, he found he had established himself as a person to be looked up to and to respect, and even the attendance at the church had grown. Louisa Evans and Jim Nesbitt had become regular in their attendance as had Mrs Corbett.

For Larry, in the weeks after the funeral, it was more nuanced. While he had clearly earned the respect of many people and he now had a status in the village, at the Trevinian house, things grew markedly worse. Sid Trevinian resented Larry's popularity; he made it clear that he did not approve of his relationship with Anna and that his friendship with Father Aloysius was like a red rag to a bull. He looked for every opportunity to pick on both his brother's children and was not averse to using physical means to make his feelings known. When Philippa accidentally spilt some milk on the table one morning while making her breakfast, he had sworn at her and cuffed her round the head. Larry had immediately gone to her aid, remonstrating with him, but his foster father had caught him by the throat and threatened to beat him to pulp.

From that day on, both Larry and his sister did their best to avoid him. They would get up very early in the morning and creep out of the house before he came down for breakfast. Larry would take his sister to the shop, and he would buy them both breakfast. If it was raining, they would eat it in the bus shelter while Larry waited for his lift to work. If it was dry, they would sit on one of the benches on the quay. When Larry left to go to work, Philippa would go to a friend's house, and they would walk together to school. In the evening, they would make sure they were in their rooms with the doors locked before he came home from the pub. Fortunately, Sid Trevinian was often away on long-haul assignments. They learnt to use these times to get their clothes laundered and to do anything else that might necessitate their being in the house for any length of time.

At the weekends, Larry spent much of the time at the Evans' house with Anna and, apart from breakfast, ate all his meals there. Louisa Evans benefited from having a willing and able handyman to help out when she needed one. Larry also proved useful in the garden, and he certainly pulled his weight when it came to lending a hand with cleaning chores and clearing away after meals. Above all, he was cheerful and polite. He seemed to enjoy her cooking and was for ever thanking her for the food that was on his plate. This caused her to wonder who did the cooking in the Trevinian home. She wasn't surprised when he started to ask her how she prepared a dish and made requests for recipes. The third time this happened, she suggested that the best way for him to learn was to help her cook. He was more than willing to help, and so the cooking lessons began.

Larry was a quick learner, and Louisa Evans enjoyed sharing her culinary skills.

Larry, for his part, had long since given up depending on his aunt for meals and had been preparing food for himself and his sister for some time. It was all very basic and hit-and-miss, but it was that or nothing. Now, he was eager to put his newly acquired knowledge to the test and to prepare the dishes he and his mentor had made during the week. He made it a principle that he bought his own ingredients and he cooked for the whole household and not just Philippa and himself. Lastly, he was grateful to Mrs Evans for teaching him; the best way of showing his appreciation was to become a teacher too, and to involve his sister. He would teach everything he learnt to Philippa. His first attempts coincided with a time when his stepfather was away, so he only had three people to cater to. His aunt spent most evenings at the pub where she cleaned. When she came back late and found a meal waiting for her by the microwave, she was more than a little surprised, but she soon came to expect it and appreciate it. She was slow to show her appreciation, but after her fourth meal of the week, which she particularly enjoyed, she left a note on the table for Larry to find when he got home. "Thank you, a very nice meal last night," was scrawled in pencil on a scrap of paper which was left on the table. The following week, Larry found himself cooking for four. His stepfather had a week of short-haul jobs. His dirty plate was left to the morning on the table or in the sink. There was never an acknowledgement or sign of appreciation.

At first Larry was concerned for his sister. Weekends were a particular cause of worry, but Philippa proved just as resourceful as her elder brother. She had friends she could go to, and these were not confined to her peers from school; there were older people, too. On the first Saturday morning after her stepfather had given her a cuff round the head, she had decided that if her brother could earn money, she could too. She would go round the houses of the older people she knew and see if she could earn some pocket money by doing odd jobs for them on Saturday mornings. That first morning, she called on the presbytery. Father Aloysius was out. Miss Farrow answered the door. Disappointed but unabashed, she had asked the priest's housekeeper if there were any odd jobs that needed doing.

Miss Farrow had known Philippa all her life. She suspected there was more behind the request than just earning a bit of pocket money. She was aware that Philippa and her brother turned up early every morning at the shop to buy their breakfast, and that was a cause for concern for a start. She invited Philippa in, and over a glass of squash and a biscuit for her guest and a cup of tea for herself, they discussed what sort of things Philippa might be able to do. For that morning, they settled on dusting and hoovering the lounge. She noted the care the child took over dusting each of the items on the mantle shelf above the fire place and the sensible way she managed to deal with the lights and lampshades. She was impressed to see how Philippa removed all the books from the bookshelf and methodically stacked them on the floor so that she could return them to their place on the shelves in exactly the correct order after the shelves had been cleaned. All this was noted from the vantage point of the corridor where the housekeeper had set up the ironing board and kept herself busy ironing the priest's shirts, glancing up every now and again to see what her young helper was doing.

Miss Farrow contrived to complete her ironing just as Philippa was finishing the hoovering. There was no doubt that Philippa was keen to earn herself pocket money, but there was undoubtedly more to it than that. Perhaps the child was looking for ways to spend time away from the house. Miss Farrow decided to help extend that time by inviting Philippa to accompany her to the church to clean the brasses and the candle sticks. That would help keep them occupied until lunchtime when the stew in the slow cooker would be ready, and they could share a good, nourishing meal. Father Aloysius would probably be back by then, and there was plenty for all three of them.

Father Aloysius had already returned to the presbytery when Miss Farrow and her helper came back from the church having completed their chores there. If the priest was surprised to see Philippa walk in the door of the kitchen he did not show it.

"We have a visitor, Father," announced Miss Farrow as she ushered Phillipa into the kitchen. "This young lady has been helping me clean the candles and brasses, and I have to say she has been most helpful. I hope you don't mind I have invited her to lunch. She also cleaned the lounge for me."

"Of course, I don't mind. You are more than welcome, Philippa, and thank you for helping clean our church brasses. Our cloakroom is just down the corridor, so you can wash your hands there, and I will get another chair." Father Aloysius helped show his visitor to the cloakroom and fetched a chair from his study. The meal was a great success, Philippa was relaxed and plied the priest with questions while she ate. She clearly enjoyed her meal; she had two helpings of stew and a banana to follow.

Father Aloysius, for his part, answered her questions as best he could and took care to make no reference to either the school or the Trevinian home. After the meal, Philippa helped him wash up before leaving to call on a friend who lived close by. The priest gave his housekeeper a big thumbs up when they returned to the kitchen after showing Philippa to the door. Miss Farrow smiled.

"I expect that won't be the last time that young lady will come knocking on our door."

She was right; the Saturday mornings became part of a new routine for Philippa.

Nor was that the only new routine she was to adopt. When Miss Farrow returned to the shop that afternoon, she had a quiet word with her brother-in-law. By coincidence, shortly afterwards, Philippa came to the shop. She wanted to spend her recently earned pocket money. There being no one else in the shop, Mr Fowler decided that this would be a good time to follow up on his sister-in-law's suggestion.

"Philippa," he asked as he handed her her change, "You come to the shop early most days of the week. I'm short of someone to deliver the papers on one of the rounds. Would you be interested?

The girl was clearly surprised to be asked, but she quickly recovered, "Yes, please, thank you, Mr Fowler."

"It would be every day of the week, mind it, and I know it's not a fortune, but you'll be earning about ten times more than I did when I delivered papers."

"That's fine, Mr. Fowler, when do I start?"

"Tomorrow, if you like, you will have more time on a Sunday than during the week, so it would be sensible. You can see how long it takes you before Monday."

"What time do you want me?"

"Seven o'clock if you can make it, not later than a quarter past."

"Fine, I'll be here tomorrow at seven."

"Good, I tell you what, I could give you a list of all the people you'll be visiting now and you could have a trial run this afternoon. Then, if you have got any questions, we can get those sorted before you do your first round."

When his new paper deliverer returned, Mr Fowler had already got the bag ready for the next day. There were also some leaflets he wanted delivered. These would have normally gone with the Sunday papers. However, he had decided that sending them that afternoon would give his trainee another valuable experience; finding the front door was one thing, but getting the paper through the letter box was another. Some of the letter boxes were quite awkward. It would be good for her to meet these in advance, and delivering these leaflets would help.

"Now, young lady, you certainly got round in good time, well done. Have you any questions?"

"Yes, Mr Fowler, I found a door for number twelve Church Lane, but I couldn't find the letterbox, and number seven Spinnaker Drive has big gates, and they were locked, so I couldn't get to the letterbox."

"Ah, I should have told you. I'm sorry, I forgot to say the lady at number twelve has no letterbox. She has a plastic bucket with a lid; you put the paper in that, and she takes the bucket back into her house. It will be out in the morning. Number seven, Spinnaker Drive, did you say?

"Yes, it's all posh and got big iron gates."

"I think you'll find they will be open in the morning, but Mr Devonshire does have dogs. Their bark is a bit off-putting, but they are quite friendly, really, and usually you don't see them. Is that all?"

"Yes, but I think I'll go round again just for a practice."

"Mr Fowler grinned, "Funny you should say that. I have got some leaflets here which need delivering, if you took these round today instead of tomorrow when you have all the Sunday papers which can be quite large you could have a go at putting things through letter boxes. That way you'll get to know which are the tricky ones in advance. Customers object to papers that are delivered wet, so if it's raining you have to work out a way of getting them in the letter box quickly and of keeping them dry."

"OK, and I'll also get used to walking with a bag."

"Good thinking, you may have to make two trips tomorrow. Sunday papers can be quite bulky and heavy. Now here's your bag all ready. This is a good waterproof bag in case it's raining, the leaflets are already inside."

Philippa picked up the bag. She took a leaflet out to look at it before she set off. "They're all the same, are they?"

"Yes, all the same."

"Fine, see you later." She waved as she went out of the door. Mr Fowler looked at his watch. "A bright button that one," he said to himself, as he set about checking the shelves.

When Philippa got back she found Miss Farrow behind the till. "Mr Fowler has gone off duty, he says for you to leave the bag here under the counter with the others."

"Thank you Miss Farrow. Do you do a lot of shifts?

"No, not really, just this one and Monday and Thursday afternoons, but I do help restock the shelves in the evening as well."

"That, on top of looking after Father Aloysius, keeps you pretty busy then."

"Yes I suppose it does, but they say the devil finds work for idle hands, so that's probably a good thing."

"I see. Is it all right if I go now?"

"Of course, dear, but before you go, Mr Fowler says he is not going to pay you for today, but you may take a drink and a packet of biscuits if you like, and he'll see you at seven tomorrow."

Philippa reached in her pocket for her change, "I bought some sweets earlier with the money you gave me for helping you this morning but I think I've still got enough for another drink. I'm meeting my friend in a minute and we could share the biscuits and have a drink each."

"Of course, dear, help yourself, but you can keep the change. Have this one on me."

"Oh, thank you, Miss Farrow." As Phillipa left the shop, she couldn't help thinking that this Saturday had been a very good day, all things considered, so far.

Philippa quickly adapted to her new routine. Larry was more than willing to help her and together they got the round completed in good time for them to have their breakfast together. Mrs Fowler had kindly suggested should they prefer it they might like to eat it in her kitchen rather than in the bus stop shelter. This generosity was further extended when she offered them a space in her fridge and a shelf in one of her cupboards. This meant they could have a proper breakfast and could budget for the whole week. In return Larry volunteered his services as a handyman.

That first Friday was another good day for Philippa. She got paid. When she got back from her paper round she found an envelope on the counter with her name on it. The other two deliverers had already taken theirs. She knew of course what she was going to be paid but none the less opening the envelope and taking out a crisp ten pound note was the cause of a great sense of excitement. Smiling broadly she held it up to Larry.

Larry smiled his approval "Well done little soldier, but now what are you going to do with that then ?"

His sister thought for a moment "Can you keep it for me?"

"Me, yes but why don't you let me open an account for you at the post office here in my name and then it will earn some interest."

"Can you do that for me?"

"I think so, we can ask, I'm old enough and some of my wages go into an account here."

"Let's then. Let's do it."

"The post office side of the shop doesn't open until later, so I'll look after it now and we will do it tomorrow morning." In the duration of a week young Philippa had become an earner for the first time in her life, and was now capable of saving her earnings such as they were. Her newly acquired role had introduced her to the world of work, and had given a new structure to her days. In joining her brother as a worker, albeit at the lowest rung on the workforce she was now no longer solely a taker, an acceptor of other people's largess, she was also a contributor with a status, and with the responsibilities that demanded she was sensitive to expectations and kept to certain rules. She found that being punctual and reliable earned her respect from her employers, she found that being cheerful and polite to the people she met on her paper round helped her to feel better and them too, to see her in a new light. She wasn't just that scruffy kid with a poor home background, she was a person who despite the disadvantages of being brought up in a dysfunctional household could be genuinely a nice person. At first her earnings did not amount to much but they were enough for her to be able to buy the odd treat for others, to express her gratitude to others for their hospitality with a small gift. She had discovered the joy of giving and that people responded with gratitude and more often than not responded in kind. As she grew in confidence her desire to improve her self grew too, she realised that she could probably increase her earnings and she started to look for opportunities to do so. She was learning to be ambitious. When Mrs Hazelmere was laid up with a nasty cold Philippa offered to walk her dogs for her. At first this was accepted with gratitude as an act of kindness but Mrs Hazelmere was not one to take things for granted and having found Philippa to be reliable and punctual and most importantly, good with her pets, she decided to pay her. It was not long before she had two other dog walking commitments. In two months her earnings had doubled. Commitments and responsibility had consequences and Philippa found herself having to make choices. Once she had been free to do what she liked, to pop round to friends whenever she pleased, to go wherever she wanted and do whatever she wanted. Now, with commitments the opportunities to socialise were less. She found some of her friends reacted unfavourably when she felt obliged to turn down offers to join them in an activity they had planned. She could no longer join the gang mooching about on the quay after school when she had dogs to walk. If she wanted to join the others of her peer group on the beach on a Saturday or Sunday afternoon she had to be aware of the passing of time and to give herself enough time to return to the village to meet her responsibilities. Some of her peers perhaps out of envy began to call her a snob and to say things about her that were hurtful. This of course was not a new experience. Since her parents split up and she had become the youngest member of the Trevinian household she had been different to most other children in her class. Being different meant you were more vulnerable to being picked on, as one of the lowest of the pecking order you could be a target for the bullies, being a Trevinian meant it was harder to establish yourself as socially acceptable and when you managed to establish a friendship in your anxiety to keep that friendship you could be jealous and resentful of any who might be a rival. Being an earner meant respect from some but not all. There were friends you could trust but they were few and you had to develop a thick skin. Philippa was young to have entered the world of work, she was growing up fast. Working at the presbytery each week she found in Miss Farrow someone she could confide in. Father Aloysius's housekeeper had been born in the village and had grown up there. There was not much that she didn't know about the village and its inhabitants all of whom used the shop. She was kind, understanding and a good listener. Cleaning the brasses in the church each week was opening up a whole new world for the girl and she was curious about what the different things she cleaned were used for. She kept asking questions. Miss Farrow for her part, while she always answered her companion's questions, did not do or say anything in the way of persuading her attend a church service and to see the chalice, the plate and the candles she helped clean each week being used. Instead she quietly said her prayers. She was not surprised when a month after Philippa had first come knocking on the presbytery door the girl slipped into church one Sunday morning shortly after the Mass had started and came to sit beside her.

Larry was pleased to see how his sister had taken the initiative to find ways of coping with the challenges of weekends and the need to avoid confrontations with their foster carers. It meant that he could feel free to spend more time with Anna. He and Anna had signed as regular helpers at the Tarrants' youth club. When he learnt that his sister was attending Sunday morning Mass at St. Prodricks he suggested to Anna that they might accompany her mother and do the same. Father Aloysius quite unexpectedly found the average age of his congregation reducing quite significantly. He was quick to take the opportunity to give the younger members of the congregation responsibilities. Philippa was given the responsibility of assisting Miss Farrow with serving the refreshments after the service and it was not long before Anna joined her. Larry was enrolled to help keep the grounds around the church tidy. This did nothing to improve relationships at the Trevinian home.

Chapter Thirty-Three

*It is only during a
storm that a tree knows how strong it is*

-Douglass Malloch

The long summer break came, the weeks turned into months, July became August and August became September. The youth club continued to function throughout the holiday break. A lot of the sessions were held outside. Rounders was very popular game among the club's clientele, and Father Aloysius found himself in charge while the Tarrants looked after those children who preferred to spend the time on other activities. For the priest rounders was something new. He enjoyed it immensely. In the winter term the rounders equipment was put away. With the shortening of the daylight hours for those children whose parents could not collect them, the Tarrants committed to escort their children back to their homes. Father Aloysius was on the way home after completing his escort duties taking children who lived the other side of the bridge back to their homes. He had had a busy day visiting the old and the unwell on his bike. He was weary but in a buoyant frame of mind, he enjoyed his evenings at the club, where he could relax and indulge in an evening of fun. It always lifted his spirits. He had crossed the bridge. There was a van parked just to the right. The rear door was open. A groan caught his attention, he noticed a pair of legs sticking out from under a van. He walked over to investigate, and bending down to ask if any help was needed. That was the last he was to remember of that evening. Lurking in the shadows was Sid Trevinian. Moving silently he swung a sock full of sand in his right hand. He hit the priest over the head and grunted with satisfaction as he fell to the ground. The owner of the legs emerged quickly from under the van. Sid and his brother Mick had waited long for this opportunity and after observing Father Aloysius's coming and goings for a time they had come up with a plan and had contrived to ambush him. Hastily they bundled their victim into the back of the van. Mick followed and set about tying Father Aloysius's arms and legs together. Sid went to the front of the van and opened the door on the driver's side. He activated the cab light, then flicked the switch so it would remain on. He returned to the rear of the van to shut the rear door and then drove the van off down the quay. There in the dark at the end of the line of boats tied up at the quay side was his brother's trawler.

The noise of the boat's engine muffled Farther Aloysius's groan as he came to. There was no one in the vicinity to hear it anyway, his two assailants were in the wheelhouse. He was lying where they had tossed him in the stern of the boat. He had been fortunate in that he had landed on a heap of nets. He lay still, his nostrils filled with the putrid stench of fish and diesel. His head throbbed. Where was he? What had happened to him? His scalp seemed sore and why this terrible headache? He was lying face down, his vision was restricted to a close up view of something rough and abrasive. Desperately he turned his head. It took him a while to register that the rough material was netting. He tried to sit up. His hands were tied behind his back, his feet were tied too. He tried wiggling his fingers to see if he could locate the knots, all he could feel was rope. The boat, buffeted by the wind, pitched and rocked. A wave broke over the bows sending a deluge of water careening down the scuppers. It gradually dawned on him that he was in the bottom of a boat, and that the boat was at sea, As to how he came to be there he had no idea. He tried rolling over onto his back. After some squirming, he managed it and lay back breathing heavily. He felt the roughness of the netting on his scalp. Above was the vast expanse of sky. He struggled into a sitting position. The light through the wheelhouse rear window spread in a warm yellow glow over the stern deck. What he saw confirmed his fears, he was on a boat at sea. With another groan he sank back. How had he got here and why was he here all trussed up with heavy rope. He lay still gazing up at the night sky and tried to put his muddled thoughts into some sort of order. He had been at the youth club. Then he had walked a group of children home. He was on his way back to the presbytery and had crossed the bridge. There was this van. There were legs sticking out from under it. He had gone over to see if he could help and then. Then was a blank. Now he was tied up in the bottom of a boat at sea. How did he get here? It was a mystery. Someone must have got him here but how and why? Could it be he had been kidnapped? Why would anyone want to kidnap him? Then in a flash it dawned on him. Sid Trevinian's brother was a fisherman. He lived in one of the cottages along the quay. Was the van his, were those legs his? It was Sid Trevinian who had got him here. It was Sid Trevinian who had threatened him not once but twice, he recalled the man's very words. He had threatened death. The realisation sent a cold shiver down the priest's spine. Death by drowning.

In the small wheelhouse, the two men argued how best to dispose of their victim. Sid was all for just tossing him over the side as he was, all trussed up in his cassock. Mick had other ideas. While it might be unlikely that his body would be found there was an outside chance that it would be washed up somewhere. If that happened then people would immediately know there had been foul play. Their alibi would not be fool proof and if the police traced the time of their departure from Pondreath and also the approximate time of the priest's disappearance then that would make them suspects.

He argued that they should untie the priest and then toss him overboard. Further he continued to argue they should remove his cassock because if his body was found and he was wearing his clerical garb that too, would be suspicious. Perhaps the best thing to do was to strip him altogether and to keep his clothes which could be left on the beach. That would suggest he had been for a swim. If the body was washed up the conclusion would be that he had gone for a swim. They had choices. If he was naked having gone for a skinny dip than all his clothes would be on the beach. It was more likely for a priest to have retained his underwear. Mick after some deliberation settled for the latter. The one option to throw the priest overboard as he was in his cassock was a complete non-starter. At first Sid was not convinced, but eventually Mick prevailed. With the sea as it was Mick was loathed that they should both leave the wheel house. It was down to his brother to do the deed but he had his doubts that he would do as he had suggested and keep to their agreement. The removal of the ropes and the stripping of the man would take time and what if were to regain consciousness. If his brother were to do the job could he be trusted not to just tip him overboard as he was? A huge wave threatened to breach the boat. As he wrestled with the wheel to get her head back into the wind and the prevailing direction of the oncoming waves he made a snap decision. They would split the job. He would do the untying and the stripping and then return to the wheelhouse leaving his brother to do the deed. "I'll go, you take the wheel, when I've got him ready you can tip him overboard." He said it as an order. He was after all the skipper of the boat. He gave Sid no time to argue, he had got the boat back on course, he left the wheel and headed out through the wheelhouse door. As he did so another large wave broke over the bows and the rushing water threatened to knock him over. Sid was obliged to take charge of the wheel.

In the stern of the boat Father Aloysius had heard the door open. Someone was coming. He needed to be unconscious, or at least to feign unconsciousness and he needed to be on his front. Hastily he turned over. He was fortunate the wave breaking over the bow of the boat and threatening to knock his approaching assailant over, had distracted him and he did not witness the manoeuvre. Father Aloysius held his breath and waited. He prayed that he would be able to remain inert and appear to still be out for the count whatever happened. He heard Mick Trevinian scrambling down to the stern clutching at anything he could in order to keep his feet. He reached his victim and steadying himself bent over and untied his legs. Father Aloysius had not expected this. What was he doing? Surely he was not going to release him. When Mick Trevinian untied his arms he wondered for a moment whether he should take this opportunity to make a break, but quickly dismissed it. It would be too risky. Another blow to the head and he would be unconscious again and not able to do anything towards saving himself. Better wait. Mick turned him over. Father Aloysius let his head flop back. He kept his eyes tight shut as his assailant wrestled with his cassock. It was more difficult than he had bargained for but he got it done. This was taking too long. Hastily he pulled off the priest's shoes and undid his belt. Removing his trousers and underwear was easier than the cassock had been. Just the shirt left. He struggled with the buttons but eventually got it off. Father Aloysius was almost naked, and completely still. Gathering the garments together he headed back to the wheel house.

Father Aloysius, his eyes tight shut lay inert, unaware that he was for a moment or two to be on his own. He had no idea who it was who had released him, or why? At any moment he expected something else to happen and when at least a minute had passed and the 'What next?' question remained unanswered, he opened his eyes, just a little at first then when there was no immediate reaction he opened them fully. Lying on his back with his head tilted back his vision was limited, he would have to move his head. Taking care he lifted his head and dropped his chin. He looked around him He had moved just in time to see his assailant reach the wheel house door.

Mick entered the wheel house and tossed the clothes into a corner. Sid Trevinian turned his head. He swore "Where have you been, took your time didn't you?"

His brother knew better than to rise to the bait, provoking Sid Trevinian by arguing could get you into trouble. He ignored the implied rebuke, stepping forward to take the wheel, he announced with some bravado,

"All ready for you stripped all but starkers."

"About time."

Father Aloysius pushed himself up to a half-sitting position. He was free! He could get up. He could....At that precise moment, the door of the wheelhouse swung open again. Too late. Hastily, the priest flopped back down into his former position. Sid wasted no time in getting to him. With the boat buffeted by the big waves, pitching and tossing in a most unpredictable way, he was anxious to get the deed done and to return to the wheelhouse. He grabbed the priest by the ankles and dragged him to the side of the boat, then bracing one foot against the wall of the gunwale in one swift movement, he stooped and, wrapping his arms round his victim's waist, he heaved him over the side. With his usual expletive, he muttered, "Good riddance ..... black n----r!" The violent movement of the boat almost caused him to lose his balance. Steadying himself without another glance at the sea, he turned and headed back to the wheelhouse. Had he spent a moment longer to check what happened next, he might have seen his victim come spluttering to the surface. Sid Trevinian slammed the wheelhouse door behind him. He grunted,

"Job done, time to go fishing."

"He was still just in his pants, was he?"

"What do you think? Wrapped him in silver paper and tied a label on him, with love from Sid? You heard me it's time to get this tub down the coast to get fishing."

"What about the clothes then?" his brother snapped.

"Clothes?"

"The n---- r's clothes. We need to leave them on the beach." There followed another heated argument during the course of which Mick Trevinian swung the boat round and set a course to take them back to the harbour. His brother was no sailor, he could rant and rave but he needed Mick and would have more sense than to try to force the issue, they needed a cast iron alibi and leaving the clothes on the beach was the best one he could think of. They had time to dump the clothes and get to sea again but the sooner they did it the better. Mick knew his craft and had weathered many a rough sea, and got through many a storm but the sooner they got out to sea again and well away from land the better. Thanks to his good seamanship by the first light of dawn the little boat was well away from land and he could plot a course to take them up the coast. When they had got a good distance from the scene of the crime, should the weather deteriorate further they could look for a good harbour. They could hole up there and their alibi would be all the more convincing. With all hatches well battened down the little craft chugged on and with every nautical mile Mick grew more confident. Sid's dark mood improved too.

Miss Farrow was at the presbytery at her usual time. She was not surprised and so not at all concerned when she found that Father Aloysius was not there. He was obviously still out on his early morning run. Perhaps he had met someone on the way home and had got delayed. However as time passed she began to be a little concerned. In order to distract herself she turned to clearing out the kitchen drawers. They had had a good clean out just recently after the robbery but another one would do no harm. The housekeeper was a methodical worker and she decided to make a list of all the contents. It would act as an inventory, and should they ever have a burglary again it could be used to check what might have been taken. At first the task achieved its purpose but when the kitchen clock showed eight fifteen and there was still no sign of him she abruptly put aside her task. What could have happened to make him this late? Then she had another thought, what if he wasn't late at all and had completed his run early and had had something to eat and gone out to the church or gone on another errand? Hastily she checked to see if his cassock was in the usual place hanging behind his bedroom door, it was not. That was it. After all, he had returned really early from his run, had something to eat and then gone out again.

The thought was reassuring but it wouldn't hurt to call at the church just in case he was there all the time. He wasn't, the church was locked. She hadn't thought to bring the key with her. She hurried back to check if the key was still hung on its peg in the office. It was there. That left the other possibility. He had gone out on an errand. Just what that might be was not at all obvious. She went to his office to see if she could locate his appointments diary. It was there on the desk. Quickly she flipped the pages. There was nothing for Thursday December the sixth. She slammed the book shut in her frustration. She glanced to the clock on the wall. It was eight forty. She had better open the church, Angelus was at nine and people would be arriving soon. She would open the church and that would leave just enough time for her to phone the shop to see if he had called there. There was no one yet at the church but it would not be long before there was. She drew a blank at the shop. Her brother-in-law was serving and Farther Aloysius had certainly not called in that morning. He like her, had no idea where he might be. She had been foiled at every attempt to solve what was becoming quite a concerning mystery. Disappointed, she had hung up and hurried back to the church. As she went she chided her self. She should have asked her brother-in-law to enquire of every customer that entered the shop about Father Aloysius. If anyone had seen the priest he could have then given her a call. Now it was too late, Mrs Hazelmere and Louisa Evans were standing in the porch waiting for the church to be unlocked. Commander Nesbitt was striding down across the field. Miss Farrow opened the church door and went down to meet him.

"Good morning Miss Farrow," he greeted her, "To what do I owe getting a special welcome?"

"It's Father Aloysius."

"Yes, what?"

"I'm not sure, he is just not here."

"I see."

"He was not at the presbytery when I arrived this morning. I didn't think anything of it at first, I presumed he was still out on his early morning run. It was only later I started to get worried. His cassock is not on the usual peg so I concluded he must have come home early and gone out again before I arrived but he wasn't here at the church, and they haven't seen him at the shop, and now it's time for the service and he is still not here so I don't know what to think."

"Um, do the others know?"

"No, not yet. I wanted a word with you first."

"Thank you. Have you any suggestions as to what we do now?"

"Other than going out to look for him, I can't think of anything else."

"Well, we could certainly do that, but we need to tell the others first."

"Would you do that, please?"

"Of course." Mrs Hazelmere and Louisa Evans had already entered the church and were sitting in a pew near the front. Miss Farrow joined them.

"Ladies, I'm sorry to say Father Aloysius is not here. He may be on his way and has just got held up. However he was not at the presbytery this morning when Miss Farrow arrived. I suggest we wait for five minutes and then perhaps if he has not turned up we might discuss what we ought to do, that is unless any of you know where he might be or have seen him this morning?" The question was met with a shaking of heads. No one had seen the priest. "Well, in the meantime there is the organ over there, so if it is acceptable to you I'll play for you." This suggestion being met with approval the commander settled down on the organ stool and played. It was Danny Boy. He did not have the music with him but he clearly knew it well and showed himself to be an accomplished organist and with a little improvisation managed to extend the piece to the suggested time. His efforts having been applauded and there being no return of Father Aloysius, there followed a discussion as to what might usefully be done to ascertain where he might be. Miss Farrow it was agreed, should remain at the presbytery. She would be recipient of information and be able to disseminate any news to the others. Mrs Hazelmere volunteered to return to her home and phone all the people she knew who were on Father Aloysius's regular visiting list and should there be any news, to relay it to Miss Farrow. The commander and Louisa Evans would be the search party. They decided to go together, two pairs of eyes were better than one. Telephone numbers were exchanged and the group departed. The commander was familiar with the route that Father Aloysius usually took when he went on his morning runs. He and Louisa decided to check that first.

It was twenty past ten when Louisa stumbled across a pile of clothes She and the commander had made their way down to beach.

The evidence of the previous night's storm was clearly apparent in the shingle and the litter. The sea was a powerful sculptor of the shore line and it was clear that the storm of the previous night had shifted a lot of shingle, it had also left a lot of litter at the high tide make. The commander was a little way away searching for footprints in the sand, she was combing the shore line where the beach met the cliffs. The clothes were folded and piled up on a rock. She called out and the commander came hurrying over.

"Clothes," Louisa announced as he approached.

"I don't think we should touch them. Are they Father Aloysius's?"

"Well, yes, I'm sure that's his clerical shirt." Louisa pointed to the garment.

"Shoes too, they look like his?"

"What are you thinking?"

"I really don't know, it looks as if he decided to go for a swim."

"Um, possibly, but there is no towel."

"True, but I suppose it could have been a spur-of-the-moment decision, and he decided to go skinny dipping."

"Maybe, but anyway I think it's time I phoned the police." The commander took his phone from his pocket. "Can you take a picture on your phone please. I'll phone the police and then we can contact Miss Farrow and let her know what's happening, agreed?"

"Agreed."

Five minutes later Louisa Evans was walking back the way they had come. The police were on their way and she had agreed to wait on the quay to meet them and to guide them to the site. The commander was busy doing a thorough search of the area.

Twenty minutes later, he was joined by Mrs Evans and two police constables.

A careful examination of the clothes led the to the conclusion that they had not been left that morning, they were too wet for that, which meant they had probably been left the previous evening or night. There was no cassock but the shirt was a clerical one and the trousers, socks and shoes were all recognisable as of the type used by Father Aloysius. There were no underpants, so if the priest had gone for a swim, modesty had prevailed. It was fortunate that they were on a rock, just above the tideline so they had escaped the waves. Since then the tide had washed any trace of footprints in the sand. It was time to involve the air sea rescue.

By midday Trawler P426 was five miles up the coast. A helicopter passed high overhead. Sid swore."What do they want?" "Relax," his brother reassured him as he watched the bright orange aircraft heading off down the coast. "It's good to see them. It means they have found the clothes, they obviously think that the n---- r has taken a swim. Just what we wanted. Search all they like, it's a hundred to one they'll find anything, and if they do so what, the evidence will all point to a foolish skinny dip."

"When are we going to head for a port then? I need a drink."

"We'll be in Newquay in a couple hours, where that chopper came from. You'll be able to get a skinful then."

Sid grunted," It won't be a moment too soon. I'm gagging."

The search for Father Aloysius went on all afternoon. An R.N.L.I. lifeboat joined the helicopter in the search. Police frogmen, taking advantage of the low tide, searched among the rocks of the headlands at opposite ends of the beach. The news of the priest's disappearance had spread quickly. Larry had heard it from the commander who had phoned him. He had informed Anna. With her mind full of forebodings Anna had rushed down to meet Larry on the quay. She thanked God it was the weekend and they were able to respond immediately. They hurried down to the beach. Other villagers gathered to help too. Commander Nesbitt organised the volunteer searchers to comb different sections of the beach. As the tide receded they were able extend their search further out from the shore. Speculation was rife. What could have happened to the cleric? Searches put together a picture of his movements from the day before. It gradually became clear that the last people to see him were some of the children he had delivered home after the Friday evening youth club. It seemed he had disappeared some time after that, but how and why and where? With a chill wind it was cold work, some searchers sensing the fruitless nature of the task drifted off home. Others went only to return with hot drinks and sandwiches for the more hardy. With each passing hour the prospects of finding anything grew increasingly bleak but still Anna and Larry and a few more hardy souls pressed on. The tide turned and still they combed the beach. Both of them refused to succumb to the thought that their search might be in vain.

Chapter Thirty-Four

There are no desperate situations.

-Heinz Guderian

The shock of the cold took Father Aloysius's breath away. Spluttering he got to the surface. The boat, already beyond his grasp was moving away. Gasping for air he was struggling in its wake. Desperately he looked about him, keeping his head just above the surface it was hard to get his bearings. A wave lifted him up. A light, was that a light? He lost sight of it as the wave moved on leaving him in a trough. Moments later he was raised up again. It was a light! A light meant the shore, he knew which way to swim. The trawler was disappearing into the darkness behind him. He did the only thing he could do, he struck out for land.

Farther Aloysius had not learnt to swim until he was an adult at his seminary. He had been taught by a fellow student and had come to enjoy regular visits to the local swimming baths, but he was certainly not a good swimmer. The coldness of the water at first lent an urgency to his strokes, he had to keep his limbs moving, but he soon began to tire. It was his good fortune that the wind and the currents were on his side. His strokes grew more and more feeble and soon it was all he could do to keep his head above water. There were times when he was engulfed by a wind driven wave and had to claw his way to the surface spluttering and gasping for air. Each surfacing was a victory and a triumph over adversity, but each took its toll. If the Trevinian brothers had taken him even only a short distance further before dumping him he would certainly have perished. Exhausted by the efforts to stay afloat he would have succumbed to the cold long before being confronted by the rocks and towering cliffs that suddenly seemed to be looming ahead. The sense that he was near to land raised his hopes and spurred him on to attempt a few more feeble strokes. He must get there. That the rocks were land was enough for him, that they presented a great threat was something he was only aware of in the back of his mind. It was a threat he could do nothing about.

As he was carried inexorably on by the current and the wind-driven waves, he encountered the backwash and the ensuing increase in turbulence. The angels were on his side. He escaped the undertow, and a large breaker carried him forward, sweeping him down a narrow channel between the rocks. Everything happened at such a speed he had no time to think; only an instinctive intake of a gulp of air saved him as he was dragged not into the sheer rock face immediately ahead but down, down and down, and then swept on under the lip of the cave, on rushed the water. He felt the rough abrasion of rock and sand as he was cast up on a shingle bank, not that he was to know it was a bank as all was pitch black.

Again instinct came to his rescue as the retreating water threatened to take him with it he dug one hand into the shingle and grasped at a rock with the other. It was enough to prevent him from being dragged back. If there was a pattern to the nature of the waves as they marched across the ocean again he was unaware of it, and if there wasn't then the Angels were still on his side. The wave that had carried him down that narrow passage way between rocks and had forced him under the lip of the cave and cast him onto the shingle had been large, the subsequent three were smaller and barely reached his feet. Completely spent and almost rendered unconscious Father Aloysius was tempted to give in to oblivion and to close his eyes and just lie there. The wetting of his feet by another wave awoke him to the need that he could not relax yet. Desperately he squirmed his way forward. He had no idea what lay ahead all that mattered was that he move further away from where he had been unceremoniously dumped. He reached some rocks. Perhaps he had gone far enough. He rested for a short time and then eased his body forward. They were unforgiving, hard and colder than the shingle. He gritted his teeth and prayed. The rocks were slippery too. Had he made a mistake. Moments later an outstretched hand felt sand. He slid forward centimetre by centimetre until at last he could feel nothing but sand beneath him. Was he safe? He could not say, but he was beyond caring and he succumbed to unconsciousness. His final thought was praise the Lord.

Some hours later Father Aloysius came to. At first he wondered where on earth he was. Then it all came back to him and he was conscious of a strong feeling of thirst. He had survived, he had not drowned. Praise the Lord. Then as he turned his head slightly he realised something was different, something had changed. He could see! It was not pitch black he could see the sand he lay on and by raising his eyes and glancing up there were rocks. He raised his head a little - sand and rocks, he lowered his head. He groaned, he was stiff with not having moved for so long. He lay still assessing in his mind his situation. Then he became aware of a sound he had not heard before, the sound of drip, drip, drip dripping water. But where? Water he needed water. Where was the sound coming from? Another thought struck him, apart from the drip, drip, drip of water there was not another sound, all was still and quiet and strangely calm. The sea, the sea..... he could not hear the sea, where was the sound of waves?

After a long moment of deliberation he turned himself over onto his back and immediately shaded his eyes with his hand. A narrow band of sunlight was streaming down straight into his eyes. He felt its warmth on his forehead. He realised he was no longer cold, at least he was no longer numb with cold, and he was no longer wet. Praise the Lord. He was in a cave, as to how he got to be there he had no idea.

Gradually he raised himself into a sitting position. The band of light from above was coming from a narrow slit, an opening in the roof of the cave but Father Aloysius decided that that could not be the only source of illumination. His gaze shifted from the roof down towards the end of the cave. He was looking for the entrance, the place presumably he had entered. What he saw puzzled him. The cave roof sloped downward and then became a wall, almost vertical and at its base was a lagoon.

The lagoon seemed to be the source of light. Gingerly he stretched each limb in turn and then braced himself for a moment to make a seemingly herculean effort as he pushed himself to get upright. He brushed the damp sand from his chest and thighs. Gingerly he edged towards the lagoon. It stretched back some two metres, and the light was filtering up through the water. The entrance to the cave was below water level. The waves must have washed him under its lip and washed him up to the patch of sand on which he was now standing. If that was his way in, it could be his way out. Out, but out to what? Almost certainly it was not going to be a beach, and if it wasn't a sandy cove then it was likely to be a rocky headland. He thought back to his last moments before that wave, that mighty force of water had plunged him on his way. It had been dark, but not complete pitch black. He sensed more than saw the cliffs towering above him. the cliffs of the headland had a jumble of boulders at their base. Somewhere in that jumble of boulders there must be a passage that ended here inside this cave. A wave had forced him into the cave, would he have enough breath in his lungs to swim out? There was no knowing how far that underwater swim would have to be. Once out what would he find? If it was the headland, which more than likely was the case, then there would be another swim to get away from the rocks and it could be some distance to the beach. If that was not going to be his escape route, then unless he could find another, he was imprisoned.

The dripping of water from the cave roof reminded him of his thirst. He could explore the possibility of escape later. Now, he needed to slake his thirst. He located the source of the drip. It came from the roof of the cave. Father Aloysius made his way over a stretch of rock to where the drips were landing in a pool. Stretching out his hand, he caught one in his palm. He licked it. It was saline. Perhaps the salt came from his skin. He held his hand under the drips and, opening his hand and closing it, washed it as best he could. He made a cup with his hand, and when he had enough for a sip on his palm, he raised it to his lips. It was saline. He would have to look for another source of moisture. He turned his attention to the far end of what looked like a jumble of rock ending in a sheer face. And peered into the gloom. The floor of his prison sloped upward.|It seemed to turn a corner. He made his way over the rocks to try and see beyond the bend. The walls narrowed, and the slope grew steeper. As he rounded the corner and peered upward, there high above was another source of light. His heart leapt. Perhaps that might lead to a way out.

The priest clambered upwards, grasping the rocks to assist his balance. One was soft and spongy under his hand. Moss, where there was moss then there might be water. He located a rock where the moss was thick and scraped off a handful. It was moist. He squeezed it catching the drop in the cup of the palm of his other hand. He raised it to his lips. It was earthy but it wasn't saline. He spent the next twenty minutes gathering moss and squeezing it directly into his mouth. He washed the salt from his lips and soothed his parched throat. Feeling better he continued his upward climb. To his amazement he found some small ferns growing, and then best of all emitting from a hollow he saw a trickle of water. This, like that he had gleaned from the moss, tasted earthy but less so. Bending over the hollow he was able to scoop a mouthful up and to drink it. He sat on a rock and rested. He looked at the small clump of ferns and addressed his prayers to them.

"Praise God, the water that sustains you has sustained me, too. We both have been blessed."

Refreshed he turned to look up. He had managed the increasingly steep slope of the cave up to this point but the way ahead looked even more difficult. There seemed to be a ledge not far below the source of the light that he was heading for. Father Aloysius plotted a route he might use and then getting up he stretched. The clambering so far had served to keep him warm and to loosen his stiff joints, but after sitting to rest, he had begun to feel cold again. It was time he got going. He clambered upwards until he was directly below the ledge. He reached upwards. Its rim was an arm's length beyond his groping fingers. There above him was a hole and he could see blue sky. It was so tantalisingly close, so near yet out of reach. Getting up onto the ledge was going to prove more difficult than it had appeared from below. He searched about for hand holds and bulges on which to put his feet. There was a crack in the rock. Reaching up he managed to secure his first handhold. He found himself precariously balanced clinging by the fingers of one hand with his feet feeling the strain of bearing his weight on small protrusions from what was now a nearly vertical section of the cave. If he could just stretch a little higher he might be able to hook an arm over the lip of the ledge and to lever himself up onto it. Sensing that his position was becoming increasingly dangerous as his fingers and feet tired he took a deep breath. Taking one hand off its hold, lunged upwards and grabbed the edge of the ledge.

He heaved himself up and scrabbling against the rock with his feet managed to reach out with his other hand and find a hold on the ledge, then with a mighty effort pulled himself to safety. Panting he lay on his stomach, his forehead beaded with perspiration. When he had got his breath back and had composed himself he looked to left and to right. The ledge was both wide enough and long enough for him to sit or lie on it. He manoeuvred his body so he could look up for the hole above him. He could see the blue of the sky and some vegetation, "Praise the Lord." However when he gauged the distance between the ledge and the hole it was far greater than he had first thought. Gingerly he stood and stretched his arms above him. The rock face was vertical and smooth, the hole was some half a metre above his outstretched arms. The priest's heart sank. Carefully he sat down and peered back and looked down over the edge of the ledge. It was going to be very difficult to get back down. Unless he could do so he was trapped.

He lay back to think and to pray. He could hear the gulls calling, could he hear the sea, he wondered? The tide had possibly turned and perhaps waves would once again be washing into the cave under the ledge. He had to make a plan, how could he reach the hole? What would he find when he got there? What if the hole was half way down a towering rock face, but then again it might be at the top of the cliff. It might be the way out. The only way to find out was to get there and look, but how? Perhaps his best escape route was at the bottom of the cave. Perhaps he would have to take a chance and swim out. If he was going to attempt a descent it would have to be soon, or at least in the light. There had to be enough light for him to risk attempting to swim out, and in any case if he left it too late to swim out and was going to have to spend another night in the cave he would need time to get down to an area where he could lie down.

Then another thought struck him. Surely people would have missed him and have been searching. So far he had been concentrating all his thought and hopes on a successful escape, but what about rescue.? What were the chances he might be rescued? He wondered if anyone knew of the existence of the cave, and if they searched the shore would they think of the cave, or even if they did know of its whereabouts, would they think there was any possibility that he might have been washed into the cave.?

The more Father Aloysius thought about it the greater the odds against it, seemed to be. If there was no rescue how long could he survive? If he were going to survive, he would have to descend to get water. He sat up and looking over the edge of the ledge studied the route he had used to climb to where he was. He visualised every move in his mind and searched for possible alternatives. If he were to attempt a descent the he would have to lower himself feet first over the edge of the ledge. He would not be able to see where the footholds were He would be relying on memory and his ability to grope for them. What if he fell, what sort of damage might he inflict on himself. The drop would not be excessive but any landing would be onto a jumble of rocks. If he broke an ankle or even a leg he would have dramatically reduced his chances of escape. He was contemplating this sobering thought when the coast guard helicopter flew overhead.

At first the sound didn't register but then as the realisation that what he could hear was indeed a helicopter dawned on him, he felt a sudden surge of excitement. He got to his feet and in his haste almost over-balanced. Having steadied himself he stood and having cautioned himself against any more rash moves he made himself as tall as he could and searched the sky above. Nothing. All he could see was the sky with a few fluffy clouds drifting across the blue, but just to hear the machine was surely a cause for hope. Perhaps after all, the odds of being rescued were better than those of being able to escape. He filled his lungs with air and shouted as loud as he could. It was a cry for help. Not that the priest really expected it, but there was no answering call. As the sound of the machine grew fainter, realising that shouting was probably a waste of energy he sat down. The sound faded almost to nothing before gradually growing louder again. It was on its way back. He deduced it was probably flying up and down the coast. After sitting for a while he realised there was indeed a pattern to the rise and fall of the noise and this confirmed that his deduction was probably accurate.

As time passed he grew resigned to the fact that if he was going to pin his hopes on rescue then he would have to be patient. He prayed for patience. He realised too, that there would come a time, a critical time when he would have to make a decision as to where he was going to spend the night. He was hungry but, worse, his feeling of thirst had returned. Each time the noise faded he wondered if this should be the time for him to make a move. Each time it grew louder his hopes rose and delayed the decision. The consideration as to when that critical time was approaching would depend on the sun and the light. He needed to err on the earlier side to allow for the possibility of an early dusk. With these thoughts churning around in his mind Father Aloysius studied the sky. Had the sun started to dip towards the horizon? Was the quality of the light changing? When could he be sure it had changed? One thing he knew for certain was that that the time was getting ever closer.

On the beach a crowd of people had gathered some to comb the shore, some to support the searchers with bottles of water, a minority just to watch. The efforts of the more hardy searchers did not slacken as the afternoon ticked away, in fact with the approach of evening they grew more urgent. Philippa was one of the searchers. As evening drew closer she realised that she still had other responsibilities which she needed to think about. There were the dogs to be walked. It struck her that searching and walking the dogs might be compatible. She considered this as she splashed in the shallows working her way up the beach towards the headland. Having the dogs with her on the beach might not be the best idea, having them barking at all and sundry would not be a help. In any event she and the other searchers had been made aware that another storm had been forecast for that evening. With the clouds banking up in the west it would not be long before they all abandoned the search for that day. Perhaps she could take the dogs up along the cliff walk. Then she could look down and scan the shore line from up there, she might get a better view than at sea level. Having made the decision she did not tarry but strode off to collect her charges.

Mrs Hazelmere was pleased to see her, the dogs had been waiting expectantly at her front door. After ascertaining that there was no positive news she handed over her pets and watched them until they disappeared round the corner to follow the road up the hill heading for the cliff walk.

It was while she was climbing the hill to get to the cliff path that the helicopter pilot having been in communication with his base, had decided to call the search off for that day. He swooped low over the beach before heading for home. He was cheered on his way by all the searchers. The life boat out in the bay was on its way too. There was a blast from its fog horn. It too got a cheer. Commander Nesbitt using a hand held speaker called the search off on the beach. He thanked all for their participation, before hurrying up the sands to be the first at the place where the path led to the village. He was joined by Larry. Together, they gave a personal thanks to all who came plodding past. Their cheers for the helicopter and the life boat had been heart felt but as they made their weary way home the realisation that their search had been in vain struck home. The implications were stark. The likelihood of ever seeing Father Aloysius again had been reduced from hopeful to the grim acceptance that the sea may have claimed another victim. Yes, a few would come the following day to search again but they would not come in hope.

Father Aloysius sitting with his legs dangling over the edge of the ledge in preparation for his descent could hear the sound of the helicopter's final fly past, he did not know what it meant but when the sound of its engine finally faded to nothing he guessed the worst. The honk of the lifeboat's horn seemed to confirm his fears. He too had to accept the bitter realisation that the search had been called off. He would be spending another night in the cave. He was tempted to cry out in anguished disappointment, but resisted that urge to succumb to despair. Casting his mind back to the night before when he was alone in a heaving ocean what chances did he have, yet by some miracle here he was alive. Then there was his search for water, what about the ferns? Finding them and that trickle of drinkable water of was another sign of hope. He at least would not have to succumb to thirst. This was no time for self pity. This was a time to believe, to think positive and to hope. Hope and faith should inform his actions.

The priest turned over on his stomach and braced himself for the difficult manoeuvre he had to make. He had to put his disappointment and fear behind him and to give the present challenge all his concentration. He completed the manoeuvre successfully but at a cost. His hands were shaking as his feet touched the rocks below. Wearily he sank down to sit on a large boulder to recover and think. First he had to get water, he could do nothing about the hunger pains that had been nagging away in his stomach all day, and water must in any case be his first priority.

Having found the little pool of water below the ferns and quenched his thirst he turned his attention to looking for a place to spend the night. The light was fading. It was too late to attempt to try to swim out. He stepped on a stone. It moved, he stumbled and fell. As he got up chiding himself for his carelessness, he grasped the stone in both hands meaning to toss it out of the way to the edge of the cave where he would not encounter it again. But in the very act of lifting it to throw it a thought struck him. Stones, what if he could gather enough stones to build a heap high enough for him to stand on it to reach up to the foot of the hole at the top of the cave. He could escape, or at least he could reach the hole and ascertain if it did present a way out.

High above him on the cliff walk, Philippa gazed down at the beach. The lifeboat had gone, disappearing round the headland not long after the departure of the helicopter. The last of the stragglers were making their way up to where Larry and the commander had stationed themselves. Her brother once again had shown his ability to galvanise others in the village to action. He and the commander made a good team. She gave him a wave as a salute, not that she expected him to see it but more as her way of showing her respect for him. She scanned the shoreline; she had been correct. From this vantage point, she could get a better view of the water's edge than when she was wading in it.

Be that as it may, the sea did not reveal any of its secrets to her probing eyes. She reached the headland. It had been difficult to see the shoreline for the last stretch of the walk, as the path was set back a short way from the cliff edge. Nonetheless, she decided when the search resumed tomorrow, she would come up to the cliff path again; it would serve as her route for the dog's morning walk.

It was while she was engaged in this reverie that Min, the slightly larger and certainly the more adventurous of the two Pekingese, tugged at his lead and pulled it from her grasp. He scuttled off through the heather towards the cliff edge. The ground sloped steeply down, just above the cliff edge, and the dog stopped sniffing the wind. He appeared to be looking intently at something right on the brink of the precipice. Philippa followed as quickly as she could, dragging the errant dog's sister along with her and calling the escapee back. He ignored her. Taking care not to stumble as she descended the slope, she reached out and grasped his lead. It was a flustered but relieved dog walker that remonstrated strongly with her charge as she dragged him and his sister back to a safe distance from the cliff edge. She had intended to follow the path a little further beyond the headland to see if there was any merit in scanning the beach of the next bay, but deciding safety was the better part of valour, she concluded it was time to take the dogs back along the path and down the hill to return them to their owner. She was not a moment too soon; the storm clouds that had been slowly gathering through the day and steadily moving their way had arrived, and with them came the wind and the rain, a deluge of rain blown almost horizontal by the driving gale force winds.

Father Aloysius set his stone on a sandy swathe that ran between two areas of rock. He set about gathering other stones, piling them up round the first stone. The thought of possible escape gave him hope; the task of collecting stones kept him moving, and that helped to ward off the cold. There was an urgency about his work as dusk fell and the cave grew increasingly gloomy. As he worked, he became more and more conscious of the waves of the high tide invading the cave with an enhanced vigour. Was there another storm brewing outside the cave, he wondered. He took comfort in the fact he and his pile of stones were some distance into the cave and that there was height, too, in his favour. He was a little above the lagoon and the cave entrance. By the time he was forced to call it a day, he had amassed quite a pile. Buoyed up by the thought of escape, Father Aloysius settled down for the night. Had he not stumbled on that stone, it might have been a very bleak time. As he stretched out on the sand, he commended the stone to God, and his prayers started with thanks and praise. That the difference between hope and despair, between possible escape and certain doom, should be determined by a chance encounter with a humble stone was the cause of much wonder on his behalf as he reflected on the mysterious workings of fate. Truly, he thought as he shut his eyes and wished for sleep, his God worked in a mysterious way. He recalled with a smile that hymn that expressed those very sentiments. He had heard it, indeed had sung it, when he had attended his first service at St Jude's. The Revd. Burns had invited him to talk to the Sunday School, and that's when he first heard the hymn being sung in Pondreath. How did it go? 'God moves in a mysterious way his wonders to perform.' "Thank you, Lord, for that stone,'" were the words on his lips as he drifted off into a fitful sleep.

It was a sleep that was not to last long. The cold and hunger woke him, and the sound of the waves thundering against the cliffs and thrusting themselves under the lip of the cave and sweeping up to within some three metres from his pile of rocks. He had no option but to endure both the cold and the hunger in the inky blackness of the cave. He dared not move about. He did what little he could, moving his arms and legs about as he lay on his back. He did this as vigorously as he dared. This did stimulate his circulation enough to prevent him from succumbing to hypothermia, but it certainly didn't make him warm how the hours dragged as he waited for dawn. Conscious of the storm raging outside he worried that it might shift enough shingle and sand into the cave to completely block the entrance. He chided himself for not attempting to swim out when he had the chance. He tried to distract himself by endeavouring to name all the people he knew and including them in a silent prayer. This did help and led to another stretch of fitful sleep. When he awoke, the cave was no longer pitch black; dawn at last had arrived. The sea, by the sound of it, had calmed somewhat. The storm, if there had been one, had blown itself out. As with his previous waking the day before, he was stiff, and now he was further weakened by hunger, but he refused to give up on hope. Movement about the cave was restricted at first, but by the time the light had improved enough to see to the edges of the cave, the priest had added a good number of fair-sized stones to the pile. It was time to start ferrying up to the ledge. As he approached the difficult climb, the rocks appeared to be wet. The previous day, they had been dry. Clearly, the rain had come into the cave through the hole through which he hoped to escape. He trod with care on the slippery surfaces. Near the wall of rock that rose up to the ledge was a pool of water nestling in a hollow among the boulders. This was good news. The realisation that in order to get onto the ledge, there was a need to build two plies of rocks, one below the ledge to help him onto it without the necessity to climb, the second on the ledge itself to allow him to climb up to the hole, was not so good.

This was going to be more of a challenge than Father Aloysius had first envisaged. Weak for lack of food and exhausted by the emotional strain and lack of sleep it was going to be a huge challenge. At least he now had two sources of drinking water. The Lord giveth and the Lord taketh away, he reflected, as he dumped the first stone at the foot of the rock face.

The business of carrying stones from his pile down near the bottom of the cave up to the top was a slow and taxing business. The time taken to make each journey was getting progressively longer. Father Aloysius struggled on. Time passed. It was Sunday; he should be taking the Mass. He wondered what his congregation would do. Would the bishop have been informed, he wondered. He should at least pray. The stone he was carrying was a heavy one, he staggered up to the pile and gratefully put his burden down. He should pray. He bent over the hollow where the water had accumulated and scooped some up to drink. He should pray.

Chapter Thirty-Five

Hope springs eternal.

In Plymouth, the bishop had heard about the disappearance of his priest and that a search was being undertaken. The news had come from Miss Farrow. He had been out when she had called and he had picked it up from his answer phone but not until mid-afternoon. He made several attempts to phone her back, but her phone was always engaged. It was obvious that Father Aloysius was unlikely to be there to take Mass in the parish the next day whatever the outcome of the search. His engagement diary for the Sunday was full. It was too late to find someone to deputise for him, and there was no one else he could ask to take the Mass. He decided it would have to be cancelled, however, he felt it was imperative that he visited the parish at some time the next day.

He continued to try to get through to Miss Farrow but was unsuccessful. In the end, events overtook him. He had a service to take. After fulfilling his commitment to take the Saturday evening Mass at the Cathedral, he decided to make one more attempt to contact his priest's housekeeper. To his relief, Miss Farrow answered. The news was not good. The search had drawn a blank. After a brief discussion, it was agreed that Miss Farrow would take responsibility for cancelling the Sunday Mass and that he would make a brief visit to the parish in the evening to lead a time of prayer. Miss Farrow would spread the news. In the village, the talk of that evening was all about the missing priest. Speculation was rife. At the Trevinian's home, Charlotte heard from a neighbour. Fortunately, Sid Trevinian was away, although his wife did not seem to know where, not that she was too bothered. Nor was she at all concerned about the missing priest. Larry, weary and depressed, had returned and cooked her meal for her. He left to find his sister. He found her at the Evan's home with Louisa and Anna. It was a sombre household.

Larry refused to give up hope and thought of as many positive reasons for Father Aloysius's disappearance as he could, and each hypothesis ended in a happy return of the priest.

"What would Father Aloysius want us to think and do in this situation," he asked.

"Have faith and pray," was Anna's reply. And so they prayed with earnest fervour and, in doing so, found comfort.

Larry and his sister were up at their usual early hour that Sunday morning. Larry helped Philippa with her paper round, and they had had their usual breakfast in the shopkeeper's kitchen. It was there that Miss Farrow found them and told them about the arrangement regarding the bishop's visit. Larry volunteered to help her spread the news. His sister had her own obligations to meet. She had the dogs to walk. Larry had arranged with Anna that they do a comb of the beach early. The storm may have washed something up. Philippa had decided she would do another cliff walk. She was up on the cliff walk when the helicopter appeared. It did a single pass down the beach before disappearing beyond the far headland. She saw Larry and Anna on the sand; they waved as it passed. She waved, too. It was her way of saying a thank you for trying and of joining in solidarity with her brother. Scanning the shoreline, she continued along the path towards the point. Suddenly, Min started to tug on his lead. He seemed to be wanting to head towards the cliff edge. The girl pulled him back.

"What's the matter? What's bothering you?" She bent down to look her errant companion straight in the face. "What's the trouble then, you silly old thing? That's not the way home, that could be dangerous, too. You can't go exploring the cliff edge."

The dog gazed up at her with imploring eyes and whined. Philippa looked about her. It was exactly the same place Min had escaped from her grasp the previous day and gone exploring. Perhaps she should investigate, but that would be difficult with both dogs. If only she had someone else with her. Larry would be good, but he was on the beach, and she had no way of contacting him. Maybe Mrs Evans could look after the dogs for her or even contact Larry. She decided to go back and call on the Evans' house in case Louisa was at home.

Mrs Evans was at home in the middle of baking a cake. She phoned Larry and gave the phone to Philippa. Having heard her concerns, he decided that they would respond immediately. They could always search the beach later. Philippa could even join them. He estimated he would be half an hour. The girl decided to spend the time returning the dogs to their owner. If she hurried back, she might be able to meet Larry on the quay. On the way, another thought struck her. What if they couldn't find what Min had found so enticing? What if they still needed the dogs or at least needed Min, the intrepid, inquisitive one?

Father Aloysius felt dizzy. He put a handout, reaching for the rock face. He needed to steady himself. He needed to rest. He slumped down into a sitting position. He needed to pray. He became vaguely aware of the sound of a helicopter. He raised his head to listen. Yes, it was the helicopter. If he had only been able to get that ramp on the ledge completed, he could have reached up out of the hole to wave. He made a half-hearted attempt to get up. The nausea overtook him, and he sank back, leaning against the cave wall. He needed.......everything went black; he had drifted into unconsciousness.

Mrs Hazelmere sensed that Philippa was in a hurry as she knocked on the door to return Min and Muffet to her. Usually, the dog walker came in for a biscuit or a piece of cake. They would chat. On this occasion, her little friend was happy to forgo a treat and get away. However, she also needed to talk. Hastily, she explained the situation and asked the widow if she could possibly borrow Min for a further period of time. Mrs Hazelmere had grown to trust and to like her young dog walker. If she could help towards solving the mystery as to what had happened to Father Aloysius, well, then she should. She gave Philippa her blessing and thanked her for all she was doing to help in the search for the missing cleric. It was a relieved and grateful young lady who turned away to hurry off to the bridge. Mrs Hazelmere watched her go and waved her goodbye.

Crossing the bridge with the dog in tow, she looked down the quay towards the path that led to the beach. She could not see them. Had she missed them? Surely not. She spent some anxious moments waiting, but at last, they appeared. Soon, they were striding up the hill together, with Larry carrying the dog in his arms. When they got to the Evans's house, his sister insisted, they paused a moment to get the dog a drink. While Min was slaking his thirst, Anna snatched a moment to speak with her mother. It would soon be time for the cake to come out of the oven when it did, she would be free to join the search party on the cliff.

It wasn't until they reached the spot on the cliff path where Min had first given an indication of wanting to explore the area at the very edge of the cliff that Larry put the dog down. At first, the Pekingese showed no inclination to go exploring; he had other concerns and sniffed about to find a suitable place to relieve himself. That having been achieved, Min set off for the cliff edge with Larry holding firmly onto the lead and his two companions following close behind. When they got to the final steep slope to the precipice, Larry dropped to his hands and knees, and they proceeded with caution. Once there, Min stopped and peered over. He began to whine. "What is it? What is it? What can you smell?" Larry coaxed. He crawled the last few feet to the dog, winding the lead round his wrist. "I'm going to have to lean out over the edge," Larry explained to his companions. You had better hold my feet. The two girls complied, grasping his ankles with a firm grip. They, too, were in a crawling position.

"Be careful, Larry, please." Anna got a grunt by way of a reply. He wriggled forward.

"What are you doing with the dog? Stop." It was Philippa's turn to express her anxiety.

"Relax, I've got him tight, and the lead is wrapped round my wrist. He can't fall unless I do, so just concentrate on holding me, please." Holding the dog in both hands, Larry inched forward. Then, looking over Min's back, he wriggled out so his head and shoulder were over the edge. There was a deep intake of breath as he found himself looking into an abyss. If he were to dislodge a stone, it would fall straight down and splash into the waves breaking against the cliff face. The dog was clearly perturbed and started to wriggle and whine. "Shush!" Larry spoke soothingly and held Min closer. There was an urgency to his sweeping glance as he searched the cliff face for any signs of an opening; there was nothing. He looked left, nothing, he looked right, ah, that might be it. "Pull me up, please. If there is a hole, it's to our right." The two girls inched backwards up the slope and pulled him back from the edge. Once safe, he was able to assist them by wriggling back himself. As he did so, he talked to the dog.

"Good boy, good boy, you've been a star. If only your mistress could have seen you," he said, stroking Min's back. This remark got an immediate response from his sister.

"What, you must be joking! Mrs Hazelmere would be having a fit. Don't you dare do that again?"

"Sorry, Sis," Larry pushed himself to his knees with one hand while he held the dog cradled close to him with the other.

"We've got to do it one more time." Larry, carrying the dog cradled in the crook of his left arm, moved along the cliff edge some two metres before lowering himself onto his stomach and wriggling his way to the edge of the precipice. As he went, he kept talking reassuringly to Min, then checked with Anna and his sister that they were secure in their positions, holding his ankles. Having learnt from his previous experience, he kept Min facing him as he made his final move. With a grunt of satisfaction, he saw what must be a hole. It was directly below him. It was smaller than he had expected. He lowered the dog so it could look directly into the cave.

Farther, Aloysius drifted in and out of consciousness. In his more lucid moments, he knew he ought to pray, but that struggling up onto his knees was beyond him, and he would drift back into an unconscious state. Was that a dog barking? He fought to make sense of the sound he was hearing: a dog? A dog would mean someone was close. He raised his head and with an effort, took a deep breath before calling out as loud as he could, "Help." Then, lying back, spent by the effort, he forced himself to listen. If someone were there and he had not been imagining the dog barking, and if someone had heard his cry, then he could hope again.

"Who's there? Where are you?" Larry could hardly believe his ears. Surely, that was Father Aloysius. Pulling the dog up to him, he lay still for a moment, waiting for a reply.

Father Aloysius had slipped back into an unconscious state. Larry needed to be able to look into the hole. "I'm coming back? Did you hear that?"

"Help, yes. It was Father Aloysius, I'm sure of it." Anna reached forward to grasp Larry's belt and to pull him towards her. Once safely beyond the cliff edge, Larry rolled over onto his back, sat up and held Min up.

"Here, Philippa, take the dog." He was unwinding the lead from his wrist, "I need to be able to look into the hole. You've got to hold me tight." Larry did not wait for a reply. Flipping onto his stomach again, he crawled back to attempt to look directly into the hole. It was a difficult and risky thing to do, but with Anna and his sister hanging onto him, he managed to lean out over the cliff and bend down far enough to look into the hole. It was indeed a cave. Inside, there was a vertical drop to a ledge. There below, he could see something, legs, brown legs, Father Aloysius's legs, surely it was Father Aloysius.

"Pull me back, It's Father Aloysius, I can see his legs." Larry, red in the face and visibly shaking, gratefully accepted the hands outstretched to help pull him to his feet.

"Well done, Larry." That must have been tricky."

"Thanks. You, ladies, did a great job holding me. Good team effort." He bent down to pat Min, "And that includes you."

Philippa joined him in stroking the dog, "Yes, you're a hero. Without you, we never would have known about the hole, and to think I told you off for going exploring in dangerous places. I'm sorry."

The trio moved hastily back away from the cliff edge before Larry spoke again. "It is definitely a cave. There is a drop-down to a ledge, and then below the ledge, I could see these legs. I'm sure it's Father Aloysius, although how he got there beats me; he must be in a state. After that call for help he didn't answer when I called out, but now we have got to get help to get him out." Anna held her phone up.

"Good, I'll call the police and you can call Commander Nesbitt, he'll know what to do."

"OK here's my phone, you'll find him on that, I'll use yours to get the police. Then we had better phone Miss Farrow. Philippa, you mark this spot so it's easy to find again and we won't waste time searching for the hole." There were a few minutes of frantic activity, then came the wait. Fortunately, the time waiting for the police, which could have been a tedious strain was broken up by the arrival first of Louisa Evans, and then a little later by the Commander and Miss Farrow. Commander Nesbitt had all but given up finding his friend. When the phone call came the Commander could hardly believe it. He had collected Miss Farrow from the shop in his car and they had driven up the hill and parked in Mrs Evans's drive.

Each new arrival brought their questions. When Louisa Evans arrived with hers, she addressed them to Larry. He immediately deferred to his sister to explain the situation. Philippa was reluctant at first to take this responsibility on, but grew in confidence with each new arrival at the scene all with their own questions to be answered. She left it to Larry to describe what he had seen when he leant over the cliff edge. It was then that Anna was struck with the thought that any rescue operation might take some time. Perhaps they would need refreshments. Louisa agreed and she and Miss Farrow hurried back to prepare sandwiches and thermoses for hot drinks. By the time the police arrived Philippa had benefited from her previous briefings and she was able to brief them. The first two policemen to arrive came on foot. They were dressed in their normal uniforms. Not long after a Land-rover came bumping along the path. Four men emerged in bright orange overalls. They were the cliff rescue squad. They brought with them their specialist equipment for climbing rock faces, along with ropes, a stretcher, emergency survival gear as well as a comprehensive first aid box. After a quick briefing they set to work.

With Philippa to guide them the Land-rover was positioned just above the last slope to the cliff edge in line with the entrance to the cave. One of the team threaded some webbing round the vehicles bumper for a belay point while another put on a waist harness and tied the rope to it. The other two members of the team assembled items of equipment they might need on a slab of nearby rock. They worked at speed with a practised efficiency. Not many minutes after their arrival their climber was disappearing over the cliff edge. One police officer remained on the path to greet any new arrivals. Miss Farrow and Louisa Evans opted to stay with him. The others, wanting a closer view accompanied the second policeman to watch from a vantage point a little distance away along the headland where they would not be in the way but could look back at the cliff face.

Supported by the rope and leaning well backwards the climber walked flat footed down the vertical rock face just to the left of the hole. Once below it he traversed across so as to be able inspect the cave entrance and to reach inside. All the while he described what he was doing and what he saw to his companion at the other end of the rope. "Hole in cliff face, small, too small for me to get in, too small for a stretcher. Vertical drop two metres ledge two metres wide. Another drop to jumble of rocks, Cave sloping steeply down, Legs of victim visible. No sound from victim, suspect unconscious. Right, time to come up. Moving right, then pull me in." The climber ascended in the same manner he had gone down and was soon in deep conversation with the other three members of the team.

From their vantage point Larry and his friends could not hear what was being said, but their curiosity was aroused by the occasional glance in their direction by the climber, and then the whole team looked over. It was as if they were being inspected.

"What are they doing?" Philippa wondered aloud.

"Probably making a plan of action," The Commander volunteered.

"And it looks like it might involve us," suggested Anna. "Ah, here they come."

The climber had uncoupled himself from the rope, and he and a companion came striding over.

"I'm Patrick, no relation to the Saint, this is Michael nothing to do with the archangel either, and you are?" he pointed to each of the group in turn and for each one he repeated their names back to them. "Thank you, this is going to be a tricky job and we are going to need your help." He scanned the group looking each one in the eye before moving on. "The situation is this. The victim is in a cave and from what we can ascertain is probably unconscious. There are two vertical drops separated by a ledge between the victim and the hole. You can't see the hole from here," He turned and pointed, "Its hidden by that bulge. Its small, too small for a person my size to get through, certainly too small for a stretcher. The victim did not get into the cave through the hole. It must have another entrance almost certainly at sea level. We have radioed base and a team will be arriving soon to search for that entrance. Finding it may take time. When it's located, it may prove to be the best way to get the victim out. However, we have to think of all eventualities. It may not. It may for example be submerged at high tide. That would mean we have to find another way, and this hole is the only obvious solution. We will have to enlarge the hole in order to remove the victim. That will take time and care and will involve machinery. The victim will have to be moved so as to be safely out of the way of any falling rubble created by the operation. Whatever way ends up being the one, this operation will need skill, speed and patience. Time is of the essence. The patient needs attention now. We have to get that patient assessed and in a stable condition quickly, then we have to be patient.

A fellow cave climber is on her way. She is a nurse, currently on duty at the hospital in Torquay, half an hour away at best, probably more like three quarters of an hour away, although by now she may be on her way by helicopter. She is your size," He pointed to Larry, "Or perhaps a bit smaller. I can't get through that hole but she could and so could you. She will be able to deal with the medical side but she will need help to move the victim, and this is where you come in, I'm asking you two, if you'd be willing, to go down into the cave now. You'd be on a rope and perfectly safe. You will have to take care not to dislodge any stones. We need you to make an initial assessment of the victims condition. Pulse, breathing, skin temperature, then signs of any physical injuries, breaks or wounds. It would be helpful to know the victim's identity that is if you know it."

"It's Father Aloysius." Anna was emphatic and accompanied her words by banging her right fist into her left hand.

"Possibly, perhaps even probably, but to have it confirmed would be good."

"We hope and pray so," Commander Nesbitt put a reassuring hand on Anna's shoulder.

"I know it, I just know it, trust me it's Father Aloysius," Anna was adamant. Patrick looked over to the Commander.

"Thank you, Jim, I'll say Amen to that. Now you, Philippa and the ladies can help us too. We are likely to be here some time, it would be good if possible to have some refreshments and also to have someone like you Jim, and you young Philippa to act as a liaison between us and the village. We don't want crowds of people up here but when they see police cars and helicopters, they will be curious and they need to be kept informed."

"Sorry to butt in again, but my mum has already brought along some drinks and sandwiches."

"That's great, thanks. Will there be enough for us all, do you think?

"I'm sure she can provide more."

"Wonderful, now you two better come with me and get roped up." Patrick talked as he walked. "Have either of you done any rock climbing?"

"There was a climbing wall on one of the camps I went on with the school. We didn't do much climbing but we abseiled down. What about you Larry?"

"Nope, Philippa and I were among the few who never got to go on school trips let alone camps. We learnt it was best to give school a miss on those days. Come to think of it, I did go on one day out. The whole school went. Your dad must have paid."

"Well I wouldn't worry," Patrick remarked reassuringly, "You'll be fine, what about first aid?"

"I got my first aid badge when I was in the Girl Guides, but that's all. It was quite a while ago now."

"Larry?"

"Sorry, nothing."

Anna and Larry were handed a harness and a helmet. Each helmet had a headlamp. Larry was also given a small walkie talkie on a lanyard. The two other members of the team, Sam and Adrian, who would be their anchor men helped their two volunteers into their harnesses and checked their helmets were secure. Next, they went through what to expect as they descended over the cliff and what the procedures were for uncoupling after their decent into the cave. During this time Patrick had been getting ready to descend again to the hole and preparing the ropes. Larry was attached to an orange rope, Anna to a blue rope.

"All set? Patrick smiled as he asked the question.

"All set." Larry and Anna replied in unison. She was glad that Larry had spoken with her, it made her sound more confident than she really felt. She wasn't good with heights but now was not the time to tell anyone that.

"Fine, now just a few words about what you do when you get down and come to check the victim. First of all check the breathing and the pulse, there are two of you so you could do it in tandem, one the pulse, the other the breathing. To check the breathing kneel beside the victim and place a hand lightly on the chest to feel for any rise and fall, place your cheek near to the victim's nose or if the mouth is open, the mouth. You are checking to see if you can detect any inhalation, breathing in or exhalation of air, breathing out. The pulse you find here above the clavicle in that hollow that is roughly in line with your Adam's apple, you use these two fingers," Patrick held up his fingers and demonstrated the position, Anna and Larry copied him. "The other place is the wrist, turn the hand palm upwards and feel just on the outer side of the tendon there. That's sometimes easier to pick up than the neck, but it may be very weak in either place. Please report everything to me as you find it. I will remain at the entrance with my walkie talkie. Michael has one too, that way we all keep informed. All clear so far.

Again, the reply came in unison. "All clear."

"Great, one last thing, I go first, you go second, Larry, but wait for me to tell you, when you are safely on the ledge, I told you about you wait for Anna. There is room for two. You may need her there to guide your rope as you go down that last drop to the victim. When you come to going over the edge, concentrate on looking at the cliff face and then the hole, try not to look down the drop." Patrick gave them the thumbs up. He and Michael strode over to the cliff edge. Michael stopped a pace away. The webbing that attached him to the Land-rover wouldn't allow him to get any closer. But he could lean forward and just about keep Patrick in view when he went over the edge. Patrick faced them. "You'll have to go a stride to your right, my left if you are to be over the hole, Larry, but, wait, I'll be right at the hole so you'll be able to see where to go over. Watch me and do as I do." Patrick leaned back on the rope and stepped back over the cliff keeping his feet flat against the wall. It all looked so straightforward. Michael kept him on a tight rope just paying it out slowly. "Easy, you'll be fine," he called reassuringly back to Larry.

"Ready when you are," it was Patrick. It hadn't taken him long to get in position. Sam, Larry's belay man nodded, "That's us."

Larry looked at Anna and gave her a smile, "See you," He and Sam walked together to the cliff edge. Larry peered over. Don't look down he had been told, it all sounded so simple, but he had to look down to check that they were right over the hole. They were. Patrick was just over a couple of metres below looking up at him. Try as he might Larry could not help looking beyond Patrick down, the long vertical face to the rocks and the sea below. It was a long, long way down. He felt the tight knot of fear in his stomach, he waved back hoping his gesture was nonchalant enough to give the impression he was totally confident. He felt far from it. He turned round, his back to the sea, Michael nodded and he stepped down keeping his feet flat on the rock and leaning back on the rope. He was just five steps from the hole. Patrick was right there at the hole edge. Larry kept stepping, his confidence growing with each short step down. He was secure on the end of a taught rope.

"Good, well done. Just step down into the hole and lower yourself through."

Larry gripping the rope hard with both hands stepped into the hole, thrusting his legs out in front of him he endeavoured get his hips to follow. His harness caught a protrusion in the rock. The hole entrance was far from smooth. With a grunt he pulled himself up to try to free the harness. It came clear. He reached with one hand into the hole groping for something to grip hold of so he could pull himself in. Patrick below reached up and with one hand tried to assist him pushing against his shoulder. Larry was breathing hard, he was stuck. For a horrible moment he felt completely helpless, he was well and truly stuck. He took a deep breath, desperately trying to think out his next move. His face was hard against the cliff face.

"Try wriggling over to your right, and turn your right shoulder down. You want to turn onto your stomach. You'll have to leave go of the rope to do it."

Larry felt a desperate urge to scream. He gritted his teeth and, dropping his shoulder wriggled himself over onto his stomach. He was still half in and half out of the hole. Reaching back with both hands he felt for the inside lip of the hole, grunting loudly he pulled himself through, chest, shoulders, head. He was hanging from the rope inside the cave.

"Well done, kid, well done. Sam will lower you down to the ledge." Larry looked down. The ledge was just below. Slowly he was eased down. He felt his feet meet the rock, with a huge sigh of relief he stepped back from the face. He was shaking violently He was drenched in sweat.

"Are you there?" It was Patrick. Larry pressed the tips of his fingers into his forehead, desperately trying to control his shakes.

"Yes," he replied shakily, then, mustering all his self-control, called out as loudly as he could, "Yes, safely down on the ledge, thank you, just getting my breath back."

"Well done, take your time, and let me know when you want Anna to join you."

Larry looked around him. The ledge was wide enough to lie down on. He seemed to be in a large chamber. He looked down. There below was a body. It was Father Aloysius. He was lying completely still.

"Slack, please. I'm moving along a bit to give Anna space to land."

"Fine."

"It's a big chamber, pretty gloomy it disappears down round a bend."

"OK I'll call Anna over, Anna, Larry's safely there, your turn."

"Well done, Larry," Anna muttered to herself. She glanced at Adrian, then in louder voice called, "Can he see who it is?"

"He hasn't said."

"OK I'm coming." She and Adrian took their place beside Sam. Michael was just a metre away. Anna gave Adrian a weak smile, "Here we go,"

"You'll be fine." She stepped backwards. "Climber coming down," Adrian called to Patrick as he gently paid out his rope.

Concentrating hard on the cliff face in front of her she walked down to the hole.

"Well done," it was Patrick, he sounded as if he was right behind her, she hadn't even seen him so hard had she been concentrating on the cliff. "Slide yourself legs first into the hole, but don't lower yourself down to sitting position too early, your harness might get caught. "Anna grasped the rope in both hands and slipped her legs into the hole.

"Slack," Still holding herself tight on the rope with one hand she reached inside the hole with the other. As he had done with Larry, Patrick assisted her. She felt his hand on her shoulder, strong and reassuring.

"Thanks" Anna slipped easily through the hole and into the cave. She still had her back to the hole. There was Larry looking up at her."

"Well done, welcome."

"In cave, slacker, please." Adrian lowered her onto the shelf. "Phew made it. That wasn't too bad." Anna looked back up at the hole. "In cave safely down, thanks."

"Great" came back a loud chorus of congratulatory shouts.

"You did well, I got stuck."

"What, really! That must have been frightening."

"Just a little," admitted Larry with a self-deprecating grin. He envied Anna's composure. She looked as if she had just stepped out of a bus.

"Where is he?"

Larry indicated with a point of his chin by way of reply. They looked down over the edge of the ledge together. There was a sharp intake of breath.

"Father Aloysius," the girl said in an awed whisper. She sighed, "Oh it's Father Aloysius, is he alive do you think?"

"I don't know, we'll have to go down to see."

"God I hope so, please God, please." Anna turned back to call up through the hole. "It is Father Aloysius."

"Is he alive? Can you tell?

"No, he's very still. We need to go down now."

Larry was lowering himself into a sitting position on the edge of the ledge. "Get them to tell the others," he said, looking up at Anna.

"Please tell the others, and Larry's ready to go down, "

"Fine, I'll lower slowly." Anna took hold of her companion's rope to guide him over the edge and prevent him from swinging back over the prone body below.

"Going down" Larry slipped off the ledge and flexing slightly at the knees let himself be lowered down. He grounded on a boulder safely to the left of the body.

"Down."

"Good, you can release the rope from the harness. Pull it out of the way and tie the end to a rock if you can." It was Patrick giving the instructions. Looking up Larry could see him peering down into the cave. "You can use the walkie talkie to communicate now, have it on round your neck and just keep talking, we need a running commentary, like they do at a football match."

"Alright, I'll do my best."

Anna was sitting, waiting to descend. Larry looked up. He needed to ensure she came down well away from the priest.

"Ready to go." Anna pushed herself off the ledge and was lowered slowly downwards. Larry stepped forward to catch her legs and guide her to a landing position well away from the victim, as he did so he started on his running commentary. "Got Anna by the legs, guiding her down away from the body. Safely down." The girl high-fived her companion and unclipped her rope from her harness. She secured it beside her companion's using the same stone.

"Ropes secure on anchors."

"Good, you are now off belay." Patrick signalled to Michael that he was ready to return to the top of the cliff. It was with some relief he scrambled over the edge and stood up. He had been hanging dangling outside the hole for some time and he was cold. He donned his jacket and swung his arms full circle over his head forwards and backward several times.

"That's better, boy am I glad it's not raining!"

"We've got the parcels ready; you'd better let me go down to deliver them through the hole. We need to be thinking how we are going to make that entrance to the cave bigger, just in case."

"Thanks Mike. Any news from the boys looking for an entrance to the cave down below?"

"Not yet, they have started but the tides not completely out, it be a while before we know."

"OK but as you say we need to get cracking on the logistics of enlarging the hole and have the equipment ready just in case getting him out at the bottom of the cave is not on. We can't afford to waste any time."

Meanwhile in the cave Larry was already leaning over Father Aloysius. The sight of the priest almost naked had been a shock to Anna, but she quickly got used to it. He was their patient. It was up to her and Larry to do their best for him.

"I'll try to get his pulse if you check his breathing." Anna knelt down and put her cheek next the priest's mouth and nose. She placed the palm of her right hand gently on his chest and looked for signs of a rise and fall.

"I think I can detect signs of breathing although it's difficult. His skin is cold but I can't see any goose pimples or signs of shivering. His lips don't appear to be blue." she reported to Larry who was still feeling for a pulse in the victim's neck.

"I don't seem to be able to get a pulse." Larry looked anxious. Anna picked up one limp hand and turning it over palm up felt for the pulse in the wrist.

"Ah, yes I do feel a pulse, here you feel," she smiled at Larry and he came round to her side of the body and placed his fingers on the spot his companion had indicted. It took him a number of attempts. He finally found it and gave Anna a thumbs up sign, then spoke into the intercom.

"Hallo, Larry here. We have just started examining the patient. There are signs of breathing, and he has a pulse. We going now to examine his body for any signs of injury."

"Thanks, very good news, well done," Patrick's voice sounded distant and crackly.

Working together the two would-be rescuers examined first the priest's arms, then his legs. There were signs of abrasions on his knees but that was all. Gently they took their patient by the shoulders and lifted him forward so they could look at his back. Father Aloysius stirred and groaned.

"Father," Anna, startled, glanced at Larry. Placing her hands either side of his head she looked earnestly into his face, "Father, Father it's me, it's Anna, we are here, it's all right, you are going to get out of here."

The Priest's eyes flickered open for a brief moment,

"Anna," his whisper was almost inaudible. His eyes closed, and his head flopped forward.

"Father, oh Father, brave, brave man it's going to be fine I promise." The priest did not respond, he had obviously slipped back into unconsciousness. "Larry," the girl turned to her companion, "He spoke, he said my name, Father Aloysius said my name. Oh thank God you're alive, you poor brave man."

"Larry here, examination complete, no obvious injuries. Patient stirred for a moment and called Anna by her name. Now unconscious again."

"Thanks. Very encouraging. Now we are going to send down some blankets on a rope. They may land on the ledge, if they do one of you will have to climb up to get them. Just let us know and we will help haul you up. Untie them there from rope because we need to use it again for the next parcel of things. Wrap the patient in the silver survival blanket first. It's important to get it underneath him, then use the others to make him as comfortable as possible. We've got to keep him warm. There will be a woollen hat for his head. There is a jacket for each of you. It's important you keep warm as well. It's probably quite a bit cooler in the cave than outside. I'm now at the top. Michael has relieved me at the hole entrance. Got that."

"Received and understood."

Larry untied his rope from its anchor and clipped the karabiner onto his harness. Moments later the first of several bundles they were to receive on the end of the rope came swinging down through the hole. It landed tantalisingly on the very edge of the ledge.

"Parcel on ledge."

"Good, Michael here. Tell us when you are going to start climbing." Larry scanned the vertical rock for hand holds and for places to put his feet. He needed to climb well away from his patient. He clambered onto a pile of stones and reached up to an obvious hand hold.

"Climbing." His rope tightened and then he felt himself being hauled up. He endeavoured to assist in the process but would have been the first to admit that he got to the ledge more as a result of the efforts of the team above than by his own.

"Untying bundle. Rope free, thanks." Larry dropped down to lie on the ledge. He held the bundle in one hand and lowered it to Anna who was standing on the pile of stones below to receive it. He was just about to announce he was ready to be lowered down when his walkie-talkie crackled back into life. It was Michael with fresh instructions.

"Don't climb down yet, we are sending down parcel number two. A sleeping bag and a blow up mattress. You can blow up the mattress straight away but don't try to put the patient in the sleeping bag until Helen the nurse arrives and is with you. She may want to examine the patient herself. Just put the sleeping bag on top of the patient. In addition, there is a bag with drinks and food for you. You can try to give the patient the liquid in the pink bottle. There is a feeding tube, don't try to administer anything else. Helen will do that. She shouldn't be long now. Parcel number two coming down."

"Thanks. Untying parcel. Rope free. Giving parcel to Anna then will be ready to descend if that is all."

"Fine, just say the word when you are." Larry lowered the second parcel to Anna.

"Take care not to drop this one, it's got breakable items in it," Larry warned her as he handed it over. "Ready to descend."

Wrapping Father Aloysius in the silver blanket was not easy. Larry stood astride the patient and holding him under the arm pits managed to lift him far enough for Anna to pass the blanket under him. The priest grunted as he was lifted but did not open his eyes. Having wrapped him in the blanket and put the woollen hat on his head they repeated the operation to slide one of the two blankets under him. It would be a cushion, a thin one admittedly but better than nothing, it would at least keep the priest from resting directly on the cold hard rock.

"Patient wrapped up in survival blanket and others, hat on head. Proceeding to inflate mattress and try feeding from pink bottle."

"Good, have you got your coats on?"

"No, will put them on now, thanks."

I'm going up top to meet the chopper when it comes, but you can call any time and you need to carry on with your updates. I'll hand the walkie talkie back to Patrick when I get to the top. For the moment there won't be anyone just outside the hole."

"Understood, thanks."

While Larry inflated the mattress Anna busied herself with trying to give some of the liquid in the pink bottle to the priest.

"Hallo, Father, it's Anna again, we hope you are a bit more comfortable now you have your blankets. Thank you for being patient with us. It's time for a drink. I'm going to put this tube into your mouth and if you can suck that would be good. Just little sips gently, gently is best." She managed to insert the tube. The liquid dribbled out of the side of his mouth.

"That's it Father good man, just try to swallow. Steady, a little at a time." The priest stirred. His mouth opened and the tube slipped out. Anna caught it. "Whoops, well done, now I'm going to slip this tube back into your mouth again, try to suck please, I know you can do it, please." She placed the tube on his bottom lip, "Open a bit please." he opened his mouth, and as she slipped the tube in he sucked. "Oh well done, well done, Amazing, you are doing just great, well done." Anna gazed intently into her patients face, willing him to continue sucking, he did so. She counted each suck and noted each movement of the throat as he swallowed. "Wonderful." His eyes flicked open and then shut, the sucking stopped. The priest's mouth opened and the tube fell out for the second time. His eyes closed.

"Had enough, alright. You've done so well. I'm so proud of you. You rest, you can have some more later." Anna turned to Larry. He gave her the thumbs up sign. "Well it's a start, not a lot but it's a start. The mattress, large and orange completely inflated was lent against the pile of rocks under the ledge.

At that moment a loud roar of a low flying helicopter filled their ears. Larry punched the air.

"Dear God, never has a sound been more beautiful to the ears, won't be long Father and you'll have an expert to sort things out down here, and then we can really look forward to getting you out." If the priest heard him he gave no sign. Larry handed his companion her coat. "Time to smarten up and look the part."

"Time for a drink for us I reckon." Anna opened the zip on the bag, removed the tube from the top of the bottle and screwing up the top returned it to its place before retrieving a thermos and two plastic mugs.

"Let's see what we have here." The walkie-talkie crackled.

"Helicopter landing. Helen and a doctor are on board."

"Message received, great, here mattress inflated, patient has taken small amount of liquid, now seemingly unconscious."

"Good, Helen will be with you directly, might be a good time for you to grab a drink and a snack. You may not get much chance for a while once Helen gets down there."

"Understood, already have thermos out.|"

"Ahead of the game, well done you. Enjoy."

The soup was hot and nourishing and Anna delved into the sandwich box and they had two tasty ham and pickle sandwiches with it. Refreshed they decided to take the opportunity to look about them and to find out a bit more about the cave. The discovery of the pool of water in the hollow at the top of the cave gave them the important information as to how the priest had survived. The pile of rocks at the bottom of the rock face below the ledge did not look natural. Had they been placed there? Was their friend using rocks to help him reach up to the ledge and then the hole? Larry left Anna with Father Aloysius while he made a brief sortie down into the cave below. It grew gloomy as he rounded the corner. There was still enough light to see but he switched on his head torch. He moved swiftly down and arrived at the spot where Father Aloysius had gathered his pile of stones. Was this more evidence of what his friend had been up to. It was clearly man made, and there in the sand was the confirmation, footprints. The feet that made these were that of an adult, and then these other scuff marks. Was this where the priest had slept ? It looked very much like it could be.

It was no distance to the lagoon, his headlamp cast a long beam to the black wall of the cave at its far end. There was no sign of an entrance. Where could it be? Hastily Larry scanned the edges of the cave, nothing. It was a mystery. Realising that time was passing he hurried back to report his findings to Anna and more importantly to the team above.

Patrick was busy briefing the new arrivals when his walkie-talkie sprang to life, and Larry's voice interrupted him loud and clear.

"Thanks Larry, you've done well. From what you say we clearly need to crack on with enlarging this hole and getting the patient out. I'm busy briefing Helen, the nurse and Doctor Burrows. It won't be long now before you have Helen with you."

"Great, thanks."

There followed an anxious wait by the team in the cave, but hectic activity above. For Larry and Anna the wait was punctuated by a request from Doctor. Burrows who had taken the walkie-talkie from Michael and wanted an update on the patient's condition. Larry gave him as best he could a description of Father Aloysius's position and his condition, handing his phone to Anna to describe how she had come to the conclusion that the priest was alive and about his speaking to her. The doctor was impressed by the calm way both of the young carers down in the cave spoke. They were clearly in control. He thanked them warmly before signing off and their waiting and wondering resumed.

On the surface Patrick and his small team had had a brief discussion, Sam was to belay Larry to get him up onto the ledge. Michael would belay him. Larry would guide Anna through the hole when the time came. Adrian would belay Anna. There would be just time for him to phone base and to call for a drill, sledge, hammer, picks and shovels, a compressor and a cage with the anchoring ropes so they could lower it down in front of the hole as a platform to work on widening the entrance to the cave. Quickly, with a quiet practised purposefulness the four set about their tasks. Patrick had just come off the phone when Commander Nesbitt arrived escorted by the police constable.

"Excuse me, we can see you're busy but I wonder if you could spare a moment to listen to the Commander. He has some important news to relay."

"Sure," Patrick smiled at the Commander. This interruption was inconvenient, to say the least, but the Commander was a Naval man and wouldn't have made the request without some pressing reason. He stepped away from the others and took the Commander to the rear of the Land-rover.

"Fire away?

"Thank you. You might want to turn that off," Commander Nesbitt pointed to the walkie-talkie."

"Don't worry it's only active to receive, to transmit I have to keep this button pressed down."

"Good. Briefly breaking news from Pondreath. There has been a trawler washed up on rocks down the coast. Two bodies have come ashore. One is the guardian uncle, the foster father to Larry who as I understand it is down in the cave. His sister Philippa is with me and the ladies. Neither of the children are aware of the news."

Patrick took a sharp breath in and clenched his teeth together with a click. This was not the sort of news either child needed right now.

"I see. Your advice please."

"Keep it hush hush if you can, no one from the village is coming up here at the moment, they are far too preoccupied. When this is over Mrs Evans and I can break the news.. You may want to tip me off as to the appropriate time."

"Fine, thanks," Patrick turned to go,"One other thing, the ladies have prepared a mountain of sandwiches and enough flasks of hot soup to sustain an army. It's there on the path whenever you need it."

"Great, Thank the ladies please." he gave the Commander a broad grin and headed off to rope up. Clipping his rope to his harness he waved the others to him. Sensing an urgency in his signal they quickly gathered round.

"This is a difficult one but you need to know, last night's storm wrecked a trawler. Two bodies have been recovered, one is the foster father of Larry and his sister Philippa. They don't know and it's strictly hush hush from us. When we have got the patient out and safely on the way to hospital Commander Nesbitt, a friend will find a way to break the news. The village will be in shock but the kids don't need to know, not yet anyway."

Patrick looked at each of his companions briefly to check they had understood.

"Now, let's get to work." With a grim face the climber put his walkie-talkie to his mouth, "Larry we need your attention now, we are ready to go, got that."

"Understood," Larry gave a thumbs up sign to Anna.

"Rope up, we need you on the ledge to assist Nurse Helen. Then wait there we have a stretcher to follow. Sam has your rope. I am going over now to be by the hole to assist Helen if she needs it."

"Understood." Larry had hardly got himself and his rope sorted when Patrick's arm came though the hole giving him the thumbs up sign.

"Helen's on her way."

"Fine." The nurse in bright orange overalls and a tight-fitting orange jacket slipped easily though the hole. She needed no assistance.

"Helen," she announced giving a minimal introductory greeting.

"Larry, Anna's below, I'm to stay and wait for the stretcher."

"Good, thanks," she lowered herself quickly off the ledge and with easy agility landed on the rocks below. Larry was to learn everything about the way nurse Helen Strachan worked was nimble, quick and thorough.

Patrick guided the folded stretcher through the hole for Larry to hand down to Anna. By the time Larry had joined her and they had unfolded it Nurse Strachan had completed her check of the priest. She used her phone to send her observations up to Doctor Burrows.

"Doctor Burrows told me you have given the patient liquid, when was that and how much?"

Anna stepped forward, "I tried to give the patient some liquid from the pink bottle that was sent down to us about an hour ago. It was at ten forty-two. He didn't take much, just a few sips, really. It difficult to say how much he swallowed, quite a bit dribbled out of his mouth."

"Thanks, Can I have the bottle please?" The nurse was impressed that Anna had managed to give her the exact time. Larry fetched the bag and Anna handed the bottle over. She examined the level of liquid left in the bottle. "Um he didn't take much from the looks of it. Have you any idea if he had been able to get any liquids before you arrived?"

Anna glanced at Larry and nodded,

"Larry." she prompted.

"Certainly, just up here," Larry climbed up to the top of the cave and pointed to a spot just beyond the pile of stones set against the cliff wall, "There is pool of water in a hollow. It's probably water that gathers here when it rains and during the storm it may have been topped up. This pile of stones," Larry put a hand on the pile, "It's not natural, we think Father Aloysius was building a ramp to enable him to get up onto the ledge. If that's what he was doing he couldn't have missed seeing the pool. As to when he drank or how much we just can't say."

"What makes you so certain that that pile is man made?"

"Well, look at it, does it look natural, is it natural to have stones piled up like this. It's all too neat. While we were waiting for the helicopter I left Anna with Father Aloysius and I went down into the cave to see if I could find the entrance. Lower down, round that corner there, I found another pile like this, it looks like a cairn but I think it may have been stones collected by our friend and piled up there. He was busy ferrying them up here when he collapsed."

"Interesting, how do you know it was your friend that built that pile in the first place?"

"Just below that pile is a stretch of sand. It's scuffed up in places. I think that's where he lay down to sleep. Remember at night this place is pitch black dark. Not only that, I found footprints in the sand."

"And it looked like that it was Father Aloysius's foot, did it?"

"Yes."

"Um, thank you, it certainly sounds plausible. Anyway we know he could have had a drink. Have you tasted the water?" "No but I will." Larry bent down and scooped up some water in the palm of his hand. He drank some. "Tastes fine."

"Not salty?"

"No, cool and fresh."

"Thanks. Do you think that sandy spot might be a suitable place to lay the patient down while they are trying to enlarge the hole?"

"Yes, at least it's flat and soft, if a bit damp."

"What about the entrance? Any sign of that?"

"Afraid not, I did a quick search, but nothing. It's a mystery."

"How on earth did he get in here?"

"Who knows?"

"I guess at this moment in time, it's a mystery. I think I'll have another go at getting some liquid into our friend here, and then we might move him."

"OK Do you think you should have the walkie-talkie?"

"Oh, thanks, that's possibly a sensible suggestion. I don't think Doctor. Burrows has one, but he could use Patrick's when he needs to. I'll tell you what, you keep it for the moment, and when I need it, you can give it to me."

Anna watched as Helen Strachan fed the tube from the bottle into the priest's mouth. He stirred. She put her hand on his forehead, pushing up the woollen cap to do so. "Good, "she said softly, bending over her patient, "I'd like you to drink for me, please."

Father Aloysius nodded and sucked on the tube until he had enough to swallow.

"Thank you, that's a good start, just keep sucking, take your time. It's good for you, it's got all sorts of good things in it which will help you to get better." Patiently, the nurse coaxed him to drain the bottle."

"Well done," Anna and the nurse chorused together and exchanged smiles.

"You're very patient," complimented the girl. The nurse shrugged by way of reply.

"His skin body temperature has improved. You did a good job wrapping him up. He was probably pretty cold when you found him."

"Yes, but his lips weren't blue."

"Always an encouraging sign, I guess humping the rocks up here must have been quite a task, but it probably kept him moderately warm until he collapsed. Larry, is there any more of this stuff in the bag, please?"

"No, I don't think so, but I'll check just to make sure."

Anna pre-empted him, "That was the only bottle. I was the first to unpack the bag, but there is a box of sandwiches and some flasks of hot soup if you'd like some."

"Sounds good, maybe when we all get our friend here down to that spot of soft sand. In the meantime I think I'd better report to base. Phone please Larry, if you don't mind." Having reported on her patient's condition she asked for further supplies of medicated re-hydrating fluids and also for three sleeping bags, ground sheets and an additional torch. Next the nurse asked for an update regarding thoughts as to a rescue route. From the reply she and her companions learnt that the tide now being fully out, the team at the foot of the cliffs was busy searching for the entrance to the cave, but that so far they had not found any evidence of one. The storm and the high tide of the night had shifted a large amount of sand and shingle down the coast line and some had been deposited in the narrow gullies between the rocks that clustered round the head land cliffs. Attempts were being made to dig along the base of the cliff at the end of the gullies to try to find an entrance that may have been blocked but so far nothing had come of these. The search was time limited by the tides. Even if they found such an entrance, whether it would be suitable as an exit through which to take Father Aloysius was something they could not second guess. Given the time factor it was unlikely there would be enough time left before the tide came in for a rescue to take place that day. The option of enlarging the hole seemed to be the better alternative. The equipment was on its way.

Patrick's best estimate for getting a cage platform in place and the drillers to be working on enlarging the hole was at least two hours. That was all he could tell them at the moment but he promised to update them as soon as he knew more. He had made no mention of the trawler disaster.

Larry fastened himself to his rope and with Sam's help was on the ledge in time to receive the next two bundles. He was getting quite proficient at the routine. Once down in the cave Helen and Anna unpacked the parcels and ferried the contents, along with the bag that contained the food down to the stretch of sand below. This took several trips. Nurse Strachan prepared the stretcher. The air filled mattress was strapped to the frame and she moved some of the stones round the priest so as to be able to put the stretcher down relatively close alongside the patient. With just the three of them to move him they did not want to be carrying him far without the stretcher. When all was ready she instructed her companions as to the best way for them to act as a team to get Father Aloysius onto the stretcher. She included him in this preparation. The priest had shown no signs of being conscious, or even semi- conscious. However she did not want him to come to and react in some way while being lifted unto the stretcher. If he struggled in any way it could cause them to accidentality drop him. Should he be semi-conscious and hear her, he would be prewarned about his move and be able to cooperate. It was a tricky manoeuvre but following her instructions, they accomplished it without jarring their patient or tripping over rocks. He did not stir.

The journey down to the patch of sand took time. Clambering down the rocky slope was far from easy. With Nurse Strachan and Anna at the front taking a handle each side, and Larry at the rear they proceeded with great caution. Larry had to be particularly careful. He could not see where he was going to place his feet until the last minute and had to be guided as to what to expect by Anna at the front. Father Aloysius was heavier than they had anticipated and it was with great relief that they arrived at the stretch of sand and were able to lower their burden down.

"Well done, team, safely there. Good spot Larry."

"It's not exactly the Riviera, but at least it's flat, and it's lighter here now than when I first came. I think the light must be coming from that hole up there in the roof. I wonder where that is in the cliff face."

"Yes, interesting, we might have a little explore but first I'd better report our position to base and get another update from them, then we might share some of that soup and treat ourselves to a sandwich or two, after that we can have a look around. First things first, walkie-talkie, please."

While Nurse Strachan made her report Larry and Anna busied themselves unpacking the bag with the food in it. Using some of the stones from the pile that the priest had accumulated Larry constructed make shift places for them to be able to sit down. The tarpaulins with the sleeping bags on top made good cushions. Another pile of rocks acted as a table. The news from above was encouraging. The equipment needed to make the hole wider had just arrived and they were busy preparing to lower the cage platform down in front of the hole. On the beach the search party had been digging at the base of the cliffs to see if they could find an entrance that had been blocked but to no avail. Now they had located a channel through the rocks to the cliff face that seemed to be the most likely spot for an entrance to be but it was chocked with sand shingle and drift wood. As to whether they would have time to excavate it before the tide came in was doubtful. They had however sent for reinforcements and for more tools. Doctor Burrows had recommended that the patient be given another bottle of medicated fluids and then sedated. That would help when it came to stretcher him out. Nurse Strachan handed the walkie-talkie back to Larry.

"Now, how about some soup and sandwiches? I'm famished."

"We had a sandwich and some soup before you arrived," Anna explained.

"Well you've been busy since then so don't hold back. We may not get another opportunity for some time." Larry needed no second invitation and Anna seeing that there was in fact a good stock of provisions decided to join him. As they ate, Nurse Strachan was unpacking the second holdall with the extra bottles of fluid. She suddenly burst out laughing. Her companions were at a loss to understand what might have caused such mirth when she held up a packet of toilet rolls, they were mauve and patterned with images of lavender.

"Very tasteful," Larry grinned, "but I just hope we are not down here long enough to need those."

"You never know, it might take longer than we would like for that hole to be enlarged and then to get the whole business of getting out done. On these occasions it's better not to get ahead of yourself."

"Sure, well I know where to find the necessary should I need it." Anna was still giggling. "Now you've set her off she'll never stop."

"It's better than crying, and just the thought of you and lavender toilet paper is hilarious."

"How do you know; you don't know what we have at our house."

"I bet it's not lavender."

"No, sadly not, if the truth be told it's more likely to be newspaper."

"Delicious sandwiches and the soup is excellent too. Whoever made this hit the button just right for me."

"It was my mum."

"Your mum? Well thank her for me when we get out of here please, they are just what we needed. Now I'm going to try to give our friend here another bottle, I suggest you two have another look for that entrance."

There was a loud clatter and then a crash.

Startled Larry leapt to his feet. The walkie-talkie crackled to life.

"Patrick here, we are getting the cage platform into place. We should be drilling soon, you will need to keep well clear."

"Message understood. Don't worry we are well out of harm's way. Good luck with the drilling." Nurse Strachan handed the walkie-talkie back to Larry. "You look after this please; I am going to be busy."

With the drilling commencing, soon the need to find the entrance to the cave grew less urgent, nevertheless it would be a good use of the time, and should they find it, well, who knows, they might be out of the cave even sooner. He fished about in the hold-all with bottles in it and retrieved a large flash light.

"This and our head torches should do."

"Hope you find something." Nurse Strachan was already examining Father Aloysius in preparation for giving him more fluid.

"Me too," Anna bent over for a close look into her friend's face, "It's time we got you out of this horrible place; it's worse than a dungeon."

He and Anna set off on another reconnoitre of the lower regions of their prison. At the edge of the lagoon, Larry used the flash light to search all along the wall of the cave. There was nothing to suggest that there was an opening. The lagoon seemed to end at a blank wall. The water reflected the roof above, it was black. They were denied access to its depths. Perhaps he should enter the water and wade out to the end. If he ducked under, he might find something. He bent down and touched the water, it was cold. What might he find? Surely if there were an opening under the water, light would come in and they would be able to see it. He shared his thoughts with Anna. She too thought as he did, if there was an opening it would have been found by the team searching on at the base of the cliffs, and anyway light would enter the cave. She was strongly against him entering the water. Frustrated they turned to go back.

"Wait, I thought I heard something."

"Like what?"

"I don't know, a sort of thump."

"Where did it seem to come from?"

"Somewhere behind us, somewhere over there I suppose." They stood still and listened. There was some noise coming from the top of the cave where the cage was being put in place.

"Perhaps it's an echo."

"An echo, what of?"

"Well, of the noise coming from up there," Larry pointed to the top of the cave.

"Really, perhaps we should try shouting and see if we can get an echo."

OK On three we both shout help together." They turned their faces to look at the ceiling of the cave and taking deep breath both screamed "Help" sure enough, there was a slight echo.

"There you are, it could have been an echo."

"Then why didn't we hear an echo when there was that big clatter and bang when they were lowering the cage over the cliff edge?"

"Maybe there was, but we didn't recognise it."

"If we can hear a noise coming from outside, beyond that wall then presumably whoever made that sound can hear us. Let's shout help again and this time really listen for a reply." They tried it but there was no answering reply.

"It must have been my imagination. Anyway, nurse Helen must be wondering what's going on, we had better go and tell her." They returned to the Nurse and her patient. Larry let Anna do the explaining.

"I did wonder what was going on. I mean a cry for help usually means someone is in trouble. Fortunately, I could see you and wondered if you had heard noises outside. It would seem there being an entrance at the base of the cliff is not an option at the moment. Larry you'd better report to base."

Above on the cliff edge the team had already come to the conclusion that finding the entrance to the cave before the tide came in was not going to happen and that any hope of an exit that way would not become apparent until the following day. Spending another night in the cave was not an option they could risk. They thanked Larry for his report and told him they would be drilling very soon.

Nurse Strachan had managed to restore the priest to a level of consciousness that meant he was able to accept another drink. She had fed him the bottle and then had started another one with the sedative in the liquid.

"This is the sedative," she explained to Anna who had picked up the empty bottle that had just been completed. She read the label.

"Gosh, I hadn't realised this is quite a cocktail."

"Yes, the body needs all those but the sooner we get him out of here the better chance he has. We are sedating him now because when we come to move him it's going to be stressful."

At that moment a message came from Patrick. He was about to start drilling. The relative quiet in the cave was shattered by a deafening sound. Anna hoped it would not take long to enlarge the hole. Larry stood on the corner at the point the cave sloped upwards and towards the hole. He watched patiently. For some time, there was nothing but noise and dust but then bits of rock started to fall onto the ledge. Encouraged he descended to tell the others.

"I think it's time to get the patient into a sleeping bag and strap him to the stretcher. It will take all three of us. We need the bag that unzips all the way down one side." Larry removed the four sleeping bags from their covers. Anna started to unroll the first. It was not the one. She had visions of them having to open all four, fortunately the designated bag happened to be the second one she opened. It had the zip running the full length. She held it up. Nurse Strachan nodded.

"We need to try and get him into the bag just as he is, wrapped up. If Larry and I lift can you slip the bag under the patient. Unzip it all the way down first."

"Will the sedation have worked by now?"

"It should have, the length of time can vary from patient to patient but we will have to get him into the bag anyway, and getting him down here seemed not to have disturbed him." Anna laid the unzipped bag down alongside the stretcher. "Larry please take the head end and I'll lift the legs; you need to lift the patient under the armpits." They had just finished strapping Father Aloysius cocooned in the sleeping bag to the stretcher when the drilling ceased. Patrick called.

"Hallo, cave team. Are you with me?"

"Hearing you loud and clear, patient sedated in sleeping bag strapped to stretcher. Handing over to Nurse Strachan."

"Thanks, Larry, well done."

"Hi Helen."

"Helen here."

"We've completed the enlarging of the hole so hopefully we can get the stretcher through. It will take us a little time to make the necessary preparations up here, but we hope to be able to join you pretty soon. We need to lower two ladders into the cave. Can Larry get onto the ledge to receive them please."

"Larry will be with you, A.S.A.P. He'll let you know when he is ready to take the ladders. I'll stay put with the patient."

"Understood. Thanks." Nurse Strachan handed the walkie-talkie back. "Looks like we are on our way. The drilling didn't take as long as I feared." She smiled. "The ladders will make it easier to get the stretcher up to the ledge, and then to the hole. After that they will rope the patient up. The helicopter will be standing by." She looked down at the priest on the stretcher. "Better say goodbye to this salubrious mansion, we'll soon have you out of here so you won't have another night sleeping rough on the beach."

"Thank God," Anna bent over and adjusted the woollen hat on the priest's head, "I can imagine there will be a reception committee to greet you so we need to have you looking your best." Larry was already clambering back to the top of the cave.

Patrick too was on his way up. As he emerged over the cliff edge, he was handed a sandwich and a thermos of soup. "Thanks. I'll enjoy this, have you all eaten?

"Yes, we've been munching away while you've been working" Michael grinned, "I should think you're famished. There's more where that came from." He pointed to the bag at his feet.

"Great, Sam could you and Adrian get the ladders down to Larry. Then whoever's down in the cage will have to come back up to help belay Mike and I when we go through the hole to bring the patient out."

"Fine, we'd better alert the chopper pilot. He can alert the hospital."

"Will do."

"Patrick is that you? Larry here. I'm roped up and ready to climb to the ledge. The dust has settled but there is a lot of loose debris here, and I can see more on the ledge."

"Good, Sam will be bringing you up to the ledge. You had better clear any debris that will get in the way. I'm now up on the top. Adrian and Sam will get the ladders to you. Set both of them up against the face below the ledge. When you are safely down Mike and I are going to join you to bring the patient out. Stay with the ladders to hold them for us. Understood?"

"Understood."

Once set in motion the rescue plan unfolded with surprising speed. Larry cleared the ledge of the rocks that had fallen onto it when the hole was being enlarged. The light aluminium telescopic ladders were lowered to the ledge. Larry extended them to their full height, and lowered them to cave floor below. On Nurse Strachan's suggestion Anna carrying the bag containing the medicated drinks and the first aid equipment with her joined Larry at the top of the cave. She held the bottom of the ladder for him as he descended. Larry remained with the ladders while she returned to fetch more of the bags. By the time she had made the trip, down and back Patrick and then Mike had descended through the enlarged hole and were on the ledge. She and Larry held the ladders for them as they descended. Patrick took the walkie-talkie from Larry.

"Sam, please."

"Sam here."

"We are now in the cave. We will proceed down to Helen with Larry and bring the stretcher with the patient up. Meanwhile Anna has some bags for you to bring to the surface. Are you in the cage or at the top?"

"Adrian's in the cage"

"OK he will be able to see Anna through the hole and will be able to tell you when she has the bags safely on a rope. I'm taking the walkie-talkie down with me." Understood?"

"Understood."

Larry led the way down to where Helen was waiting.

"How's the patient?" Patrick responded to her greeting salute with a salute of his own.

"Sedated, ready to be moved." Patrick scanned the cave and then inspected the straps holding Father Aloysius to the stretcher.

"Pity he couldn't speak to tell you how he got in here."

"That's a mystery that is going to have to be on hold. No doubt we'll learn in time."

"Um yes, Larry, you and I will take the front, Helen and Mike the back. Sam, we are bringing the stretcher up. I'll let you know when we get to the top of the cave. You'll need to get Adrian up to belay Helen, she'll come first and then you can take my rope and you'll need the doctor with you on the stretcher rope, so get him to put on a harness. Helen can take me and Adrian take Mike. Understood?"

"Understood."

"Right, let's move." With Larry indicating the most suitable route over the boulders the four stretcher bearers moved steadily up to top of the cave. Patrick handed the walkie-talkie to the nurse, "You better alert Doctor Burrows to the fact his patient will be with him soon. Tell Sam we are roping the stretcher up now. Larry and Anna, you hold the ladders. When we are safely up fetch the remaining bags and as soon as they are up you follow, OK?"

Larry looked at Anna, "Yes, understood."

"Sam is that you?"

"Sam here Helen."

"Can you put Doctor Burrows on for me, please. We are attaching the stretcher to the ropes."

"Understood."

"Thanks."

"Burrows here,"

"Good. Any instructions, please? We are about to bring the patient up."

"Nothing from me, you have got him sedated, when you get him here, I'll make a brief inspection, and then we need to have him on the chopper and off to hospital as soon as possible. They have been alerted and are expecting him."

"Understood," The doctor handed the walk-talkie back to Sam. He had brought Adrian up from the cage outside the hole to join him as part of the belay team. Helen followed. She had just a moment for a word with the doctor before Sam gave the stretcher team the go ahead to proceed with the final phase of the rescue.

"Ready when you are."

"Coming up." Patrick and Michael, with one hand on the ladder and the other on the stretcher, climbed slowly up to the ledge. Larry and Anna held the ladders at the bottom. "Slowly now we are coming to the ledge where we need to put the stretcher down to get ready for the next phase.

"Understood."

"On the ledge, slack, please. We are lowering the stretcher to the horizontal position."

"Understood, enough?"

"That's fine. I'll let you know when we are ready. Larry, there's only room for one ladder here. Keep the other one to use when you come to get out. Sam, I'm going to use one ladder to get to the cage before the stretcher. When you pull it up, Mike will guide you from the bottom, and I will help from above. Once we have it in the cage, it will be up to you. Is that all clear?"

"Understood."

"One more thing, when Mike and I are out Anna and Larry will send up the baggage and the ladders. Then they'll follow."

"All understood." Getting the stretcher through the hole without it getting snagged and taking care to prevent Father Aloysius from being bumped against any rock was the tricky bit. Patrick using the ladder to scale the wall between the ledge and the hole was soon in the cage. He waved cheerily to the belay team above and then lent through the hole in order to be ready to receive the stretcher.

"Ready Mike?"

"Ready."

"Above slowly up, good, gently, gently, Mike's got to direct it head first up through the hole. Hold it. Hold it a minute. Ready Mike?"

"Nearly, just changing my position on the ledge. With the limited room on the ledge much of which was taken up by the stretcher Mike had to take care not to overbalance backwards, "Ready."

"Up she goes gently does it, gently, good keep going slowly, slowly." Below in the cave Larry and Anna watched with increasing trepidation as the stretcher was first raised to vertical and then guided initially by Mike then by Patrick up safely through the hole. Father Aloysius was on his way out, but they would not feel at ease until he was safely at the top.

"Good well done Mike, got it, gently above, he's coming through, gently, OK stop there, I've got to get myself in position to turn him round as he exits the hole so he's facing away from the cliff for the last lift. You may have to adjust your positions too." Patrick braced himself to take the weight of the stretcher as he guided it out into the cage taking care not to let it swing back against the cliff face as it emerged.

"Good, good, now slack very slowly I'm going to lie the stretcher out horizontal over the edge of the cage in preparation for turning it round. Once there we'll rest a moment while Mike joins me OK?"

"Understood."

If Father Aloysius hadn't been oblivious to all that had occurred over the last hour and would continue to be so for some hours to come, he might have been more than a little perturbed at being laid out on a stretcher precariously placed over a sheer fall of considerable distance to rocks below, round which swirled frothing foaming waves. As it was, he knew nothing. Patrick and Michael however were all too aware that the next manoeuvre was going to be difficult and spent some time working out the best strategy. In the end it proved to be fairly simple. They lowered the bottom of the stretcher to the floor of the cage. While Mike held it in an upright position Patrick unclipped the ropes at the head in order to avoid them becoming twisted when they turned the stretcher round. They shuffled the stretcher round to have their patient facing out to sea. Patrick then re-clipped the ropes to the stretcher making sure they would not be crossed or twisted. It was a very short distance from the cage to the cliff top, standing balancing on the side wall of the cage they could guide it up to the top.

During the course of the afternoon a number of villagers attracted by the sound of the helicopter had ventured along the path for a closer look. They had been met by the policeman who had had some quiet words with each group regarding the young Trevinians and the sensitivity of the situation with their not yet knowing of their uncle's death He had then escorted them down to the vantage point from which Commander Nesbitt, Mrs Evans, Miss Farrow and Philippa had been keeping a vigil for much of the day. The moment the stretcher appeared over the edge of the cliff a loud cheer went up from the assembled watchers. Commander Nesbitt gave Philippa a friendly slap on the back.

"He's out, and it's all down to you. Well done."

"Not just me, Commander. Don't forget Min; he raised our suspicions, and it was Larry leaning over the cliff who saw him."

"As always, a team effort. Well done all."

Below in the cave, Larry and Anna were already heading off to fetch up the rest of the baggage. When they heard the cheers, they, too, joined in the celebration. The echo of their cheers reverberated round the rock walls.

"Sam, Larry here, bags attached to rope. We'll climb up the ladder to the ledge and then pull the ladder up after us. It will be Anna next;

she'll use the ladder to get up to the hole. Then it'll be the ladder and, lastly, me. Oh, and well done for getting Father Aloysius out."

"Understood. Team effort, Larry, and you two have been great. The doctor's giving the patient a quick look over, and then they'll be taking him on the stretcher to the helicopter, it'll be job done, and we can all go home."

Anna reached the cage cave. The helicopter took off. She joined the others in the cheering and waving. Larry, too, let out a whoop of joy when he heard the sound. It was over, thank God. When Larry's turn came, he found exiting the hole much simpler than when he had entered it. Standing in the cage, he took a moment to look about him. It was then, looking along the face of the cliff and then down to the rocks and the sea below, that the scale of the rescue and its complexity really came home to him. And he and Anna had been part of it all, an amazing experience. The question remained - how did Father Aloysius get into the cave in the first place? Perhaps he would now find out.

Chapter Thirty-Six

Time has its own ways of of revealing truth. Just be patient and live life, you will get answers to all questions.

Anna was waiting for Larry as he emerged at the top of the cliff; she held a hand out to him.

"Thanks," he stood smiling down at her. She threw her arms around him and gave him a big hug. Larry bent his head and kissed her hair. For both, there was a great sense of relief and joy. Looking over to Sam, Larry nodded, "Thanks, Sam. I guess there will be a bit of clearing up to do."

"And some. It must be good to be out of there."

"It feels good to have got Father Aloysius out. I know that for sure. Did nurse Helen go in the chopper?

"Yes, she and Doctor Burrows both. It won't be long before he's in hospital, and then its wait and see."

"He's going to be OK, isn't he?"

"He should be, but he's had a lot to cope with. One thing is certain: he won't be out tomorrow or any time soon. You two going down probably gave him a fighting chance."

Anna had released Larry, "God, I hope so."

"We all do. Sounds like he was a special bloke."

Anna looked up at Larry, "Yes, very special."

"Solid gold," affirmed Larry, and he unclipped himself from his rope and unbuckled the harness." Where do I put this?"

"Leave it with me. I'll stow it with the others in the Land-rover. When all this is done, I hope we get to enjoy another of your mum's sandwiches. I could murder a drink right now."

"I'll tell Mum." The girl strode off back to the path where her mother was packing the empty thermoses into a bag. As she approached, Anna was greeted with a round of applause.

"Thanks. Wow, quite a few of you. What a reception committee for Father Aloysius! Any sandwiches left Mum?

"As it happens, yes, but how is he? We are just off to brew some tea and fetch a cake. If you want to, come and help. Is Larry staying here to help clear up?"

"Father Aloysius is as good as could be expected. He was unconscious most of the time. Before we got him out, he was sedated. We are just praying for the best. Looks like Larry is staying and Philippa too. I'll tell him I'm going with you, but we won't be long, and he can spread the word; tea and cake is on the way." She hurried back to give her message to Larry, who was assisting in the bringing up of the cage and then ran to catch up with her mother. He gave her a thumbs-up and blew her a kiss.

As with the setting up, the team worked methodically at gathering all the equipment together and packing it in the Land Rover. Larry, Philippa, and the Commander helped where they could, as did the two police constables. The rest quickly dispersed, returning to their homes and no doubt to share the news that the priest had been rescued. With the village in shock at the fate of two of their own, this would be a relief and good news for many, but there would be questions, too.

For Anna and her mother, it was a quick walk back to their home to replenish the thermoses and collect a cake before returning. The long vigil was over. It had ended well. The suspense had been immense. Now, their friend was safe and in good hands, and their prayers must be for his full recovery. It was a greatly relieved and happy, if weary, group that trudged back to deliver their supplies to the team.

Patrick set up a make shift table on the flap of the Land Rover's tailgate and called the team together. With a mug of tea in one hand and a piece of cake in the other, he addressed them all.

"Well done, it's been quite a day. I've just heard from Helen; our patient is now safely in Intensive Care in the hospital. The prognosis appears to be good. If the truth be known, I was worried at first, but now it seems doctor Burrows is optimistic, so here's to Father Aloysius and a speedy return to the village," He raised his mug, "Father Aloysius." Mugs were raised in unison as the team responded.

"A huge thank you to you all, the team worked well. This has been one of the most challenging of the rescues I have been involved in, and by and large, it's been glitch-free. And then a big thank you to our providers here for some delicious food and soup, and now this tea and cake. It makes all the difference and if this has been one of our trickiest assignments, it's also been the one we will always remember for great provisions."

This was greeted with a chorus of "Hear! Hear!"

"It's been unique, too, in that this is a first for me that youngsters have been part of the actual rescue. It was a risk, but sometimes you just have to take these risks, and this was, in my judgement, one of those times. It certainly paid off, so well-done Philippa, Larry, and Anna... and thanks."

Larry blushed and put his arm round Anna's shoulders as she smiled proudly up at him, and then he reached out to bring his sister into his embrace as the rest of the gathering clapped in agreement.

"Any questions or observations?"

The Commander stepped forward. "As a mere observer, I have to say you've all been hugely impressive, and we have to be very grateful that we in these parts have such an excellent cliff rescue team to call on, so if you will allow me, I propose a toast to the cliff rescue team." This last toast was rewarded with a cheer.

"I have a question." It was Miss Farrow, "Do we have any idea how Father Aloysius ended up in this cave? It must have an entrance somewhere, surely?"

Patrick shrugged, "I'm afraid that is still an element of mystery about the how and the when. As you say, there must be an entrance. The team looking for one at the bottom of the cliff told me they thought that they had located the most likely place. It's at the end of a narrow gully. As you will be aware the sea is a great shifter of materials. It may be that on the night Father Aloysius was cast up against the cliff, that gully had been cleared by a previous storm, and there was an entrance to the cave, then the next storm, which happened to be the next night, filled it in again, blocking off the entrance. It sounds plausible, but it will have to be confirmed."

"Thank you."

"Now we've had our tea, lads, I think it's time for home." It wasn't long before the tractor, closely followed by the Land Rover, were being waved on their way, bumping off towards the road. The villagers had long since departed and dispersed to their homes. No doubt, the news of the rescue was already spreading round the village.

The Commander thanked the police constables. Theirs had been the less dramatic role but a very necessary one. It had been a great team effort.

"Time for us to be on our way."

Larry and Anna assisted the Commander in carting the bags of tea things back to the Evans household. It was a weary but happy throng that walked the path back to the village. After all the excitement and the tension of the rescue, both Larry and Anna felt drained. It was with a mixture of emotions that they dumped their bags on the kitchen floor. Relief tinged with a sense of elation and gratitude, all mixed up with exhaustion. Larry stretched as he stood up from dropping his bags and turned to Anna. Their eyes met.

"Thank God that's over, I'm done."

With a little sob, the girl threw herself into his arms. Her tears were tears of relief and of love. She reached up to kiss him. "We did it, Larry, we did it. God help Father Aloysius and the hospital to do the rest." She sniffed and wiped her tears away with the back of her hands. He pulled a handkerchief from his pocket and handed it to her.

"I'm sorry. I don't know what's come over me. I guess I'm just so happy we did it. You and me Philippa and the team, we did it. They embraced again. Holding each other tight. Anna gave a last sniff as she finally broke away. She put her hands up to Larry's face and looked long into his eyes.

"I love you, Larry."

Larry beamed, "I love you too, and I always will."

"Now, I guess we had better get on with the washing up," the girl reached out a hand and led her admirer to the sink. "You wash, and I'll dry."

The couple were joined by Philippa, Louisa, Miss Farrow, and the Commander. As the last mugs were put away the Commander sensed that the time had come to talk to the young Trevinians. It was a duty he was not looking forward to. They were all both elated and exhausted. Now they would be faced with some extremely distressing news. With a heavy heart he called Larry and Philippa to him. He was about to take them outside into the garden when a thought struck him, Anna would have to know too. He decided to include her and take all three along the cliff path a little way where there was less likelihood of being interrupted.

The Commander was not new to the experience of having to break bad news to people. On board ship as the captain of the vessel he had had on occasion to break sad news to members of his crew. It was never easy but he had learnt that setting the scene was important. The nonverbal signals of a grave face and a quiet dignified demeanour would set the right tone for the meeting and lessen the shock of what he was about to impart. Then he needed to have allowed time after delivering the news to be able to support the crew member to whom the news was being imparted, which, given the nature of his job, was not always easy. He had always made sure that he was not the only one available to give support, before he had embarked on the task. In this case that role was to be taken by two people, Anna's mother and the priest's housekeeper. He had already briefed them and so when he had called Larry, his sister and Anna together both Louisa and Miss Farrow were already aware that they might be needed.

Moving back from the path a little way he took Larry and Philippa by the hand, Anna picking up on his cue joined hands with them too.

They stood for a moment in a silent circle, he looked at them all one by one. All their eyes were fixed on his face.

"I'm afraid I am going to have to break some bad news, sad news." There was a collective intake of breath as each of them pondered what this might be. Surely it did not concern Father Aloysius, but who else might it be, what might have happened.? The Commander continued gravely "There is no good time for the sharing of bad news and this certainly isn't a good time at all. You have been part of a very dramatic and demanding ordeal and you acquitted yourselves magnificently, but needs must and so very sadly I have to tell you, Philippa and Larry that in last night's storm the trawler belonging to Michael Trevinian was wrecked. Two bodies have been recovered, Michael and your Uncle Sidney Trevinian. They were washed ashore. This news came to the village this morning. You were already embarked on a difficult and dangerous task so it has been kept from you until now. I'm very, very sorry." The Commander paused. There was a moment's stunned silence. He continued quietly "Your mother Anna, and Miss Farrow know and we are all ready to support you in whatever way you need."

"Thank you." Larry was the first to respond then he broke away from the circle of supporting hands and strode off through the heather across the path to the cliff edge. Anna would have followed but was prevented by Philippa who clung onto her hand.

"God," she threw her arms round Anna and buried her face against her chest. Anna for her part very gently stroked her hair. Commander Nesbitt stood quietly watching, then placing a hand on each bowed head, said softly.

"I'm going to be with Larry for a moment." The Commander stopped short of joining Larry on the cliff edge and waited watching. The boy was motionless, gazing out to sea. The seconds ticked away, a minute passed then two. Finally, Larry spoke.

"I'm not going to pretend I'm sad because I don't feel it, but, he, he was family and for quite a time he and Charlotte were the only family Philippa and I had. For better or worse they put up with us and we had a roof over our heads and a place to go to after school. Their house is still our home, and no matter what I feel there is Charlotte to think of."

"Yes." The Commander shook his head in wonder. He smiled. "Well spoken. I know it's been far from easy for you and Philippa but I have to say your response is most impressive. You will all need support, and we are here to give that. I suspect your parents will have already heard the news. Right now I guess we just don't know what this is going to mean for you, for Charlotte and for them. We can only take things a day at a time and when things become clear make plans for the best outcome for all. Now I suppose when you are ready you need to be getting home. I'll come with you."

"Thanks, I think we can manage. Charlotte may not take kindly to seeing you, but perhaps if it's OK, I'll tell her you asked after her and have offered help."

"Certainly, I'm going back to the girls." Larry stood quietly, still gazing out to sea, and then raising an arm in a salute to the far distant horizon, he spoke,

"Sid, there was never much going for us, you and me. At times I hated your guts, probably still do, but nobody's all bad, you, me, none of us are perfect. I just hope the end when it came wasn't too painful. We'll do our best for Charlotte." He turned away from the sea and head bowed hurried over to the group on the other side of the path. He put his hand on his sister's shoulder.

"Thanks, Commander, Flip I think we ought to be heading home, don't you?"

"What! No way I'm not going back to that bitch!"

"Hey Philippa, I'm sorry I guess I know how you feel, but it's the only home we've got and...."

"You could stay with us, both of you I'm sure Mum wouldn't mind, in fact she'd be more than pleased to have you." Anna gave Larry an imploring look.

"I'm afraid it's not as simple as that. Charlotte is our legal guardian, and her home has been our home since Mum and Dad split. Besides she may need us."

"Need us, you must be joking, she can't wait to get rid of us, why she's probably out at the boozer already."

"Maybe, but I still think it's the right thing to do. Maybe later we can look for somewhere else but tonight I think we ought to at least go and see how she is, I know it must be hard and I know how you feel."

"You don't, you don't." The venom in Philippa's voice was apparent to all, "I hate her and don't say you know how I feel because you don't. What's she ever done for you or for either of us. The only reason she has us is because Dad pays her to have us, and how much of that money gets spent on us, almost nothing, it all goes to the pub. Without us she wouldn't have the money for her fags and booze and you know it. I don't care if I never see her again."

Larry looked at the Commander and shrugged.

"Flip, please, you mentioned Dad, what's Dad going to think? He'll be down to see us and we owe it to him at least."

"Owe! He left us with that monster his brother and his bitch of a wife, and when did he last come to see us? To go into that place will make me puke." The bitter retorts were a culmination of years of bad feeling that had finally found a way of coming to the surface. For years Philippa had endured times of shameful even cruel treatment, for too long she had lived in dread of her violent guardian Sid, and had despised Charlotte. Now on that cliff top path it had all come out.

"Sis, look, come with me just for a visit if you like, if she's not there or if you don't want to stay I'll bring you back to Louisa and Anna, promise. Just for me, to support me, just come and show your face, please." There was a long silence. Larry looked at Anna and then the Commander. "OK I'm going." He gave her shoulder a squeeze, glanced at the Commander, and then at Anna, "Thanks I'll keep you informed." He blew Anna a kiss. "Please thank your mum for me for all the sandwiches and cake. Love you."

Anna, like Philippa and Larry, was still trying in her own way to digest the news. She was aware of Philippa's hand clinging tightly onto hers. She looked imploringly at Larry, then, realising how torn he must feel she blew him a farewell kiss in return.

"See you, love," she mouthed the words.

"See you." Larry turned and walked away head bowed. He hadn't gone far when he heard a patter of feet. It was Philippa. She slipped her arm through his.

"Thanks." He smiled down at her, but she wasn't looking. After a long pause, she said

"I'm only doing it for you."

"Thanks, it means a lot."

Philippa was right, Charlotte was out, probably at the pub but she hadn't left a note so they couldn't be certain, Larry speculated she might be with Dot, Mick's wife.

"Typical of you Larry, always ready to give people the benefit of the doubt and think the best of them."

"Maybe," Larry shrugged and opened the fridge. "Let's see if there is anything worth cooking here shall we. Check the food cupboard. There should be some potatoes and maybe a can of meat. No, hello, there are some sausages here and bacon. This should do."

"I'm not hungry."

"No, but you will be and she might be too, so I'm going to knock something up for all of us."

"Alright I'll peel the spuds. How many?"

"Depends on how big they are, small three each, big two."

"Big"

"Well that's good." Brother and sister worked quietly together. "This is nice, you helping me."

Philippa huffed by way of a response, and then added "I meant every word I said you know. And if you say you know how I feel I'll be out that door before you can say."

"Sizzling sausages."

"Quicker even, that's way too long."

"Speedy,"

"That's me, greased lightning."

"I thought that was John Travolta."

"Who's he?"

"That guy in, oh, it doesn't matter. I think I'm going to phone Dot."

"What! What for? "

"To see if she's there."

"She isn't."

"Alright. To see how she is."

"She and Charlotte are both the same, but suit yourself." Philippa was right again, Charlotte was not there, and Dot had not heard from her. She had been rather taken aback to hear from Larry and when he voiced his sympathy for her situation, she was totally unappreciative. Larry had a distinct feeling she was keeping something from him but as she clearly didn't want to speak to him, he wished her well and rang off.

"So was I right."

"Yes, afraid so."

"Not friendly then."

"No."

"Waste of time then, hadn't you better be phoning Anna like you promised? "

"Yes, thanks for reminding me, are you staying or going then?"

"What's the point? She'll come in pissed long after I should have gone to bed and fallen asleep. I might as well not be here for all she cares."

"But you'll see her in the morning."

"Will we? We've usually long gone by the time she gets up."

"We could make tomorrow an exception and wait for her."

"Really."

"Yes, really. It's a bit late to be off to stay with Louisa and Anna now anyway. Come to think of it, they will probably be at the church meeting with the bishop, and tomorrow you'll have to have some time to pack your things, providing you still want to go and stay somewhere else."

"Alright you win, let's have that meal I'm feeling hungry." Larry laughed. They were half way through the meal when there was a knock at the front door. It was Commander Nesbitt with the bishop. Larry was both surprised and impressed. He invited them in. The bishop was disappointed not to meet their step mother but left her a card of condolences. He had been to visit Father Aloysius on his journey over and was able to give them news. The priest was still not conscious enough to speak to him but he had spoken to one of the nurses. He was getting excellent care and the staff seemed to be confident he would make a good recovery. The bishop expressed great gratitude to them both for their part in the rescue of Father Aloysius, and further commended Philippa on her help for Miss Farrow. Then having committed to be on hand to help them in any way he could should they need it, he and Commander Nesbitt left, they had one more visit to make before the bishop wended his way back to Plymouth and that was to see Michael Trevinian's wife Dot.

Larry wondered what sort of reception they would get, but he did not share the fact that he had already phoned.

The reception was much as Larry imagined it would be. Dot was taken aback for the second time that evening and was totally ungrateful for their concern. She was rude. She had in so many words told them to mind their own business. The bishop gave the Commander a wry smile as they left.

"It would seem the Trevinians don't have much of an empathy for the church, that is, except for the young ones, don't you think? "He remarked dryly. Commander Nesbitt could not resist a chuckle.

"I have to agree, but it makes the attitude of the younger Trevinians all the more impressive."

"I wholeheartedly agree. That boy Larry is nothing if not impressive. To be what he is, coming from that background speaks volumes. Somebody must have been a good influence on the way, Father Aloysius has not been here that long."

"Yes, it was his headmaster at the primary school here, you met his wife this evening and Anna her daughter, is his girlfriend."

"I see, she has made a good choice, then."

"Yes, and they are well suited. I wouldn't underestimate Father Aloysius's influence on them both though. He has worked wonders in this village."

"Yes, I am not totally unaware of that, Commander, but thanks. Now I'll drop you home and be on my way, next week is a busy one."

"Aren't they all?"

The bishop smiled appreciatively, "Yes, but I work for a wonderful boss, so I don't mind."

"Don't bother to drop me. I can walk; it will do me good."

"Are you sure?"

"Perfectly." The two men shook hands and went their separate ways. The Commander plodded up the hill. It had been quite a day. He felt completely drained. Wandering his weary way he reflected on the last ten hours. At first his thoughts revolved round the bishop and Dot Trevinian. There was something odd about the whole of that visit. He shook his head, the Trevinians were a strange lot with a fairly dubious role in the warp and weft of the life of the village. He had suspected that they would not get a royal welcome, but Dot Trevinian had been bristling with animosity. True, she was a woman who had just lost her husband and grief can work in strange ways. But there was something that just didn't ring true about the way she spoke and behaved. Was she trying to hide something he wondered? The bishop on the other hand had been a revelation. The Commander had met a number of bishops in his time, some, perhaps slightly over conscious of the demands of their position and their own perception of their importance had been, how, should he put it? Somewhat haughty and unapproachable. All, he had no doubt, had been men of high intellect and ability but some, in his experience the majority, were men of humility and humanity.

The Roman Catholic bishop of Plymouth was one of those. His empathy with the suffering was palpable, his sense of responsibility towards his priests was obvious, not only was he humble but he had that Irish twinkle about him and his humour. He understood the Cornish in a way a bishop from say Oxford might not, he identified with them, like them he was of a Celtish strain, he came from a people who had been on the fringe and perhaps had the same sense of pride in his heritage. A pride born out of a sense of their otherness.

He had too, that most precious of gifts, a sense of humour. The Commander had been impressed. But then so many of those he had watched as the drama of the day had unfolded had been impressive, not just Anna and Larry who had stepped up to a challenge that must have been very testing. They had played their part with a maturity that belied their young years, as of course had Philippa. True, she had not acted with the dignity and sheer decency of her brother when she received the news of her guardian's demise but that was to be expected. She was younger than he was and being a girl was more vulnerable.

Then there was the rescue team, volunteers each one, so professional and committed as they brought their own particular skills, each one vital in their own way, to a critical situation. They engendered a sense of confidence that affected all who watched them, Father Aloysius would be rescued alive. Yes, the day had been a victory over odds that could only be described as very unfavourable, and he had been privileged to have seen it all. There were still lots of questions left unanswered but he had no doubt they would be. He had arrived at his own front door. He was exhausted, but very grateful. His good friend Father Aloysius had been found and was safe in hospital. In the kitchen he found a note from his housekeeper. His dinner was on a plate in the fridge. He put the plate in the microwave and while it was whirring round he poured himself a whisky. It was not his habit to drink anything alcoholic but on occasion he found it helped. Food, drink and then sleep, precious sleep. He ate well, enjoyed his drink and his sleeping was deep and long.

Philippa slept well too. She and Larry were both very tired after their ordeals and retired to bed as soon as they had dealt with the dishes and cleared the rubbish left by their guardian. Larry on the other hand found sleep difficult, he was very tired but was too wound up by the events of the day and wondering how it was that

Father Aloysius had come to end up in a cave that seemingly had no entrance. It was not long after he had eventually drifted off that Charlotte Trevinian returned and her clattering about in the kitchen and cursing in a loud voice woke him again. He was tempted to go down to remonstrate with her but she was clearly drunk and would only react angrily and that might wake his sister. He did get up but that was to check on his sister. He was pleased to see that she was still sound asleep. As to when the racket ended and he at last was able to get back to sleep, he was not sure, but when he woke early as was his habit, he knew it had been a short night, a very short night.

Larry checked again on his sister. She had not stirred. He did not disturb her. His guardian's bedroom door was ajar, he peeped in, the bed was unmade but there was no one there. He found Charlotte in the kitchen slumped over the table, an unlit cigarette in her hand and a half empty bottle of beer in front of her. He woke her, and was sworn at for his pains. When she tried to get out of the chair her legs seemed to be incapable of supporting her, he helped her over to the sink where she proceeded to vomit. Clearly he was not going to be able to get her up the stairs to her bed. He cleaned her up and took her staggering to the sitting room where she collapsed on the thread bare sofa. He set a bucket beside her and fetched her duvet and pillows, and shutting the door left her, to clean up the kitchen. Charlotte's meal was still in the fridge but there was no milk or bread in the bread bin. A glance in the kitchen cupboard revealed there were no cereals either. He decided the sleepers would more than likely continue to slumber. He wrote a note to his sister in case she woke and having washed and dressed set off to pay a quick visit to the shop. They would need provisions for breakfast and also for their lunch boxes.

Larry was grateful that the shop was empty when he arrived. Both Mr. Flower and his wife expressed their condolences and also congratulations. They were keen to talk about the events of the previous day, but they understood when Larry excused himself and hurried off to do his sister's paper round. He was back at the shop in record time. With the same haste he went about collecting his purchases, ignoring the looks of the only two other customers who had come in to collect their own papers. Then it was another brisk walk back to the Trevinian's house. As he had hoped neither Charlotte or Philippa had woken up.

Chapter Thirty-Seven

*I sometimes wish that
people would put a little more emphasis
upon observance of the law than they
do on its enforcement*

-Calvin Coolidge

Larry had not long been back when there was a knock on the front door. It was the police. The two constables who had attended the rescue of Father Aloysius stood on the front step. Below at the gate was a police van. Having inquired after his welfare and that of his sister in a concerned and friendly manner they requested entrance. They needed to ask a few questions and would need to see Mrs Trevinian. Philippa need not be disturbed but might be required later. Larry woke Charlotte. She was furious and swearing loudly, told her visitors to leave her home immediately. The response was a polite refusal.

"I'm afraid that's not possible, Mrs Trevinian. We have come on a matter of grave concern and need your cooperation. Should you refuse, you will be arrested and taken to the police station. Charlotte unsteady on her feet and still cursing, appeared at the door.

"I suggest you sit down here, Mrs Trevinian. Larry will you please wait in the sitting room, one of my colleagues will speak to you there. Oh before you go, do you have a phone?" Larry was obliged to hand over his mobile. Confused and alarmed Larry complied. What was this about? He had a sickening feeling it might be about drugs. It was. Pacing the floor he could hear talking in the kitchen but could not make out what was being said. Outside in the road the police van had been joined by another car. Sergeant Graves got out with a police lady. Larry watched them come up the path.

The front door was open and they came straight to the sitting room. Larry ceased his pacing and stood quietly waiting, his heart thumping in his chest. He felt weak at the knees. What if they asked him about Anna. He had never seen her with drugs, for that matter he had never seen his uncle with them either, but he had suspected that both were, or in Anna's case had been involved in some way. If they asked him, what was he to say? Lies would only lead to more trouble in the end but what was the truth. He just hoped they would not ask him about Anna. Sergeant Graves was relaxed and friendly, he had heard about Larry's role in the rescue of Father Aloysius and at first his questions were all about the events of the previous day. Feeling much more at ease, Larry as modestly as he could spoke about the rescue.

"Have you any idea how Father Aloysius happened to be in the sea and then land up in a cave?"

"No, all that side of it is a mystery." He went on to explain how he had searched for the entrance and had not found one. He shared with the constables Patrick's thoughts on the subject.

"Would you say you know Father Aloysius well?"

"Yes very well." Larry did not enlarge on their relationship.

"I imagine he is a popular person. Do you know if he has any enemies?"

Larry sensed he should have foreseen this question but he had not. He had no time to consider its implications or to plan how he framed his answer, he had to rely on his instinct. He chose to be totally honest.

"Yes, Father is popular but that came because he's earned it, at first it wasn't easy for him. He is obviously different. Being so different and an 'In comer,' you know, I guess it was hard at first, but he is good with young people, in fact he is good with everybody, and most people like him or have come to like him, there are a few who didn't take to him from the start and who don't like him. He got off to a bad start with my uncle and he didn't like him."

"Do you think that 'didn't like' was enough for your uncle to want to harm him?"

"Possibly, my uncle has a short fuse. When he gets upset, he can be violent with anyone."

"Was he ever violent to you?"

"Yes, but it was his way of teaching us discipline I suppose."

"Us? Was he violent towards you sister?"

"On occasion, but as I say, he had a short fuse."

"And his wife?"

"Yes, anybody who upset him might provoke violence."

"I see. Do you know if he had any plans to harm Father Aloysius?"

"No, he wasn't really a planning type of man."

"What about drugs? Do you know if he was involved with drugs in any way? "

Larry's heart sank; what if he was asked about Anna? He paused, thinking.

"I never saw my uncle with drugs,"

"But?" prompted Sergeant Graves, leaning forward and looking Larry straight in the face.

"I suppose I was suspicious."

"Were there any particular incidents or times that caused you to suspect?"

The memory of the dance came flooding back. "It was at the dance we held to raise money for a memorial outside classroom at the school."

"And?" Sergeant Graves had been impressed at first at the candid way Larry had answered his questions, but now he sensed he was struggling. Was he worried about something? Was he hiding anything?

"My uncle came to the dance and there were some young people who came here from Pendon Bay. It was common talk that they used drugs. They were surfers. I saw my uncle talk to them but I didn't see any drugs."

"Thank you, were there any children or young people at the dance who might have been involved?"

Larry looked down, what was he to say? Did he have to mention Anna? "I don't think so but," He trailed off with out completing his answer. What did the sergeant already know about Anna and the crowd at Pendon Bay?

"But what about your friend, Anna Evans? I assume she was at the dance was she involved in any way with drugs?"

Larry clenched his fist to try to stop his hands from shaking, was Anna involved in any way? She had left the dance with the Pendon Bay crowd. The answer must be yes.

He took a deep breath and passed his tongue over his lips. "Yes." His reply was a muttered whisper. Then he added hastily "Not that I have ever seen her take anything but ...! his voice trailed off. He sat head down looking at his feet. He felt confused and ashamed, what would Anna think?

The policeman got up and walked to the window. He spent some time there deliberating in his mind as to how to continue his interrogation. Larry sat in the long silence wondering fearfully what might be coming next. Had he betrayed the girl he loved?

"You didn't see anything," The policeman had returned to his questioning. "You had no proof. We have no proof. Am I right she is not now involved in any way with her former associates?"

"Yes." Larry looked up at his questioner. This affirmative was said with much more confidence. "Are you going to question her?"

"Perhaps. According to my colleagues Anna Evans acquitted herself magnificently, that was the word they used, magnificently, in the rescue of Father Aloysius. I take it she is not now involved with the people who take drugs in Pendon Bay and that she has learnt whatever lessons needed to be learnt. We all make mistakes, especially when we are young. Perhaps she was merely associated with them because she liked surfing. There are some drugs that youngsters take that are not strictly illegal. In any case we are dealing here with another matter altogether far more serious than drugs. However, you might warn her that she risks getting into serious trouble if she dabbles in drugs." The sergeant did not elaborate. He had had a great regard for Mr Evans as a headteacher. Mr Evans had done wonders for his children when they attended the school. The headteacher's wife and daughter would be struggling with their grief. They needed each other. There were times when his sense of duty conflicted with his feelings. In this case he was inclined to side with his feelings. If the girl had been drug taking, she was probably a victim of peer pressure. Her mother needed her and she seemed to have repented of her association with the surfers. He had sympathy too, for the young Trevinians being bought up in such a dysfunctional family, and in a way he could not but admire them. Perhaps he should be content to leave the matter to rest.

"Yes, I'll tell her." Larry felt a great sense of relief.

"I think that will be all for the moment, if we need you further, we know where to find you. Oh yes, you and your sister too, were magnificent in your respective parts in the rescue." The policeman smiled.

"Thank you," Larry replied with genuine gratitude. "Will I get my phone back?"

"Yes, but not until it has been examined by our experts in Plymouth. That may take some days."

"I see, thank you. I'm sure you won't find anything."

"I hope that's the case, but it has to be done."

"OK" The two policemen left to join their colleagues in the kitchen. Larry felt an overwhelming need to visit the toilet. He felt drained and his back was wet with perspiration. He wondered where his sister was. Charlotte was sitting stony faced, at the table. Opposite her was her interrogator. Neither acknowledged Larry as he passed to climb the stairs. Philippa's bedroom door was shut. When he came out of the toilet the police woman was waiting for him, she handed him his phone.

"Your father phoned, you may like to return the call, but I am afraid we will need the phone back when you have finished." Charlotte continued to stare at the wall in silence. Her questioner merely nodded at Larry.

"Can I see my sister, please?"

"She's in her room. I'll call her, you can make the call in the lounge, she can join us. I have to be there too." Larry just shrugged and made his way to the sitting room. Philippa joined him, wide eyed with anxiety, she rushed over to him. He gave her a hug.

"Larry what's going on, why are they here?"

Endeavouring to sound relaxed and in control, he gave her an extra squeeze.

"I don't know Sis, how was your night? Hope you don't mind but we left you to sleep on, thought you deserved it."

"What about them?

"The police? Just a routine call to see how we all are, I expect they won't be here long. Dad phoned but I couldn't get to my phone in time, I'm going to call him back."

"Dad, do you think he's going to come to see us?"

"Probably, I would say so wouldn't you?"

"Yes, we haven't seen him in ages. I just hope he is coming."

"Me too."

There was no message on the phone but Larry called back anyway. He could not remember the last time he had spoken to his father on a phone. His father did answer but their conversation was brief in the extreme. He was trying to get hold of his sister - in - law but she was not answering her phone and some strange female voice had taken his call when he had phoned Larry. When Larry had explained that that would not be possible at that point in time his father had queried why not. On being told she was being interviewed by the police, he wanted to know what for. Larry had to say he did not know and his father rang off. He had not even enquired about his daughter or asked after their health or wellbeing.

Larry had thought that years of neglect had schooled him into accepting the situation as a lost cause, and that resentment was only going to embitter him and make him less of a person. He had long since decided he did not want to be defined by his father's failings. But on this occasion, he could not help but feel bitter.

Philippa had always yearned for her parents. Their mother had never contacted them in any way. It seemed she had decided it was better for them if the break was clean and final. On the few occasions his sister had seen her father he had made some effort to be pleasant and Philippa had never given up hope of a return to his care. That, it seemed to Larry would never happen, but he owed it to his sister to help her come to terms with the situation, and expressing his own anger and resentment would not help her. He steeled himself to control his emotions and put a brave face on the matter. Philippa accepted the lame excuse he made for their father's brevity on the phone but the police woman clearly realised the situation was not good for the young Trevinians. She did not mention it but showed her concern for their welfare in other ways. Realising that they had not eaten any breakfast and must be hungry she arranged for them to have access to the kitchen.

Charlotte was taken into the lounge. She had clearly been crying.

Larry and his sister were still eating their breakfast when Sergeant Graves returned to inform them that they were going to search the building.

"I thought you said it was just a routine call?" Larry put an arm round his sister's shoulders.

"Relax, they just need to have a nose around, that's all." The police woman informed them her colleagues would start upstairs so the pair could complete their breakfast and then they would be allowed to go to their rooms, while the constables searched the rest of the house.

The sergeant with the two colleagues who had come in from the van put on gloves. Each had a holdall containing plastic containers, bags, and labels. They disappeared up the stairs. Larry smiled reassuringly at his sister,

"I tell you what let's get Charlotte a coffee and a bit of toast. She didn't eat anything last night so she probably needs it. I'll do the coffee, can you do the toast."

"Me!" Philippa pulled a face.

"Please."

"For you but only for you. I mean it." Her disdain for her aunt was not lost on the police woman. Larry had put on the kettle. He turned to their minder.

"I hope it's alright to make my aunt some breakfast? Would you like me to make you a cup?" The policewoman smiled her appreciation.

"It's perfectly all right for you to make one for your aunt. I won't have anything thank you, but it's thoughtful of you to ask. I suggest you finish your own breakfast first."

Larry returned to his cornflakes. "Happy to be of service, any time just ask."

"That's my brother! Always looking out for others. He'll be inviting you round for a roast dinner next, anyway Larry where did all this come from? It wasn't here last night; the cupboard was bare."

Larry shrugged, "Fairies."

"Pull the other one, you sneaked out to the shop didn't you. Why didn't you wake me? We could have had breakfast there like usual and we would have missed all this."

"Precisely, we'd have missed out on all the fun."

"Fun!" His sister stuck her tongue out at him. Larry just shrugged and grinned.

"You needed your sleep and I was hungry. If I'd known we were going to have visitors I'd have baked a cake."

"Funny, who do you think you are, Les Dawson?"

"No, just your loving brother. Do you want toast when you have finished your cereal."

"Yes please, but you do yours and you can take the other slice to the lounge while I do my own and then wash up."

Larry made the first batch of toast, spread it with a good layer of butter, and then added some marmalade. He made a mug of coffee. "Come on, Sis, I need your help. Bring the coffee, please. "

"Oh, alright, but only for you."

Charlotte was standing gazing out of the window when they came through the door. She looked a pathetic figure. She turned as they approached to put the tray on the coffee table, her face haggard and gaunt, her hair dishevelled, she barely nodded her appreciation.

"We thought you could do with some coffee," Larry said by way of conversation.

His aunt picked up the mug and had a sip.

"Been to the shop have ya, didn't think to get any fags while you were there did ya?"

"Oh my God!" Philippa stamped her foot and stormed out, grinding her teeth in her disgust.

Her brother turned to his aunt. "I'm sorry, we didn't, but I can go down again and get some when this lot has gone."

If she heard him she gave no indication. Larry left closing the door quietly behind him. Philippa was making her own toast.

"You should be going to school."

"School, no way. Anyway, it's too late." Larry turned to the policewoman. She was looking quizzically at his sister.

"I wonder, please could I make a couple of calls on my phone. I ought to phone the school to let them know my sister will be late in, and I must phone my work too." The phone was handed over and the calls made. Larry's boss had been very understanding and had told him to take the day off, the school was grateful to have been warned and said they would be expecting Philippa to attend. Philippa was not best pleased, but with the policewoman party to both calls could not very well object. Larry had had the foresight to buy her some of her favourite biscuits to go in her lunch box and made her some egg sandwiches which she liked. As soon as the upstairs rooms had been searched Philippa got dressed and retrieved her school bag. The policewoman had offered to take her to the school but she had declined. It was bad enough having to go to school but to arrive with a police escort was the very last thing she would have wanted.

The search took some time. They found nothing, not that any of the three residents of number thirteen Carline Road were given that information until later. The other thing they were to learn later that day, well before the results of the search were shared with them, was that the police had also searched the home of Michael Trevinian. Dot, like Charlotte, was interrogated at length. Like Charlotte, the enormity of what she was having to deal with had been forced on her for the first time since the fatal news of the wreck of the trawler and of her husband's demise. She was left broken and in despair, and she had no one to turn to. Her position was made even worse by the fact that the police did find drugs. They were hidden in a trunk in the loft. Michael Trevinian unlike his brother Sid had been careless. Sid had been careful never to have any drugs at his home, partly because he could not trust his wife. She was the one who had introduced her husband to the whole business of the supplying and taking of drugs. As an occasional user she had obtained what few drugs she could afford at the public house where she worked as a cleaner. She had always taken them there, or on her way home partly because she could only afford very little of the substances offered, and invariably used the whole batch immediately, and partly because she feared her husband would take it out on her if he ever discovered how she was spending the money given her by his older brother for the upkeep of his children, Larry and Philippa. When the dealer who supplied Charlotte with her drugs learnt that big Sid Trevinian was her husband, he had approached Sid as a possible customer. Sid had declined, his addiction of choice was drink, but he became interested in what could be made out of selling drugs to others, and so had become a supplier himself. The police had no concrete evidence which would enable them to charge Charlotte but they did have the evidence they needed to charge Dot.

There were others who would be questioned. Only two lived in the village, one of whom was the subject of a visit on the same morning. That was Anna. She too found it a harrowing experience. For her the tears were of genuine remorse, but when she realised that the implications of the investigation were serious, she had the good sense to answer all their questions honestly. They obviously knew about the involvement of her once upon a time, surfer friends and so there was nothing to be gained from trying to shield them. It quickly became clear they were more interested in obtaining information about a far more serious matter than drugs. They asked her about Father Aloysius and his relations with the Trevinians. She was honest and confirmed that Sid Trevinian hated the priest. Then Sergeant Graves moved on to the question of drugs. He told her that there was no evidence that she had been taking drugs but that her associations with others like the Pendon Bay surfers might make her a possible suspect. He warned her that taking drugs could get her into serious trouble. However, unless any more evidence that she had been guilty of serious crime came to light, the matter was closed as far as he was concerned. Before leaving, Sergeant Graves had thanked her for her help and had commended her on her part in the rescue of Father Aloysius. For her this, as it had been for Larry, was a huge relief.

For the community of Pondreath the presence of so many police personnel in their village on one day was most unusual, so much so that in times yet to come that year would be distinguished from others by three things: it was to become remembered as the year of many storms, the year of the invasion of the village by the boys in blue, and of course the year when the sea claimed two more of their own who were later to be implicated in the attempted murder of their Catholic priest. It was the year too of the passing of their much-respected headteacher. It had been the year of mourning.

Among the others who would be questioned were the surfers. The police conducted a late-night raid on the cottage in Pendon Bay They had a sniffer dog with them and found evidence of drug taking and there were a number of stolen items that were due to appear at a car boot sale in Plymouth the next weekend. Three adult males were charged and pleaded guilty and were given a sentence appropriate to their crimes and their age. Two females received an official warning. Then of course there was Father Aloysius..

The priest was in no condition to be asked any questions for three days. Anna, meanwhile, had been shocked by the police appearance at their door in order to question her. At first she had assumed they were merely checking up on her welfare after the events of the previous day, or maybe they had come to give news of Father Aloysius, but no, they had come to question her. She hadn't even had her breakfast and had been on the verge of trying to contact Larry. Her mother too, had been taken by surprise by the visit but had hidden her concern from her daughter. While the interrogation was going on she busied herself in the kitchen. Realising if she had been taken aback by the visit from the constabulary, her daughter would have been even more surprised and would need support when the police left. She had taken Sergeant Grave's assurances that their visit was a formality, and that they wanted merely to ask her daughter a few questions at face value. Would the police question her she wondered? She had meant to tell them about Mr Trevinian but had put it off. There had been so much to plan and do. Now it was too late. To take her mind of this worry she determined she should make that breakfast special, a celebration of the achievements of the successful rescue of their mutual friend. When the police lady accompanying Sergeant Graves informed her that their mission was complete, she felt a deep sense of relief. She had shown them politely out, before greeting her daughter warmly. Anna, the tears glistening in her eyes, embraced her mother.

"Well done, love. I've got your favourite breakfast. You must be famished." Anna wiped her eyes.

"Thanks Mum, I felt awful, but I suppose they are just doing their job. I am so glad this didn't happen when Dad was with us. As it is I feel so ashamed, but if Dad had been there, it would have been so much worse. I told them the truth. Dad would have expected me to. Sergeant Graves was really quite nice. He asked me about Mr Trevinian and his relations with Father Aloysius. He did mention drugs but said there was no proof that I had been guilty of taking anything illegal. He gave me a warning. I'm so sorry Mum. All I can do is ask you to forgive me."

Louisa just gave her daughter another hug. "What's been has been dealt with, love. I am just grateful lessons have been learnt. You and Larry, and Philippa too were so good in helping me with your father's passing, and then yesterday, well, you made me very proud. Your Father would have been so proud of you too, so let's make this breakfast a celebration of the rescue of Father Aloysius and his safe return to us."

"Yes. I guess I won't stop worrying until he is really back but, yes, let's celebrate. Thanks, Mum. I ought to phone Larry first." She already had her phone in her hand. Eagerly she keyed in his number, anticipating hearing his voice, her disappointment when there was the standard reply, telling her that he was unavailable registered clearly on her face.

"No joy?"

"No." She tried again. The result was the same.

"Don't worry love, he's probably still in bed fast asleep and after yesterday I am not surprised." Her daughter merely shrugged, and putting her phone away decided to put her anxiety about Larry and the whole business of the interrogation on hold until she had had her breakfast. Both daughter and mother were hungry and relished every mouthful of the feast of eggs, bacon and waffles with golden syrup. Both had very clean plates when they were done. Breakfast and the clearing up complete she tried phoning again and once more was disappointed. Not wanting her daughter to fret Louisa Evans determined that what was needed was a good distraction. She had been giving some thought to the dilemma that Larry and clearly Philippa faced over their future accommodation.

"Do you think Philippa was serious about not wanting to go back to number thirteen yesterday?"

"Most definitely, she can't get on with Mrs Trevinian and was frightened of her uncle."

"Do you think it would work if we had them both here?"

"Well, we'd have to clear out Dad's study to make the fourth bedroom but might not be such a bad thing. How about beds and furniture?"

"We could leave the desk in there and a chair. As for a bed, Duncan and I have always had single beds pushed together so that wouldn't be a problem. It might be best to put Larry in there and he could help with the shifting of the bed, but first we had better get down to sorting out his desk and cupboard. Larry would be more likely to use the desk." Sorting out her husband's desk was easier said than done, and it was a challenging and emotional experience for Louisa going through her husband's things but it had to be done some time and even if the young Trevinians did not end up coming it would be a good thing to do. Anna made another attempt to phone Larry but once again there was the standard reply that he was unavailable. Encouraged by her mother she set to with a will, fetching boxes from the garage and bringing in the dustbin. Louisa got the roll of dustbin bags. Anna was ruthless but her mother had to see everything and to check each page, pencil, pen and photograph. She was also practical and in sorting papers decided on five categories personal papers, finances, school, family holidays and the house, and that's where they ran out of boxes. They would need to get some more but for the time-being the papers appertaining to friends, the car and anything else mechanical could be stacked in piles on the desktop, and then there was sport and the garden. Once you started sorting the categories could go on and on.

Half way through the morning they had a break for a coffee and a piece of cake. That was when Anna decided that she should go down to the shop to see if she could get any more boxes. Before she went, she rang Miss Farrow to ask if there had been any news about Father Aloysius, and also to check whether she knew if the shop would have any empty boxes to spare. To both questions she got a positive answer, the priest was in a stable condition, but it was not yet advisable to visit, and the shop would more than likely have boxes.

Going down the hill towards the bridge she saw Larry appear round the corner and start to walk towards her.

"Larry!" Her scream startled more than one passer-by. He looked up and seeing her waved. She ran helter skelter down the pavement, weaving in and out of the shoppers and other pedestrians and where necessary taking to the road. Panting she threw her arms round his neck.

"Oh Larry." Feeling somewhat sheepish he returned her embrace.

"Hi, you gorgeous girl?"

"Oh you, it's so good to see you, you've no idea it's been awful, just awful!"

Suddenly, mindful that their meeting had provoked a number of interested looks from fellow pedestrians she released herself from his arms and taking his hand asked "Where are you off to?"

"To see you of course."

"But I've tried to phone, but you are always unavailable."
"I know, I'll tell you in a minute."

"I've got to go to the shop, we can talk on the quay and then you can help me get some boxes, Mum wants good strong boxes. Miss Farrow says they are bound to have some. They'll probably be out the back."

"Boxes?" Larry looked puzzled.

"In a minute, when we get to the quay." The couple hand in hand hurried down the hill. Just as they had hoped there were far fewer people on the quay. The seat down on the edge of the water, in front of Mrs Hazlemere's cottage was not occupied.

Larry took out his handkerchief and wiped the slats dry. They sat close, Anna with her head on his shoulder. They held hands.

"So what was awful?"

"The police, I had the police come to the house to question me?"

"Snap."

"What you too?"

"Charlotte and I both and then they searched the house, but there is something else I have got to tell you." Larry took a deep breath. He was obviously struggling. The girl squeezed his hand.

"What is it? What's troubling you, my love."

"I have an apology to make."

"Apology? I don't understand what for, and who too." The girl was looking at him earnestly.

"To you.."

"To me why? I can't think what for."

"They asked me about drugs."

"And so what."

"I had to tell them, about the dance and my uncle and the surfers. I'm so sorry I felt, I feel awful, but I did say I'd never seen you with any drugs. I'm sorry. You must feel I've betrayed you but..."

"Oh Larry darling," the girl put a finger on his lips, "You were just telling the truth. I wouldn't have expected you to do anything else, I promise. It's me who should be feeling ashamed, and I do. All those times I treated you badly.... and well didn't appreciate what a special person you are, but now I do. I'm sorry Larry. I love you. You are so honest and so good. I don't deserve you. Now kiss me darling and don't think about it anymore please."

Larry sighed. They kissed. "Thanks. You are so precious to me."

Anna was able to share the news of her mother's decision to clear out her father's study in case he and Philippa should want to stay. Larry was touched. He was grateful but he needed to talk to both his sister and his aunt first before making a decision. He was aware that if they left number thirteen, her brother-in-law would almost certainly stop sending his aunt the allowance he paid regularly as a contribution to their upkeep and that might leave his aunt very short of money. They had been so engrossed in recounting and comparing the events of the morning that they had lost track of the time and were surprised when Anna got a call from her mother who was wondering why collecting boxes was taking so long. When she learnt her daughter had met Larry, Louisa was relieved. Feeling a little guilty the couple rushed up the hill to the shop. Fortunately, Miss Farrow had thoughtfully set aside a number of good cardboard boxes for them. Larry brought a box of Louisa's favourite chocolates as a peace offering and they hurried back across the bridge and up the hill to the Evans' home. Louisa had anticipated that Larry would be joining them and was busy laying the table for a light lunch for three.

"Don't worry, Larry, you'll earn it we are going to need you to help with the moving of furniture." Larry took this as a sign he was forgiven. Another worry could be crossed off the list.

For Father Aloysius the police visit came on his fifth day in hospital when for the first time he was allowed visitors. Up until then, only the bishop had been permitted to visit and that for a very limited time. For a time, the priest was in a critical state in intensive care. With skilful nursing he turned the corner and started to improve. On his fourth day he was showing signs of recovery and was able to eat. By the fifth day he could sit up and start to take note of his surroundings, the changing skies as seen through his window, as well as his immediate surroundings. He recalled the hope that just the sight of the passing clouds gave him when incarcerated in the cave. It had been a very different window but in the end, it had been his route to freedom, not that he knew the details of his rescue yet. For the most part he was content to leave it that way, it was enough just to be alive, and to thank his God. He was alive and that was miracle enough to be grateful for. The visit of the police changed all that, it obliged him to face reality and bits of that reality were not pleasant. Sergeant Graves with a lady constable were made aware of the need to be gentle and not to take too long over their business. Both were well used to making such visits.

"Well, Father Aloysius, it's good to see you looking better, you may not remember but we met in Truro some time ago. You were on a mission to help a great friend of mine, Duncan Evans. You may not know it but once I lived in Pondreath. My two children attended the village school. Duncan was a brilliant headmaster, all the children loved him and the parents too, for that matter. He was very grateful for your help with his daughter. This is Constable Rosemary Taylor. We were wondering whether you might be able to help us?"

Father Aloysius smiled at the lady constable and held out a hand, "Pleased to meet you. Of course, I'll help if I can."

"Well, if you don't mind, we'd just like you to tell us what happened and how you came to be in the cave. We found your clothes on the beach."

The priest sighed, he turned and looked out at the clouds. Then he looked down at his hands resting on the bedclothes.

"I guess I went for a swim." There was a long pause, the police constable had to prompt him to continue.

"You must be a strong swimmer." His reply was just a shake of the head. Miss Taylor looked at her companion and shook her head.

"Thank you, Father, you must be tired I think we should call it day. If it's all right we'll come back tomorrow. Is there anything you need, anything we can get you?"

"That's kind of you, thank you, I think I've got everything I need. If you see Anna or Larry just thank them for me."

"Of course." The constables excused themselves and quietly left. Farther Aloysius sighed, and turned over and tried to sleep but the reality of what had happened was preying on his mind, perhaps he should have told them, but what about Larry and Philippa, if the truth be known how would that affect them and what about Sid and his brother? It would mean a long prison sentence. Did the police need to know?

Anyway, did he really know for certain it had been them. After all it was dark and the boat was pitching about and he had never really got a good look at his captors. All that mattered was he was alive. He reached for his rosary, said his prayers. Comforted he fell asleep. It was later, that afternoon that his prayers were answered in the form of a visit from the bishop.

It was the bishop who was to help him come to terms with his dilemma as to what to tell the police. As with his previous visitors Father Aloysius was at first very reluctant to talk about the events surrounding his apparent near drowning. The bishop had not pressed the matter; however he found an opportunity to touch on the subject when the priest asked him if he had heard any news from the village and his congregation.

"Well, as it happens, I was able to visit the village and to meet your congregation on Sunday evening. There was not time for me to take a Mass but we did say some prayers. You have a faithful flock there Father and they were very concerned about you. Not only that, I was able to make a couple of pastoral visits on your behalf."

"Pastoral visits, that was very good of you but who did you visit?"

"Your friend Commander Nesbitt was most helpful, and I was able to call on two Trevinians, the first up on that street with the council houses and the other down on the quay." Father Aloysius looked surprised.

"You don't mean Sid Trevinian and Michael Trevinian?"

"The very same, although it was, of course, their wives I was visiting, but I see from your surprised reaction that you haven't yet heard of the second of the two tragedies that the Village was having to grapple with on Sunday. That is before you had been rescued."

"No, please, what tragedy?"

"How silly of me, I was assuming you would have heard. Your friend," the bishop mimed two speech marks and an exclamation mark, "Your friend Mr Sydney Trevinian and his brother were on a fishing trip. It seems they left the day before you disappeared. There was a storm that night, the first of two storms on consecutive nights. They took shelter in Newquay harbour, but on the night of the second storm they were at sea, and their trawler was wrecked. They lost their lives. The bodies were discovered washed up on a beach some miles west of the village. I was visiting their widows.' There was a long silence while Father Aloysius grappled with the implications of this news.

"I didn't know, I guess I've been out for the count for the last few days. I'm so sorry, the village must have been in shock."

"They were, they still are. In the event I didn't get to meet Sid Trevinian's wife, she was out, but I did meet young Larry Trevinian and his sister, a very impressive pair. Apparently they and Anna Evans were part of the rescue team that got you out of the cave."

"Team?"

"Yes, the Cliff Rescue team, there were a number of them including a nurse and a doctor and of course a helicopter. It seems Larry Trevinian and Anna are, how shall I put it, dating. Lucky girl, he is quite a lad." Father Aloysius detected an element of humour in the way the bishop related this last observation. This was confirmed when the priest looked up at him and saw his bishop wink. Father Aloysius chuckled.

"I take it you didn't give Larry advice on red lights!"

"Nah, not really appropriate in his case."

"I do remember a helicopter. The sound of it whirring about above gave me hope but as for the Cliff Rescue team that's all a blank, except I was aware Anna and Larry were there with me in the cave, and there might have been someone else too. I wonder what sort of reception you got from Dorothy Trevinian. I have to confess neither of the Trevinian wives were on my visiting list."

It was the bishop's turn to chuckle.

"You surprise me Father Aloysius, anyway joking apart, what shall I say? It was interesting, and no, we were not given a royal welcome."

"We, being you and Commander Nesbitt?"

"Precisely, a very helpful gentleman."

"That doesn't surprise me at all."

"As I say, it was interesting. I couldn't help feeling there was something that Dorothy Trevinian was trying to hide."

Father Aloysius made no comment but turned his head to look out of the window.

A large dark cloud had blotted out the sun.

"I understand from the nurse I am the second visitor you have had today."

"Yes, the police came."

"Ah, and how did that go?"

"They were very kind and considerate."

"Good. May I ask were you able to help them?" Father Aloysius shrugged and turned back to look out of the window.

"I see. Can I just say when I face a bit of a dilemma about sharing something difficult, I remind myself that our heavenly Father knows everything, and that in the long term, all things are usually revealed. I find that a great help and I usually end up just telling it how it is, in other words, the truth."

There was another long pause, then his priest turned back from looking out of the window, and, looking his bishop in the eye, he smiled.

"Thank you."

Shortly after this, the bishop, having prayed with Father Aloysius, took his leave. A prayer had been said, and a prayer had been answered. There were no further visitors that day, but there were several phone enquiries. Miss Farrow had phoned and was advised that it would be better if she put off her planned visit until the next day. Father Aloysius, she was told, was making good progress but was tired and would probably be pleased to see her the next day.

When Sergeant Graves with Constable Rosemary Taylor arrived the next day, they found Father Aloysius sitting in a chair beside the bed. He greeted them with a warm smile. They had brought a suitcase with them and also a black dustbin liner which seemed to contain a bulky item. In the suitcase were some of his clothes, they asked him to confirm that they were his. He was informed they had been found on the beach and was asked how they might have got there. He had to reply that they were indeed his but he didn't know how they got to be there, however he told them he had thought long and hard about his disappearance and the events related to it and was happier about sharing them. With his consent, the rest of the interview was recorded. The black dustbin liner was opened. It contained his cassock. As with the clothes he confirmed the cassock his. He then described the events as best he could recall them, that led to his being washed up in a cave, and how he had sought to escape.

His visitors were very appreciative of the efforts he made and thanked him for his cooperation. Inevitably they had some questions to ask arising from what he had told them.

"Have you any idea whose boat you found yourself in and who your captors were?"

"I've got no idea about the boat. There were two men. I thought they might be Sidney Trevinian and his brother Michael, but as I told you it was dark and I was trying to appear unconscious so I can't say for certain it was them, except when I was thrown into the sea I remember hearing the man responsible say something about a nigger. It was an expression I had heard Mr Sid Trevinian use before."

"Father Aloysius, you have been most helpful. I think we owe it to you to tell you something you may not know. On Saturday night, the night after you disappeared, a trawler was wrecked on some rocks further down the coast. Two bodies were washed ashore."
"I know they were Sidney Trevinian and his brother Michael. The bishop told me."

"I see. Well, there is something I doubt the bishop knows that we are going to tell you. We have had people go aboard the wreck of

Michael Trevinian's boat. They found your cassock in the wheelhouse. That would seem to suggest the two men were almost certainly who you say you suspect they might be. They found something else, too. Hidden on the boat was the largest consignment of drugs that has ever come into our possession from a boat clearly heading for a Cornish port."

There was a long silence. Father Aloysius was clearly contemplating what he had been told. His voice when he spoke was soft, and he shook his head sadly.

"Thank you. I'm sorry. As you know, Sidney Trevinian and I had our differences, but I had hoped if I was patient, I might be able to bring about a reconciliation."

"While I admire your intention, I am afraid that such a possibility was always highly unlikely. What we have told you is not for public knowledge."

"I see. Do Larry Trevinian and his sister know?"

"No, however, we suspect both Charlotte and Dot Trevinian might well know about the drugs. They might also be party to their husbands' intentions regarding you, but they probably don't know about your cassock. It may be in our interests that they are not aware of the cassock and the implications of where it was found. That is why we want to keep this information confidential. We will be continuing our investigations into attempted murder as well as into drugs."

"I understand."

Constable Rosemary Taylor had repacked the suitcase with Father Aloysius's clothes and had returned the cassock to the plastic bag.

"I'm afraid investigations into this case may well go on for some time, and any possible outcomes could be months away. We all need to be patient and keep our counsel. We are very glad to see you are on the mend and hope it won't be long before you return home. In the meantime, is there anything we can do for you or get for you?"

"No, thank you, you have been most kind." The two constables were about to leave when a thought occurred to the priest.

"I do have a question you might be able to help me with."

"What will happen to the bodies?"

"They are with the coroner and will be kept in the mortuary probably until we have completed our investigations. Then they will be handed over to the relatives."

"Thank you, Sergeant, but what about funerals?"

"That will be up to the relatives."

"And if they can't afford a funeral?"

"Then the council might help. They could have what's called a pauper's funeral, and most of the costs are paid by the council, and there are other charities you can apply to."

"I see. I've had to take funerals on occasion for people without the means to pay for them, and we had to help them apply, but this is different. I've not had the experience of dealing with the funerals of bodies washed up after drowning at sea, and under these circumstances, I presume they still have to apply?"

"Yes, in normal circumstances, they would need to apply."

"Thank you, you have been most helpful."

"Is that all? Anything else?"

"No, no thank you. It's highly unlikely I'll be involved in any way, but I have been quite involved with the young Trevinians and wondered what the position might be."

"Understood, I recommend you concentrate on getting better. As I've said, these investigations may take some time, and the bodies may not be released for burial until they are complete. We may have to talk to you again, but I hope that won't be until you are better and out of the hospital. Then you would be best advised to keep what we have told you strictly to yourself."

"I'll do my best to follow your good advice. Thanks for your help."

"Our pleasure." The two police officers bid Father Aloysius farewell and departed. For them, it had been a very satisfactory visit. Father Aloysius, too, felt a burden had been lifted from his shoulders. His bishop had been right.

The priest was moved from intensive care to the general ward, but on the recommendation of the police, he had his own room.

That evening, he had his first visitors from the village. Commander Nesbitt brought Miss Farrow, Larry, and Anna. He had been warned in advance that they were coming and had had time to prepare himself. He was sitting up in his chair and greeted them with a cheerful grin.

"Well, this is a great joy. Welcome to my luxury apartment, so Commander, what's the news of the village? It seems ages since I was last there. I understand the bishop has been checking up on you!"

The Commander, having the first shout, was able to tell his friend that the rescue had been the talk of the village ever since and that everywhere he went, he was asked for the latest news of his progress. Miss Farrow had kept everyone informed and had put a notice on the window of the shop giving a daily bulletin from the hospital. The bishop's visit had really impressed the congregation, but of course, there had been no services since he went missing. Miss Farrow was able to update him on some of the older folk he visited. All this was music to the priest's ears.

He had given his condolences to Larry and had asked after his aunt. Larry had shrugged. The priest had learnt that Charlotte Trevinian was acting predictably. When faced with a difficult situation, she reverted to drinking. Philippa had moved out and taken up on a generous offer from Anna and her mother to live with them. Larry would have liked to do the same but felt obliged to remain to care for his aunt. Not that they saw much of each other, but he was able to provide her with one good meal a day and clear up the mess she made when she returned from the pub. The police had interviewed her twice. There was one further piece of news. He had had a phone call from his father and, more significantly, from his mother. His father had called from time to time and used to visit very occasionally. His last visit had been over two years ago. His mother had clearly decided to make a complete break with her past, and they had heard nothing of her since she had left. This call from her was completely out of the blue. At first, he couldn't believe he was actually speaking and listening to his mother; it was the first time he had heard her voice in four years. He had taken the call at work, and so Philippa had not been able to speak to her, but she had promised to phone again and even hinted she might come and see them. Unfortunately, she was calling from a phone box, so Larry could not get her number to call her back. When it came to Anna's turn to speak, she was more anxious to hear his news and to learn when he might be returning. At that point, the doctor arrived, and that proved to be the end of the visit. Both patients and visitors were greatly buoyed by their time together. Father Aloysius had a lot to mull over when the doctor left him to his own devices.

Commander Nesbitt's passengers spent the whole of the journey back to Pondreath talking about their friend. There was a lot of speculation as to when their priest might return to the village. Estimates varied from a few days to several weeks. There was a suggestion that when he was discharged, he might need a period of convalescence.

It was Anna whose estimate was the closest. To her, he looked almost ready to leave. It was two days after the visit that Miss Farrow got a phone call from the hospital to say Father Aloysius was ready to return to his home and that he was being discharged. She was preparing to set off when her brother-in-law came hurrying out of the shop. He had had a call from the bishop. He had tried calling the Presbytery but had got no answer so he had phoned the shop. He was on his way to the hospital and would collect Father Aloysius. He thought it best if the priest spent a few more days recovering from his ordeal and preparing himself for a return to duties. He would be a guest at the bishop's residence in Plymouth until the end of the week, and then, if he felt ready, he might return to take Mass on the Sunday. They would call at the presbytery to collect some of his things. If Miss Farrow could have a suitcase ready and anything she thought he might need, they would collect it in an hour or so's time. He would phone when they were approaching the village. Miss Farrow was delighted it would give her a bit more time to get the presbytery cleaned and the garden tidied to welcome her Father Aloysius home.

Chapter Thirty-Eight

Home is where the heart is.

-Pliny the Elder

Father Aloysius was surprised to see the bishop. He had been expecting his housekeeper. When he learnt that he was to spend a few days as a guest at the bishop's residence, he felt a twinge of disappointment. He had been anticipating getting back to his church and was looking forward to it. However, he soon came to appreciate his bishop's kindness and the wisdom of his decision. Both he and the village needed a few more days to get used to the idea of the return of their Catholic priest. The police were still calling, and speculation about what they might be investigating was rife. While most were overjoyed that for Father Aloysius, the outcome of his disappearance had been a good one, they were still reeling at the news of the trawler disaster and the death of two of their own. There were still a lot of unanswered questions appertaining to both incidents. They needed time to get used to the idea of his return, and he needed time to prepare himself for a return to a community in shock.

The bishop was a busy man, but they got to meet for morning Mass and for meals. At first, the bishop allowed his guest time just to enjoy being looked after, to get out to exercise as he wanted, and to reflect on his ordeal. He could use the bishop's library and come and go as he pleased. On the third day of his stay, the bishop made time to be in his library at the same time as his guest. It was an opportunity for them to talk, or rather for his guest to talk and he to listen. He was a good listener, and on this first occasion of their being together for some time - apart from a few carefully thought-out questions, which he used as prompts, listen was all he did. On the fourth day, the bishop again found the time to be on his own with

Father Aloysius. They went for a walk together. As the pastor of his flock, the bishop needed to be confident that his priest was ready to return to duty and was keen to gauge how well he had prepared himself.

This time, his questions were more direct, and the answers to them were followed by some of the bishop's own thoughts as to how best to approach difficult situations. It was a subtle way of giving advice. How was he going to minister to a grieving village? How was he going to prepare for his return to a teaching role? How was he going to deal with any backlash to his return from those who were very much anti-church and who, in the past, had shown they resented him being foisted on their community? When Father Aloysius finally found himself at the cathedral, it was natural for both men to enter the building and to pray. The bishop was confident his priest was ready, and Father Aloysius was happy at the prospect of getting back to work. There was one last task for him to complete before the bishop would make the offer to take his priest back to his home, and that was to preside over the morning Mass. So, as the last question of the day, the bishop turned to his guest and asked him, "Would you like to take Mass tomorrow?"

Sensing that this was to be the final hurdle, Father Aloysius was very happy to take the opportunity. He had never presided over a Mass in a cathedral. For him, it was an honour, and in later years, he was to look back on occasion with some pride.

Perhaps in anticipation of that, he had raised the matter of humility in his confession with the bishop the night before. His confessor and mentor had reassured him that such pride, if coupled with gratitude, was not the deadliest of sins. After all, the bishop had explained that a young person looking back on the occasion of taking their first communion naturally felt a sense of pride; it was when pride was coupled with a sense of superiority that it was dangerous. Having received his absolution, Father Aloysius was surprised to be asked to reverse the roles and to take his bishop's confession. On later reflection, he concluded perhaps it was the bishop's way of teaching him a lesson in humility. Saturday was to be a big day for Father Aloysius; he would take the Mass in the Cathedral, and then the bishop would take him home to Pondreath. He phoned Miss Farrow to warn her that her priest was coming home.

Taking the Mass was an emotional occasion, but no more than that of his return to his home. The bishop had warned his housekeeper that she should keep everything low-key. And so it was. Saturday lunchtime with the sun shining meant there were few people about, and he managed to deliver his guest unnoticed. Miss Farrow was at the presbytery to greet him. She reached out her hands to take his and smiled up at him,

"Welcome back, Father. You don't know how good it is to see you. I'm sorry there is no bunting, but we were advised not to make a fuss. However, your lunch is ready, and there is enough for you, bishop, so you are very welcome to stay." The bishop politely declined, and, having accepted his priest's profuse expressions of gratitude, he left.

"Well, Miss Farrow, God has worked a miracle, your prodigal has returned. And before you say anything thank you, thank you a million times thank you for coping so well while I was otherwise engaged. As for the bunting, I am grateful that there has been no fuss. The bishop has been marvellous. You all have. It will take me a little while to get back into the swing of things and I will need your advice, but for this afternoon, your lunch smells delicious and I have a sermon to complete, then it will be early nights for a while. I feel fine but the bishop in his wisdom has advised me to make a gentle start, not just for my own good, but for the good of the community.

Many people here will be in a state of shock and be grieving and we need to be sensitive to that."

"I understand, and we will go softly, softly to begin with, but it is so good to see you back. I know, we all wondered for a while whether we would ever see you again."

"God is good,"

"To him be the glory." his housekeeper chimed in. "Now you get yourself sorted, and I must make the finishing touches to our lunch."

Farther Aloysius had a somewhat fitful first night back in his own bed. He had slipped off to sleep quickly enough but something had woken him in the night and he had found it hard to settle again. It was clear to him that he was probably the only one in the whole of Pondreath who knew of the true reason for his disappearance. Being custodian of that secret was a difficult burden to bear. He had heard that the police had charged Dot Trevinian with the illegal possession of drugs. The police had not however divulged anything more. There might be some in the village who knew about the consignment of drugs found on the trawler, but that did not mean that they knew about the cassock. One day it would all come out, but until that day people were free to speculate. Some might even want to ask him the question direct, how had he ended up in the cave having left his clothes on the beach some distance away from the cliffs? The truth he knew had not yet been revealed to them. How would he answer them? Would he have to lie? Eventually sleep returned, but when he rose early the next morning he felt ill at ease and certainly not rested.

The congregation at Mass was the largest since his arrival in the village. There was no bunting nor a fanfare but a lot of ladies had been baking and he was made very welcome. The prodigal had returned and they were very pleased to see him. He preached on miracles but made little reference to his own, save in passing to mention he did have some experience in that area. When the after-service refreshments were done and all clearing complete he was left with quite a pile of tins and boxes to take back to the presbytery. Larry and Philippa had helped him and he made them promise that they would assist him in consuming their contents.

That afternoon he resisted the temptation to visit any of his regulars and only made one call and that was to see Charlotte Trevinian. She was out. Feeling a little relieved he left a card expressing his condolences. After a long walk along the cliff path he returned to spend a restful evening reading. That night he slept well.

For Father Aloysius that first week after his return to his duties in the village was a quiet one. The priest continued to rise early for his morning exercise and then to conduct the usual acts of worship but after that he would retire to the presbytery to work in the garden or slip away on his bicycle. He spent the evening reading and writing letters.

For Father Aloysius keeping himself to himself and limiting his opportunities of meeting others was one thing. He had no control over people who came visiting him. Among those who came knocking on his door were friends like Commander Nesbitt, who came with Mrs Hardcourt as representatives of the school. The bishop had taken the trouble to advise them that the priest should not be expected to return to his school duties until the new year and they came not to talk about that but to welcome him back and to bring him messages of support from the staff, and a number of cards from the children. These he found very touching. Another visitor he was happy to see was Mr Tarrant. He had come bringing the good wishes of the Youth Club and to reassure his friend that while he would be missed, there was no expectation that he would return soon. Then there was the Rev. Burns and his wife who called with a cake and joined Father Aloysius for his evening prayers in the church. None of these visitors expressed any interest in knowing why he had disappeared that fateful Friday, and all had been most discreet in their conversations with him and subsequently with others who had asked after him. For this Father Aloysius was very grateful.

On the Thursday afternoon he decided to visit the graveyard. It was some time since his last visit and he anticipated Frederick Towzer's grave would need tidying up. He was right. The grass had grown since his last visit and the pansies had long since completed their flowering. Kneeling in front of the stone he removed the pansies and started to use the shears to clip the grass, when he sensed he was being watched. Wondering who it might be without turning, he spoke.

"Hello."

"Hello, Father." It was Anna. He, conscious of the last time they had met at this place and of his feelings then, and the bishop's red lights, resolved to remain calm and dignified. "I hope you don't mind my joining you."

"No, not at all, but I thought you were at college sitting your examinations."

"I was this morning but we didn't have an exam this afternoon."

"I see, and how are they going, if you don't mind my asking?"

"All right, nothing too unexpected yet, but of course, I won't know until the results come out. I called at the presbytery, and you weren't there, so I went to the shop, and Miss Farrow said you were here."

"Yes, as you can see, I've been a little neglectful of my duties."

"How are you?"

"Me? I'm fine thanks to you and Larry and the rescue team."

"Good, have you spoken about it to anyone since?" Her question surprised him.

"No, I mean yes, yes of course."

"The police?"

"Yes, the police and Miss Farrow and also the bishop."

"Anyone else?"

"No, I guess not."

"Sometimes it's good to talk."

He did not reply.

"You can always talk to me if you want to, I won't tell anyone." There was another long silence. The priest got up and looked at the grave inspecting his handy work.

"That's better, don't you think?"

"Much. I suppose I could tidy Granny's grave."

"Would you like me to help?"

"That would be nice. I really wouldn't tell anyone."

"Thank you. I'll bear it in mind." They found the grave. It looked as if someone had already been recently.

"It doesn't look too bad."

"Yes, Mum and I came after Dad died. The grass just needs a little trim I guess."

They knelt side by side. He clipped and she raked up the bits with her fingers and put them in the black dustbin liner he had brought with him for just that purpose. The priest was careful not to let their hands touch.

"I, I came to find you because I need to talk, please."

The priest put his shears down and looked at the girl beside him. He sensed she was near to tears. There was a moment when he nearly put his hand out to her, but then he drew back.

"Is it Larry?"

"Yes, partly, but more about Mum."

"I see."

He got up and pointed to the bench by the wall. "We could sit over there." Anna followed him to the seat, fiddling with the bracelet on her wrist for a moment she sighed as she sat down.

"Mum got a letter from her sister yesterday." There was another sigh. "Aunty Gwyneth wants her to return to Wales. She and Dad grew up together in the same village. Both their families are still there, some have moved away of course but a number are still there. Some years ago, Dad bought two cottages in the village, they were semi-detached and he had them knocked into one. He always aimed to retire there. Anyway, he let them out and the present tenants have just given their notice and will leave in a month. So Aunt Gwyneth thinks it would be an ideal time for us to move back," she paused, "I don't know what to do."

"About Larry?"

"Yes. It's quite a big house with four bedrooms so he and Philippa could come too. Mum thinks he could get work there, or at least in Swansea and it still has a school - the school Dad and Mum both went to, but I'm afraid to ask him."

"So you haven't talked to him yet?"

"No, I'm afraid he might not want to come to Wales. You see the thing is a lot of people speak Welsh there. They speak English as well of course but for a non-Welsh speaker it can be difficult. And there is another thing, now that Sid has died I don't think Larry's dad will want to keep on paying Charlotte to look after his children, and Philippa, as you now know, has moved in with us. Jack Trevinian has no intention of taking his children to live with him. Larry's mum has already phoned him. She may make a visit to see her children. If that happens, she might want them to live with her. I don't know whether you know this, but Larry and I were quite close when we were at school together. I was a year ahead of him, but most of the time that didn't seem to matter. He struggled at school especially with writing. He was good at Maths. I was the opposite. Dad took an interest in all his pupils; he would analyse their learning styles and try to cater for them. Larry wasn't a book person. He often had good ideas but struggled to put them on paper. He found spelling very hard. Dad saw however that he was good at modelling and making things. He learnt through his using his hands not from reading books. One Saturday he took us both to the tip. He had some rubbish to get rid of. He saw these old beat-up bicycles there and he bought three of them. He gave Larry some of his tools and left him to work out how to fix them. Larry chose the best one to fix and used the others as spares for parts. He soon had his own bike. His mum and dad always worked weekends. That was when the garage was busiest. They were always short of money, Larry's Dad saw to that, he was Pondreath's big spender, always in the pub and he gambled. Larry and Philippa were looked after by their grandmother. She was sweet, but often on Saturday Larry came to us. He got on very well with Dad and with Mum. He would take the bus to Pendon Bay and go to the tip. He'd buy up old bikes and bring them back on the bus. At first the bus driver was not best pleased but dad had a word, and it was alright after that. He lent Larry the fare for the first three trips. Larry would earn the money to pay him back by fixing things and he'd do odd jobs. He mowed the lawn for Dad. Then he fixed up an old mower and started offering to mow lawns round the village. What with fixing bikes and selling them, and the mowing he started to earn the pocket money his mum and dad could never give him. Then came the marriage break up. That was awful. Larry and Philippa took it really badly. And, worse still, his grandmother died. His mum had a break down. That was before she married again. Anyway, they ended up with Sid and Charlotte. I think it was the bikes and the mowing business and dad and mum, but especially dad who helped Larry to cope, and Philippa too. Having a little business of his own made him independent in a way, from his guardians. He was always out of the house and that suited his aunt and uncle. We were still good friends but after the breakup he became very possessive. I guess he felt insecure after his mum and dad left, and needed to feel he had at least one special relationship that would not let him down. I reacted. I had started at sixth form college. He was still at secondary school. I got in with a very different crowd of girls and boys. I thought he was immature and silly. In a way he was, but in another he was growing up and I was the silly one. He had made himself almost independent of his aunt and uncle, and he had taken on the responsibility of looking after his sister. She doted on her brother. She would sit and watch him working on his bikes, and go with him when he went mowing. He bought some garden tools at the tip, an edger, clippers and trowels. She would edge the lawn he mowed and do a bit of weeding and later she became an earner too. It was when Dad became ill, he really started to show how grown up he was becoming. He was still jealous, jealous even of you, although he looked up to you. He was also very caring of my dad. He would visit every week. He'd bring Mum flowers. He would sit and talk with Dad, and that's when I was off with the surfers. When you made me see sense and brought me home, I started to see Larry in a different light. When Dad was really ill, he was with us a lot and our old friendship was rekindled, and for me it started to become more than that. I think he had always loved me. Now I was falling in love with him. I am worried. Whatever happens Larry and Philippa have to make up their own minds. They might want to come with us, but if there was another alternative what then? They might want to be with their mother. I don't want to put pressure on them."

"But?"

"But what?

"What do you really want?"

Without hesitation Anna replied. She turned to look at the priest.

"I know what I should want and that is to support Larry whatever he decides, but of course that could mean us being apart for long periods of time, me in Wales and he in Glasgow, and that would be hard."

Father Aloysius allowed himself to take a moment to think.

"Please, Father, what should I do?" He looked at the girl. Their eyes met, his full of compassion, hers pleading for help.

"Yes, it's a difficult situation with a lot of buts, ifs and mights. You can't cross bridges before they even exist. We can only work on what we know. All the rest is conjecture. There is no point in worrying about what may never happen."

"I know, but surely it does help to consider what might happen so you can prepare yourself."

"Maybe, so I guess you expect me to say pray about it, and of course I do, but that alone seems to be a bit of a cop out, so firstly we don't know what his mum might do at the moment, but you do need to talk to him about your worries and even your mother's offer."

"Yes, I guess I should."

"You can mention your fears as to what might happen too. It might help if we went through the possible options."

"Yes, please, that would help." The priest went through them all starting with Anna accompanying her mother to Wales along with Larry and his sister, to at the bottom of his list Anna going to Wales with her mother and Larry and his sister remaining with their aunt.

"Thank you, Father, you have been a great help. I knew you'd put me back on track."

"Wait a minute, what about the praying bit."

"Oh sorry I forgot, yes can you pray please?" The girl gave her mentor another pleading look.

"Of course, I'll pray, but you must too."

"Me? But I'm not very good at praying."

The Priest just smiled and shook his head. He was not going to accept any excuses.

"Don't tell me you're not good at talking. Forget about the praying word, just talk to God, I'll start off but then it will be your turn. Some people like to think about the word ACTS when they pray, A adoration, C confession, T thanks and S supplication.

I'll do the first two, you do the second two."

"OK, but by supplication, do you mean the please God bit?"

"Yes, precisely."

And so priest and girl prayed. He in a soft measured voice, she somewhat hesitantly at first but as she grew in confidence, she become more fluent.

"Well done, it wasn't that hard, was it?"

Anna smiled. She felt better, so very much better.

"No, it was good, thank you. As usual you know just what to say. Thank you so much you've been a great help."

"Well, I'm glad to have been able to do a little to address the debit side of the amount of gratitude I owe you. If it wasn't for you, I'd have been bleached bones in that cave."

"Ah, but I should be grateful to you for our cave adventure."

"What do mean? I don't understand."

"Larry was so wonderful when Dad was ill, as were you, and he was amazing when Dad died. I realised then what a special person he is and as I said I started to fall in love I suppose, but it was the cave challenge that really bonded us. You see neither of us had done anything like that before. The cliff rescue team were wonderful and I don't suppose we were in any danger, but going over the edge of that cliff on a rope was scary for both Larry and me, but we did it. Then when we got into the cave and found you there, we had to work as a team, and.... well, we were, and together we did our bit until the nurse came. And when we got out of the cave, I knew then that Larry and I were made for each other. Without you being in the cave that may never have happened. Not many young lovers get that sort of opportunity to grow together. So I think we are quits."

Father Aloysius chuckled. He shook his head in amused wonder.

"Wow, and all I had to do was lie and look helpless."

It was the girl's turn to laugh, and then she shook her finger at him.

"You didn't just look helpless, you were, and it's not surprising after what you had suffered. In fact, it was a miracle you had survived. I don't know how you came to be in the sea during that storm but it must have been awful. And then you found yourself in a cave and you are trapped. You were there for two whole nights and nearly two full days, without food and in the cold without clothes, except for your pants, it was a miracle you survived. But you didn't just survive. Was it you that piled the rocks up at the top of the cave? If it was you, it looked like you were trying to build an easy way onto that ledge?"

"Yes, it was me. I was going to have to build two sets of steps to get to the hole, one to get onto the ledge and one on the ledge to get to the hole. That was the plan, and it gave me hope; it's just I ran out of strength and energy. Then, as you say, you came, and it was a miracle. To God be the glory."

"To God be the glory. Now we need to finish tidying Gran's grave, and then will you come to tea? Larry will be home soon, and you can be there while I talk with Larry."

As they tidied the grave, Father Aloysius reflected that the bishop would not be displeased with how he had handled his afternoon with Anna. He was learning to use the red lights more consistently.

Louisa Evans was delighted to see Father Aloysius when he and her daughter returned from the graveyard. True, she had seen him each day at the morning worship, and he had phoned once to ask after her welfare, but he had not ventured up the hill to see her and she had sensed he was reluctant to get too involved in village life with so many questions as to the reasons for his disappearance yet to be answered ....so much speculation about how he came to be found in a cave almost naked, having left his clothes on the beach. She was pleased too because she, like Anna, wanted to talk to him about her own situation and her possible move to Wales. Larry was yet to arrive and Anna had gone straight to her room to spend as much of the little time she had left on revising for her mock examination paper the next day.

Father Aloysius was ushered into the kitchen where along with drinking a welcome cup of tea, he worked alongside Louisa in preparing the evening meal. They talked while they worked. Louisa was careful to confine herself to seeking his advice as to how best to handle her possible move to the country of her birth and did not ask any more of him than advice. The priest was more than happy to share his thoughts on how best to prepare for the difficult decisions that would, or rather might, soon challenge them all, much as he had with her daughter. He was pleased not to be interrogated about anything to do with his disappearance and was glad to be able to express his own feelings about her prospective move back to the land of her birth. He was able to tell her that he was full of admiration for her generous offer to have Larry and Philippa join her.

Larry did not arrive until just before the meal. Anna was grateful in a way because it had given her more time for her revision, but she realised that she would have limited time with him after the meal. They excused themselves from helping with the clearing away and retired to Anna's bedroom. Larry had listened quietly while she poured her heart out. He put an arm around her shoulders and gave her a tender kiss.

"Wales eh, well there's a thought. I'd have to learn Welsh too and I'm not very good at that sort of thing but I'd give it a shot. Your dad is probably having a good old chuckle at the very idea of it."

Anna smiled, then with some trepidation, she asked the question she had been so dreading having to ask.

"But it could be Scotland?"

"Oh, would you still fancy me in a kilt?"

"Of course, I would, Larry, be serious. This is our future, it's important."

"I'm sorry, quite right. Well, seriously, Father Aloysius is right, we can't cross any bridges before they are even built, so let's just see what happens. We don't even know if your mum is coming. All I know is wherever you go I'll want to be there with you. With that in mind you had better settle down to some revision, you beautiful Welsh mermaid."

"Oh, you, give me a kiss then."

He did and then left. He had a lot to think about but his heart was singing. The girl he had always loved wanted him at her side.

It was early on the Saturday morning after the return of Father Aloysius, that Larry received his second phone call from his mother. He and Philippa were at the shop sorting out the papers for her delivery. As with her first call, Larry was taken by surprise and it wasn't only the fact that his mother was calling so early in the morning, but also the thought that he was hearing her voice again that was a shock. He had beckoned his sister over and led her into the Fowlers' kitchen where they could speak in private.

"Mum, you're up early, it's great to hear your voice again."

"I thought I'd lost you for a second."

"Don't worry, Philippa and I are at the shop sorting out the papers for her paper round. We just had to find somewhere private."

"The shop, I'd forgotten about the shop, so Philippa has a paper round has she, good for her."

"Yes, she has been dying to speak to you ever since you last phoned, I'm going to hand over to her and she can tell you all about it."

Larry handed his sister his phone and put his arm round her shoulder. His sister was overcome with emotion and the tears streamed down her face. It was all she could do to tell her mother she loved her and missed her.

"Larry, I'm sorry, I seem to have upset Philippa."

"Don't worry, it'll be alright. The last time you called you mentioned you might come to see us."

"That's what I'm calling about. Bruce and I are in London but are staying with friends in Plymouth tonight, and plan to be in Pondreath tomorrow. We could meet then if that's convenient for you."

"Great, what time?"

"We thought we might take you to the pub for lunch."
"Lunch is fine, but not the pub. I'll make a picnic, and we can have it by the pond."

"Pond, where's that I don't remember the pond. Are you sure about a picnic, I mean it is December?"

"I should have thought, it's up by the school. Yes we could have a picnic. This is Cornwall remember, and I'm sure you have picnics in December in Scotland. If it's sunny like today that would be ideal, if not we could meet at the presbytery, I'm sure Father Aloysius wouldn't mind. And you ought to meet him anyway."

"Well if you are sure you don't mind and it won't be too windy that sounds nice."

"Certain, I'm certain."

Larry walked to the end of the room, "Sis, I think someone is calling us in the shop, can you take a look please, "Mum, you still there?" His sister had left the room.

"Yes." The pond is nice and private. I'm thinking of Philippa."

"Oh, I see now, very thoughtful of you, thank you. Is there anything I can bring?"

"Just yourselves, dress up warm in case. See you tomorrow, you can always call if you can't find us. Love you."

June Grant felt a great lump in her throat. She blinked away the tears. And taking a deep breath replied.

"Love you too, I think I know where the school is, after all I did go there. The pond it is tomorrow at twelve. Now I must go, we need to be getting off to get to Plymouth for lunch. Tell Philippa I love her too. Bye."

"Bye" His mother rang off before he could hand the phone to his sister to have a last word. It took a moment for Larry to take it in, he was going to see his mother again. He gave his sister a big squeeze.

"Did you get that, we are going to see Mum tomorrow, I can't believe it, it's just too good to be true. She told me to give you her love."

"There was nobody in the shop but Mr Fowler and he said he didn't call. You said something about a picnic, are we getting that and where are we having it anyway?"

"You bet we are getting it. You can show off your cupcakes and I'll make the bread. I thought by the pond would be good, nice and private. I wonder what Mum likes to eat."

"Miss Farrow might be able to help us, and perhaps Father Aloysius still has some cakes left from last Sunday."

"Good thinking, why don't you ask Miss Farrow, and I'll talk to Father Aloysius. I've got to ask him if we can meet in the presbytery if it's raining."

Larry was pleased to see that his sister, who had been overawed by the sound of her mother's voice, was now clearly looking forward to her visit. He left her to get on with her paper round and went to keep his side of the bargain. Father Aloysius was more than happy to make the presbytery available if he should need it. His next task was to tell Anna. The news was something she had been half expecting. It had been obvious to her that the arrangement between Larry's father and his brother to foster his children had been unravelling and that it was only a question of time before it collapsed altogether. When that happened, it would probably mean a re-establishing of a relationship between Larry and Philippa and their mother. When Sid had departed the scene, she knew that time was imminent. She was so glad that she had taken Father Aloysius's advice and had talked to Larry about her own situation.

That morning helping at the presbytery and cleaning the brasses in the Church all Philippa could talk about was the impending visit. She had been just six years old when the breakup of the marriage occurred. Miss Farrow remembered it had caused quite a stir in the village. She had always thought that the pair both born and raised in the village were ill matched, June Moor, a Doctor's daughter, and he a Trevinian, a fisherman's son. True he, Jack, had a certain charm and as a youngster had been a likeable lad, and he was intelligent. His charm had served him well when he became a salesman. He quickly gained a reputation as a very effective operator. The saying was he could and would sell his grandmother. She was pretty and capable but quite shy. They worked in the same garage in Newquay, he in sales and she as the personal assistant for the manager. Bruce Grant was a Scotsman, and an astute business man as well as being a good engineer. The garage was part of a large chain. He had been seconded from London to take on the job in Newquay when it was in bad shape. He was sent to turn it round, which he did. In this endeavour he owed more than a little to his personal assistant.

Jack and June both earned a good wage, but he was addicted to gambling and always short of money, consequently June had always had to work, even when the children were young. When they were small her mother, a widow, had been able to look after them in the day. Sadly, she had died, and her passing coincided with the breakup of her daughter's marriage. Jack was not only a gambler but he also had a wandering eye. He was known to have had a number of affairs before he took up with his boss's wife. They had gone off together when he had landed himself a job in London. June had sued for divorce, as had her boss. Over the years Bruce Grant had come to value his personal assistant. She was loyal, industrious and capable. In their adversity they had found mutual support and they had decided to make a fresh start together in Scotland. As is so often the case it was the children who were to suffer. Jack was determined to make it as difficult as possible for his former wife, and there was an ugly battle over custody of the children. June, with the loss of her mother, and all the trauma surrounding the divorce had a break down. It was deemed she was unfit to continue to care for them. Jack had won but had no intention of being a hands-on father. His new partner was certainly not going to take on bringing up a youngster and a teenager. Sidney, Jack's younger brother, and his wife Charlotte had no children and were struggling financially. Jack decided he would pay them to foster his children. Bruce Grant, to his credit, stuck by his personal assistant, and with his care she recovered, but it took time. What Miss Farrow and no one else knew was he also made a contribution to the money paid to Sid and Charlotte to look after his wife's children. Now Sid's demise had thrown everything up in the air again. Miss Farrow prayed that it would not be the children who would suffer this time. Larry had proved himself capable of weathering the worst situations and making the best of them. Philippa was far more vulnerable. She chastened herself for thinking it but perhaps Sid's passing would, for Philippa be a blessing.

For Philippa, Sunday twelve o'clock couldn't come quickly enough. She spent much of Saturday afternoon and evening deciding what she should wear. Her brother found this mildly amusing. Prior to this she had shown little sign of caring much about looking smart and making the best of her limited wardrobe, she was far more inclined to opt for the leather jacket than a dress. Her clothes were now all in her bedroom at the Evans's cottage which was an advantage in that there they had benefited from regular washing and ironing. She tried everything on and inspected herself in a mirror. Anna was constantly being badgered to give her advice or comment on possible alternatives. Her anorak was a bit of a mess and that's all she had in the way of a coat. Anna put it in the washing machine. She promised it would be dry by the morning and if not, she'd put it in the tumble drier. Larry had his work cut out to persuade his sister to spare the time to make the cupcakes for the picnic tea. He occupied himself preparing for the picnic while he waited his turn to use the mixer and the oven. He made a batch of six loaves of bread. One was for sandwiches, one could be a gift to his mother. Both Miss Farrow and Mrs Fowler were a great help, they too deserved a loaf and he needed one at number thirteen Carline Road. The last was for Louisa and Anna. The shopkeeper's wife had lent him a wicker picnic basket, two thermos flasks and a chequered table cloth to put over the picnic table. Miss Farrow provided cushions for the benches.

It was early evening by the time Larry had made the bread for the sandwiches. He would make those before church on Sunday, and arranged to leave them in the presbytery's fridge until it was time to set up the picnic at the pond. Anna insisted he join the family for supper. It proved a wise decision. It gave him a chance to talk about his mother and to get Philippa to join in with her memories. Hearing her talk about her childhood, her mother and her grandmother helped him establish how she now felt after the years of separation. He had been careful to keep his description of his memories as positive as possible and not to be judgemental in any way about either of his parents. This he hoped would influence his sister as she was confronted with having to think about her past for the first time for a while, perhaps ever since she had realised she might never see her mother again and had, consciously or unconsciously decided, remembering her mother was too painful and had buried her early childhood as a subject in the deep recesses of her mind. For both, the opportunity to talk in a safe place helped. Both Louisa Evans and Anna were patient sympathetic listeners and Larry was confident his sister was in a good frame of mind when she finally retired to bed.

Anna saw Larry to the door. She was not happy about him going back to his aunt's house but did not mention it. Instead, she put her arms around him and gave him a good night kiss.

"Larry, you are so special. I love you and I'll always be there for you. Promise."

"Oh, Anna," He held her to him and kissed her hair, he drank in the scent of her. The firmness of her young body, and the softness of her skin, his voice was hoarse with emotion as he fought to control his desires.

"You are so precious and so good. I am so lucky. I don't deserve you, but I love you. I have for a long, long time, you know that. Thanks, my love, for all you have done this evening. You and your mum have been such a help. I wish I could stay, but..."

"I know that love, I wish too, but I understand..... one day..."
"One day." He sighed. "Thanks, darling love, good night."

There was a final kiss and he was tearing himself away and striding off into the dark. She with a sob ran into the house to her bedroom, and throwing herself on her bed cried into her pillow. Larry, she whispered between the sobs I love you so much. For Larry there was the mixture of heart thumping desire and elation, and the thought of one day that set his thoughts singing as he murmured his loved one's name, repeating it softly to himself as he went striding home to make his aunt a meal.

Louisa Evans heard her daughter's hurried entry and the bedroom door close, sensing that all was not well quietly opening the door she tiptoed over to the figure sprawled on the bed. She placed a gentle hand on her shoulder and bending down kissed the top of her head.

"Sorry, Mum," her daughter sniffed, "I'm alright, really, I'll be alright in a minute."

"Sure?"

"Yes, I don't know what came over me. All I know is I wanted a good cry."

Anna sat up wiping her eyes with the back of her hand, she pulled a tissue from the box on the bedside cabinet blew her nose.

"That's better, we all need a good cry sometimes. Would you like a drink?"

"That sounds nice, a hot chocolate, please. I'll come and help clear away."

"No hurry dear, take your time."

While Larry was preparing his aunt's dinner, Anna was helping clear one away.

For Larry there was, as he had expected, a mess of half smoked cigarettes and empty beer cans to clear away, and the washing up of the last night's plate to deal with before he could get down to making a meal. At first, he had resented his aunt's callous slovenly behaviour and was angry when he found her discarded clothes scattered over the bathroom floor and the basin full of dirty water. On one occasion when he found the tap still running, he had scribbled his aunt a rude note, but realising it was just a futile gesture of his frustration no sooner than he placed it on the kitchen table than he was screwing it up. Fortunately, the plug was not in the basin. He had decided he would not give her the satisfaction of knowing she had riled him. After that he resigned himself to what was the inevitable and something he could not change. He was no longer angry or resentful and made the best of the situation. On this particular evening he had other things on his mind as he went about his chores. He was thinking of his mother and in doing so it struck him that he probably owed it to his mother and her orderly ways and meticulous tidiness that he too valued cleanliness and order. He wondered what else he had inherited from her. Certainly, he looked more like her than his father, and perhaps, too, the shyness he felt as a boy came from her as well. Unlike the Trevinians she was very even tempered and patient. Perhaps he had those qualities too, he hoped he had her kind nature.

His sister in sharing her memories of her mother had emphasised her kindness, and her generous loving character. Philippa would be expecting a lot from their scheduled meeting. He would need to be sensitive to the way she reacted and to help set the tone of their time together, he would need to be relaxed and confident. Being preoccupied with these thoughts helped make the unsavoury task of setting the kitchen and bathroom to rights less of a chore. With the meal on a plate in the fridge he wrote his aunt a note telling her about his mother's visit. He was weary, his bed beckoned, he would clean his shoes in the morning, it would be a day for a sweater and the leather jacket. If he got up to the Evan's home early, he could shower there and wash his hair. His last thoughts before he fell asleep were of Anna. He wondered what his mother would think, God, he hoped she liked her.

Chapter Thirty-Nine

*The sweetness
of reunion is the joy of heaven.*

-Richard Paul Evans

Larry woke late. Normally he had no trouble in waking and getting off to an early start in the morning. He never bothered with an alarm. The light or the dawn chorus was usually enough. Even in the winter when the nights were long he seemed to wake at his usual time. This morning was a rare exception. He had overslept. He could not believe his eyes when he read the time on his phone. With a loud groan he leapt out of bed. Larry was not usually one to panic, but this morning as he rushed to the bathroom to wash his face and found his aunt had left her usual mess in his frustration and anger he trampled over her discarded clothes and sloshed water over his face and slammed the door as he left. He would take the clothes he had selected to wear with him and his shoes could wait until later for a clean. Halfway down the stairs he realised he had forgotten his wallet. When he dashed back to his bedroom it was not in its usual place in the drawer of his bedside cabinet. Frantically he searched about. He finally located it under his bed on the side that was against the wall. He had already looked under the bed twice but had failed to notice it.

It was a flustered young man panting heavily who rang the bell of the Evans's front door. He was grateful it was Anna who had opened it, not her mother. She sensed immediately that he was not his usual calm self. Hiding her concern, she gave him a warm smile.

"Well, done love, you're nice and early. Here let me take those from you." She gave him a kiss on his cheek as she took his clothes from him, "I expect you would like a hot shower?" Suddenly all the frustration and tension drained away as he found himself marvelling that this lovely girl who had greeted him so warmly loved him. He chuckled.

"You are such an angel, I overslept, I couldn't find my wallet and I ran all the way here, and, yes, I'd love a shower."

"Fine, Mum's in there at the moment, but she won't be long. How about a cup of tea, and I'll clean those, while you in the shower," she pointed to his shoes. "I hope you brought your razor. You don't want your mum to have to kiss that bristly chin."

"Yes, you darling, precious girl, I have brought my razor, but ."

"But what?"

"I don't expect she will want to kiss me, I mean."

"Of course, she will, and I hope you will kiss her. Oh Larry, isn't this exciting It's going to be such a happy day, I just know it."

"Well I hope so, if only for Philippa's sake. Is she up yet?"

"Up! You're kidding! She's been up for hours. While you were still snoring and dreaming of tropical islands and some dusky maiden she was probably in the shower. She's in the kitchen making a start on the sandwiches."

"Amazing. I hope she left you and your mum some hot water."

"Yes, and anyway I've got the boiler on booster."

"You are so good, and for your information, the only girl I dream of is you."

"How boring."

"I don't think so. To change the subject to something that can be boring, talking about the weather. Have you heard today's forecast by any chance?"

"Oh, yes, the usual for this time of year, a storm, lots of rain and lightning round twelve, I think he said."

"Oh no, I can't believe it. It said it'd be fine all week."

Anna shrugged, "That's Cornwall for you." Then she couldn't suppress a little smile.

"You little minx, you're kidding me."

"Well, now, minx certainly makes a change from Angel and Darling."

"You are kidding me, aren't you?"

Anna put on a hurt expression, "Oh Larry, how could you think I'd do that!"

"It'll ruin my day, and Mum was surprised I suggested a picnic, and I guess she was right. Now what will she think?"

"I guess she'll think you have a strange taste in girlfriends, fancy falling for a minx and a teasing one at that."

"Oh you," he caught her and pulling her to him started to tickle her."

Struggling, she protested, "Stop it, you, you'll crease my dress, and your minx has done her best to look good for you." He stopped and gave her a big hug and a kiss on the top of her head.

"If you were dressed in rags, you'd still be beautiful to me."

"Flatterer." With that Anna took him by the hand and led him into the kitchen where his sister was smiling away to herself as she buttered slices of Larry's homemade bread.

"Good morning, Sis, you're up early."

"Somebody's got to be; there's a lot to do before Mass, and you know Father hates people straggling in halfway through the service, so I'd cut out your goings-on and get yourself ready. "

Larry put on a mock face of contrition, "Yes, Madam, of course, at once, anything you say, oh yes, and just one other thing, where did you get that black leather jacket?"

His sister turned round and made a face in return, which included sticking her tongue out at him.

Normally the family would have walked to the church, but with the picnic to leave at the presbytery Louisa drove them in the car. Father Aloysius had helpfully left the door unlocked. They were last to arrive at the church door, the four smartly dressed people who had turned up for Morning Mass just in time.

It would be hard to say who was the most nervous, June, Bruce Grant or Larry and Philippa Trevinian as the hour approached twelve. Bruce Grant was one of those people who liked to be near enough dead-on time. His wife liked to be early but often found herself running late, but she always did her best not to make her husband late. On this occasion they had arrived in the village earlier in the morning before the end of Mass. They had called on number 13 in the hope of seeing Charlotte. June had some flowers and a condolence card. Despite having read Larry's note on the kitchen table Charlotte was surprised to see who was at the door when June rang the bell, just before eleven. She had done nothing to prepare for visitors and looked her usual dishevelled self. Her greeting was terse.

"Oh you." For a moment June had wondered if they were going to be invited in, Charlotte stood so long on the front step but eventually she had let them in. There was no offer of any refreshments and their host kept all the answers to their questions short and blunt. It was a difficult visit. Charlotte sat on the edge of her chair and looked out of the window or at the far wall, anywhere to avoid looking at them. The sitting room looked as if it hadn't been cleaned for some time, the ash tray was overflowing. It was cold and there was a musty smell. June couldn't help wondering what the rest of the house was like. She was not given the chance to see. Charlotte abruptly brought the visit to an end, announcing she had things to attend to, she left the room. The Grants saw themselves out. They walked in silence to their car. June fastened her seat belt and turned to her husband.

"That was awful."

"Yes it wasn't very edifying. I'm sorry, love."

"To think my daughter has been looked after by that woman, it's just too horrible."

"Our daughter." Bruce reached over and put a hand on hers. He gave it a squeeze,

"Our daughter."

His wife stifled a sob, then dabbing her eyes with a tissue whispered, "Yes our daughter, thank you." Her husband gave his wife a reassuring smile. Neither of them spoke for a few minutes as they grappled with their thoughts.

"How could Jack leave them with her, it's beyond belief. I should have realised; I should have done something sooner."

Bruce pulled into the side of the road and stopped the car.

"Please don't blame yourself. I think now we need to put this morning right out of our minds as if it had never happened. We need to concentrate on the picnic. I know it won't be easy, but I sense this meeting is going to be very important. This meeting could change all our lives. Change our lives for the better. Remember what we said, we need to be relaxed. It's a reunion, let's make it a happy one. Let's think of it as potentially one of the happiest days of our lives."

June dabbed her eyes again. "Yes, you're right, the happiest day of my life, wow."

It was too early to arrive for the picnic but June felt the need to have a chance to go to the toilet before the picnic. They drove past the school and found the pond before going to the Ship Inn on the quay where they had a coffee. Nancy, the publican's wife recognised June and was welcoming, and considerate in that she confined herself to complimenting June on the way she looked and her questions were tactful. Despite this, June could not help her growing feeling of anxiety and nervousness. Her hand was shaking as she held her coffee cup. Bruce Grant, sensitive to his wife's feelings was careful to be gentle and attentive as well as appearing as relaxed as possible.

"I think we ought to think about making a move."

"I'll pay a visit."

"Me too. I'll just put these on the bar on the way and settle up." Her husband placed a pound coin in the saucer of his cup and took the tray back to the bar. "Very nice coffee thank you," He paid by card.

"I'm glad you enjoyed it, staying long?"

"No just a brief visit to old haunts."

"Notice any changes since you were last here?"

"If you don't mind, I'll just make a visit first, but I'll think about that one and tell you on our way out."

"Help yourself." Nancy pointed to the sign on a far door saying 'Sailors." Bruce wondered what the sign for the ladies said. His re-entry to the bar coincided with that of his wife. He was glad to see she had tweaked her make up and that there was a spring in her step as she hooked her arm through his. He led her back to where Nancy stood by the till.

"Well?"

"That was very nice coffee, thank you Nancy."

"Good, I was asking your husband if he had seen any major changes since you were last here. It must be four or five, even six years."

Bruce made a show of scratching his head, "Four years," he was quick to clarify the guesstimate. "As for changes to tell you the truth I didn't get to spend much time here while I was in Cornwall. I was Newquay based, so I didn't get to know the place that well, but my wife tells me the pond and that garden up by the school is new. It looks very nice."

"Um, maybe."

"You sound as if you don't approve."

"No, no, I guess I do really. Actually, June your boy Larry played quite a role in helping establish that."

"Oh, that's good to hear. It probably kept him out of mischief."

"Larry? I don't think he is the mischievous type, from what I hear he a good lad. I expect you're off to see him."

June turned away, "That's even better to hear." She declined to say anything more other than to wish the publican's wife a polite goodbye as they left. They arrived at the picnic venue with half a minute to spare.

Larry and his sister had been at the pond some time. They had spread the table cloth. Larry had brought some large smooth pebbles from the beach to weigh it down in case of wind, but it was a still sunny day, with hardly a cloud to be seen. Philippa arranged the cushions. They left the food in the cool bag, but they put out the cutlery, plates, glasses and mugs, along with the flasks. The paper napkins, a contribution from Mr and Mrs Fowler and the shop, had be placed under a pebble. The cold drinks were in another cool bag. Larry and his sister had considered every eventuality, and every detail of the picnic. In this they had benefited from the help of Miss Farrow, along with Anna and her mother. Everything had been carefully thought through. Now all they had to do was wait. All was in place and it was still only eleven forty-five. Sensing that his sister must be feeling much as he did, and that a mounting feeling of excitement combined with anxiety might influence them to act unnaturally, Larry had proposed a game of I Spy. With the two of them sitting on the bench together they could keep an eye on the road and also have a wealth of objects to be the subject of their I spy question. The game had the advantage of allowing Larry some thinking time while his sister searched about for ever more obscure objects to challenge him with. For his part he settled for the simple. He wanted to boost his sister's confidence, so choices were deliberately chosen to be easy to spot. He used his thinking time to try to imagine how his mother might be feeling and how best to get over the hurdle of the initial moments of their meeting. He asked himself what would she appreciate most, and how might they achieve that. His happiest memories of his mother were of the times she took him into her arms and cuddled him. He was older now and much bigger, so perhaps that was too much to expect or hope for, but Philippa was not.

It was his turn to ask when at last a blue Volvo estate came into sight. They saw it simultaneously.

"I spy something blue with four wheels?"

"It's them, Larry it's them!"

"Come on, let' s give them a warm welcome."

"You go, I'll stay here."

"No way, I need you, we must do this together." He took her hand and dragged her to her feet. The car drew up at the side of the road.

"I bet Mum will be wearing a blue coat."

"Like her eyes." Larry was leading his sister out through the gate of the enclosure and out onto the field. "I'll beat you there!"

"But you know you're much faster."

"I'll give you a head start. I'll count up to ten."

"And if I win?"

"A pound."

"No way"

"Ten."

"Ten, OK. I told you her coat is blue."

"Counting. One!" Philippa set off. "Two. Three." Bruce and June were heading towards them. "Nine. Ten." His sister was fast closing the gap between her and her mother. Larry had no hope of overtaking her. Philippa was looking round to see where he was. June opened her arms and reached out. The girl stopped and turned.

"Beat you. You owe me ten."

Larry held up his hands part in recognition and part in resignation. Then waved her on. To his relief, she threw herself into her mother's arms. The image of the look of joy on his mother's face, of the sparkle in her blue eyes as she took her daughter in her arms, would be one of his most treasured memories for the rest of his days. In that moment, all his anxieties slipped away. He knew that all would be well. For what seemed an age, he stood entranced, grinning broadly, then seeing that Bruce Grant was standing transfixed too, he stepped forward to shake his hand. Their eyes met, and it was clear they both understood they had just witnessed a very special moment.

"Welcome back to Pondreath, sir."

"Thank you, Larry, it's good to see you and to see your mother so happy. Larry gave him a thumbs up and turned to his mother. She was standing there holding her daughter's hand.

"Mum."

"Am I going to get a kiss from you too?"

"Come on, Larry, you can't save them all for Anna." Larry raised his eyes to the heavens and shrugged.

"Sure, little sister, anything you say. Mum, it's so good to see you." He stepped forward and, bending, kissed her on both cheeks. Turning to his sister, he queried

"Happy with that, Madam?"

"Four out of ten."

Larry laughed, "Some people are never satisfied."

"I'm sure there will be other opportunities. Now Larry, where's this picnic? I'm famished." June turned and led by Philippa, they made their way over to the fenced-in environmental area.

"We hear you had quite a hand in creating this school resource."

"Me? Well, I helped. It was my old headmaster's idea, but sadly by that time he was too unwell to manage it, so he commissioned Father Aloysius to do it. The school P.T.F.A. were great and it became a sort of village project. Parents helped, former parents and their grown-up children helped. We had a dance to raise money for the materials. A lot of it was given. For example, the garden centre down the road donated the pond liner. So many people got involved, which was all down to the respect everyone had for Duncan Evans, my old headmaster." They followed the fence round skirting the pond.

"June nodded, "Yes, Mr Evans was certainly popular and had my full respect. You did well. What a fitting memorial. That pond alone must have taken some digging."

"We had a digger, a former pupil is a digger driver."

"A team effort."

"Yes. Duncan drew the plans, and we did our best to follow them. Sadly, he never saw the results."

"How sad. He was a remarkable man. If my memory is correct, he got you into your bike refurbishment business. Are you still doing that?"

"I haven't lately. Now, I'm working at the garage, I have less time, and recently, other things have been more important."

The picnic was a great success. Larry's bread proved to be a hit, and Philippa's cakes too, received lots of compliments. June was able to talk freely about her life in Glasgow, where she was still Bruce's P.A. but in a very different business. She tactfully did not ask any questions about her children's lives but let them share their stories as they felt free to do so. Philippa talked extensively about the disappearance and rescue of Father Aloysius. Her version of events included a number of teasing references to her brother and his relationship with Anna. He took it all in good heart. He was just very pleased she seemed so relaxed and happy to chatter away. He for his part, contented himself with listening and making sure everyone had what they wanted. For him, the three hours flew by. When it came to clearing away June insisted, they load everything into their car and they would all go up to see Louisa and Anna Evans. She wanted to thank Louisa for giving her daughter a home. Larry phoned to give Anna and her mother prior warning.

Anna was there at the door to welcome them.

"I hope you don't mind us calling on your Sunday afternoon, but just wanted to see you before we left to go North and to bring the picnic things back."

"Not at all. It's lovely to see you again, have you had a good lunch? The weather has certainly been kind?"

"Hasn't it? And the picnic was splendid thank you." Before June could continue Philippa stepped forward.

"Now, Larry, I was thinking, is it all right for you to give Anna a kiss in front of Mum, hadn't you better ask permission?" June laughed and Larry gave his sister one of his despairing looks.

"Maybe I don't want to be kissed." Anna was blushing.

"Maybe I do want to kiss you. I don't need permission and to ask would only set an unfortunate precedent, so young lady." Larry tapped his nose with one finger to indicate to his sister that he would appreciate it if she minded her own business. He stepped forward. Anna had her head bowed, gently with a hand on her chin he lifted it, and kissed her on her forehead. She responded by putting her arms round his neck and kissing him on the lips. June and Bruce clapped as Larry took Anna by the hand and led her to the back of the Volvo where they started to unpack the picnic bags. Louisa came to the door.

"Lovely to see you, June," she smiled at Bruce. "It's been a long time. Come in, please. I've put the kettle on for tea. "

"That's very kind of you but I think we had better not. We have an early start tomorrow. Bruce has a meeting on Tuesday and we need to get back. We just wanted to say a big thank you for all you have done for Philippa and Larry."

"Oh, that's no bother I assure you, they are both so helpful and Larry was a great support to us when my husband was ill. When Duncan passed, I don't know what Anna and I would have done without him."

"I'm sorry about your husband. I have my own memories of him. He was such an inspirational man and a gifted teacher. It's good to hear that you have been well supported but I know it must be hard."

Bruce bought a bouquet of flowers from the car with a condolence card attached. He presented them to Louisa.

"Oh, that's kind, thank you so much. They are beautiful!"

It's the least we could do. Now if you don't mind, we need to be slipping away, as my wife has said we have a long drive tomorrow. No doubt you haven't seen the last of us, perhaps we can all have a picnic together on our next visit."

June Grant disliked protracted farewells, and after promising to keep in touch, she gave both her children a hug and with a last wave through the car window they were gone.

During their brief meeting with Louisa and Anna Evans she had managed to keep her emotions in check, but once in the car she was overcome and cried all the way back to their hotel in Newquay. Her tears were tears of sadness and of joy. For Philippa hers were tears of frustrated anger.

Larry was busy in the kitchen washing up the picnic things. Anna joined him.

"Do you know where Philippa is by any chance?"

"No, why?"

"I couldn't find her in the house. I think you better have a look."

"I don't want to leave you with this lot."

"Don't worry, I'll handle this; your sister is more important."

She wasn't in the house or the garden. Larry stood at the entrance to the drive wondering which way to go to look first, town or cliffs. He opted for the cliffs first, it would be far easier to see her from a distance on the cliff walk than search the whole village. Sure, enough as he rounded the corner in the path and he could see the whole length of the walk along to the point there she was in the distance. He set off running. She had almost reached the point when he caught up with her. Not wanting to give her a fright he gave his sister a call well before he reached her. She ignored him. He was panting when he drew alongside her.

"What do you want?" Philippa was in one of her belligerent moods. He wondered why; it had been such a happy day.

"I just thought I needed a bit of fresh air and when I saw you doing the same, I thought I'd join you."

"Go away, I don't want you."

"OK but just before I do. I wanted to say a big thank you."

"What for?"

"This afternoon and the picnic, you were great, you made our mum feel very welcome. It was thanks to you we had such a happy time. It was very special."

"Ha, a lot of good it did me!"

"Oh, why? You're upset. I'm sorry. Is there anything I can do to help?"

"Just go away!"

"Fine, but it'll cost you that tenner I owe you."

"No way, that's not fair."

"Oh I don't know about that. Let's just say it's what you owe me for doing all the washing up of the picnic things, your share and mine. In fact, I might just add another fiver to cover the clearing away too."

"You pig!"

"Oink."

"Don't be silly, Larry, this is serious."

"Oink, Oink, Oink!"

"All right, if you'll be sensible, I'll tell you why I'm upset."

"Fine, please do."

"It'll cost you another tenner."

"Well, if that's what it costs for me to be able to help my sister, so be it."

"So you owe me twenty."

Larry sighed, "I owe you twenty pounds, but if I were you, I'd be careful you don't want to kill the goose that lays the golden eggs."

"What does that mean?"

"It means if you carry on like this, I'm likely to go bankrupt, and what's more, I won't bother to help."

"All right twenty. I'm upset because of what Mum said when we're saying goodbye. I had thanked her for coming and she told me she'd keep in touch. Well if keeping in touch is once every four years! Do you want that?"

"Hey, slow down, wait a minute. I think we need to be patient. I suspect we haven't heard the last word from Mum and Bruce, this weekend."

"What do you mean by that? How do you know?"

"I don't know, but think about it. They are bound to talk about today together. You did such a brilliant job of welcoming them that Mum and Bruce can't help but take note. Another thing, when Bruce and I were loading picnic things into the back of the car, he asked me why you were staying with Louisa and Anna."

"What did you say?"

"Just that you were happier there."

"Is that all?"

"No, he then asked me why I wasn't staying there. I told him I needed to look out for Aunty."

"What did he say to that? He told me they had visited Aunty Charlotte before coming to see us."

"And?"

"That was it, but you think about it. They have seen her and the house. They now have some idea of what's it like. I wonder what their reaction might be when they saw what it's like."

"The mess, it's a tip, why don't you say it?"

"All right, when they saw the mess. Think about it. I don't think we have heard the last from them. We need to be patient. They need a little time to think things through, and then it could all be very different."

"Maybe but how long do we wait? What about Louisa and Anna and going to Wales?"

"What about it? You know we can go there if you really want to, and as for time, a day, a week, a month. I don't know. All we can do is wait patiently."

"A month, no, you're joking."

"Think about it. What's a month when you have waited four years." They walked on in silence. At that point, Philippa stopped.

"Thanks, Larry."

"Good on you, I fancy a cup of tea and big bit of cake. Let's get back. We can't let Anna do all the washing up."

Larry left early that evening. He was conscious that Anna had one more examination to take and needed time to revise. He was weary after the excitements of the day and he wanted time to sort out his possessions. He needed to be ready just in case a move suddenly became a probability and not just a possibility. Charlotte, as he had expected, was not in. The kitchen was as usual in a mess.... it always was. Wearily he set about clearing up the cigarette buts and the beer cans on the floor. It was then he saw the flowers. They were part of the rubbish scattered about under the table. He picked up the bunch still in its cellophane wrapper. He read the attached card. 'To Charlotte, our sincere condolences, yours, June and Bruce.' In an instant weariness was replaced with rage. How dare she. This was the last straw. Clutching the flowers he was about to throw them into the bin when he realised these were the flowers his mother had chosen... these were the flowers that she had probably held.... hers was possibly the writing on the card. Charlotte could discard them without any respect, let alone gratitude, but he should not. He filled a saucepan with water and placed the flowers in it while he searched about for a vase. Quickly realising that his search was more than likely to be in vain, he settled for a large tin. Filling the tin with water and using newspaper as a wadding he carefully arranged the bunch of flowers to make as good an arrangement as he could. He placed it in the centre of the table and beside it put the card. Somehow just handling the flowers his mother had chosen and held was a comfort to him. It helped sooth his anger. He felt he was doing something for her, and when it was done, he felt a glow of satisfaction. He then with some effort put a meal together. He cooked a fish pie and as he cooked, he planned, he was determined not to spend another night in the house. He would pack his case and leave. Grateful that he had left the Evans' house early he set about choosing what to take with him and what he would leave to collect at a later date. It was relatively early when he shut the front door behind him for what he was determined would be the last time. Feeling a sense of relief, he walked down the hill towards the quay. He would go to Anna's, but wasn't it a bit late and surely, he would disturb her revision... he should have phoned first, where else could he go?

Father Aloysius and the presbytery was the only place he could think of. He found his phone and rang. The priest was in the kitchen reading. Unless he lit a fire in the hearth in the sitting room it was the warmest room in the house. It was Larry, he felt quite relieved that it was not a call out. Larry wanted to speak to him and was on his way up the hill. That was far better than having to descend the hill himself. He put the kettle on and got out two mugs.

Larry declined the tea and was very apologetic at having disturbed his friend without much warning on a Sunday evening. He was in a quandary. Larry related the events of the evening and shared with the priest his feelings of rage and despair. What should he do? Father Aloysius smiled.

"Well, you can always stay the night here, but what do you think you should do?"

"I don't know. I can't bear the thought of having to stay another night in that place."

"So, what do you think you should do?" Larry was silent. He looked down at his shoes. He was so grateful to Anna for cleaning them.

"Some years ago, now I attended a clergy retreat. The person leading it was an old Monk. It wasn't just silence; although there was a lot of that, we also had role-play. We were put into a variety of scenarios and had to work out solutions. We were obliged to think about challenging circumstances and situations which were difficult, and there were no obvious ways of handling them and of achieving solutions. In situations like that, Father Joseph said, "I usually find myself asking myself a question. What would our Lord have done in this situation?" So, what do you think Jesus would do?"

Larry looked up and met Father Aloysius's questioning eyes.

"He would have turned the other cheek, I guess."

"Well."

The priest had to wait some time before he got a reply. When it came, he was relieved. "Thanks Father. You've been a great help."

"Now, how'd you get on with your mum and Bruce?"

"Oh, Father, I'm so sorry, of course you wouldn't have heard. We had a great afternoon. Yes, it was a really happy occasion. I was really nervous, but it turned out fine."

"I'm so glad, but what about Philippa? How did she cope?"

"Oh, she was overjoyed to see her mum, and Bruce was very good with her. She was a bit disappointed at the end that our mum didn't make a definite date to see us again. I think I talked her round to the view that Mum and Bruce had a lot to think about and would almost certainly be in touch soon."

"Well done, Larry. Things seem to be working themselves out well for you both. You deserve it. It's amazing how God works for good for those who let him."

Larry smiled, "Yes, as you say, to God be the glory. Now I've disturbed you long enough, I must leave you in peace. Thanks, as always, you've been a complete star."

Larry had a spring in his step as he strode down the presbytery path to the gate. That's when his phone rang. It was his mother. She was very apologetic for having rung so late but she felt she wanted to see her children one more time before she headed North. She wondered what was the best time. They settled on seven at the shop over breakfast. Father Aloysius was still standing at the door.

"Good news?"

"Wonderful, just wonderful. Thank you, Father. You have been such a help. A moment ago, I was walking down this path full of confidence and at peace with myself. Now, I am elated. Philippa and I are to have breakfast with our mother tomorrow. Thank you, Father. Good night."

"Great. Good night. God Bless."

Larry waited until he was round the corner before calling Anna. She was just taking a short break from her books and was very pleased to hear his voice. He told her the news and asked if he could speak with his sister if she wasn't already asleep. She wasn't and let out a wild scream of delight when he informed her of their breakfast date.

"Oh, Larry, I can't wait."

"Exactly how I feel but we both need a good night's sleep, so off you go to bed and don't be late in the morning. Good night." Feeling he was walking on air despite the heavy suitcase, Larry made his way back to number thirteen. He had expected the place to be shrouded in darkness, but to his surprise, he could see that although the front of the house was dark, there was obviously a light in the kitchen. Surely, Charlotte was not home already. It wasn't even nine o'clock. Had he left the light on, he wondered. His aunt was sitting at the kitchen table eating her supper. A half-smoked cigarette rested on the rim of the saucer she used as an ashtray, and there was a can of beer placed perilously close to the table edge. The flowers were still there in the middle of the table. He decided on a cheerful greeting. He was in far too good a mood to let the unexpectedly early homecoming of his aunt dampen his spirits.

"Good evening, Aunty, nice to see you back early. Lovely flowers. How's the fish pie?

At first, he thought she was ignoring him, but eventually, she spoke.

"What's it with the suitcase then?"

"I thought I might sleep somewhere else tonight, but it didn't work out."

"What, wouldn't that fancy bit of yours let you in?"

"If you're talking about Anna Evans, she is not my fancy bit, and no, I was not at her house."

"Saw your mum, then?"

"Yes, we did. We had a picnic. It went well."

"Picnic!" His aunt's language was invariably accompanied by a string of obscenities, "Whatever next! Did she say anything about having you back?"

"No."

"Shame, weren't you good enough for her then?" Larry chose to ignore this remark.

"We are meeting for breakfast tomorrow before Philippa does her paper round."

His aunt's reply was again accompanied by a string of swear words, "Not here, you're not, I'm not having her and that stuck-up prig of hers here in this house."

Larry forced a laugh, "No, don't worry, we are certainly not meeting here, anyway, you won't be up. Oh yes, I got some more bread in and milk, cornflakes, and sugar, so you won't go without for breakfast."

"Cigarettes?"

"No."

There was further cursing followed by a question, "If she were to ask you... though I can't think why she would, what would you say?"

"Yes."

"Right, before you go, just make sure you settle up. I'm not having you sneak out before you pay me what you owe."

"Owe? No, Aunt Charlotte, I assure you we won't sneak away. I'd be glad to have a settling up, and when we do, don't be surprised if you find you owe me money."

His aunt was in the middle of taking a swig of beer from the can. Spluttering her annoyance at his reply, she told him not to cheek her and asked where his gratitude was after she had looked after him and his sister all these years. Refusing to be intimidated, Larry walked over to the table and, looking his aunt in the eye, he made his reply in a quiet, measured voice.

"I'm sorry you see it that way. I'm not cheeking you. I am grateful that our father didn't completely abandon us and that we have had a roof over our heads, but as for owing you anything, I am very aware that he paid you to do it, and it wasn't a pittance. Of course, there were expenses, but you spent a great deal of that money in the Smuggler's Arms or the Ship. I can't remember when you last bought either Philippa or me any clothes, and for some time now, I have been buying all the food as well as cooking your evening meal. If you want a proper reckoning, I'll get Dad down here and let him know just where his money went. Furthermore, I suspect he wasn't the only one contributing to the cost of our stay here, so I'd advise you to be very careful how you speak about my mother and her partner in the future. Another thing, it's Dot's hearing soon, and you have already had the Police search this place. I've got a funny feeling they still suspect Sid was involved in the drugs business, and it wouldn't be hard to trace your own role in any of his activities. Now I'm going upstairs to bed, and if you've got any sense, those flowers will be exactly where they are now when I come down in the morning, and for a change, try not to leave your clothes all over the bathroom floor and this place in such a mess. Good night."

His aunt was clearly taken aback. She stared at the opposite wall with a fixed look of vehement anger. Larry was careful to place his chair and suitcase in front of his bedroom door before he retired to bed. As he lay there reflecting on the day, the memory of his mother's face when Philippa had thrown herself into her arms was the balm that filled his thoughts as he fell into a deep sleep. It had been quite a day.

Chapter Forty

A dream is the bearer of a new possibility, the enlarged horizon, the great hope.

-Howard Thurman

Larry had taken the precaution of setting his alarm on his phone to ensure he woke early enough to have a bath before going to meet his mother and Bruce for breakfast. On rising he went downstairs to turn the boiler on and to make himself a mug of tea. He was pleased to see the flower arrangement was still safely standing in the centre of the kitchen table. The saucer that acted as his aunt's ashtray had been emptied, and she had even washed up her plate. Perhaps his forthright outburst the previous evening had had an effect. This was given further credence when he came to take his bath and found that the room, too, was tidier than he had seen it for a long time. He wrote his aunt a note of thanks and left it on the table. By half six, he was ready to leave. He gathered his bag and was about to turn off the boiler prior to leaving when there was a knock on the front door. Wondering who it might be at this early hour, he hurried to open it. To his surprise, it was Anna. She stood on the doorstep, her breath white in the cold air, the wind tugging at her hair, a look of concern on her face. Clearly, she had come in some haste and was anxious. She apologised for calling so early and explained she wanted to talk to him before he left for his breakfast date. They agreed they would talk as they walked down the quay.

"Larry, I've been thinking about you and your mum and this meeting. I just needed to say, you know I have to be there for my mum and support her in this move to her old village home?" Anna stopped and, taking his hand, looked earnestly up at him.

"Yes, of course."

"Well, I know you have to be there for your mum too. She needs you and Philippa; she needs to be your mum again."

"Yes, but."

"Please let me finish. She needs to be able to make it up to you for, well, you know, for you ending up with your uncle and his wife. You both need to be there for her. I know that. For both of us, we have got to put our mums first."

"But, but what about us? I understand what you're saying, but?" Larry was worried, he had an awful feeling of fear about what Anna might say next, what she might be implying. His concern was reflected in the worried look on his face.

"Shush," she reached up and put her finger across his lips. "Listen, you know I've got this provisional place at Cardiff University if I get the right A levels in July. I think these mocks I've been taking haven't been too bad and so I'm hopeful. What with the move and my studies for the real ones it'll be a busy time? If you and Philippa are with your mum up in Glasgow you'll be busy too, but we could have the weekends together. There is a train on Friday afternoon that gets in to Glasgow at ten. You have to change at Bristol. There's a similar one on Sunday from Glasgow down to Bristol, and then there are several trains from there to Cardiff."

Larry sighed; it was a sigh of relief. "I see you've thought this all through. For a moment I thought you were giving me my P 45."

She laughed gently as she shook her head and reaching up took his face in her hands and gave him a kiss. "You silly boy, where would I be without you? We, we are made for each other, you and I. I realised that for the first time in the cave. We, we are a team, and

I knew it was meant to be. For me it's us or nothing, but now we both have to think about our mums. It won't be forever. There will be a time when things have settled down when we can think again, but you know how it is now and we can still be us and especially us at the weekends."

Larry nodded and enfolded her in his arms. "Oh you precious, precious girl, I am such a lucky boy, I don't deserve you but one thing I promise I won't let you down."

"It's me who is the lucky one, you chump." She patted him on his chest, "Come on, we had better get on, you don't want to be late."

"You could join us for breakfast."

"No, I don't think that would be right. I've got a feeling that this is going to be a special time for you both and for your mum. It's not for gate crashers, but you could let me know how it's gone before you go to work."

"Sure."

By the bridge they had come to parting of the ways. "Good luck," they kissed and Anna was off. He watched her as she walked across the bridge and disappeared up the hill, he shook his head and muttered to himself, "Larry Trevinian, you are one very lucky boy, that girl is always full of surprises and the biggest one of all is that she cares for you. She's right, whatever happens this morning she's right."

June checked her face in the car mirror. She adjusted the brooch fastening to the scarf round her neck and took a little box from the glove box. She opened it. The sapphire centre stone, a deep blue matched almost perfectly the blue of her coat, and she knew too the blue of her eyes. It had been her mother's engagement ring. She and her father had had a good life together. They had been well suited. She clicked the box shut. Bruce was drumming on the steering wheel with his fingers. She knew the sign.

"Time to go?"

"Yes, we haven't got long with them, Larry has to be off to work and Philippa has to have time to complete her paper round before school, I think on this occasion it might be better if we were a little early."

Larry was laying the table in the Fowlers' kitchen, but his sister was in the shop. She was arranging her newspapers in her bag when her mother and Bruce came through the door. She looked up as the bell on the door that signalled to Mr Fowler the arrival of a customer rang loudly.

"Mum, Larry they are here!" She dropped the bag and ran straight to her mother. "Come." she said grasping her by the hand, "Larry is in the kitchen." Bruce approached Mr. Fowler.

"This is very kind of you. Are you sure it's all right for us to meet in your kitchen?"

"Perfectly, when Larry asked, I was only too happy to agree. Between them those two are my most reliable paper deliverers. They have their breakfast here every day. Two more in the kitchen is fine. Enjoy your cornflakes, but leave room for the waffles. Oh and please feel free to use the facilities, they are just through the door at the other end of the kitchen."

"Thanks. Thanks, very kind of you. I'm much obliged."

Mr Fowler just smiled. Bruce bought a paper before joining the others in the kitchen. June was busy stirring the porridge.

"Come and sit down, we thought we'd start with porridge, it's warmer on a cold day." Larry indicated the chair at the head of the table.

"That's good for me, this is a very handy arrangement."

"Yes, the Fowlers are very good to us."

"I take it your aunt has yet to get up?"

Larry just grinned and shrugged. He confined himself to a brief "Yep. Late to bed, late to rise. But it suits us, and this is great too."

"I can see that. It appears it also suits Mr Fowler, he seems to think highly of you both."

Again, Larry just shrugged. June handed out the porridge bowls. His sister proffered a jug of creamy milk. There was a choice of sugar or maple syrup. Larry brought glasses of fruit juice. Bruce waited until everyone was seated.

"Well, this is the second meal you've provided for us, so thank you. Your mother and I just wanted a word before we head back home and we appreciate your hospitality. We know you are both busy so June would you like to share what we have been thinking." He nodded to his wife.

"We were wondering whether you would consider the possibility of coming to live with us in Glasgow. I know your father has legal custody but the reality is he has not exercised that in person. Bruce kindly contacted him yesterday evening and he agreed it might be sensible to reconsider the position. We have a large enough house and, Larry, you might think about joining the Grant's engineering company as an apprentice. There is a very good engineering college in Glasgow and you could have the same sort of arrangement you have here. I'm sure we could find a school you would like, Philippa.

We realise it will be a big challenge for you leaving Cornwall but we wanted you to be able to think about it, and we wanted to tell you face to face rather than on the phone, so there you are. It's entirely up to you. The decision will be yours, and we will happily go with whatever you decide." June looked enquiringly at her children. She made a good job of hiding her anxiety and appearing calm. Larry looked at his sister, and nodded.

Philippa pushed her porridge bowl away and got up; with tears welling up in her eyes, she came round the table to June and, putting her arms around her, burst into tears. Between her sobs, she managed a mumbled,

"Yes, please, yes, yes yes."

Bruce thoughtfully provided a handkerchief and Larry waited until his sister had calmed and dried her eyes. His mother looked over her daughter's head enquiringly at her son.

"Thank you. It's a very generous offer, and I think the apprenticeship would be a big opportunity."

"But," prompted his mother, her heart in her mouth. She had sensed that her son had more to tell her.

"I, I don't know whether you know but Louisa and Anna are going to move to Wales. Louisa has a property there in the village where she grew up. She still has family and some friends from her school days there. She has offered to have Philippa and me."

"I see, I was going to ask you about Anna?"

"Anna came to see me this morning."

"You mean before you came here."

"Yes, we talked things through. She's got a provisional place at Cardiff University if she gets the right grades. She told me there are lots of trains to Bristol and there is one that goes to Glasgow on Friday afternoons and you can also return to Bristol on Sunday. For me the challenge about Wales is in the village where she is going to live a lot of people as you might expect speak Welsh, I don't and it might be quite difficult to find comparative work there to what I have now."

"I see, so do you need more time to think?"

"If Anna came for weekends, could she stay with us in your house? Philippa asked her mother.

"Yes, of course, she'd be welcome any time."

"Thanks. I will also visit her."

"Yes, she seems to have thought this through and done her research."

"That's Anna for you," again it was Philippa who spoke on behalf of her brother. Larry just nodded in agreement.

"Now, that's given us all something to think about. So, Larry does that mean you would be happy to come and be with us?"

Larry looked at his mother, Anna's words rang in his ears, 'For both of us we have got to put our mum's first.' His mother was waiting expectantly. He gave her a reassuring smile. "It's a very generous offer, yes please." The look of relief and joy on his mother's face was all the confirmation he needed to know he had made the right decision.

"Oh Larry, you don't know how happy you have made me, how happy you both have made me."

Bruce raised both hands his fists clenched. "Good, that's settled. I am sure you both have made a sensible decision, and for us it is a relief to have our worries all cleared up before we head up North. We can start planning to welcome you to Scotland. Perhaps we need to finish our breakfast. Then I think it would be a good idea if I go with Philippa on her paper round while you Larry help your Mother clear up here. When we get back you will be free to go to work and we will spend time with you, Philippa, before you go to school, and we head North. This porridge is very good, thank you both, and do I see some of your homemade bread over there?"

"Toast and marmalade and tea, or would anyone like jam and coffee. Then we also have waffles.?" Philippa had dried her eyes and was clearly taking charge.

"The porridge was just what I needed now a cup of tea will do for me, but Bruce I'm sure would love some toast and marmalade and perhaps coffee." June got up and helped her daughter clear away the porridge bowls and make the coffee for her husband, while Larry made the toast.

The meal over, Philippa and Bruce left to collect her bag of papers. Bruce accompanied her helping to deliver them. Larry was left with his mother.

"That was another lovely meal, Larry. How about I wash, and you dry, and we can talk while we work,"

"Fine."

"I guess you will have to give the garage some notice, and it might be best to get Philippa's term over and Christmas done. Then there is the whole business of school and college dates. In Scotland it is slightly different. When do you complete your first year at technical college?"

"We have our first-year examinations at the end of May."

"I see, would it make sense to complete those before moving North?"

"It might."

"Would you mind delaying the move until then?"

"I haven't really thought about it, and of course, there is Philippa to consider."

"Yes, but for her it might be less critical. I think we need time to think things through and for you both to consider what best for you."

"Yes, I think that makes sense."

"You clearly do a lot for your aunt; how do you think she'll cope."

"I don't know, she has friends and I think she's a survivor but the loss of her husband has been a big shock."

"What were they like? Was it a good marriage?"

"That depends on what you think a good marriage is, I suppose. They had a sort of love-hate relationship. She depended on Sid but he was a bully and could be very difficult."

"Was he violent?"

"Yes, if you upset him, he could be."

"So did he hit her?"

"Yes, it occasionally got to that."

"What about you and Philippa?" His mother was looking at him anxiously.

"Yes, nothing too dramatic, a cuff round the ear was his way of asserting himself."

"How awful! Oh Larry, I'm so sorry, I feel terrible, I should have realised."

"Mum, please don't beat yourself up over it, it sounds worse than it really was, we learnt not to upset him and in the end we kept out of his way as much as possible. He was often away and when Philippa got her paper round we were out of the house before he or Charlotte got up. Then in the evenings they were both out at the pub and we were in bed before they got in."

"You seem to have coped, but I can't help feeling guilty and angry too. Didn't your father know?"

"No, I don't think he did, but Mum, please don't feel guilty. The way I look at it is, the school of hard knocks sometimes does one a favour. As Father Aloysius says 'whatever doesn't kill you strengthens you.' You learn to cope and come to terms with things you can't change. Philippa took it harder than I did, but you know there are a lot of children who suffer far worse, and quite a few of them live here in this village. The Trevinians are Cornish and the Cornish have a tough streak. We get by, and we did, and now, well, it's a new chapter and a new challenge for us all, it won't be easy but I'm sure we can do better than just get by."

"Oh Larry, you've certainly got a grown up head and broad shoulders. You're amazing. I suppose you had a wonderful headmaster, and Anna must have helped."

"Yes and Father Aloysius too, I'll miss him."

"Well perhaps he could come up and stay. It would be nice to get to know him."

"That would be great, he is a very special person."

"And Anna too, I take it you two are very serious about each other."

"Yes Mum, I'm a lucky boy, Anna is the only one for me and always has been. We just click."

"That's wonderful, but you are both very young."

"Sure, but her mum and dad were too when they got married, and if we wait until Anna gets her degree, we won't be that young."

"Right, she certainly seems a very sensible girl."

"She is, and she loves me, so it's all good."

"In that case I've got something for you. June dried her hands and collected her bag from the table. She took out the little jewellery box and handed it to her son. "You might want to give her this, it was my mum's, and she got married very young too." Larry took the box and carefully opened it. There nestling in its velvet cushion was the most beautiful ring he had ever seen.

"Oh Mum, it's beautiful, it's exquisite, but are you sure?"

"Yes darling, I just hope Anna will like it too."

"Oh, she will, she will. You are so clever. This will be our engagement ring and I can't wait to give it to her, oh Mum thank you, but."

"But?"

"What about Philippa?"

"Don't worry I've got something for her too that I'm sure she will like and is appropriate for her age."

Thank you Mum, thank you. Mother and son embraced.

"Mum, I hope you don't mind me asking, but what about our father?" There was a lengthy silence which filled Larry with misgivings.

His Mother eventually sighed. She looking enquiringly at her son. "What about your father?"

Larry was at a loss to think of what to say. He took refuge in asking for clarity, "I'm not sure what you mean."

"June shrugged, "How many times have you seen your father in the last four years I wonder?"

"Not many, I guess, and this last year not at all."

"I don't want to be uncharitable but my feeling is simply this, your father wanted custody not because he wanted you. That at least must be clear to you. I am afraid the arrangement he engineered wasn't based on wanting the best for you and your sister. It suited him at the time. He needed to support his brother, he wanted to get his own way in the battle for custody because he was always a bad loser. He was quite happy to absolve himself of any responsibility for your welfare and of regular visits if he could possibly avoid them. He's only agreed to relinquish his right to custody now because, well, probably, because he's short of money and now his brother is no longer about to demand his financial support, he is free of that obligation, and so he is only too happy not to be paying a contribution for your keep."

Larry's mother smiled at him. Coming over to put her hands on his shoulders. She looked her son straight in the eye. "Larry I won't stop you having a relationship with your dad if that's what you want, and if you do, so be it, I won't think the worse of you in any way. It's sad but I have to be honest with you, I would prefer never to see him again. I am happy, married to Bruce. He is a good man, wise, faithful and very caring, things your father in my opinion never was. I will regret to the end of my days that I did not contact you or your sister once until now. I honestly thought it was for the best. I didn't want you to be constantly pining for me. I guess I thought you'd forget me. But I promise you I never forgot you or your sister. I did the only thing I could do and that was to pray for you, which I did every night. Of course, I should have visited, and if I had I would have seen how unsatisfactory things were for you. The fact is I didn't. Now I want a chance to make up for what turned out to be a mistake, by building a relationship again and walking along side you both in the next phase of your journey of life."

"Larry swallowed hard as he fought back the urge to cry. "Thanks, Mum, I'll do my best to make you proud of me. I love you." He took his mother into his arms and held her tight.

It was June who had to battle with the urge to cry when he released her.

"I already am very proud of you, very proud indeed."

At that moment Phillipa, with Bruce in tow, returned. It was just in time for Larry to have a few minutes before having to run down the hill to catch his bus to work. He spent the time asking about the engineering firm and about apprenticeships. Philippa had enjoyed her time with Bruce. Now was to spend time on her own with her mother while Bruce excused himself and went to make business calls from the car. Her mother was able to share with her the possible time line involved in the working out of their plans for the move

North. Philippa at first seemed disappointed not to be moving sooner but then came her mother's surprise gifts and that helped. Like her brother she was overcome with gratitude as she put the pearl necklace round her neck and tried on the colourful silk scarf with a jewelled brooch. She wanted to know what Larry had received, but her mother had just given her a smile and told her that that would have to be a mystery. She did assure her she would find out possibly quite soon but that it was not appropriate for her to know immediately. On June's insistence they took Philippa back to the Evans' house so she could deposit her gifts safely there. They then delivered her to school. As her husband had commented earlier, there was a lot for them all to think about and to look forward to. This future was the topic of conversation for much of their journey home.

Larry had phoned Anna just before he got his lift to work. He gave her the good news as briefly as he could and thanked her again for her early morning visit. She sounded very pleased for him. That evening he resisted the temptation to work overtime and took the early bus back to the village in order to arrive in daylight. He sent Anna a text on the way suggesting they take a walk along the cliff path. They could talk about the implications of the morning's decisions in private. Anna's reply came almost immediately. She assured Larry she would be ready and was looking forward to hearing his version of the breakfast meeting, she had already heard Philippa's version. Philippa, she reported, was very excited and couldn't stop talking about it all.

Conscious that a cliff walk would necessitate her wrapping up well against the cold wind and would not look her best, Anna compensated by using some of her mother's lipstick and even a dab of perfume. She was ready waiting by the front door and on seeing him coming up the drive went out to greet him. Hand in hand they strode along the cliff path. The light was already fading and Larry set a fast pace. He talked as they walked.

"It was so good of you to come this morning. You spoke so much sense and those words of yours about us needing to be there for our mothers were ringing in my ears when Mum spoke about us going to live with them in Glasgow and Bruce put the question to me. Philippa had already said yes she would go. I, in fairness, had to tell them about your mum's generous offer and that prompted the question, and I looked at my mother and I could hear your words in my mind. I had to say yes."

He felt his hand being squeezed, "Well done you, I bet she was pleased, but what did you feel?"

"Relieved, I think we all were, and as you say June especially so. I thought the picnic and seeing Mum's face when Philippa ran to welcome her and threw her arms around her was special, but this morning was just as special too. I don't think I will ever forget the look in her eyes on both occasions, such a look of joy."

"I'm so pleased for you Larry; I'm pleased for you all. It's just so right don't you think?"

"Yes, yes, I do, but if you hadn't have come this morning and prepared me, I don't know what I would have done. You're right about so many things and when you said that about us being a team you were so right again. I needed you and it was as if you were there. I'm so grateful."

"Well, that's love for you."

"I guess." They walked on in silence, it was as if there was nothing more needed to be said, together they both knew they were a team mutually dependant on each other. They reached the spot where they had cast Duncan Evans' ashes to the winds. A watery sunset tinged the thin wisps of cloud pink, it would soon be dark. Larry stopped. "This is where we stop."

"It's special I know, but why what's on your mind.?"

"You'll see." Larry took a small box from his pocket and handed it to her.

"What's this?"

"Mum gave it to me for you, open it and see," As she opened it he dropped down onto one knee. She gasped her eyes brimming with love she looked down at him.

In a voice choked with emotion, she whispered, "Oh, Larry, it's beautiful."

"Anna Evans, would you please do me the honour of agreeing to be my wife?"

"Yes, yes, yes. She dropped to her knees and smothered his face with kisses. "You darling, darling boy, yes, but the honour is all mine." For a long moment, they knelt, clinging to each other. A gull swooped low overhead and screeched. Anna laughed and disentangled herself from his arms.

"I do believe you have even arranged to have a witness. I think you had better put the ring on my finger and see if it fits." Larry took the ring, raised it to his lips and then, taking her hand in his, slipped it onto her finger.

"Oh Larry, it's exquisite. I hardly deserve such a beautiful thing, and I haven't anything for you."

"Me, you know I don't need a ring, I'm not into that sort of thing, you are all I need and I'm the happiest boy in the world." The gull swooped with another screech. "Yes mate you heard me I am the happiest boy in the world." The pair got to their feet.

"I think I had better take you home, Mrs. Trevinian, to be, take my arm. I think we need to drink a toast."

"Certainly, I think we might just have a bottle of lemonade. Tell me, Mr Trevinian, am I to be spending my first months at Uni planning my wedding as well as studying?"

"No, I don't think so, 'Hurry hurry has no blessing,' to quote Father Aloysius. I don't want to distract you from your studies and I will be studying too."

"You mean we wait until we are qualified."

"Yes, something like that."

"That long?"

"Well let's get the first year over with, then we can review. After all we are both very young."

"Alright, but my mum was a teenage bride, and Dad was still at college. I'm not renowned for being patient."

"I know, but let's just get ourselves settled in our new situations and we can decide then."

"It's a deal. I don't think I want to be waiting three or four years, and I suspect you'll be qualified well before me. But, as you say, it would be sensible to get ourselves and our mums sorted and then decide, but I tell you what I can't wait to do and that is to tell Mum and to say a huge thank you to your mum too. Oh Larry, you are such a darling."

"And so are you. Hey do you think we should get Tee shirts made with Anna is my darling and Larry is my darling printed on them.?"

"Now Larry you are being frivolous, don't spoil it, I'm so excited. How are we going break the news to Mum and Philippa?"

"I'm not sure, I mean I don't want to be frivolous!"

"Oh you, you are exasperating. I hope this is not a foretaste of things to come."

"Exasperating and frivolous, and all within an hour of taking on the awesome responsibility of pledging to love the most beautiful girl in the world for the rest of my days, I wonder how many accolades I can clock up in twelve hours!"

"Ooo you!" Anna dug him in the ribs, "I could smack you."

"Wow violence already, am I going to have to add battered to frivolous and exasperating?"

"Please, Larry, do you want me to have to give your ring back to you?"

"Alright, how about this from serious Larry, we go into the house holding hands so no one can see the ring. Then I let go of your hand and we see who is the first to notice, and that person has the honour of supplying the wherewithal for the toast to the loving couple."

"Alright, but what happens if it's Philippa?"

"If it is, then either she is going to have to fork out a bit of the money she has squeezed out of me in the way of bribes and nip down to the shop to buy a bottle, or alternatively she could just fill the glasses with water."

"Sounds a bit wet."

"Now whose being frivolous! Actually, there is one thing I ought to do that I really should have done before."

"Really, what?"

"Well, I should have asked your mum's permission."

"Do you really think so? I'm sure she wouldn't have expected it."

"I could still do it. Hopefully she will say yes and then."

"What, we act as if you haven't already proposed?"

"I could do it all again, I mean we could treat what happened just now as a rehearsal."

"No, it wasn't a rehearsal, it was so special, and we can't replicate it."

"What then?"

"I think Mum will be delighted even if you haven't asked her permission, so, yes, we go in hand in hand, and we just share the good news."

"Who is going to do the sharing?"

"I will. I'll just say, Mum, Larry has asked me to marry him, and I've said yes, and then we will reveal the ring."

"And what do I do?"

"You just look adoring."

"I see, that won't be too hard, I guess I can manage that."

Larry did. It wasn't hard. It didn't work out just as Anna had planned. When hand in hand they entered the house, her mother was in the kitchen preparing the evening meal. It was not a good time to make a special announcement. Anna decided the safest place for her to be was her room. There were still a lot of unanswered questions for she and Larry to consider, the most pressing being the timing of the various moves. Anna had intimated that it might be better to delay their move until the middle of the year after her finals were complete. Moving and taking her final examinations was hardly ideal. For her, to take her examinations in Wales would be challenging, and a lot would hang on the results. For Larry and Philippa there were challenges surrounding their move too. Larry had to share with Anna the whole question of dates. His mother had told him that Scotland had different term dates to schools and colleges in England. She had suggested he might be better to delay his move until he had completed his first year at technical college. For Philippa too there were choices to be made. The timing of her move was less critical but she might find herself moving on her own and Larry following later. They were in the middle of discussing the various scenarios when the call came that the evening meal was ready. It was time to deal with the only certainty they had, they needed to announce their engagement.

Louisa was not surprised when her daughter walked in hand in hand with Larry. She had sensed that something was in the air when Anna had helped herself to her lipstick and perfume, so when Anna had announced they had something to share she had an inkling as to what it might be. She had a second or two to prepare herself and her thoughts immediately went to Duncan and one of their last conversations. She was able to greet her daughter's quiet and slightly nervous attempt to share her news with a show of genuine delight and joy. Moving round the table in a flash, Louisa had enfolded the couple in her embrace. When, with tears in her eyes she persuaded herself to release them, she gave her feelings a voice.

"Oh, this is wonderful, and I know your dad would be over the moon."

Philippa meanwhile was jumping up and down chanting, "I knew it, I knew it, come on let's see the ring," and then when Anna held out her hand to show it off, she screamed with delighted amazement, "Wow, it's, it's just amazing. Larry where did you get that?" Philippa held Anna's had by her finger tips and bent over examining the ring closely.

"Oh Gosh, it's so beautiful. Are those stones real?"

"Yes, as far as I know."

"Was it Mum's ring?"

"Not originally, it was Gran's."

"Like my pearls and brooch."

"Yes, apparently, Granny was a teenage bride."

"So when is the big day?"

"Tomorrow."

"Don't be silly. Anna, when is the big day?"

"Undecided, probably after I've done my first year at Uni, that is if I get in."

"Can I be bridesmaid?"

"Ah, we haven't got that far yet, but if we have a bridesmaid, I promise you'll be top of the list when and if we have to choose." Eager to change the subject, Anna turned to her mother, "Mum what was that you said about Dad?"

"Your dad will be delighted as I am, we had a conversation about it. It was towards the end when I was with him in the hospital. Larry he always thought a lot of you, and I remember earlier he told me he thought you'd go far. Then in this conversation he held my hand and said, 'I worry about Anna, I think Larry would be a good choice you know.' I agreed with him and then he said, 'I think I'll have a word with Anna.'

"And he did."

"When was that?" Larry was looking at his fiancée."

"In the hospital just before he died."

Larry sighed, "Oh, well, God bless Duncan. I think we should drink a toast to him."

"What a good idea, Philippa, be a pet; there are some glasses on the kitchen table, and the bottle is in the fridge. Could you bring them, please?"

"Mum, you knew, you knew all along."

"No, no, but when we got the news this morning that Larry and Philippa had had an invitation to go and live with your mum and dad in Glasgow, I just wondered what might happen, then when you borrowed my lipstick and the perfume, I had another little wonder. Anyway, I thought I'd get a bottle out, and we could drink some to celebrate the Glasgow move, if nothing else."

"Is that all?"

"Well, as I said, I did have a little wonder."

"And what's this bottle business?"

"You know your dad always got lots of presents at the end of the year, mostly from the leavers. A lot of them were bottles. He wasn't a great drinker, just the odd beer or shandy. He gave most of them away but he did keep a couple at the back of our cupboard. One he set aside was especially for this occasion. It was called the engagement bottle."

"Do you know who gave it to him?"

"I do."

"Who?"

"It was Larry." Her revelation was the cause of great laughter. Anna picked up the bottle of Champagne.

"You are a dark horse, Larry Trevinian. Did you give this to Dad hoping to be able to drink it at my engagement?"

"No, I'd like to think I did, but those weren't the best of times in our long-standing relationship if you remember. I saved up for that for weeks. I wanted to give the best headmaster in the whole of England a special gift. Anyway, he wrote to me to thank me. I've still got the letter. He wrote that he would set it aside for a special occasion. Little did I know it would be my engagement to the most beautiful lady in England, his daughter."

"What a story. Are you sure you are not making this all up?"

Larry was busy opening the bottle, "No way, it's completely true." he poured out four glasses and, turning to his future mother-in-law, asked, "Do I have permission to make a toast?"

"Of course."

"Please raise your glasses and drink to the best headteacher in all England and to the most beautiful girl in England too. To Duncan and to Anna."

"To Duncan and to Anna."

"Thank you, Larry, that was very gracious of you, well done. Now I feel it's my turn to propose a toast to the happy couple, to Larry and Anna, may they love long and love well, and if you two are half as happy as Duncan and I were then I'll be more than best pleased. To Larry and Anna." At this juncture the bubbles got up Philippa's nose and set her off sneezing violently which was the cause of more laughter as well as sympathy. Laughter and sympathy, both were to be much in evidence and much needed over the weeks and months ahead.

For Larry his next action was to phone his mother. She and Bruce were overjoyed at the news. Two days later her card arrived along with a big bouquet for Anna and the message 'Great news, Congratulations, lots of love June and Bruce." They too were able to open a bottle to toast the young couple.

"Mum always said that ring brought her luck," June smiled at her husband as she raised her glass.

"They'll need more than luck; it will take patience and hard work for those two just as it did for us, but somehow, I feel they are up for it, and I am sure that boy of yours will make good, he's got a very level head on those broad shoulders." June found her husband's comments a great comfort. She had come to respect her husband's ability to judge character, it was not something that had come naturally, but something he had learnt over the years. After his wife's defection, he recognised that he was not always right; it had taught him a harsh lesson, and he became more careful and guarded in sharing his observations about human nature.

Chapter Forty-One

There are no goodbyes for us.
Wherever you are you will always be in my heart.

-Mahatma Gandhi

The news of Larry and Anna's engagement spread quickly in the village. The first person in Pondreath to know of it was Father |Aloysius. The priest had prepared himself for this moment. He had long anticipated that one day Anna and Larry would come to him with such news. He had wondered how he would feel and how he should feel and now, he had to face the news, how he did feel? He was in the presbytery when Anna had phoned him. She had sounded very happy. She had expressed her gratitude to him for his advice and kindness over the time she had known him. He was touched. He had congratulated her. They had talked briefly then she had rung off. He had gone straight to the church, and to the steps of the sanctuary where he knelt to look up at the cross. It was where he had come before to reflect and to examine his own thoughts and his conscience. Was he in anyway resentful of their relationship, jealous even, or perhaps envious? As he asked himself these questions and considered his relationship with Anna first and then with Larry he prayed. He recognised that God had created him with the body of a man and with the natural desires of his species. He knew too he had pledged himself to a way of life that involved the sacrifice of curbing these desires and of devoting himself to the service of another relationship, his relationship to his God. But as with any of his species he found staying faithful to such a commitment had its challenges. He needed to reach deep into himself and his spiritual resources to meet those challenges. Kneeling at the foot of the cross helped, and when he finally rose from his knees he was at peace and he knew how he should react.

Anna and Larry took the opportunity to show him the ring before the morning service. He was overjoyed for them both and when they asked him if he would marry them when the time came that only added to his pleasure and widened his grin. For most, the news was welcome if not unexpected. There were a few detractors, those loyal to Sid Trevinian scoffed, but they were a very small minority who hated anyone who took a stand against their own nefarious doings.

The days after that memorable evening passed, days turned into weeks. Anna and Larry had a new focus to their lives. To both it was important do well in their examinations but especially for Anna. Supporting each other, they settled down to their studies and worked hard. Otherwise, their lives continued much as before, with the addition for Larry and Philippa of regular calls to Scotland. Christmas being the other major exception. Larry resisted the temptation and his mother's urgings to move out of number thirteen and continued to care for his aunt. She had taken his engagement with her usual disdain, but when he showed his continued commitment to make number thirteen his home, she mellowed. He did have a few nights over the Christmas feast staying in the room, formerly Duncan's study, at the Evans' home. As they had expected, his father had ceased to make a financial contribution towards his children's upkeep. Charlotte was left to manage as best she could and she now relied on Larry for providing the weekly food shopping, her own earnings were meagre.

Larry was concerned how she would cope when he left. He shared his worries with Father Aloysius. The priest reassured him and committed to look out for her welfare which was a relief. The priest suggested to her that she might take in lodgers, or run an Airbnb, but the house was such a mess that such a thing would only be possible if it was redecorated. Larry decided that that would be his parting gesture. At first, she had resisted but soon saw sense and accepted his generous offer. The challenge for him was he had never done any decorating before. Again, Father Aloysius came to his aid, he volunteered to help and even mustered others to join him. Charlotte was careful to keep clear of the house when Larry and his crew were at work. She was made aware that the priest was one of the party and she was determined not to meet him. His involvement however proved to be to his advantage. While the Police continued with their investigations into Dot's part in his abduction and attempted murder, he was left having to live in a community that was still hoping for answers to a lot of hitherto unanswered questions. He did not find this a comfortable position to be in. There were some in the village, a small minority who used his silence to spread rumours and stoke old prejudices. It was difficult for him to take a stance against the gossip and tittle tattle. However, when he reached out a helping hand to Sid Trevinian's widow it helped stem the tide of speculation and innuendo.

Louisa, conscious that this would probably be her last Christmas in Pondreath determined to make it particularly special. For her and Anna it would be their first Christmas after her husband's death. She knew he would not have wished her anything but a joyful time and so she felt emboldened to make it special. Duncan was no believer but, he was not a kill joy either and their Christmases had been a time to get out old board games and to do quizzes. Presents were exchanged but only three each, however there were lots of prizes to be won in the quizzes and family games. All three were involved in the preparation of the meal. Louisa continued with what had become a family tradition, with two additions they all went to church in the morning, and the number of presents were four each as June and Bruce had been exceptionally generous. For Philippa and Larry it was one of the happiest and most enjoyable Christmas days they could remember. For them their experience of Christmas at number thirteen was bleak. Their aunt and uncle invariably went on a bender and got very drunk. If it had not been for their class Christmas parties the season would have passed by without a hint of a celebration.

The police investigations into the drug dealing and the disappearance of Father Aloysius dragged on until just after the New Year. Eventually the team on the case concluded they had enough evidence to prosecute. Dot Trevinian was charged with two indictable offences. One was appertaining to the possession of drugs with the intent to traffic them for personal gain. The second was being an accomplice to attempted murder. Dot pleaded not guilty to both charges. She was detained on remand until her trial. As with all such serious criminal trials the wheels of justice worked slowly and the date was some thirteen months away. With Dot's appearance in court and her imprisonment awaiting trial and the publication of the facts as reported in the local newspaper, as Father Aloysius had predicted, all was revealed. The questions round his disappearance on that fateful night were answered. Sid and Michael Trevinian had abducted him and had attempted to kill him. His clothes on the beach were just part of their alibi. The unpalatable truth was out and the village had to make what they could of it.

For Father Aloysius this was both a relief and a concern. He was relieved that the speculation would now cease to have any credence. His concern was for Larry, for Philippa and their aunt. His immediate reaction was to visit Larry and Philippa. He found them at the Evans' home. As with every household in the village the news had come as a shock, and was the topic of much conversation. For Philippa, it was a vindication for all her feelings of antipathy towards her guardians. For Larry it was more of a concern, would he and Philippa find themselves stigmatised by association, and then there was his aunt. How would she come out of this and cope with the news and the notoriety? And of course, there was Father Aloysius. Larry felt ashamed that his guardian had almost brought about the death of his friend, and worse still that he knew nothing of it and had not been able to prevent it. Father Aloysius had enfolded them both in his arms and had held them close.

"My dear friends I know this news brings lots of challenges for you and indeed for us all. As we grapple to understand the whys and the hows of it all our biggest challenge is to find a way in our hearts to forgive. For me, part of that is the knowledge that not one of us is perfect, and me least of all. Why, Larry, was your guardian like he was? I don't know. My great regret must be that I was not able to come to some sort of reconciliation with him over our differences. I had hoped for an opportunity to attempt such a thing, but it never presented itself. Could I have tried harder? Probably. Both Sid and I, as do we all, need God's forgiveness. Our consolation must be that God understands us, and if we come with contrite hearts, he will forgive and also provide us with the support we need to move on to trying to be better." He released them from his embrace and stretched out his hands to Anna and Louisa and then motioned that they should all hold hands and form a circle. "One thing is certain I stand here today with some of the very best friends any one could have, friends that saved my life, and I am eternally grateful. Then looking each one in the eye he continued, "Thank you Philippa, thank you Anna, thank you Louisa, and thank you Larry, thanks be to God for you all."

Wide-eyed and hoarse with emotion, it was Larry who led them all in saying Amen."

At that moment the phone rang. It was June. She had received the news from Miss Farrow. Her immediate reaction was to offer to travel straight down to Cornwall to collect both her children. Larry cautioned her that acting in haste was not in this case, wise. For them to disappear suddenly might be conceived as them running away. It might be better to wait and to see what happened. In this he was supported by Bruce, who counselled that they should give themselves time to think it through carefully.

"Mum, darling thank you for your concern, I assure you we are quite well and happy. Yes, this news has been a shock but please don't worry. I love you and now I'll hand you over to Philippa, and Anna too I think, would like a word."

Despite her son's reassurances, June was not completely happy and it was left that she would give the matter some thought before making a final decision.

While Anna was on the phone talking to June and thanking her again for the beautiful ring and also the flowers, Louisa had taken the opportunity to put the kettle on for a drink and to get the cake tin out of the cupboard. Father Aloysius excused himself, he needed to make a second visit. Louisa made him promise to return for the evening meal.

Charlotte had taken the news of her husband's involvement in an attempted murder badly. For the first time in many years, she had not gone out to the Smugglers Arms but had shut herself away in her house. She did not answer Father Aloysius's persistent knocking on the front door. He went round the back of the house and found the kitchen door open. He called out to her and eventually she responded. She stood awkwardly at the door.

"Oh, it's you, what do you want?" Her tone was a mixture of resentment and aggression.

"I've just come to say I am sorry, sorry for what has happened and sorry too that I was not able to come to some sensible reconciliation with your husband."

Charlotte swore. "If you hadn't meddled in his affairs, it would never have happened."

"Well that's as maybe. As a priest you can't ignore a situation that you believe to be wrong and know to be potentially very damaging to people you know, but that's all in the past. As far as I am concerned that is where it will stay. As for the future I would like to forget the past and to start with a clean slate, so if I can help in any way, please ask." This offer was firmly rejected with a string of curses and a slamming of the door.

Father Aloysius had half expected that his visit might provoke such a reaction. As he left to return to the Evans's home for the evening meal, he said his prayers.

Larry met him at the door.

"Hi Father, you've been to see aunt, haven't you?"

"Yes,"

"I see, by your look, I guess you didn't get the red carpet treatment?

"You could say that."

"Don't worry, Father, you know you will win in the end." Larry gave his friend a gentle punch on the arm.

The priest shrugged. "I wish I could be so sure, but ...."

"Remember the first time we met, the arm wrestle? You took on the strongest man I've ever known, and you won!"

"Thanks, I think this is going to be even tougher."

"You'll still win in the end."

"God willing."

"Well, there you are, you will win! Now supper's almost ready, come in and get warm."

Father Aloysius was somewhat subdued but for all that it was a happy evening. Later Larry was to walk part of the way back to the presbytery with him. As they went, he whistled a tune. Father Aloysius joined in with the words, words they sang together all the way to the parting of their ways. "We shall overcome, we shall overcome some day." Each still humming the tune when he arrived at his destination.

The reaction by the village to the news that Sid and Mick Trevinian had conspired to murder Father Aloysius was for many yet another a shock. Their deaths coming on top of Father Aloysius's disappearance had been bad enough, but now they had this to contend with. When the priest arrived home that night, he checked his answer phone. There were a number of messages, the first was one from his bishop to say he would be calling the next day early and would accompany Father Aloysius in the service of morning prayer. He suggested that they would need to have a plan as to what would be the best way to proceed now that the village knew the truth. The priest had other messages of support from Commander Nesbitt and the Rev. Burns.

True to his word, the bishop had arrived early the next morning. Over a cup of tea, the two men planned their approach to the service, and how best to deal with any repercussions to the news that was bound to come as a shock to many in the village. Father Aloysius was gratified to see that the congregation was considerably larger than was usual for a weekday morning prayer, and among them was the Rev. Burns and his wife. His entry with the bishop caused quite a stir. The priest led the service. There was not normally a sermon or even a homily but on this occasion the bishop requested to be allowed to say a few words from the pulpit. He was conscious that among the congregation were people who might need to get back to jobs and one who might be late for school.

"Father Aloysius has kindly allowed me the privilege of saying a few words from his pulpit. I just want to say two things. Firstly, I want to thank you all for your tremendous support for this church and its priest. Father Aloysius is, in the estimation of the church, and I am sure in yours an outstanding priest. You must take a large amount of credit for that, so thank you. Then as we are all aware there is the sensitive matter of his disappearance. I am very aware that here in this church today is at least one member of the family of those responsible for what can only be described as an evil act. I am also aware that this person was also responsible for finding him and of helping in his rescue, for which he and I too am hugely grateful. What looked like a tragedy has thanks to you and a lot of brave people turned out to be a triumph. Praise the Lord your priest is alive and well and here serving you and this community today. Now how should we move on from here? It is not for me or the church to judge. The law will run its course and justice will be done. For the church it will be business as usual, the business of living out our saviour Christ's love, Christ's forgiveness and Christ's compassion for all his people. We are called to forgive our enemies and to turn the other cheek, we are called to build the kingdom of God in this place. This is the vocation that your priest has embraced, and I am sure you will support him in following his calling, but not only him but also each other, for we are all church here and all are called to follow Christ's example and live his love in our lives. God Bless you all, and thank you." The bishop then concluded the service with a prayer and a blessing.

In years to come, Father Aloysius would look back and reflect on that service and the last months of Larry's time in Pondreath and draw strength from the memories. He would recall their walks, their talks, their labours on the redecorating of number thirteen. How he had come to admire his friend's quiet determination, how Larry, busy with his work and his studies, still found the time to undertake what was to be a time-consuming project. The support of Anna and Louisa and the experience of working with a team were all part of what was for him a rich experience, an experience of doing what his bishop had called for, building the kingdom of God in Pondreath.

It was Commander Nesbitt who finally won Charlotte Trevinian over. He had taken advantage of discovering the date of her birthday. His housekeeper had made a cake and he had given her a gift voucher to be spent at one of the more prestigious ladies dress shops in Pendon Bay. He had briefed the staff in the shop and encouraged them to be as helpful as they could. He was gratified that with their guidance the very generous sum he had pledged was spent well. Larry, Anna, Louisa and Father Aloysius combined to make a similar arrangement for Charlotte to visit a hairdresser. Again Commander Nesbitt, along with Miss Farrow, called to prime the staff. Charlotte's clothes' purchases since her marriage had been few and all from Charity shops. She had never been to a hairdresser. A friend had trimmed her hair for her and her birthday presents from Sid had been a few beers in the pub. Although it took some time for her to admit it, that birthday was to be the best she had had in years, and she was proud of her new outfits. She had taken the trouble to wash her hair before her visit to the hairdressers, and was pleased with the end result. She had resisted the temptation to have it died a shocking green or purple and had settled to have her pony tail in a bun.

That evening Larry had cooked his aunt her favourite meal, a steak and kidney pie. Miss Farrow had provided an apple pie and a tub of cream. He had arranged the table with her birthday cards, one from each of the contributors. To his surprise, his aunt was back earlier from the pub than usual. He had only just retired to bed when he heard her come in. In the morning he found a note on the table. The one word, 'Thanks' had been written by a shaky hand on a scrap of note paper. When he left for work Larry took it with him and it did the rounds of all who had contributed.

It took a while longer for his aunt to even acknowledge Father Aloysius, but she gradually came round. Larry had been only partly right, he had won in the end, or if the truth be told the team had won in the end. The priest was to remember it all and the memories invariably made him smile and mutter to himself "To God be the glory."

For Philippa, her departure to travel North came shortly after the revelations concerning Sid Trevinian and his brother. June had decided it would be best if her daughter did not complete the Spring term but opt for an earlier move. Philippa was delighted. She had never been further from her home village than Newquay, she embraced the idea of going to Scotland as a great adventure. She would miss her friends and Anna and Larry until he joined her, and she would miss Father Aloysius and Miss Farrow, but for her, the thought of making a clean break with the place where she would always be looked on as a would-be murderer's brat, far outweighed any misgivings she might have had at the prospect of leaving the village she had grown up in. Louisa had thoughtfully arranged a farewell party for her on the day before she was to be collected. Father Aloysius and Miss Farrow, her class teacher and the Tarrents as well as her friends from school and the youth club were all invited. Philippa had strongly rejected the offer to include her aunt in the list. It was a happy farewell and a happy Philippa who embraced her mother the next day when June and Bruce came to collect her. She waved good bye to the small gathering that had turned up to see her off with a mixture of happiness, tinged with sadness and trepidation. Saying goodbye to friends she had known all her life was not easy. Would she ever see them again? How would she find making new friends? Being with her mother was a great joy.

When his sister left, Larry took over the paper round. The Fowler's had been good to both of them, he did not want to let them down. The money he earned was not a lot but he had learnt the truth of the old maxim every penny counts and so the few pounds he got from delivering the papers would help towards the cost of his aunt's meals. Without Jack Trevinian's contribution towards the upkeep of his children she was hard pressed to make ends meet. She had lost the income she used to have from pushing drugs for her husband and so had to rely on her wages as a cleaner. As a result, she had to cut down on her drinking and smoking and Larry began to see her change. She made more of an effort to keep the house tidy. He no longer found beer cans strewn over the kitchen floor and she emptied her own cigarette ash tray putting the stubs in the bin. Her language became less coarse. She began to thank him for the meals he cooked. When Commander Nesbitt decided to purchase a new television set he gave her his old one. He paid for an aerial to be installed and also for her license. She wrote him a letter of thanks.

Father Aloysius was concerned for the welfare of both the Trevinian widows. He had phoned the prison chaplain at Truro jail where Dot was being held pending her trial. The chaplain had been most helpful and had agreed to ask Dot whether she would accept a visit from the priest. At first, she declined. Dot and Mick like Charlotte and Sid had no children. She had no visitors. Her cottage home was lying empty. Father Aloysius had an idea that might help both ladies. His plan was simple, the cottage should be let to holiday makers. Charlotte could manage the lettings and clean the place between lets. That way both women would have an income and the cottage would be clean and tidy. He discussed this with Commander Nesbitt before broaching Charlotte. His plan was to get her to raise the subject with Dot but they would have to be patient. He needed permission to visit Dot. To do that he needed to earn Dot's trust. He had to get Dot to accept him as one of the people who was welcome to visit her. First he wrote a number of colourful cards. He also paid a call on a number of her friends. One, Barbara Ferris agreed to accompany him. Miss Fowler kindly agreed to provide the transport. Father Aloysius contacted the prison chaplain again. This time Dot agreed that he could visit her as long he brought a friend. The priest decided he would take Barbara on his first trip, and Charlotte on his second. They could alternate and perhaps after two visits if they went well, he might get Charlotte to broach the subject of letting the cottage. He was careful to keep his time with Dot to the minimum and to slip away to allow her to be on her own with Barbara or Charlotte. He provided cigarettes for both ladies to give to her. On her second visit Charlotte had suggested the idea of letting the cottage for the summer months. At first Dot had been hesitant. She hoped that she would be acquitted on both charges and then it would be returning to her home, and she questioned as to whether it was worth the bother for just a year. However, having thought about it between visits she had changed her mind. Charlotte and Barbara were to put all her personal things into one bedroom and lock the door. They would then advertise it for summer lettings. Father Aloysius helped them produce an inventory and a letting form. With Commander Nesbitt's help they dealt with the advertising and the procurement of several changes of bed linen, towels, and some new kitchen utensils. Over the course of that letting season both Dot and Charlotte benefited from a good number of lettings.

Larry's examinations preceded Anna's by two weeks, and there were not so many papers for him to sit. Having completed them and passed the practical tests well, he was able to concentrate on getting the redecoration of number thirteen done and to start helping Louisa with her preparations to move to Wales. Anna finished her examinations almost a month later. Both had felt that their intensive revision programme had paid off and were happy with the way they had coped. They would not get their results for some time, but with that hurdle over, they could both look forward to the next chapter of their lives. Larry kept in regular contact with his mother and sister.

Philippa was settling in well to her new life North of the border. Of course, there were challenges. June and Bruce had persuaded her to join their church youth choir and to attend the church youth club. She had a good singing voice and the positive encouragement she had from the lady who ran the choir gave her confidence. Her choir mistress had eclectic tastes, and she found herself singing a great variety of compositions. Within a month of joining the choir she was being challenged to sing duets and then solos. June and Bruce were thrilled, but there had been already another incident that had given them an even greater sense of pride.

Their daughter's introduction to the youth club was not without its challenges. A number of those attending came from a more deprived area of the city where the church was establishing an outreach and building a new congregation. Inevitably, within the group as a whole, there were cliques and groups of like-minded youngsters, which sometimes resulted in relationship difficulties. Philippa, being new, had to establish herself. The youth leaders introduced her to a number of different children, and she found herself being accepted and drawn into a clique that was made up of young people from the outreach congregation.

On the occasion of her third week of attending, she was in conversation with some of her new found friends when she happened to mention Father Aloysius. The realisation that he was an African had provoked a racist response from one of the girls. Philippa was furious, and there was a confrontation. Fortunately, the adult leader of the club was nearby and intervened just in time to prevent the outbreak of violence. The next week, Philippa was reluctant to attend, but June had a word with the youth club leader.

He visited Philippa, and with his encouragement, she agreed to take part in a debate at the club on the subject of racism. All the young people were given the opportunity to express their views. Philippa was asked to speak. It was a new experience for her. At first, she found it difficult to put her thoughts into words. Sensing she was struggling and feeling embarrassed, the youth leader quietly suggested she just tell the group the story of her relationship with Father Aloysius and of her part in his rescue. As she described Father Aloysius's first attendance at the Pondreath's youth club and his arm wrestle with her foster father and saw her audience listening with interest, she gained confidence, and the words just seemed to tumble out.

Realising that this might be a very significant moment not just in her life but in the lives of all who heard her, the youth leader had let her go way beyond the time allotted to each speaker. She told of her foster father's attitude toward people of colour and of his confrontations with Father Aloysius that finally led to him trying to commit murder. She told of his drug dealing and of his death, and of her part in finding Father Aloysius and in the rescue. When she concluded with the words that Father Aloysius was one of the best friends she ever had, so kind and so gentle, yet so brave and strong, the whole gathering got the message. Colour prejudice and racism were wrong. She got an extended round of applause.

In the course of a few minutes, she had moved from being an outsider to one with heroic status. She was now someone who others could go to with their own stories of maltreatment and get advice. To others who had not had such challenges in their growing up she was someone to look up to and admire. All this was a great help as she started out at her new school. Philippa was never going to shine academically, nor was she gifted at sports, but she had a powerful personality, and in that, there was great potential. In her second term at the school, there was a vacancy on the school council. A child from her class who had held the position had left. Philippa was elected to be the class representative. That, too, was to be formative. With all this success, she might have become over confident and big-headed. Fortunately, Father Aloysius's words of advice on humility were to be her guide, 'Humble you must be if to heaven you go, the roof is high there, but the gate is low.'

A week after completing his examinations, Larry and his team finally finished the redecorating project at his aunt's house. Whether it was her new clothes purchased with her birthday vouchers, or the experience of living in a transformed house, or a combination of the two that was to lead Charlotte Trevinian into deciding to turn over a new leaf and not only try to stop smoking but also to drink a great deal less, it would be difficult to say. Whatever the cause, the result was that Charlotte became a far more agreeable person. She modified her language and started to look for opportunities to help others. There was still a lot of unfinished business in her life, not least the continued interest of the police in her goings-on and the fact that her husband's body had yet to be released from the mortuary for burial, but she was in a much better position to deal with these challenges than she had been in the weeks after Sid's death.

Larry, at last, felt comfortable about moving out and handing over his catering duties to a new team. Father Aloysius had undertaken to look after Charlotte when Larry ceased to be able to. In reality what happened was Miss Farrow and Mrs. Trimmer, Commander Nesbitt's housekeeper, combined to provide Charlotte with her evening meal. Miss Farrow undertook to see that the essentials for a basic breakfast were also provided.

An advertisement offering lodging at number thirteen was placed in the shop window. For two weeks, there was no response, but then a new family moved into a recently vacated council house just up the road from number thirteen. Prior to their move, they had had the wife's father, a widower, living with them. He had accompanied them, but there was scant room for him in their new abode. He became Charlotte's first lodger. As he ate his meals at his daughter's house, he was the ideal person for Charlotte to welcome into her home.

With the departure day of Monday for Larry and Anna, that preceding Saturday was their last one at the Tarrents' youth club. It was to be their farewell party, and there was to be a disco. Father Aloysius was invited to make a farewell speech and present them with gifts, a matching pair of his and hers Welsh love spoons intricately carved out of rose wood. They were to act as salad servers for the cut-glass Waterford salad bowl. It was bound to be an emotional evening, but Father Aloysius had determined that it would be a very happy one. He had spent some time in the church quietly preparing himself. Speaking from the heart, every word he said carried the weight of sincerity as he spoke of their faithful attendance, of how the Tarrants had seen them grow and mature to become the lovely young couple they were, contributing to the efforts of the leadership team, and how they would be sadly missed. Tears were shed, but there was much laughter, and it was for the laughter of a very happy occasion that that evening was later to be remembered.

Commander Nesbitt helped the priest at the drinks table, and both men managed to resist being enticed out onto the dance floor until the very last conga, which ended up with everyone joining hands to sing 'Auld lang Syne.' For Larry and Anna, it was a moment they would never forget, as was their last service at St. Prodrick's. Again, there were tears, mainly from Anna, as she went round hugging the people who had been such a part of her growing up. There was also much laughter when, after the service, the congregation presented them with their own token of affection, a Celtic cross carved from a chunk of Cornish granite. For Louisa, there was a picture. This had been especially commissioned. It was of the cliffs over which her husband Duncan's ashes had been cast. Louisa joined her daughter in tears of gratitude. Eventually, the congregation dispersed. Only Larry was left with the priest and his housekeeper. He had a request to make, and that was that he and Anna might have some time with him after the Angelus service that evening. Weather permitting, they would meet at eight at the school's garden. They could sit on the bench by the pond, the site of Larry and Philippa's reunion with his parents and the place that Duncan Evans would have loved to have seen. The place that was his last project.

Chapter Forty-Two

*Don't worry about making waves
simply by being yourself. The moon is doing
it all the time.*

-Scott Stabile

Larry and Anna spent the rest of the day helping Louisa make the final preparations for their departure the following day. They had one other task to fulfil before their date with Father Aloysius. When Louisa was finally satisfied that they had done everything possible to leave her property in good order and to make the leaving go as smoothly as possible. Larry and Anna went together to say goodbye to his aunt. To Larry's surprise, Charlotte seemed genuinely pleased to see him. They had been invited in, and they spent a happy quarter of an hour chatting before saying their farewells. Charlotte stood at the door and waved as they departed. Larry felt content. What might have been an awkward meeting had been cordial and pleasant. He could leave secure in the knowledge that he had done his duty by the Trevinian family.

The young couple were sitting on the bench quietly holding hands when Father Aloysius arrived. He noted the bicycle; Larry had obviously come by bike. The priest greeted his friends and stood admiring it for a moment.

"I didn't know you had a new bike, Larry; it looks to be a good one, very smart, bet it cost a penny or two."

"I'm glad you like it, but it isn't mine, it's yours."

"Mine! Really?"

"Yes, it's part of our farewell thank you gift from us."

"Thank you, gift? It must have cost an awful lot of money, you are so kind, I can't believe it. I hope you haven't emptied the piggy bank when you should have been saving your money for your move North, but thank you so much. I won't know myself as I peddle round on my visits."

"We are so glad you approve, and don't worry, I got it for a very reasonable price, so there is lots left in the piggy bank. A friend of mine, a former pupil of our old school, got it for me. He runs the bike shop in Pendon Bay, and I asked him to look out for one for me. It's second-hand, but it's in good condition, and we only had to do a few minor repairs."

"The bike shop in Pendon Bay, I'll remember that when it needs any attention in the future."

"Good idea, it's a lot closer than Scotland. Graham will be glad to see you. I think Anna has already told you how her dad got me into the bike repair business. When I started to do up old bikes from the tip, I was pretty raw. He lent me tools, but there were lots of jobs when specialist tools were needed, and anyway, they were beyond me. Duncan arranged for me to spend time there shadowing him and his mechanic as they repaired bikes. I learnt a lot, and we became good friends. I used to get all my parts from him, that is, those I could not get at the tip."

"That's good to hear. Your gift will remind me of him and you two. Thank you so much."

"It's our pleasure, Father. You have done so much for us both, and so we just wanted to say our thanks," Anna took a parcel from the bench beside her.

"But life is not all about work and biking, so this can be a little reminder of us all when you are off duty in the presbytery." She handed him the parcel.

"More, oh my, is there no end to your kindness? If I felt overwhelmed by the very generous gift of a bike, now I'm getting all wobbly."

"Then you'd better sit down to open it." Anna patted the seat beside her.

Gratefully, the priest complied and unwrapped his gift. It was a pullover knitted in soft blue wool. "Mum and I knitted it; she was the expert. I was the learner; we hope it's big enough." Father Aloysius removed his cassock and put it on; it fitted him nicely.

"Ah, it's so lovely and soft, and just the thing to keep me warm in the winter, I don't know what to say."

"You don't need to say anything, at least not about these small tokens of our gratitude, but we do want to talk about something else."

"Well, I will treasure these, they will remind me of two of the best friends I have ever had. God Bless you both." The priest rose, and, putting a hand on each of their shoulders, he added, "Thank you both so much. Anna, please give my thanks to your mother. You have made me feel very humble. I shall miss you; we all will, but I understand you have your lives to lead and new horizons to explore. But we will never forget you, and of course, we will meet again from time to time."

The priest's two friends returned his gaze. They were smiling, but there were tears in Anna's eyes, "Oh, Father, now I've got a big lump in my throat. Yes, saying goodbye is sad," She sniffed, "But yes, of course, we will meet again."

"Don't forget, Father, you will be taking our wedding."

"No, I hadn't forgotten Larry, I'm looking forward to it. Now, what's on your agenda? What do you want to talk about?

It was the girl who replied. "When we were planning Dad's funeral, I asked you about your childhood in Africa and whether your father had had a Christian burial, and you didn't want to talk about it. You said it wasn't the right time. We hoped now might be."

Father Aloysius sighed and shrugged; the memories came flooding back, as they always did, the cracking of the whips and the bleating of the goats, then the screams and the overpowering stench of the hyena as he crawled into its lair.... a hole dug into an ant hill. It became his refuge. He remained there paralysed with fear, his thighs wet with his own urine. The vultures gathered; he heard their squawks and the flapping of wings; he imagined tearing at the flesh and wondered what flesh it was. It was the thirst that drove him to leave his hiding place, and there were the corpses, what was left of them by the vultures, the smell of blood and the flies, incessantly buzzing, buzzing among the remains of his family. What could he say about Karamoja? How could he explain about his father? He sat for a moment, looking at his hands. He laced his fingers together, then open-ended them again to look at his palms, and after looking at each of his companions for a moment, began, hesitantly at first but then more fluently, to tell them of his childhood as a pastoral nomad, of the then situation in that part of Uganda, of his father and how he herded his father's goats, and then later his cattle, learning to be a skilled stockman from an early age. He described his father and how he had been a warrior, too, and how, as a young boy, he had looked up to him and wanted to emulate him.

He explained the customs of his tribe, their primitive beliefs, and the role of witch doctors. He told them that he could not remember being subjected to the scarification on his cheeks, but he explained that they were possibly to serve as amulets to ward off evil spirits or to denote which clan of the tribe of Karamajong he belonged to. He told them of the practice of cattle raiding and of the raid in which all his father's livestock had been stolen and in which his father and all his family had lost their lives, leaving him as the sole survivor. He told them of how he had been found starving in the bush and had been taken to the mission station miles away and how he had been so traumatised at all that he lost that for days, he could not speak. He explained how one priest, who could speak a little of his language, helped him learn to speak and had then taught him English. He told them how he had got his name, Aloysius, warrior. He explained how he was converted to Christianity, how, for the first time, he had gone to school, and of his years of study that eventually led him to become a teacher and a priest. He told them of his time at the seminary in Ireland and then of his posting to Zimbabwe and explained how he had become involved in politics, which had led to him being beaten up and put in prison.

At this point, Father Aloysius had paused. The sun was setting, and the clouds above were tinged with pink. He gazed up at them, and the tears glistened in his eyes. Anna noticed. She was holding hands with Larry. She glanced at him, and then, reaching out with her left hand, she took his right hand in hers. She gave it a gentle squeeze. He seemed to gather himself. In a hoarse whisper, he thanked her and then recounted the horrors of that experience, of the torture, of the unspeakable abuse, and of the things he had seen happening to others and that then had happened to him. He told them of how the bishop, who had been on a visit to Zimbabwe, came to the prison to see another person there but had also seen him.

Father Aloysius explained how very bravely the bishop had demanded an enquiry, and when he was ignored, he went personally to the president. When, again, he was fobbed off, he phoned the pope, who had contacted the president on his behalf. The president had capitulated, and he had been released. He was a broken man, physically and mentally damaged. The bishop had brought him back to the seminary in Ireland. He was there for a year. With the help of a psychologist, he recovered, but it had been a long, painful journey.

"The man was an atheist; he was very caring and understanding. He helped me to get to a position where I could forgive my torturers and those who had abused me. It was not easy. With his help and with lots of prayer I was helped to get better. Later, I learnt he had had a conversion and that he put it down to the time he had spent with me and his meeting with the other monks in the seminary. That also helped me. Good had come out of the suffering I had endured. When I recovered, I wanted to return to Africa, but then the bishop here contacted the seminary and requested that I might serve here. And here I am, and here I met you and your dad, Anna, and all my other friends here, which has been another amazingly good thing to have come out of what happened there in Zimbabwe, so thank you. Thank you for listening."

Anna lifted his hand to her lips, her cheeks were wet with tears. "Thank you, Father. I'm sorry I didn't realise."

"Please don't worry. I'm sorry to have taken up so much of your time on your last evening here."

"Thank you, Father," Larry reached over to pat the priest on the back and then put his arm about Anna's shoulders.

"We knew you are an amazing man, but we didn't know just how amazing. For us, we couldn't have spent this evening in a better way."

"To God be the glory," It was Anna who had started them off, but after the word 'to,' it was all three voices that completed the response. Father Aloysius removed his hand from Anna's and repeated what seemed almost a ritual, the interlacing of his fingers, the examining of his palms before looking into the faces of both his listeners.

"Lovely people, it's home time."

They stood and joined in a three-person hug of farewell.

It was a long story, and he had spared no detail in the telling. He had told them things he had shared with no others except for his psychologist, not even the bishop. During the course of his telling, the sun had set, and the moon, a majestic full moon had risen and had climbed high on its journey across the night sky. For him to tell his story had been cathartic. For them, the listening had been inspiring. They saw their priest in a new light, as a vulnerable man who, in his life's journey had faced so much and who had overcome so much.

Later that evening he went to the church. Kneeling before the altar he was half-conscious of the sound of footsteps. Two people joined him. On his right knelt Miss Farrow, on his left Commander Nesbitt. Moments later, they were joined by two more, the Rev. Burns and the bishop. Father Aloysius raised his eyes to the cross. He thanked God for his friends and a sense of peace in his heart that he had finally laid to rest the ghosts of his past.

Printed in Great Britain
by Amazon